DIANA FINLEY was born and grew up in Germany, where her father was a British Army officer. After a move to London, at eighteen, Diana spent a year living with nomadic people in the remote Pamir mountains of Afghanistan – an experience about which she wrote several stories and accounts. These helped secure her first job, as copywriter and then as writer and editor of children's information books for Macdonald Educational Publishers. A move to North East England meant changing direction. Diana took a degree in Speech and Psychology, and worked for many years as a Specialist in Autism, publishing a professional book. In 2011 she completed an MA in Creative Writing with distinction at Newcastle University. In 2014 her debut novel, *The Loneliness of Survival*, a moving family saga, was published.

Diana enjoys exploring complex and often contradictory characters and emotions in her writing. *Finding Lucy*, her second novel, is a dark, intriguing, psychological story about every parent's worst nightmare – a stolen child.

Finding Lucy

DIANA FINLEY

ONE PLACE. MANY STORIES.

HQ
An imprint of HarperCollins*Publishers* Ltd
1 London Bridge Street
London SE1 9GF

This paperback edition 2018

First published in Great Britain by
HQ, an imprint of HarperCollins*Publishers* Ltd 2018

A catalogue record for this book is
available from the British Library.

ISBN: 9780008310158

MIX
Paper from
responsible sources
FSC
www.fsc.org
FSC™ C007454

This book is produced from independently certified FSC™ paper
to ensure responsible forest management.

For more information visit: **www.harpercollins.co.uk/green**

Typeset by Palimpsest Book Production Ltd, Falkirk, Stirlingshire
Printed and bound in Great Britain by
CPI Group (UK) Ltd, Melksham, SN12 6TR

For Harvey, who may read it one day.

Chapter One

1984

Alison

It was after seeing the grave that I finally decided to take a child. There was nothing special about it – the grave, that is. Not one of those ghastly, over-sentimentalised affairs sprouting angels' wings or teddy bears. Quite plain. A simple stone and a concise message:

In memory of our dearly loved little girl
Lucy Sarah Brown aged 2 years
Born 20-9-1982 – Died 16-10-1984
Safe in the hands of Jesus

Somehow, imagining little Lucy's life – and her demise – touched me deeply, coming as it did just a month after Mother's death. How desperately tragic. What might have killed a child so young? A car accident? Meningitis? A hole in the heart? How her parents must have suffered. How they must have grieved for their "dearly loved little girl" – still be grieving, in fact; she'd been gone only two months, after all. So very sad.

As I thought about it, I almost wished I could share my plans with them: with Lucy's original parents. Let them know that, in a sense, their Lucy was going to be brought back to life; *I* was going to bring Lucy back to life! Perhaps they would be comforted by that thought. Of course, telling them would never be possible, and anyway, she would cease to be *their Lucy*. She would become *my Lucy*. Lucy would be my secret. She would be my daughter, my secret daughter. How perfect! Lucy Brown. A fine, tasteful name – yet "normal". Not one that stood out too vividly, just like the sad little grave.

It wasn't as though I had planned the whole thing beforehand, thought it through – not at that stage. The idea grew out of a medley of thoughts that had been swirling in my mind; indistinct, like miscellaneous letter-shaped noodles stirred into soup, sometimes emerging for a moment to make meaningful combinations on the surface, then breaking up and disappearing into the depths of the pot. Stumbling upon the grave that day drew the letters together, began to make order and sense of them. I had decided.

It was a bright, crisp December day. Long shadows streaked the wet grass. Early afternoon, but already the sun was starting its descent towards the rooftops. As often before, I had been wandering through one of the city's urban cemeteries. Not that I was attracted to such places for any macabre reasons. No, it was the quiet I yearned for, the peace, and perhaps the sense of the past. This was a particularly agreeable cemetery: serene, well maintained and cared for, with mature trees and shrubs creating a screen from the surrounding suburban streets, emphasising the separateness of the graveyard.

At first I had been drawn to the grave simply by the fresh, bright flowers arranged in neat vases, which contrasted with the faded, bedraggled blooms nearby. But standing there in front of the grave, my attention soon moved on from the flowers. I was mesmerised by the name: Brown. It is natural to notice one's own surname. I stood and gazed at the neat letters, the scrolled stonework marking the boundary of the pitifully small grave and containing shiny gravel of various colours: pink, brown, yellow and green. On the headstone, carved stone hands curved beneath the words "Safe in the hands of Jesus" as though gently lifting them – or perhaps Lucy herself – upwards, heavenwards.

All the while, as my eyes absorbed these details, my heart was beating unevenly and with great excitement. A plan started to take shape in my mind. It was so simple; Lucy Brown would become my child – indeed, my invention. Just as, years ago, Mother had created me as Alison Brown. I could hardly wait to get home and begin to put my ideas onto paper.

Chapter Two

Once back in my own house on the other side of Nottingham, I made a cup of tea, sat down at my desk and started to write a list. I love to make lists. So reassuring. Firstly, the birth certificate. Having that in my possession would make it all seem real. This first item on the list occupied me for quite some time. I worried about the application process though. Would proof of identity be required?

As it turned out, discovering the details of Lucy Brown's parents' names and dates of birth was extraordinarily simple. All I had to do was to write to the General Register Office giving Lucy's first name, surname and date of birth – and requesting a copy of her birth certificate. An address was required. I provided my own, of course. I sent the modest payment as indicated – and a week or so later the precious document was in my hands. I studied it with a trembling thrill; it was almost as though I held Lucy herself, as if she was reborn!

Her mother's name was given as Audrey Brown, and her father's as Russell Brown. That would need some adjustment in time of course. *I* would be her mother, Alison Brown – but then people often used a different first name to the original one.

This was just the beginning. Much needed to be done, but

that did not deter me, not at all. Indeed, anticipating the tasks ahead filled me with great pleasure and excitement.

I had already decided to stop working for a time. Mother's death had left me feeling deeply unsettled. It had always been just the two of us. Apart from my brief and unhappy sojourn at university, I could scarcely remember spending a night apart from her. Or rather, the very few occasions when we *had* been apart stood out in my memory as rarities; exceptional – and a little frightening.

Now suddenly I found myself completely alone. During those initial weeks of bereavement, I found it impossible to enjoy anything of ordinary, domestic life – for example, mealtimes. I ate almost nothing at all. Sitting alone at the table where, all my life, Mother and I had sat together, sharing the small events and anecdotes of the day, felt almost as though I were in the grave rather than Mother. I found little pleasure in my own company.

Sleep was even more difficult. I tried to postpone the moment of plunging myself into darkness by reading for as long as possible – often reading the same passage over and over again – until exhaustion forced me to switch off the light. As if by signal, this act heralded a succession of morbid, disturbing and often terrifying thoughts, which would not be still. Sometimes I was obliged to get up and make myself a cup of camomile tea, and sit with it in the armchair in the soft light of the kitchen, until a fitful sleep eventually overcame me.

Dr Munroe, who had known me since I was an infant, suggested a mild sleeping pill might help – 'just during these sad and difficult early weeks, my dear'. I accepted his prescription, but never swallowed a single one of his pills. No, it was not my preferred way. It was important to remain in control of my consciousness.

At the office, my mind would not focus properly. Every task seemed difficult, yet nothing seemed to matter to me as before. I felt the need for a complete change, a time for peace and reflection; a time to reconsider my life and my future. Perhaps it was something to do with having turned forty last year. Not that I believed in phenomena such as "mid-life crises", but it was surely reasonable to regard forty as a chance to embark on new endeavours. So, back in November, not long after Mother's will was read, I had handed in the obligatory three months' notice at Chambers.

'So what are you going to do, Alison?' asked Mrs Anderson, the administrative manager (promoted well above her capabilities, I always believed). 'Have you found another job to go to?'

'Not exactly. I feel it's time to re-evaluate, to think about the next period of my life and work out exactly what I want to do with it.'

Mrs Anderson sniffed. 'Re-evaluate? Sounds a bit of a luxury to me. "Re-evaluation" isn't something most of us can afford. Still, I suppose it's unsettling to lose your mum when you've always spent so much time together – is that it?'

'Certainly losing Mother has been a blow …' I paused for a moment.

Mrs Anderson sighed and glanced at her watch.

'Yes,' I said hastily, 'you're right, very unsettling.'

Despite this unsatisfactory exchange, I was touched to note the genuine regret expressed by most of my colleagues at my leaving – both the legal team and the administrative staff.

'S'pect you'll miss us 'ere in the office, won't you, Alison? What you goin' to do wiv yourself all the time?' Julie was the newest office recruit. Her long nails clacked away on her typewriter.

'I'm sure I'll find plenty to occupy my time, Julie.'

'Oh yeah, goin' to museums and libraries and that?' She winked at Debbie and they giggled, without revealing the source of their amusement. Certainly, I mused, I would not miss the banality of office conversation.

It was clear that Mrs Anderson was at least sensitive enough to register the strength of my determination, because at no time did she try to dissuade me from my decision. She had never been generous with praise, so it was a particular pleasure to see myself described with words such as "efficient", "invaluable", "intelligent", "loyal" and "highly valued" in the brief note about my departure circulated to the staff. It would have been perfectly proper for Mrs Anderson to have written a personal note or card to me at home, and perhaps to have wished me well, but this was not her way.

At the end of my last day at Chambers, a select gathering had been arranged in the main office by way of a "leaving do". Cups of my favourite Earl Grey tea and a tray of tasteful and dainty iced cakes were handed around by the juniors. I was seen off with a gift token, a bunch of flowers and a jovial peck on the cheek by Sir Julian, delivered amid the usual waft of winey fumes – he had not long returned from his usual lunchtime expedition.

'A new year, a new life! Eh, my dear? Jolly good for you.'

I tried to smile benignly. He could never have imagined how true those words were!

Chapter Three

I had wanted a child of my own for as many years as I could remember. I might even admit to having felt a desperate longing for a child. I frequently recall Mother's words to me during the last days of her life.

'Don't live alone, Alison,' she had said. 'It's not good for you, dear. I do so wish for you to have a child – a child to love, and to love you. I won't be a grandmother, of course – it's too late for that – but if only I could know that you will have the joy of being a *mother*, as I did with you; that would be such a comfort for me.'

'You're right, Mother,' I had told her soothingly, Mother's hand in mine as frail and fleshless as a chicken's claw.

'Please don't worry – I want to have a child. I *will* have a child, I promise.'

Perhaps it was a rash promise, but I had genuinely meant those words. Three days later Mother was dead. I had underestimated the impact her loss would have on me. She had been right; I needed someone to love, and to love me. I needed a child. That need grew in me until it was all-consuming.

* * *

Of course, I had tried all avenues: conventional means some might say. But none felt truly right for me. Why not give birth to a child of your own, some might ask. The fundamental barrier is that first a man is required. My attitude to men had been permanently coloured by the event at university some years before. I didn't dislike men, but neither did I trust them, and they had never played a significant role in my life. I could not envisage the constant presence of a man in my home, in my life. Above all, I regarded acts of physical intimacy with a man with the utmost revulsion.

Some women might even pursue what I understood were referred to as "one-night stands" – a revolting term – but this was not a path I could ever have contemplated. Even thinking about it caused me to tremble and feel quite nauseous. Thus I had dispensed with the idea of "natural" means of having a child.

Next, I considered the possibility of artificial insemination. However, I could never have submitted myself to such a humiliating procedure – little better than the means by which a prize cow might be used for breeding.

Having dismissed all these avenues, I looked into legal adoption. One would imagine that a respectable woman, still in her thirties at that time, and willing to offer a home to an unwanted waif, would be welcomed with open arms. Not so! After weeks of visits from social workers and their ceaseless interviews and questionnaires, I had been told that I was not considered suitable to adopt a child. *Not suitable!* "The team" had decided – "regretfully" – that I was not suited to bringing up a child, especially a young and vulnerable child, they said. Words like "judgemental", "lacking in empathy", and "rigid personality" had been bandied about; meaningless psycho-babble straight out of some left-wing social work textbook, no doubt. And thus this questionable group of people had passed their own judgement on me.

There had been no means of appeal. As will be appreciated by anyone with a scrap of insight, I had been left with no choice but to take the matter into my own hands.

Chapter Four

By February, I was taking the first steps towards a fundamentally different future. I had decided on Newcastle for its distance from Nottingham, and as a fine, distinctive city in its own right. Only Newcastle's proximity to Durham, with that city's sad associations for me, made me hesitate over my choice at first. Yet the advantages were clear and I resolved to overcome my doubts, and to look firmly down at a book rather than out of the window as the train passed through Durham station.

I made my very specific wishes quite clear to the Homefind estate agency. As a widow with a small daughter, I explained, I was looking for a smallish house, with three bedrooms, preferably detached, with a neat, easy-to-manage and secure back garden, to allow the child to play safely. I felt no qualms about presenting myself in this way – in my mind I was already Lucy's mother.

The agency soon found a very suitable house on a predominantly post-Fifties estate on the edge of the suburb of Gosforth. It was perfect for my needs, having one bedroom off the "half-landing", and two further bedrooms with dormer windows set into the slope of the roof. It was described as a "Dutch bungalow". I liked the term. It gave my new home a touch of the exotic, while retaining a wholesome image.

The house was freshly whitewashed and stood at the end of a quiet cul-de-sac, its garden backing onto a pleasant area of trees and fields where people strolled and walked their dogs. There was even a small playground nearby – ideal for Lucy. The neighbouring houses were far enough away for me not to feel overlooked. My – sorry, *our*! – new home (I would have to get used to using the plural pronoun) had been well maintained by the elderly couple who were selling it. Certainly, the decoration was a little old-fashioned, but that didn't matter to me. Thanks to Mother's carefully invested estate, added to the anticipated sale of our house in Nottingham, and my own smaller savings, I was able to contemplate not working while caring for a young child. This was very important to me; far too many young children were placed in the care of nurseries or childminders. I had no intention of Lucy becoming a "latch-key" child.

Fortunately, there were spare funds to put in a new kitchen and bathroom, and for fresh wallpaper and paint throughout. Mother had never been a great spender, but she would have enjoyed discussing decoration and soft furnishings with me, especially when it came to Lucy's room. At times like this I missed her terribly. In fact, if I am truthful, not a moment went by when I did not miss her, but at least having so much to occupy my mind did help.

It was vital to be able to come and go freely at the new house over the coming weeks, without arousing curiosity or suspicion. One of my first tasks was to visit the next-door neighbours on either side and introduce myself. I'd never been one for dropping in and out of other people's homes, so I felt a degree of anxiety about these initial contacts. To the left was a youngish couple, Susan and Mike Harmon. They had a nice polite little girl of about nine called Claire, and a younger boy, Charlie, who seemed somewhat boisterous and over-excitable.

'Come on in, it's just lovely to meet you, Alison!' said Susan, eagerly taking my arm as I hesitated on the doorstep. 'Come into the kitchen and let's have a cup of tea.'

Susan didn't think to ask what sort of tea I might prefer. In fact, she served what Mother would have called "builders' tea", but I drank it and made no comment.

'So you see, we'll be coming up in a while – my little girl Lucy and I – just as soon as the house is ready,' I explained.

'Ooh, how lovely! It'll be so nice for all of us to have a younger family next door. Charlie – did you hear that? A little girl next door for you to play with!' Susan turned back to me. 'How old is Lucy?'

I almost panicked for a moment. I felt a rush of colour swarming up my neck and cheeks. How could I know exactly how old Lucy was?

'She's … er … a bit younger than Charlie.' I lowered my voice. 'The thing is, Susan, we lost Lucy's daddy recently …'

This was a useful device to distract Susan from her question. Her eyes widened and she put her hands up to her face, which adopted a tragic expression.

'Lost …? Oh no, how terrible! I'm so sorry … er … how …'

'Accident …' I whispered under my breath. 'Yes, that's why we had to move, you understand … to allow us to rebuild our lives together up here in Newcastle. A completely new start.'

I was getting into my stride now. I noted Susan's agonised expression and continued. 'I'm looking forward to making a happy, loving home, for Lucy's sake. That's what I'll live for now.'

Susan nodded at me knowingly. To my astonishment, her eyes filled with tears. She squeezed my arm tenderly. I gulped and looked at my lap.

'Right now,' I said, inserting a slight tremor into my voice, 'Lucy has been staying with … um … an aunt back in Nottingham whenever I make these visits to the North East to get things sorted. She's been very supportive, but I'm hoping we can both settle here properly soon.'

19

Susan continued her nodding, while biting her lip in a rather foolish way that I supposed was intended to denote empathy. I took a deep breath, and concentrated on brightening my facial expression.

'I'm sorry, Susan – I didn't want to upset you with all this gloomy talk. Just listen to me, I've done nothing but talk about myself! How rude of me – please tell me more about you.'

Susan didn't need asking twice; she looked relieved to change the subject. She was a naturally talkative person, and seemed keen to tell me all about the family; her husband Michael ('most people call him Mike') was a GP and she herself was a part-time solicitor. There was an excellent first school on the estate, which Claire attended. She had the rest of that year there before moving on to the middle school. Charlie had started going to the nursery part-time.

Susan was sure Lucy would love it too, when she started. I quickly intervened and explained that I felt Lucy was too young for nursery just at the moment. She would need some time to settle down first.

'Of course she will, Alison. Dear little Lucy will need her mummy more than anything at the moment,' she said, 'but don't forget she can come and play with Charlie any time, any time at all – and Claire will just love playing the older sister. Also, we know most of the people around here and can easily introduce you. That'll help *you* to settle and get to know people. Everyone's really friendly.'

I wasn't at all sure I liked the sound of these introductions, but decided that at least it showed that Susan and Mike were welcoming and accepting.

The neighbours on the other side were an older retired couple, Frank and Molly Armstrong. They were equally warm, rushing about to produce tea and homemade scones for me when I called. I told them the same story as I'd told to the Harmons. Molly Armstrong shook her head and patted my hand sympathetically.

Frank said if there was anything he could help with, anything at all – he was handy with tools or a paintbrush – just to let him know.

They both said how nice it would be to have a little girl growing up next door, and they would be happy to babysit at any time – they didn't go out much. I almost responded that I didn't go out much either, but decided it was best to reveal as little of myself as possible.

Chapter Five

I found the next stage of the preparations highly enjoyable. I got up early, took the train to York, and spent the morning in the city centre buying the necessary items: a navy blue gabardine coat (a bit dull) and some clumpy navy shoes; a more stylish, pillarbox red, lightweight wool coat; and black knee-length boots for me. Then I went into British Home Stores and Marks and Spencer for a number of sets of girls' clothing, including pyjamas and underwear, all sized for age two years, and one set of boys' clothes: dungarees, jumper, hat and parka, also for age two years.

Next, I allowed myself a break – a delightful light lunch and pot of tea at Betty's Tea Room. Mother frequently said I should allow myself more "treats". As always, she was right – I found I could relax and enjoy myself as I nursed a good cup of my favourite Earl Grey tea in the comfort and warmth of Betty's.

It was pleasant strolling through the historic lanes and looking in at the shop windows. Mothercare was not far. With some helpful advice I selected a lightweight Maclaren pushchair, which the assistant referred to as a "buggy". I also bought a potty, some nappies (just in case), a set of child's plastic crockery and cutlery, and a few toys and books. This was all I could manage, but by putting several of the carrier bags into the buggy I was able to make my way back to York station, and from there I caught my train to Newcastle.

The next day I ordered a child's bed, mattress and bedding, a wardrobe and chest of drawers, a little table and two chairs to match, some cheerful pictures, and a few more toys, all from Bainbridge's excellent department store in Newcastle city centre. These items were to be delivered to my new house the following Friday, by which time Lucy's room would be decorated and carpeted.

* * *

At home, I tried on the navy coat and shoes for the third time, together with the dark brown wig I'd ordered previously from a discreet company dealing mainly with cancer sufferers. I'd never taken great interest in fashion, much to the scorn of my school-mates, but I knew exactly what I *liked* in the way of clothes.

I gazed at my reflection in the mirror. The effect on my appearance was immediate and striking. I was totally transformed – how very satisfactory. I even *felt* different in my new outfit: older and, it has to be said, somewhat dowdy. Removing those clothes, I delighted in observing the metamorphosis wrought by switching to the red coat, the delicious high boots, and the return to my natural fair hair. Not exactly a "scarlet woman", but certainly a more lively and attractive persona.

The following week I arranged for some of my furniture and household possessions to be moved from Nottingham to Newcastle. I had stocked the new kitchen cupboards and the freezer with suitable food for me and a young child. The house was ready.

I invited Mike and Susan Harmon, together with their children, and Frank and Molly Armstrong to come in for drinks to celebrate. Mike and Susan opted for a glass of wine and I'd got in Kia-Ora and Ribena for Claire and Charlie. I'd laid out some toys, books, paper and drawing pens and crayons on the dining table for them, as well as some crisps and snacks. It pained me a little to see Charlie sift through the objects I had so carefully ordered. He seemed to have no thought for rearranging the colours of the crayons, nor the size order of the books and toys. Oh well; I resolved to do it myself later.

'Oh, aren't you thoughtful, Alison!' said Susan, looking around.

'Well, I know what it's like for children when adults are talking together.'

''Course you do. We can't wait to meet Lucy, isn't that right, children?'

Claire looked up from her drawing and smiled. 'It'll be nice to have a little *girl* next door,' she said emphatically, glancing at her brother.

'Have you got a photo of Lucy, Alison?' asked Mike, looking around the room. My mouth dried up suddenly.

'No ... well ... yes, of course I have ... er ... but they're still in boxes. Lots of things still to unpack – or at my other house, you see.'

Charlie was looking around too. What would they ask for next? 'Alison ... got no TV?'

I don't approve of children being allowed to use adults' names without permission, but I let this pass.

'No, sorry, not yet, Charlie. But it won't be long before Lucy's here for you to play with – just another two or three weeks, I hope.'

After all my preparations, I thought, all Charlie could think about was television! Never mind. My Lucy wouldn't be glued to a screen – I was certain of that. I turned to the Armstrongs.

'Now, what would you like, Molly?'

'Eee, I'd love a cup of tea, pet, if it's not too much trouble, and Frank's noticed you've got some beer over there. He's not really a wine man, are you, love?'

'Yes of course. Here, Frank, here's the opener and a glass. Just help yourself while I get Betty's tea.'

24

'Thanks, pet, that's grand. I hope we're going to get the guided tour after, are we?'

'It'll be a pleasure, Frank.'

'You've done an amazing job here, Alison,' said Mike, looking around the sitting room.

'Thank you, Michael ... Mike. I'm pleased with the way it's turned out. That's partly down to the decorators you recommended. They've been wonderful – completely reliable. I'm really grateful.'

Mike followed me out to the kitchen. The back of my neck began to prickle uncomfortably to feel his physical presence so close behind me. However, he seemed rather a nice man – quieter than Susan, and thoughtful.

'Wow, what a difference!' he said, looking around.

'Well, it was basically a sound house, and the Turners had left everything in pretty good condition. All I've done is a bit of window-dressing.'

I put the small teapot on a tray with a milk jug.

'Can I get the cups, Alison?' Mike asked.

'Just in that cupboard above the bread bin.'

It was a relief to watch him walk to the other side of the kitchen.

'Oh, that's very tidy,' said Mike, opening the cupboard and smiling back at me. 'You're a woman after my own heart.'

'Cups in the front, saucers at the back on the left.'

'Thanks. I'm so sorry you've had to do all this on your own, Alison. Susie told me ... It can't have been easy.'

I sighed tragically and nodded. 'I'll be very glad when Lucy joins me up here at last – it has been a bit ... lonely ... on my own.'

Mike gently touched my shoulder, sending a shock down my spine as I carried the tray through. I gripped the handles tightly.

I decided that the evening was turning out to be a great success, although I worried that Charlie might break something with his frenetic racing about. I hoped Lucy wouldn't turn out to be quite so lively. I wasn't sure I could deal with that. The children were both thrilled to see Lucy's room, though.

'Oh it's so pretty. Look, Mum – all the animals on the bed! Lucy's got her own little desk. Look how tidy it is! Can we sit on the chairs, Alison?'

Even Claire was using my first name.

'Of course you can. I'm sure it won't stay as tidy once Lucy gets here.' Everyone laughed. Although I secretly hoped it might.

Chapter Six

1985

Next came the trickier part of the plan. After weeks of research I had decided on Riddlesfield. All the indices showed it to be one of the most "disadvantaged" towns in the country, with certain districts such as Thornhough, Hollerton, Woodhope and Frainham consistently reported as areas of the highest child poverty in England. Studying a map of the town and its surrounds, it was Frainham that stood out as most suitable for my needs. Not only was there street after street of small, tightly packed terraced houses, but the area was easily accessible from the city centre, and more importantly, from Riddlesfield railway station. I pored over the map so often that soon I was able to close my eyes and picture the exact pattern of streets, squares and landmarks required for my purpose.

The morning after the house-warming party for the neighbours, I returned to Nottingham for a few days, awaiting rain. On the third day, I woke to a dank and gloomy morning. By the time I'd had breakfast it was drizzling steadily. A solid bank of lowering grey clouds sat over the houses and foretold of more to come – perfect.

I put on my navy coat and shoes, and the brown wig. Then I tied a large paisley headscarf over my head, using kirby grips to make sure all the hair was firmly tucked in beneath it. For extra anonymity, I put up a large umbrella as I emerged from the front door. If I'd been of a more dramatic inclination, no doubt all this would have been a source of great entertainment, but not for me. I felt sick with anxiety. Over and over again, I rehearsed in my mind exactly what I had to do. Nothing must go wrong.

I needn't have worried. By now the rain was falling heavily. The few pedestrians I encountered on my way to the bus station hurried head-down to their destinations, clutching their collars around their necks, striving only to get out of the wet as quickly as possible, and scarcely glancing in my direction.

Nottingham to Riddlesfield was not a straightforward journey, but I felt that this was in my favour. The number of necessary changes – though daunting – made it less likely that I would ever be linked to my destination. After a bus ride to Derby station I bought a day return to Leeds, where I had about forty-five minutes to wait for a direct train to Riddlesfield.

Thankfully, by this time the rain clouds had cleared and I was able to dispense with the unpleasantly damp headscarf, revealing my dark hair. The train to Riddlesfield was not too crowded. I tried to read the newspaper, but found I couldn't concentrate. Nevertheless, I kept the paper open, and sheltered behind its protective screen. An hour and a half later the train arrived at Riddlesfield.

I found myself increasingly nervous as I stepped onto the platform and made my way out of the station, my heart pounding unpleasantly. I had to pause a few moments, breathing deeply, while I calmed myself by picturing the map with which I had become so familiar. Sure enough, the layout of the actual streets before me precisely matched the image in my mind.

I quickly crossed the road and walked southwards until I came to Churchill Square, with its shops and cafés. One café looked bright and welcoming. I noted it as somewhere I might allow myself another cup of tea later on that day. I continued along Holbrook Street and, after a few minutes' walk, turned right into City Road. After perhaps a quarter of a mile, I turned left and soon found myself in precisely the right area of narrow streets, densely built with mean and coal-blackened terraced houses, just as my research had indicated. This must be Frainham, I thought, recalling the map, this must be it.

As if to confirm that it was indeed the poor, run-down neighbourhood I wanted, two small boys, aged only about three or four – both dirty and inadequately dressed for the time of year – were playing unsupervised in the gutter at the end of a back lane strewn with rubbish. An overflowing dustbin provided the little urchins with playthings; they were rolling tin cans noisily over the cobbles.

I stopped and made a deliberate effort to smile at them. The children stared back at me impassively. Then the slightly larger boy stood up, and, looking both impish and defiant, he stuck his tongue out at me! I knew it was ridiculous to allow myself to feel intimidated by two such tiny children, barely out of babyhood – but nevertheless I did feel it, and so hurried on, fearing the boys might have started throwing stones or items of rubbish.

I explored the streets systematically, working my way southwards, wandering up one terrace, and then down the next – all the while trying to look as unobtrusive as possible. As I rounded a corner, I encountered another small boy – this one of maybe five or six years old – who almost bumped into me. He wore shorts much too long for him and a torn jersey. His hair was tousled and unwashed-looking.

''ello, missus,' he said, standing sturdily in my path and grinning up at me.

'Hello ...' I said, beginning to edge around him. He shifted sideways, as if to bar my way again.

'Wanta see what's in me box, missus?' he said, thrusting a battered cardboard box up at me. I looked about uneasily.

'Well … um … yes, all right.'

He carefully prised off the lid, to reveal a scrawny, greyish house mouse. It twitched its nose and regarded me with glittery black eyes. Horrified, I took a step back.

'It's me mouse,' the boy informed me unnecessarily. 'He's me pet. I call 'im Billy. You got ten pee for Billy, missus? For 'is dinner, like?'

With trembling fingers I searched my purse for a coin. Finding two ten-pence pieces, I held them in the air in front of the boy.

'Put the lid on the box,' I urged him, dropping one ten-pence piece into his expectant palm. 'That's for your mouse's food,' I said, 'and here's ten pence for you to spend.' The child smiled a gap-toothed smile.

'Ta, missus.'

I hurried onwards.

I could have no doubts that this was a suitable area. Greyish, shabby-looking washing hung in many of the yards, and in places was draped right across the back lanes. A group of young men clustered around a motorbike outside a corner shop, talking and laughing loudly and crudely, in a way I could not help finding unsettling. Some were drinking what I assumed was beer from cans or bottles. One threw an empty can at an advertisement hoarding just behind me, causing such a sudden clang that I jumped with shock, which only made the youths laugh louder still.

I turned quickly down the next back lane. Here and there women smoked and chatted with one another in pairs or threes. The local dialect was so broad that I could scarcely make out a word of what was said, although their frequent use of profanities was clear enough. Some held babies on their hips, while toddlers swarmed around their legs. Bigger children chased each other about, screaming like savages.

At one street corner a bigger girl pushed two younger children in a large cardboard box, careless of broken glass strewn across the ground. The scene struck me as more reminiscent of the Twenties or Thirties than the Eighties. I made sure not to linger, anxious to remain inconspicuous. It was essential that no one should notice my presence too readily, or engage me in conversation.

Just as my resolve, in this hostile environment, was beginning to falter, I came to a row of houses that appeared to hold some promise. My attention was drawn by a woman's voice shouting.

'Will youse two ger'out from under me effin' feet right now! Go on – ger'outside!'

I slowed my pace. A boy of about five yanked open a battered door hanging by one hinge, and ran out of the yard. He looked from left to right, and then ran leftwards until he was out of sight. I caught my breath, gasped, and stood still. For a moment I hadn't noticed a second child emerge from the door. But yes, there she was: tiny, elfin; two or perhaps two and a half years old. She stood in the yard doorway looking about her, a finger in her mouth.

'Wy-yan …?' she called plaintively.

I guessed the child was calling her brother. Her fair hair was tangled and matted at the back, her face extraordinarily grubby. She wore a stained yellow dress and an equally grimy cardigan, which had once been white. In her hand she held a filthy, one-legged doll by what remained of its hair. I paused and watched her, scarcely breathing. The little girl put the doll on the pavement and squatted down, crooning softly to it. She picked up a paper wrapper from the gutter and smoothed it carefully across her knee. Then she laid it over the doll with great tenderness, muttering something like 'Dere y'are. Dere y'are, Polly.'

I tiptoed towards the child, holding my breath, longing to linger, but knowing I could not. As I reached her, the child looked up and noticed me. She raised her little face to gaze up at me and give me a startlingly beautiful, radiant smile. I paused and smiled back for a moment, and then, reluctantly forcing myself to turn away, I walked on. My heart was pounding. I had found my Lucy.

Chapter Seven

I scarcely noticed the journey back to Nottingham. I even forgot to spread my clean handkerchief on the back of the seat behind my head. Somehow I made each connection and boarded the correct trains. Ticket collectors came and went. I must have presented the relevant ticket, though I had no memory of doing so.

One cheery conductor on the Leeds-to-Derby stretch said, 'Penny for them, duck!' as he punched my ticket – such a foolish expression. But he shrugged and quickly moved on, disappointed, I suppose, that I had failed to respond in the same spirit. He could have offered me a fortune for them, but I wouldn't have shared them; my thoughts were all on Lucy. How could such a dreadful place, such a dreadful family, have produced a child of such beauty and perfection? My mind drifted unbidden to my own history.

Could I have been born into just such a slum? Certainly my "birth mother" must have lacked morals. "Unmarried mother", the adoption agency had written in the sketchy notes Mother had shared with me, when she felt that, at fourteen or so, I was mature enough for such information. Mother had always been open about the adoption. From my earliest memories, I knew I'd been "chosen" and that somehow this made me special. Mother had emphasised that it was unnecessary to share this information about my roots with anyone else. It was just for the two of us. Well, Mother was my real mother in every true sense of the word, wasn't she?

When thoughts of this "unmarried mother" occasionally surfaced, I shuddered at the image of a slovenly, unkempt woman – such as those I had seen today in abundance on the streets and back lanes of Frainham. I screwed up my eyes tightly and forced myself to concentrate on Mother, neat and decent, her morals intact, and felt I could breathe easily again. Thank goodness I had decided years ago never to attempt to make contact with my birth mother.

Finally, the bus from Derby deposited me and I walked the last half-mile or so home in the dark. As so often happened, sleep did not come easily that night, although I was exhausted, both physically and mentally, from the day. I had had nothing to eat since breakfast, except an egg and cress sandwich hastily bought at Riddlesfield station, of which I could swallow only half. I knew I should eat something when I got home, but the very thought of food was repellent.

I lay back in a soothing hot bath and then fell into bed. My mind spun and my whole being was as tense as a spring with excitement. If it had been possible, I would have returned to that street, that house, the very next day, indeed that very minute. I would have scooped the beautiful child up in my arms and run off with her.

But impulsiveness was not in my nature. I knew it was an impulse that, like so many urges, had to be resisted – and a good thing too. It was vital to concentrate on the longer term. By focusing solely on my immediate longing, the whole future could be jeopardised. Self-control was everything. The final stages were approaching, and that made it all the more important to adhere absolutely to the plan.

* * *

The last day in Nottingham came soon enough. I stood in the chill of the empty house, and spent some minutes listening to the echo of the many years gone by. I checked each room one last time. Here, where we sat comfortably by the fire, Mother with embroidery or knitting on her lap, me with a book, or my stamp album (how I loved those colourful stamps, especially the ones sent by Mother's friend Maureen from New Zealand, with their bird pictures).

Here, too, where we shared the evening meal together, the table always perfectly laid – not for us a plate on our laps in front of the television. Here my bedroom to which I had loved to retreat during difficult times as a child, for peace and solitude. And here was Mother's room with its pink carpet and white built-in cupboard. The delicate smell of Mother lingered still, hung softly in the air, like a gentle ghost.

Now was the time for leaving. I locked the front door and went next door to say goodbye to Sylvia Blythe, our elderly neighbour, and leave the key with her for the agents to pick up. I took her two large carrier bags full of the non-perishable remnants from the kitchen cupboards: tins of soup, dried fruit, pots of jam and the like.

'So kind of you, dear, just like your mother, aren't you? I can't believe you won't be here any more. Not you, nor poor Dorothy.' Sylvia's voice broke with a sob. 'After all these years – oh Alison, I shall miss you terribly.'

'I'm sure the new neighbours will be nice.'

'Maybe, but that's just what they'll be: new. Dorothy and I were friends for nearly fifty years – fifty years, Alison!'

Tears wound a crooked path down Sylvia's wrinkled cheek. I held my breath, bent over her armchair and hugged her. I couldn't help recoiling slightly at the feel of the soft, loose flesh of her face and its powdery smell. Sylvia recalled memories of her friendship with Mother: anecdotes I had heard many times.

When at last I was able to say my final goodbyes and extricate myself, I left by Sylvia's back door and returned through the side gate to the garden. It was still only half past eleven. I fetched the pushchair and bags from their hiding place in the shed, put on my navy coat and brown wig, checked that no one was about, and departed through the back gate. I left the house I'd lived in for all of my forty-one years without a backwards glance.

Chapter Eight

There was nothing to guarantee I would be able to take the child that day, or the next, or the one after that, although I hoped, of course. What was vital was that I travelled to Riddlesfield from Nottingham, and never from Newcastle. That connection must never be made.

If the opportunity to take Lucy did not arise that day, I had planned to stay the night in a bed and breakfast in Brayling, an ancient village in a quiet rural area just outside Riddlesfield, and to return again by taxi the following day, and the day after that if necessary.

In the event, there was no need to stay overnight. My plan went miraculously smoothly. The journey seemed much simpler this time, having experienced it all before. It was late afternoon as I pushed the pushchair – empty but for a large carrier bag – from the station and through the streets. The sky was already darkening, which was greatly to the advantage of my disguise. I was concerned, however, that even the most neglectful parents, as the child's appeared to be, would surely not allow such a tiny girl to play alone outside in the dark – and I might have missed my chance.

I needn't have worried. As I approached the now familiar street,

I recognised the small figure on the pavement near the yard as before, playing with some sticks. She wore the same yellow dress, this time with a boy's green jersey over it, clearly a hand-me-down, as it was far too big for her, the sleeves turned up in lumpy rolls.

No one was about. I walked rapidly straight towards her, fishing in my bag for a lollipop. Her parents must have been inside. I could hear raucous shouting, shrieking and coarse laughter coming from the house. They sounded drunk. The little girl stood up, holding a bundle of twigs and sticks. She looked at me as I approached. I crouched to her level.

'Hello, dear,' I said quietly. The child stuck a dirty finger in her mouth and smiled. I held the lolly in front of her and she reached for it.

'Do you like trains? Would you like to go for a ride – on a train?' I said, holding the lolly just out of reach.

'Tain,' the little girl said, her eyes on the lolly.

I gave the lollipop to her and she immediately stuck it into her mouth. I pulled a pink anorak out of my bag and pushed the child's little arms into it. She looked at it admiringly and did not resist. I put the hood up and tucked the fine, fair hair in.

'It's cold,' I explained, 'let's go and see the train.'

'See tain,' the little girl replied.

I looked carefully all around us. No one; no sign of her parents, or anyone else. Just howls of laughter, screeching and braying from inside the house. They appeared to be completely unaware of their child, of Lucy. I picked her up and sat her in the push-chair, quickly fastening the straps, as I had practised. I set off at a fast walk. Lucy sat in the pushchair completely relaxed, sucking her lolly, looking about her with interest. I talked constantly, frantically, as if a gap of silence might somehow cause the child to beg to turn around and go home, to cry for her mother. I gabbled about a car, a tree, a dog, a blue door – anything we passed by, anything to engage her interest.

'Look, Lucy – a black dog! What a big dog! Oh, there's a bus.'

Lucy looked in the direction of whatever I remarked on in this way. There was nothing wrong with her comprehension. I might have known my Lucy was no fool.

As we approached Churchill Square I said, 'Let's go in a shop now, shall we?'

'Sop,' Lucy agreed.

We went into British Home Stores, down the escalator to the lower ground floor, and straight to the toilets. No one inside. Good. I lifted her out. I paused for a moment and held Lucy tenderly to me, breathing her in. It was as if I breathed Lucy into my very heart, which beat hectically. I felt something for this child – whom I'd only just met – that I had never felt before. The feeling was so strong and so unfamiliar that for a moment I was afraid.

I put Lucy down, took a flannel from my bag, and wet it thoroughly with warm water at a basin. We squeezed into a cubicle, leaving the pushchair in a marked area by the basins. From the carrier bag I pulled out a spare bag and retrieved the blue dungarees, a red and blue jumper, and a pair of boys' socks and shoes. I lifted Lucy onto the toilet and said 'Wee wee' encouragingly. Lucy looked a bit doubtful, so I gave her a little clown figure to hold, which made her laugh. To my delight, after a moment I heard the sound of success.

'Good girl, Lucy!'

'Tacy,' she replied. 'Done wee.'

I wiped her with toilet paper, and used the wet flannel to wash her face and then her bottom. We heard the sound of someone entering the end cubicle. Lucy pointed and I smiled and nodded. Lucy nodded back. It was an understanding we shared. Lucy allowed herself to be dressed in clean underwear and the boys' clothes, including a khaki parka in place of the pink anorak. She watched a little regretfully as I stuffed the anorak into the bag. She studied the sleeves of the parka with some disdain, but did not protest.

39

The shoes were slightly too big. She gazed at them and banged her feet together. I put all of Lucy's clothes into the spare bag and quickly took off the navy coat. I put on my red coat instead and pulled off the brown wig. Lucy laughed and pointed.

'Hair!' she said.

I folded the blue coat and put it in the large carrier bag, together with the wig. I gathered Lucy's hair gently into a little band, and put a boy's woolly hat over it, careful that no long strands had escaped. Lucy put her hands up to touch the hat. I sighed gratefully when she did not try to pull it off. She looked very much like a little boy now. We opened the door of the cubicle. My heart was thundering. A woman was combing her hair at the mirror and smiled down at Lucy. I helped Lucy wash and dry her hands. Then I washed my own.

'Eee, what a clever lad,' said the woman. 'Mine'd make a terrible fuss! You've got 'im well trained, God bless 'im.' We laughed together wryly, as mothers do.

Next, we hurried to the station. I was relieved to see from my timetable that there was a direct train leaving in less than ten minutes. At the ticket office I bought a single to Newcastle for myself and we found the platform. I gave Lucy a shortbread biscuit. She nibbled it daintily. She jiggled with excitement every time a train arrived or departed, flapping her arms up and down.

'Tain, tain!' she cried, pointing.

'This is our train, Lucy,' I told her.

'Mam?'

'Yes, I'm here – Mummy's here. What fun to go on the train!'

A kind man helped lift the pushchair on. I lifted Lucy up the high step and she ran ahead into the carriage. We folded the pushchair and deposited it in the luggage store and found a seat with a table. The carrier bags fitted in the overhead luggage rack. The train was only half full and, predictably, most other passengers avoided sitting near to a small child, so we had the area to ourselves.

Initially Lucy took delight in the journey, seeing the lights flashing by, watching other passengers walk past, clambering on the seat to peep at those sitting in the next section, but I had to restrain her from this. It was important to avoid attracting anyone's attention. Also, Lucy was still wearing her boys' woolly hat to conceal her hair, but I was increasingly anxious that she might try to pull it off as the temperature in the carriage rose. I gave her a carton of chilled fruit juice I'd bought at Riddlesfield station, the loud slurping sounds as Lucy sucked on the straw clear proof of her enjoyment.

After that she sat very quietly for a while, looking at me.

'Mam?' she said, her lower lip starting to quiver. A tiny convulsive sob escaped from her. I pulled her onto my knee and whispered,

'Don't worry, Lucy – *I'm* Mummy. Mummy loves you, Lucy.'

'Tacy,' she said, a little fractiously. 'Tacy!'

She had said this before and I was unsure what she meant. Was it some toy she was missing – the dreadful doll I had seen her with the first time?

She began to whimper a little. I guessed she was tired. It was nearly eight in the evening – probably past her bedtime. Rather against my principles, I took out a little plastic box, in which was a sterilised dummy I'd been keeping in reserve, and held it in front of Lucy. She grabbed it and immediately pushed it into her mouth. I took a copy of *The Very Hungry Caterpillar* out of my bag and, rocking Lucy gently on my lap, I read the story to her. Her body went limp and relaxed. She sucked rhythmically on the dummy.

When the book was finished, Lucy patted it to indicate she wanted it read again. By the time I had finished the third reading, she was nearly asleep, her head heavy against my arm.

41

Chapter Nine

As the train doors opened at Newcastle Central Station, a blast of cold air surged in and enclosed us. Lucy was fast asleep in my arms. I hugged her close, as once again a helpful fellow passenger intervened to carry the pushchair down the steps and onto the platform. It was a relief the woman knew how to unfold it and I was able to deposit Lucy straight in and tuck the parka around her drooping form. The woman handed me the carrier bags.

'There's a little fellow who's ready for his bed,' she remarked kindly. I nodded and thanked her. We joined the queue for taxis. At the sight of Lucy, several people urged me to go ahead of them and take the next taxi. I hadn't realised how sympathetic people can be when confronted with small children. It must be a human instinct.

'Here you are, pet. You take the bairn and I'll put the buggy in the boot.'

The taxi driver regaled me with anecdotes about his own children's antics on the journey home – I was unable to absorb these stories, my mind focused on our imminent arrival. I was terribly anxious that the neighbours might see us – with Lucy in her "boy-guise". But it was dark and late in the evening. As the driver pulled up in front of the house, I had his money ready and added a largish tip, eager to be rid of him. Thankfully, not a soul was about.

By now Lucy was writhing and wriggling in my arms, and making strange animal-like moaning sounds. I struggled to hold her and unlock the front door. I put her down in the hall, grabbed the pushchair and bags, pulled them into the house and hurriedly slammed the door shut. I started to pull Lucy's hat off and unzip her outer clothes, but she wrenched herself free. She threw herself onto the carpet in the hall and kicked her feet on the floor. She started to howl.

'Maaam!' she yelled, the sound emerging in great stuttering gulps. 'Mam-Mam-Maaam! Mam-Mam-Maaaam!'

I stared at her for a moment, deeply alarmed by the noise and unsure how to proceed. I steadied my breathing and tried to recall what Mother might have done when I was upset as a small child. I faintly remembered being taken up to my room to "calm down". I took off Lucy's coat, picked up her writhing form, and carried her up to her bedroom.

'Look, Lucy! Here's Lucy's room. Isn't it lovely! Lots of toys, just for you. And here's your cosy little bed. Mummy will run you a nice warm bath and we'll put some lovely clean pyjamas on. Look, here's Teddy.'

Lucy frowned furiously. She flung the bear across the room and lay sobbing face down on the bed. I was aghast – I hadn't expected this. In fact, I was trembling, a feeling of panic taking hold – pinching at my spine. Why was Lucy so distressed at leaving behind a sordid home and such unsatisfactory and neglectful parents? Couldn't she see what a wonderful home I had prepared for her, what a wonderful life I'd planned?

And then I realised. Of course Lucy could not see. I tried to calm myself and allow reason to return, remembering what Mother had always said: "Children have no sense of time." I had so much to learn about children. It seemed that Lucy had no ability either to evaluate the present or to envisage the future.

That dirty, impoverished home and those worthless parents were all she had known and experienced. How could she possibly understand how much better life could be, how much better a *mother* could be? I resolved to show her, however long it took.

Chapter Ten

I do not regard myself as an intolerant person, nor am I politically minded. I have nothing against poor people; decent, caring, hard-working poor people. No doubt some of them make admirable parents. But equally, there is no doubt that certain types of people do not deserve the privilege of having children. Perhaps some do not even realise that it is a privilege.

Lucy's parents – Gary and Shelley Watts – spring instantly to mind. Social workers may have had the audacity to decree that I was unworthy of parenting a young child – but no end of feckless individuals, like the Watts, appear to have the right to bring children into the world willy-nilly, with no mention of the responsibilities that go hand in hand with those rights – and without a thought or care for the well-being of the children. Of course, I don't go so far as to advocate sterilisation, but the balance of rights appears all one-sided to me.

Yet, however much they might have brought the situation upon themselves, I couldn't help feeling a few transitory moments of pity for Gary and "Shell". I had ultimately submitted to buying a television set, much as I disapproved of them. Perhaps in the future, Lucy would enjoy some educational programmes, I reasoned. Meanwhile, I felt, it was important for me to keep up with news of the police search, and with their dealings with Lucy's birth parents.

The usual "television appeal" (media circus, you could call it!) did Gary and "Shell" no favours. To be sure, they were not a photogenic pair. Gary, with his shifty, rat-like features, lumpy shaved head and extensive tattoos, looked the epitome of a vicious criminal rather than a responsible, loving father. Most people would hardly trust him to wash their windows, let alone entrust a small child to his care. Indeed, the *Daily Mail* reported that according to their information, Gary Watts had served a prison sentence for burglary in the past.

The image projected by Shelley Watts was no more appealing. Her pudding-like face was red and blotchy. Her shapeless body appeared entirely boneless; enormous breasts like vast jellyfish, swelling and spilling over the table in a repulsive way, as she leaned towards the camera. An unfortunate habit of regularly swiping her eyes and nose with her sleeve elicited disgust rather than sympathy. I shuddered. How had such an unprepossessing pair produced an exquisite child like Lucy? It was a mystery.

'Please, please …' Shelley sobbed and spluttered on the screen, 'please don' 'urt her. Please don' 'urt me Stace!' (The name was bad enough without the shortening.) She sat up straight and stared directly into the camera.

'Stacy baby, we love ya, we miss ya. Please, please, we jus' want 'er home …' She dissolved into gulps and wails, her great, hunched shoulders shaking. The police inspector supervising the case – Detective Inspector Lawrence Dempster – was a rather handsome man in his early forties, about my age in fact, I noticed. He was tall, his temples reassuringly streaked with silver. His manner projected intelligence and authority. He patted Shelley's lumpen back and handed her a bunch of paper tissues. Gary, the father, then had his turn at inarticulate pleading.

'Was the little girl playing outside on her own, Gary?' shouted one of the gathered journalists.

'We 'ardly let 'er outa our sight,' mumbled Gary. 'We was in the back room – so we could check 'er all the time, like. 'Er brothers and sisters keep a watch on 'er.' (This was rich, I thought, remembering how Lucy had been playing entirely alone outside – a two-year-old child!) 'Yeah, they miss 'er something rotten – Ashley, Sean, Kelly and Ryan – they want 'er back an' all. We all do. She was just playin' out the back, like. She was all right.'

He gazed at the cameras open-mouthed, his expression one of challenging idiocy.

'Then …' he said, 'a moment later she was gone. Just … just gone in seconds.'

He shook his head in apparent disbelief, and clasped his forehead with both hands.

The roomful of reporters was silent for a moment, the camera stilled on Gary's face.

'Why are no photographs of Stacy being published?' a woman at the back enquired. 'Surely that would make it easier to identify the child?'

Gary opened his mouth to respond. Inspector Dempster placed a hand on Gary's arm and intervened.

'Unfortunately,' he said soothingly, 'the family had no camera beyond Stacy's babyhood, so they were unable to provide current photographs.'

'We did have a camera, like, but it broke …' said Gary. A murmur rose from the gathered press.

'Is it true you've previously had two other children taken into care?' someone called.

The parents looked dazed and exchanged shifty glances. They both turned and looked at Detective Inspector Dempster, as if for guidance. He stood and raised his hands towards the room, as though preparing to conduct an orchestra.

'No more questions today, ladies and gentlemen,' he said firmly. 'I can assure you that every line of inquiry is being pursued. We will spare no effort to find little Stacy. If any members of the public have any information about Stacy and her disappearance, anything at all, however small, please contact us on the number now on the screen – or via your local police station.'

He narrowed his eyes and swivelled his gaze to take in all the members of the press in the room, like a stern teacher eyeing an unruly class.

'You will be informed of any further developments, but please understand: this investigation is at a very early stage. Thank you.'

The weeping parents were ushered out.

For some days the newspapers and television news programmes were full of accounts of Stacy and her family, of the search for the child, with long lines of police reinforced by volunteers tramping shoulder to shoulder over grassy slopes, searching any nearby parks and open ground. Ominously, ponds and rivers were dragged repeatedly.

At first the press was largely sympathetic to the parents, but as time went on there were murmurings about whether they themselves might have been involved in her disappearance. The back yard was dug up. Both parents were taken in for questioning by the police on several occasions, although, of course, this was always expressed as "helping the police with their inquiries".

Next-door neighbours were interviewed and appeared eager to share their impressions of the Watts. They talked of frequent loud arguments, furniture and household objects being thrown about. Domestic violence was hinted at, as was heavy drinking, and possible drug-taking. The older children ran wild; their behaviour was out of control and their school attendance erratic. A picture of a highly dysfunctional family was emerging. What a blessing I had removed Lucy from such an environment.

There were one or two reported sightings of a child of Stacy's age in the nearby area, and a few from further afield, but they were vague and lacked details. None led to any significant findings. The police tried to put a positive slant on the investigation. They were seriously concerned for the child's welfare, they said, but were confident that she was still alive. They were pursuing several lines of inquiry.

It was reported that an elderly woman who lived in the next street had seen a dark-haired woman in a navy coat, pushing a buggy with a child of Stacy's description towards Safeways and British Home Stores in the town centre. A sales assistant in British Home Stores said she thought she might have seen someone a bit like that too, but then again, she thought it might have been a little boy in the pushchair, not a girl, and she wasn't sure if the coat was blue – maybe it was. After that, I read with interest, "the trail went cold".

I felt compelled to watch the news programmes about Lucy's disappearance. Of course, if it hadn't been absolutely necessary, I would never have obtained a child in that way. The papers and television reports frequently referred to her being "taken", but I couldn't accept the term in the sense of stolen or kidnapped. No, her removal from that family was more an act of liberation, of charity, one that relieved her of a life of potential misery, neglect, poverty and ultimate under-achievement.

The more I saw of Lucy's family and learned of their lifestyle, the more convinced I became that taking her away from her parents could be regarded as salvation.

Chapter Eleven

The time came when I had to admit to myself that the initial period with Lucy was not easy, not easy at all. Should I have expected such difficulties? Yes, I realised, perhaps I should, but my direct experience of small children and their responses had been extremely limited.

It took my little daughter much longer to settle in her new home than I had anticipated. All my careful preparations – with Lucy's happiness in mind – seemed to mean nothing to her. The pretty bedroom with its colourful matching curtains, cushions and bedding depicting amusing cartoon-like jungle scenes; the carefully chosen toys and books; the cheerful pictures and friezes decorating the walls: none of these things elicited the slightest interest or pleasure in Lucy.

The first week was the hardest. During the daytime, Lucy mostly lay on the floor, crying and moaning. She would kick and scream when I tried to comfort or even approach her. She woke frequently during the night, and her screams were pitiful. So often did she wake with soaking sheets that in the end I had to put nappies on her during the night.

For some days after her arrival, she would eat and drink nothing but a little water, and I began to fear seriously for her health. At last, in desperation, I added a little sugar to a saucepan of milk, warmed it and filled a baby's bottle. I lifted her onto my knee. At first she arched her back and howled like a wild creature, but I persisted, holding her firm, and after a while she submitted to being rocked gently on my lap. She sucked rhythmically on the teat, and took the whole bottle, her eyes rolling up into their lids. Her body went limp with exhaustion. At last she fell into a deep sleep.

This was a turning point. I realised that perhaps Lucy had missed out on some crucial early stages of babyhood. Of course she had, with neglectful parents like hers. Why had I not thought of it before? I endeavoured to restore these vital experiences to Lucy, even though she was now about two or two and a half years old – hardly a tiny baby. Yet, what did it matter if, in private, I rocked Lucy to sleep like an infant, hummed and sang to her when she was distressed, allowed her a dummy and fed her with a baby bottle?

Lucy talked little at first, but every now and then she repeated a tedious little litany in a plaintive questioning voice.

'Mam? Dad? Wy-yan? Polly …? Tacy … Mam?'

By this time I had learned more of Lucy's former family from television and newspaper reports. I knew that "Tacy" referred to her previous name. What a fortunate chance that Stacy and Lucy sounded not totally dissimilar. Surely she would soon adjust? "Wy-yan" of course was Ryan, the brother nearest to Lucy in age – whom I had witnessed paying her little enough attention, indeed, abandoning her on the pavement outside her former house. He was, in my opinion, quite undeserving of her affection. It took me a while to remember that Polly was the name of the filthy, naked and disfigured doll, with which Lucy had been playing when I first set eyes on her.

* * *

51

The first time I dared to take Lucy out of the house was many weeks after her arrival. I suggested we should go and buy a "new Polly" for her. Lucy's little face lit up, and she actually smiled! My heart turned to liquid and I nearly wept aloud.

'Buy Polly,' she said, nodding eagerly.

We made our way to the High Street, where I had noticed a small toyshop. The assistant immediately stepped forwards and asked how she could help us.

'We're looking for a doll,' I explained. 'In fact, my little girl has lost a favourite old doll, and I'm hoping to find a similar one for her.'

We were shown the rows of baby dolls, brown dolls, black dolls and white dolls, boy dolls and girl dolls, dolls with plastic heads and dolls with hair. I found one that seemed to me the closest in size and features to Polly, although this one was in pristine condition, quite unlike the stained and discoloured appearance of the original. The doll had blond hair tied up in a bunch on top of her head with a pink ribbon. She wore a frilly pink dress and knickers.

The box in which she reclined also contained a tiny plastic brush and comb, a baby bottle and a small yellow potty, all held to a cardboard base with rubber bands. The doll's face wore an expression of exceptional stupidity. When upright, her eyelids fluttered open to reveal large blue, sightless eyes. Her red lips were pursed in a look of perpetual astonishment, heightened by the small round hole in their centre, presumably into which the bottle could be inserted.

'She wets an' all,' the assistant informed Lucy, who regarded the doll balefully.

'Not Polly,' she said. I crouched down in front of the pushchair, facing Lucy, and spoke in a quiet whisper.

'No, Lucy, but she's *like* Polly, isn't she? You'll see, when we get home we'll take her clothes off and give her a bath, shall we?'

She frowned. 'Not Polly.'

52

I quickly paid and we pushed out of the shop. Lucy did not want to carry the doll on the way home and maintained a resentful silence. Once in the house, she yanked all the clothes off the doll and flung them aside. She took the ribbon from its head and pulled violently at the pale, yellow hair, until it stood in rough tufts.

'Leg off,' she said, her little hands tugging ineffectually at the doll's limb. She looked at me. I sighed. Defeated, I prised the right leg out of its rubbery socket and handed the doll back to Lucy.

Chapter Twelve

I knew it was important to introduce Lucy to our neighbours, but the thought of how she might behave filled me with apprehension. I took her first to meet Frank and Molly Armstrong. Molly tried to lift her up into an embrace, but Lucy immediately uttered a squeal, wriggled free and retreated behind me.

'Oh I'm sorry, Molly – she's very shy at the moment,' I said. Molly nodded knowingly and went to a low cupboard in the corner of the room. She extracted a decorated box, crouched on the floor and took the lid off. Lucy watched with interest from behind my legs.

'Frank, bring that blue and white tin tray from the kitchen, would you, pet?'

Molly emptied a cascade of buttons from the box onto the tray with a satisfying tinging noise. She poured the buttons back into the box and then emptied them onto the tray again. Lucy was mesmerised.

'There you are, Lucy. You have a look at the pretty buttons, but don't put them in your mouth, mind.'

Lucy spent half an hour picking up one handful of buttons after another and letting them drop onto the metal tray, time and time again. She didn't utter a word during the entire visit.

Molly and Frank seemed unperturbed. They watched her absorption in the activity with satisfaction.

'I'm afraid she's been very quiet ... since her daddy died ...' I mouthed at them behind my hand.

'Don't you worry, Alison. Your Lucy's been through a difficult time. She'll come round before you know it,' Frank said softly, as Molly made us some tea.

* * *

A few days later I took Lucy to see the Harmons. Michael was at work, but Susan and the children were home. Claire and Charlie were delighted to see Lucy. They brought lots of their toys to show her. She stared wide-eyed at them from the safety of my chair, her expression frozen.

'Why won't she play?' asked Charlie, frowning.

'Just leave her alone; let her do what she wants,' said Claire. Such a mature, sensible child.

'Charlie, will you come and help me get some squash and snacks, please?' said Susan. They disappeared to the kitchen together. Claire brought a pile of picture books, put them on the floor near Lucy, and retreated. Lucy looked at her and then looked at the books. She looked at me, and then at the books again.

Susan and Charlie brought in a tray. After a few minutes, when Claire and Charlie were occupied with a bowl of crisps and a plate of chocolate animals, Lucy crawled hesitantly across the carpet towards the books and began looking at them. Claire looked at me and her mother, and smiled. Susan winked at her.

I began to realise that Susan had what I had always felt lacking in myself: an instinctive understanding of the thoughts, feelings and reactions of other people. What a wonderful ability it seemed

55

to be, and clearly something that Claire had inherited, or perhaps learned, from her mother. Perhaps, in time, I could learn such skills myself.

Chapter Thirteen

People like Susan and Molly, close neighbours who had extended friendship to me, expressed no surprise that Lucy was quieter and more withdrawn than other children of her age. It was natural, they said, in view of her experience of losing her father, and the disruption this tragedy had imposed on our lives. Molly told me it was important for Lucy to play with other children.

'She's such a serious little mite, bless her – be nice to see her running about with some other little bairns her own age.'

'Why don't you take her to the playgroup next to the church?' suggested Susan. 'It would be good for her to play with other children. Charlie absolutely loved it. Be good for you to meet some other mums too. It's just a couple of hours three times a week, and Harriet Grant, the playgroup leader, is absolutely fantastic at involving all the children, no matter how shy they are. Go on, Alison, it'd be good for both of you.'

So everyone seemed to know what was good for Lucy, and me – what was best for us. But shouldn't Lucy be with me? Wasn't it best for young children to spend as much time as possible with their mothers? Yes, my supporters replied – united in their opinions, it seemed – but it's just as important for them to have the company of their "peers" – they need to learn to play cooperatively, to communicate, and develop their social skills.

I resented this interference, but in the end their perseverance won and I gave in. Susan came with me – just to introduce me to the playgroup staff and some of the mothers, she said. Lucy sat on my knee clinging tightly to my sleeve for the first half-hour. She'd been eyeing a dolls' house on a table close to us. Eventually she slid cautiously off my lap and walked hesitantly towards her goal. Susan nudged me.

'There you are,' she whispered. 'What did I tell you?'

A little girl was playing with the dolls and toy furniture, arranging them in one room, then moving them somewhere else. Lucy stood watching her for a few minutes. Then she sat down on the small chair next to her. The other little girl smiled and chatted about the toys.

'I like that one, that mummy one,' she said, pointing to a toy figure. 'I gonna put her in the bath!' She looked at Lucy and giggled.

Lucy watched her solemnly. She picked up a boy figure, bent his legs and sat him on a chair. She nodded. 'Put Wy-yan on tair,' she said.

Every now and then, as she explored the toys, Lucy turned around as if to check what I was doing. Watching her seeking me out for reassurance, I felt a terrible pain in my heart; a feeling that was both intense and mysterious, yet not altogether unpleasant.

Chapter Fourteen

I worked hard at building our life together, and ultimately felt confident that anyone who understood the situation would agree I was very successful, despite the difficult start. Of course, no one did truly understand – I had convinced myself that it was vital that no one should know, and that therefore no one *could* understand. Although I had never been someone who depended on friends and confidantes, my awareness of this conviction made me feel very lonely at times.

That first summer I rented a cottage for Lucy and me in southwest Scotland, just a hundred yards from the beach. We went for walks, dug endlessly in the sand, paddled and splashed in the shallows, collected shells, ate sandwiches on the beach for lunch, and fish and chips or hot dogs and ice creams for tea.

It was some weeks since Lucy had mentioned her "mam" or had cried. Very gradually she spoke more, looked at me more and even laughed sometimes. She loved stories. Some of our happiest times were spent in the library or curled up on the sofa, looking at picture books together. Every night when I tucked her up in bed, I remembered to hug Lucy and tell her how much I loved her.

Mother had been devoted to me in every way, I knew, but it

was not in her nature, or perhaps her upbringing, to express affection openly in this way – and she was aware that I was not a child who enjoyed physical closeness. I was determined that I would have no such inhibitions with Lucy. Had she shown any signs of returning affection to me during those early weeks and months, it would have been so much easier, but she did not – or perhaps, she could not.

'I love you, Lucy,' I said each night, kissing her. I knew it was important to tell her. 'Mummy loves you so, so much.'

Lucy would respond by regarding me silently with a deep, impenetrable look.

* * *

On September 20th 1985, the date I'd assigned to Lucy's third birthday, I arranged a little party for her. Of course, I was unsure exactly when *Stacy* was born, but I had created a birthday for Lucy based on the records of poor little dead Lucy, which must have been near enough correct. September 20th was the date written into my Lucy's birth certificate.

I had made a cake to look like the little house in Lucy's book of Hansel and Gretel, a story that she loved dearly. I decorated it with coloured icing, chocolate buttons and Smarties. The morning of Lucy's birthday, Claire asked if she could come in to help me prepare, but I wanted very much to do it all myself. I thanked Claire, but explained that it would really help me create the surprise party food if she would entertain Lucy while I made the preparations. I also asked her to be a special helper at the party itself.

While they played in the sitting room, I shut the kitchen door and assembled plates of tiny sandwiches and sausage rolls, chocolate animals, little cheese and pineapple cubes on sticks, and bowls of crisps and jelly. Just like Mother had made for me years

60

earlier. These preparations gave me such pleasure. There was no doubt I was a real mother now.

Both Claire and Charlie came to the party, of course; Claire enjoyed organising some simple games for the smaller children: Pass the Parcel, The Farmer in his Den and Musical Bumps. Jenny, Mark, Megan and Laura – friends from playgroup – and their parents had been invited too. We asked our neighbours on either side, Susan and Mike and Frank and Molly, as well.

Everyone agreed how much Lucy had "come on" since she first came to Newcastle in March. It was true. She was a different child from the wan, disturbed little creature of seven months previously. She spoke more clearly and confidently, and her vocabulary had grown enormously. These days she hardly ever mentioned members of her former family. I was starting to feel much more positive, more confident about her progress.

Perhaps I was becoming overconfident. When it was time to sit at the long table for tea, the children began squabbling about who should sit next to Lucy, but she kept pushing each of them away.

'No, not sit there!'

I came and crouched by her chair and spoke quietly. Claire was hovering behind her.

'Lucy dear, why not let Claire sit next to you?'

Lucy adored Claire; surely this arrangement would please her?

'She can help you blow out the candles.'

Lucy looked round at Claire and frowned. Her face reflected some inner turmoil. To my consternation, tears sprang in her eyes.

'Not Claire, no!' she said firmly, fixing me with her most determined stare. '*Stacy* sit there.'

There it was – the name Stacy again – just when things were going so well. Although, fortunately, only I had heard her say it, this incident chilled me to the core; I worried terribly about it. What did it mean? Did it just happen to be a name that lingered

61

faintly in her memory and perhaps came into her head suddenly; or had she somehow invented an imaginary friend based on her former self? If there were an imagined Stacy, whom she believed could sit next to her, what did that imply about Lucy's sense of herself – her "identity", a psychologist might have said?

In the end it was agreed that none of the children should sit next to Lucy. Instead that honour was afforded to Polly, the unfortunate, one-legged doll, which she still worshipped.

* * *

Then, about a month after Lucy's birthday, there was a great breakthrough. It meant the world to me, and went some way to setting my mind at rest about the "Stacy" incident.

It was a beautiful autumn day, the sun skittering in and out of the oak and sycamore leaves, just taking on their deepest colours. We had gone for a walk and ended up at the little playground in the wooded area behind our house. Lucy was becoming more daring and showed signs of becoming an agile climber. I had to resist the urge to be overprotective, to shield her from any perceived danger – in order to allow her to explore her own capabilities. She had learned to clamber up the bars of the metal fence that separated the playground from the adjoining pathway.

This particular afternoon I went to sit on a wooden bench, enjoying the quiet, the mild air and the slanting golden sunshine – watching while Lucy was balancing at the top of the fence in a "look, no hands" stance. I delighted in Lucy's pleasure and felt calm and peaceful. Just then, a woman with a large Alsatian dog approached on the path. The dog was busily sniffing the ground.

As they came level with Lucy, the dog suddenly noticed her and tried to leap towards her, barking ferociously. Fortunately, the owner had a tight hold on the lead, so he was restrained, but Lucy got a terrible fright and screamed out 'Mummy! Mummy!'

at the top of her voice. I rushed to Lucy, carried her back to the seat and cuddled her until the sobs subsided. All the while, as I comforted Lucy in her distress, my heart was leaping with such joy I wanted to laugh out loud. Lucy had called me *Mummy*.

Chapter Fifteen

January 1987

Lucy

I'm a big girl now. Mummy said so. Going to big school today. Not nursery any more. Got special clothes for school. I like yellow shirt best. Yellow my favourite colour – like sunshine. My sweatshirt is blue. Got a badge with words on. Wear it when it's cold. I got a grey skirt. Mummy says I look smart; I look grown-up.

We walked to the school. Mummy held my hand. Lots of children in the yard. There are some coloured lines on the ground. Wiggling about. Maybe we paint coloured lines in school today? Some boys and girls running on the lines and laughing.

I want to run on the yellow line, but my heart feels bumpy. Wish Stacy was here. Don't tell Mummy. Mummy doesn't like Stacy. Makes her sad. I'm holding Mummy's hand and watching the boys and girls.

Mummy says, 'Go on, Lucy, don't you want to play? It'll be time to go inside in a minute.'

I see Laura from playgroup. She runs over. She stands in front of me, smile on her face. She sticks out her hand to me. I look at Mummy. She smiles and nods her head. Laura and me hold hands and run. She pulls me to a red line.

'No! Yellow,' I say.

Laura says 'OK' and we chase the yellow line all round the playground, laughing and laughing.

Suddenly a bell is ringing. Big, loud bell. We stop running. A teacher lady is standing by the door with her face smiling. Another lady next to her. All the children run to near her. She shouts in a kind voice, 'Good morning, children! How lovely to see you all! Welcome to you on your first day of school! My name is Miss Carson. This is Mrs Hope, our special kind helper. We're all going to have a lovely day today: playing with toys and games, listening to stories, and *learning* lots of exciting things! Does that sound like fun?'

Some of the children shout, 'Yes!'

Laura shouts 'Yes!' but I feel shy. I look for Stacy. Some children jump up and down.

Miss Carson says, 'Well, children, say "bye-bye" to your mummies and daddies now. And say "see you later".'

Miss Carson says in a loud excited voice, 'Then – let's – go – in – and – have – a – look – at – our – *classroom*!'

I run back to Mummy and she gave me a big hug, and my special yellow schoolbag.

'Bye-bye, Lucy dear, have a wonderful day, and I'll be here to pick you up at three o'clock,' she says, and she pushes me towards Miss Carson, not hard.

Laura walking into school too, and lots of other children. Some children still hugging their mummies and daddies, and crying. The Mrs Hope lady goes to talk to them. I not crying, but I wish Stacy was here.

Chapter Sixteen

1987

Alison

At the start of the January term, when Lucy was nearly four and a half, she began attending the Reception class of the local first school. By this time the press had long tired of Stacy's disappearance and moved on to other more current or more sensational news stories. Just occasionally, one of the tabloid newspapers ran a feature headed something like "Wherever is Stacy?", followed by speculation as to her whereabouts, or presented some trumped-up theory about her fate with the white slave trade or itinerant gypsies, or made even darker references to paedophiles and murderers.

About a year after "Stacy's abduction" Inspector Dempster had made an appeal on the BBC *Crimewatch* programme. I watched it after Lucy had gone to bed. Detective Inspector Dempster looked tired, I noticed. There were dark circles under his eyes, but he was still a handsome man; distinguished, just as I remembered him. He spoke articulately, with quiet confidence, and with just a hint of a northern accent discernible. He reminded viewers of the few details that were known concerning Stacy's disappearance, and urged them to search their memories for any further information.

A reconstruction of the "abduction", as they called it, was shown. A shadowy figure of a woman in a dark coat was scurrying down one of Riddlesfield's gloomy terraces, pushing a fair-haired toddler in a pushchair. I was delighted to note that the film showed her pushing it down the wrong street! What's more, they showed only a little *girl* in the pushchair, and clearly had no idea of her transformation into a boy at that stage – a boy in a woolly hat with no fair hair showing.

The public was asked that anyone present in the area that night, who might have seen a small fair-haired girl or had noticed anything unusual – anything at all, however insignificant it might appear – should report their observations immediately. A little *boy* was never mentioned. Detective Inspector Dempster did say that Stacy might have been taken to a car parked elsewhere in the town, or possibly to the train station. He therefore reminded viewers that the child could have been taken anywhere in Britain, or even abroad. No mention was made specifically of the North East as a likely destination, which was a relief to me.

The programme had shown an artist's impression of what Stacy might have looked like at the current time. I wasn't too concerned about this – it really could have been any snub-nosed, fair-haired four-year-old. The artist had no dental records and no up-to-date photographs on which to base this likeness – the family had never taken Lucy to visit a dentist and had no recent photos of her, only one or two baby pictures. Neither were any distinguishing features mentioned, which might have marked her out. Yet I knew that Lucy actually had a diamond-shaped brown birthmark on the back of her neck, only visible by lifting her hair. I'd seen it as soon as I washed her hair for the first time. No doubt her parents had never even noticed it – it wouldn't surprise me if they'd never washed her hair.

Detective Inspector Dempster had ended by assuring the public that the case would never, never be closed – until Stacy was found. The unspoken words "alive or dead" hung in the air.

Periodically, there were newspaper interviews with Gary and Shelley Watts, well paid, no doubt, which printed nauseous quotes from the "still-grieving parents", such as 'We'll never forget our Stace …', 'We'll search for our girl if it takes for ever …' and the like. All my opinions about Lucy's birth family were confirmed. There could be no doubt she was far better off with me – and without them.

By this time Lucy's Riddlesfield accent was long gone. Despite some slight lingering immaturities, everyone remarked on how beautifully she spoke, what a wide vocabulary she had, what good manners she had. It was something that mattered a lot to me. I felt it was important to bring her up to be polite, just as Mother had with me.

At first when Lucy was given something and I had prompted her with 'What do you say, Lucy?' she would reply 'Ta'. I would have to explain to others that unfortunately my aunt in Nottingham, though well meaning, had taught her some slang and also some "baby words", of which I did not approve. The aunt had misguidedly thought it was easier for a small child to learn to say "ta" rather than "thank you", I told them. Personally, I never believed there was any necessity to alter language for children. How can "choo-choo" be easier to learn than "train", or "bye-byes" rather than "sleep"? It just meant the unfortunate child ended up having to learn two words rather than the correct one in the first place.

So, early on, Lucy had received some intensive speech training from me to great effect, and was soon using "please" and "thank you", and other social niceties. I find people always prefer a well-mannered child, as I do myself.

* * *

The first time I went to see Lucy's pleasant young Reception teacher, I was delighted to hear positive reports about how well she had settled, and how quick was her progress with literacy and numeracy – she was definitely one of the brightest children in the class. She was a polite and well-behaved little girl, and never caused any trouble.

It was true she was a little shy, Miss Carson said, but that was quite normal. It was early days. She'd soon learn to form friendships more readily. Perhaps I could help by inviting one or two of the other children to play at home? Of course I was eager to do anything to help Lucy, although I felt there was an unnecessarily heavy emphasis at such a young age on "making friends". However, that evening I began by asking Lucy what her "best friends" in the class were called. For such a bright child, she seemed to have difficulty grasping the concept.

'I've got lots of friends.'

'That's good, Lucy. So, who do you like best? Who would you like to come and play with you here?'

She listed nearly all the children in the class. I found this response a little irritating, but tried hard not to show any impatience.

'I'm glad you've got so many friends, Lucy, but can you think of one girl or boy you like *best*? Someone to come and play with you at home?'

'I like to play with Stacy best.'

I was stunned. Instantly my hands began to tremble. It was as though Lucy had punched me hard in the stomach. I took a deep breath.

'Lucy, Stacy is not real. She's in your imagination. It's like a … a dream, but not real.'

Lucy gazed back at me with her most inscrutable expression. I made a great effort to remain cool, not to show any trace of anxiety or irritation.

After yet further coaxing, still no special friend's name was forthcoming, and Lucy was showing signs of becoming distressed by the conversation. In the end I had to avoid prolonging the questioning by deciding to make the choice of special playmate myself. I did this largely on the basis of which of the parents I liked best. After all, good parents tend to have good children.

We started with Laura. She was a dear little girl, thoughtful and solemn, with a mass of dark curls, contrasting with Lucy's fair hair. I liked Laura's mother Rosemary, who was a librarian. She was quiet and contemplative. Both girls shared a love of books. Yet they did not actually share the books. When I went upstairs to Lucy's room to tell the children tea was ready, I found each girl sitting companionably on the floor cushions next to one another, leaning against the wall on the far side of the room, reading to herself. Not a word passed between them. Nevertheless, they seemed perfectly amicable and content.

From time to time we asked Charlie to play. I felt we had to – after all, he lived next door and Susan had been so kind to me, and regarded herself as a close friend. On her own, Lucy often enjoyed playing imaginative games with toy animals or figures – inventing elaborate scenes and stories. Charlie preferred lively games. His imagination focused on noisy vehicles, dinosaurs, fierce animals or monsters, fights, chases and crashes. A lot of shouting was involved.

Both Lucy and I were always quite exhausted by the time he went home. It was a relief to tidy up together at the end of the day. However, the tension Charlie's company created had a noticeable effect on Lucy, and not a positive one. On one occasion, when he was being particularly loud, Lucy closed her eyes, put her hands over her ears and screwed up her face.

'Stop shouting, Dad!' she yelled.

The room seemed to still. Charlie stopped in his tracks. He glanced at me and raised his eyebrows in a knowing fashion, as if he and I shared some special understanding. I felt an urge to smack him. He turned back to Lucy.

'I'm not your dad!' he said laughing. 'He's dead, isn't he?'

Poor Lucy looked at me in utter confusion, and burst into tears.

* * *

The following term Miss Carson called me in to school for a second time. Having had time to observe Lucy for some months, she said, she had some concerns about Lucy's "social skills". 'Nothing to worry about, but we don't want Lucy becoming isolated, do we?' She was not unpopular, Miss Carson said. The other children liked her, but were unsure how to react to her. She often appeared indifferent to them, to live in her own little world. Miss Carson wondered if it would be helpful to refer her to a child psychologist. What would Lucy's daddy and I feel about that?

Expected to respond spontaneously out of the blue, I hesitated for a moment, my hands trembling, and then explained to Miss Carson that Lucy's father had passed away when Lucy was two. There was only Lucy and myself. Miss Carson looked profoundly shocked. Then she appeared to gather herself. She nodded in an understanding way, as if this news explained everything.

'Oh, Mrs Brown, I'm so very sorry. If only you had made that clear to school when Lucy started, we could have … taken it into account.'

'Yes, you're right. Probably I should have told school staff sooner. But you see, it was so difficult dealing with my own bereavement at that stage, as well as Lucy's. I … I could hardly bear to talk about it.' I dabbed my eyes with my handkerchief.

'No, I see, I do understand – how dreadful for you. I'm so, so sorry,' she repeated. 'It's just that … if we had known, maybe we could have given Lucy some special help.'

'She doesn't need special help – all she needs is more time, more understanding. I will help her. I am helping her. She certainly doesn't need to see a psychologist.'

'No, of course not,' Miss Carson said hastily. 'I'm so sorry. Now that we do know … well … we can all help Lucy.'

* * *

Susan agreed with Miss Carson's viewpoint.

'Honestly, Alison, you're so secretive. I can't think why you didn't tell her teacher before. They need to know about such important aspects of the children's lives. They need to understand just how well Lucy's done over the past year, considering what she's been through.' Susan grasped my hand.

'After all, she's had to make so many adjustments in her short life, hasn't she? Losing her father, moving to a new city far from her previous home and family. And now, starting school – which is quite enough of an adjustment on its own for most children!'

'Yes, perhaps I should have been more open about it. It's just that … well, I suppose I am a very private person.'

Susan smiled, put her arm around me affectionately and hugged me. I steeled myself.

'Aren't you just, dear, Alison! A *very* private person.' She looked at me thoughtfully.

'You know, maybe you should talk to Lucy more about her daddy,' she suggested. 'Young children need lots of help to absorb such a huge loss; to understand death at all. Why not visit her grandparents – her paternal grandparents – so Lucy could learn more about her father from them? You could look at some photographs of him together.' Her voice rose with enthusiasm as she expanded her theme.

'What about making a memory box? Fill it with pictures and mementos, to help her remember and make her daddy more real for her? After all, she was so young when she lost him.'

Susan paused to allow me to absorb these wisdoms. She grasped both of my hands; I forced myself not to recoil and withdraw them. She peered into my face, as though a photograph of my dead "husband" might suddenly appear there.

'*You* never talk about him either, Alison,' she said. 'I know it must be hard for you, but don't you think it would help both of you to talk about him more?'

'You're probably right,' I said slowly. 'It was all so traumatic … I suppose I've tried to bury the memory, along with him. I must learn to be more open. But his parents, Lucy's grandparents … well … er … unfortunately they live abroad … so we can't visit them just yet.'

'Oh, what a shame! Well maybe one day …' She looked thoughtful. 'Well, what about that aunt who looked after Lucy while you got the house ready just after you bought it? Was she your husband's aunt? Might she help?'

Another unexpected hurdle to negotiate! I thought rapidly of a solution, and it had to be a final one.

'No … I'm afraid not,' I said, looking as sad as I could manage. 'She was very old, poor thing, and she died not long after I moved up here.'

'Oh no! How awful. Poor Alison, what a lot of bereavements you've had.'

How exhausting it was. I had never considered that maintaining a lie requires constant vigilance and effort. Just when you think you can relax and move on, suddenly a whole new chapter of the story is needed. I realised I was going to have to work on Lucy's father. I had thought that killing him off would dispose of him conveniently once and for all, but now it was apparent I would have to invent much more of an identity, more of a presence, and even a family history for him, even though he was dead.

'Do you know, Alison, I don't think I even know what your poor husband's name was,' Susan said, as we sipped our coffee.

It was true – I had never given a thought to his name, and

though I had filed it away in a drawer somewhere, I hadn't given the father's name on poor dead little Lucy Brown's birth certificate a thought for so long! I closed my eyes for a moment and applied my mind to this supposed dead husband of mine. Desperately, I scanned my memory for his name. What was it again? Something a bit unusual, something connected with writers or philosophers. A series of rapid thoughts clicked through my brain. Was it Bertrand? No, that was *too* unusual, too odd … and yet Bertrand rang a bell. I know – Bertrand Russell – that was it! *Russell*. Russell was his name.

Susan, perhaps observing my mental struggle, assumed I was overcome with emotion. Once again she put an arm around me and hugged me affectionately. Why people seem to need to express friendship in this way I'll never know. My whole body tensed.

'Russell!' I burst out. 'His name was Russell. Russell Brown of course.'

'Russell. Aaaah.'

Susan put her head on one side and adopted her sad, sympathetic face, as if there was something inherently endearing about the name Russell. Oh God, I thought, please let this conversation end.

Chapter Seventeen

1988

Just after half-term, chicken pox rampaged through the school. I had hoped Lucy might avoid it – she was one of the last children in her class to show symptoms. One afternoon, as I waited in the schoolyard with little groups of other parents, she emerged slowly, looking quite unlike her normal cheerful self. She was pale and listless, and dragged her schoolbag, as if she hadn't the energy to carry it.

At home she wanted little to eat, which was unusual for her these days; she generally had a good appetite. I gave her plenty to drink, but all she really wanted was to sit on my lap and be cuddled. There was something very appealing about her in this state; her need for physical contact and affection was rather gratifying – and also a novelty for me, never having learned to enjoy cuddles myself, even as a young child. But I did enjoy cuddling Lucy. Lucy was different. I read stories to her until she became sleepy, and I put her to bed early. In the night I woke with a start to hear Lucy crying and calling out to me.

'Mummy! Mummy!'

I ran into her room and clutched her hot little frame close. She was damp and trembling, sobs convulsing her body. Her eyes stared straight ahead.

'Shhh, my darling,' I said. 'Everything's all right, dear girl. Mummy's here.'

'Another Mummy was there! I saw her. She said, "Come with me." She had a dark coat on and brown hair that came off! I'm frightened, Mummy, don't let her take me!'

'No one's going to take you. It was just a dream. You're safe with me, quite safe.'

I bathed her forehead with a cool flannel and gave her a spoonful of Calpol. Soon her breathing slowed and she slept. My heart was pounding. Did she remember? No, surely, it was just the fever? I was deeply unnerved. Unable to settle back to sleep, I went downstairs, and made some camomile tea.

I extracted Lucy's crayon box from the toy cupboard, and tipped them out onto the floor. I spent half an hour arranging them in the shape of a rainbow on the carpet, their colours in the order of the spectrum. I counted them. There were forty-one altogether, a prime number, which was a bonus. After that I felt a bit calmer.

In the morning, Lucy's spots started to appear – a few blisters scattered on her tummy at first, gradually multiplying to form a rash all over her body. She lay limp, vulnerable and dependent. I offered to bring her some breakfast, but she was only able to drink a little orange juice.

'Poor little Lucy. My poor little girl.' I stroked her head gently. 'Never mind. I'll look after you and you'll soon be better. At least you can stay home with Mummy. No school this week. I'll read you a story later. We'll have a nice time.'

Lucy held my hand and smiled wanly.

'How did you sleep, Lucy?'

'All right, I think. But my head hurts.'

'I know, dear. I'll get you some more Calpol in a minute.'
I hesitated at the door. I turned and looked at Lucy.
'Any dreams?'
'No, I don't think so. I can't remember any.'

Chapter Eighteen

October 1989

Shelley

It's our Stacy's birthday. Seven years old today. Fancy, five years since she was took, five whole years. Hard to believe I've lived through those years, somehow – if you can call it living. I wake up each morning – not that I sleep much – and for just a second or two I wonder if it's all been a dream, a nightmare. Even after five years.

And then I remember; I realise she's gone, and it's like a dark cloud wraps itself around me and works its way inside me. I want to pull the covers over me head and stay there in bed all day, block out the memories. But I can't. I've got me other bairns to think of.

I think about Stacy; what she looks like now, where she is, what she might be doing. Is she somewhere near, or is she far away, is she happy or sad? More than anything, I think about who might be with her. A man, a woman, a whole family? Are they good to her, are they kind? I can't bear to think they might be cruel, that they might hurt her.

My head starts to hurt and I go all hot and cold thinking about the person what took her. I fill up with such a rage it's like I'll explode. I have to press all that anger down inside meself so the kids don't see it, and get back to thinking of Stacy and her little beautiful face. I think of her smiling, smiling and alive.

It's never got no easier. Like a huge part of me's missing; torn from me. An important part, like my heart. I seen a film once, one of them old Westerns. There was a big battle between the white men and the Indians. A Red Indian warrior stuck his knife in a white man; I think he was a General. He stuck his knife in the man's chest and he tore out his heart and held it up, still beating and dripping blood. That's how it feels for me. Someone's torn me heart out. Only it happens over and over, every day. I never knew anyone could feel pain like this.

'Til I lost Stacy I never really knew how important the kids were to me. I'd had Leanne and Dean that young, and never really had a proper mam or dad meself. Nobody to show me what to do, how to look after meself, let alone a kid. I found out the hard way, that's for sure. I love all my kids, but Stacy – she was the baby, the last one. I got the operation done on me tubes after she was born. There won't be no more, ever. I miss her something terrible. There's no words to say how much I miss her.

Our Ryan's never been the same since Stacy went missing neither. Started off crying and crying; waking in the night, and looking for her, searching for her like a little lost soul, bless him. Then the temper started; yelling at me and his dad, like he blamed us for not looking after our Stacy properly. Well he was right, an' all. I blame meself. I should'a watched her. The papers called me a slag, a useless mother, a heartless bitch, you name it – for letting a two-year-old play out alone. Well, I thought Ryan was with her, but I know I can't use that as no excuse.

I cried for Stacy every day – I was worse than Ryan. And for a time I took to the drink, I was that stressed. Anything to blunt my feelings. Gary didn't seem to have no feelings; his feelings was dead. He said she was gone and that was that; we had to accept it, get used to it. He'd always drank and took the drugs anyway, he didn't need no excuse. So when he got arrested for dealing – again – I could'a killed him. Just a few months after our Stacy went missing. Then not long after, he got done for breaking and entering – he got two years. Well, course he needed the money for his habit, didn't he? It's not like me and the kids saw none of it.

That was the last straw though. The social said we weren't responsible parents. They were right an' all. Me eldest two, Dean and Leanne, had got took off us three years before Stacy went missing. They'd been in care all that time. Then the social took the rest of the bairns into care, all of them. So I was on me own. How much worse could life get? The papers made a right meal of it, 'specially the local paper.

Everybody on the estate knew about us. They hated us. People called me names if I went out. Some spat at me. They put dog shit through the letterbox. One night someone threw a brick through the back window. Smashed it into thousands of pieces. I was scared all the time. I was shaking.

I asked the doctor for some pills, to calm me down, like, help me sleep. He shook his head. He patted me hand. I think he reckoned I'd take the lot, top meself, and probably he wasn't far wrong. He was all right with me though, was Dr Shah. He listened to me troubles. Said he wouldn't give me no pills, but he could try to help me get me children back. If I really wanted them. It might take time, he said. I'd have to decide to really work at making a proper home for them. With Gary gone it was my chance, he said. It would be hard. What did I want?

Well, of course I said I wanted them back. He said for a start he'd write to the council – ask them to re-house me in a different part of the town, where people didn't know us. He told me to go back to the social and cooperate with whatever they asked me to do. He even helped me get a part-time job as a cleaner at the hospital. It didn't pay much, but it was something, a start.

The social worker suggested a counselling course. Counselling! I didn't even know what the word meant, but I went on it. Then she suggested a "parenting skills" course – anyone could see I needed it – so I went on that an' all. I even went on an "everyday cooking" course – I reckon they thought we'd lived on chips long enough.

I applied for getting each of the children back, one by one, starting with Ryan – he was that needy. It was dead hard and it took a long, long time, like Dr Shah said, but I managed it in the end. Even when they were back, it wasn't all plain sailing. Ryan was playing up at school. They said he had behaviour problems. I sat him down and asked him if he wanted to go back in care. He shook his head and looked at his feet.

I told him I didn't neither; I told him I couldn't bear to lose him. I'd lost one precious child and I didn't want to lose another. If he carried on misbehaving, I told him, they'd put him back in care, and that would kill me. He cried, and hugged me, and promised to be a good boy. He really tried, and after a while he started doing all right at school.

The next ones I got back was Dean and Leanne, the eldest two. That wasn't easy, I can tell you. They'd been in care for that long they hardly knew us. They didn't trust no one, 'specially not me. They were that angry and disturbed, they nearly took the house apart. It was tough. Time was, I was nearly ready to put them back with the social. But I told them I'd never let them go again, so they might as well put up with me.

Things settled down after a while. They all began going to school regularly. Any sign of bunking off, they had me to answer to. I told them I wasn't going to let them follow the same road I had, and certainly not their dad. Once they were properly settled, Dean and Leanne turned out to be me rocks, me right little helpers. Then, one by one, the rest came home. We were quite a crowd. Only Stacy missing. Always Stacy missing.

The council give us a house in Moorside. It was a right mess to start with, even though the area seemed posh to me, what with being semi-detacheds, trees along the streets, and little gardens at the back. God knows who was in the house before us. It was filthy, and we had no carpets, no furniture; nothing to start with. The social worker – Michelle they called her – helped us get some beds and other basics from a charity. Me and Leanne scrubbed the place from top to bottom. After that I made sure to keep the house clean. I was always scared of an unexpected visit from the social.

Leanne was a good support, bless her. She did housework and kept an eye on the younger kids if I was working on a late shift. Dean cleared all the rubbish out of the garden and got busy with a paintbrush inside – he didn't need no asking.

Ashley always had her face stuck in a book and her head in the clouds, so she wasn't much help, but at least she was no trouble. Kelly and Sean did everything together – they liked to cook the tea sometimes – simple stuff like jacket potatoes and baked beans, sausages and that. I made them all eat vegetables too, even though I wasn't that keen on them meself – cabbage, sprouts, cauliflower and that. Eat them, they're good for you, I told them.

Once the kids were all back with me, we decided that every year, on Stacy's birthday, I'd make a cake and we'd have a bit of a party. Well, the first few were bought cakes from Safeways – 'til I learned how to make one. The first one I made was a bit hard on the outside and soft in the middle, but the kids didn't seem to mind at all.

So each year, we light the candles and sing "Happy Birthday dear Stacy". The idea is it helps to take our minds off all the sadness. 'Course it doesn't really. But that's what we'll be doing tonight, when the kids are all home. Her cake's chocolate this year: the kids' favourite. It has seven candles on, and a big number seven in Smarties – Ryan done that. It breaks my heart that she's not here with us all to see it. Stacy, baby, I long for you every day, every minute. We'll never, never, ever forget you. Will we ever see you again?

I've got to believe we will. One day.

Chapter Nineteen

1993

Lucy

When I try to remember my childhood, a lot of it seems very hazy, as though I was viewing myself through a thick mist, or as though I existed within a dream, a vague, half-remembered dream. Perhaps that's how it is for everyone. There were one or two difficult times, there was some confusion and some upsets, of course, but nothing out of the ordinary; on the whole I think I was fairly happy until I was about eleven years old.

Mummy was definitely not a funny, jolly sort of person, who played silly games and shrieked with laughter, like some of my friends' mothers, but I didn't mind that especially. She was quiet and a bit serious, but I suppose I was too, so maybe we got on well together because we were alike. She was OK with people one to one (some of them at least), but she didn't much like people in groups, such as at parties or gatherings, and nor did I.

One good thing at least was she hardly ever shouted at me – so when she was cross, which wasn't often, she just went sort of cold and distant and silent for a while. Actually, I hated her being like that, so it might have been better if she had shouted, and been done with it. When she was in her cool and distant mode, it felt like she was across a wide lake, and I couldn't reach her. I would have to think of something good and kind I could do or say, to try to please her. Then maybe she'd stop being cross, and the great, frightening, silent expanse between us would evaporate. Sometimes that took a long time.

I guess every child thinks its own experience is normal, just takes its own situation for granted. I know I did, at least until I got older. Of course, I realised it was unusual not to have a father at all, but then quite a lot of my friends had parents who lived apart, so they didn't all live with a father as an ever-present part of their lives. But when I thought about it, which was only occasionally, I was vaguely aware that there was something different about my family, perhaps because my daddy was so rarely mentioned. Mummy never mentioned him, and even as quite a small child I sensed that questions about him made her nervous.

At the time I just interpreted this as sadness – that she was upset thinking about him. From my earliest memories, she had told me he was dead. She said he was killed in a car crash. She didn't elaborate. I didn't feel questions were encouraged. So there was this huge father-shaped gap in my life.

Gradually, I came to realise that most other children had not only a father, but also at least one or two grandparents – many of my friends had a complete set of four. I didn't have any. There was just me and Mummy. Her own mother had died when I was so little that I had no memories of her at all, though Mummy did often show me photos of her. There was a photo of her in a frame on the mantelpiece in the sitting room, and Mummy kept another one on her bedside table. My grandmother didn't have a husband, and she'd adopted Mummy when she was a baby. So they were just a mother–daughter unit, like us. I know Mummy loved her very much. She sometimes talked about how much she missed her. She always called her "Mother".

From what I saw of my friends' families, grandparents seemed like a really good thing. They adored their grandchildren and indulged them. They often took care of them if they lived near and were always happy to take them on trips, read stories to them and play games with them. They were generally very proud of their grandchildren's every little achievement, and often seemed to be generous with presents, treats and even money too. I thought how wonderful it would be to have grandparents – not for the money or presents, but just because sometimes I longed to have another grown-up in my life to talk to, someone who really loved me and was proud of me.

I knew my father's parents were living in New Zealand – Mummy had explained about that – so they were hardly at "popping-in" distance from us. I did receive birthday and Christmas cards – and sometimes presents – from them, though. But they barely seemed real to me; more like fairy-tale grandparents. Well, I'd never even seen photographs of them, let alone met them. Sometimes I tried to think about what they might be like. I suppose I imagined them almost like fairies, or a prince and princess, rather than being able to picture real, ordinary people.

There was one time when we were doing a history project at school about how people lived in our country fifty or sixty years ago. We were supposed to ask our grandparents questions about what life was like when they were children of around the same age as us. We were expected to record their answers and then write about their experiences, and to use photographs and draw pictures if we wanted. It was the sort of task I normally really enjoyed, but of course I was at a total disadvantage.

'What am I going to do?' I wailed. 'Everyone in the class has got at least one grandparent they can talk to – and some have four! How am I possibly going to write anything?'

Mummy looked a bit worried and thoughtful. 'Well,' she said, 'Auntie Molly and Uncle Frank are like ... kind of ... special grandparents to you, and I know they'd be delighted if you asked them to talk to you about when they were young.'

Mummy was right, of course. Auntie Molly and Uncle Frank, who lived next door, were very happy to take on the role of granny and grandpa for me. Actually, it turned out they made quite interesting subjects because they had lived in a mining village when they were children. Frank's dad had been a miner and worked underground from the age of fourteen. But his mum and dad had wanted Frank to "better himself", so he had had to work very hard at school, so that he'd get a scholarship to the grammar school. He was the first in his family to stay at school past sixteen – and get a job in a bank after. His parents were really proud of his achievements.

Molly was the eldest of nine children, so she'd had to leave school and help her mum a lot with looking after the younger children, and with the cooking and housework. You wouldn't believe how crowded it was in her house! The five youngest children slept in one bed, and the older four shared another.

Molly told me how every morning her mum made a big pot of porridge and put it on the kitchen table, with nine hungry children sitting around it. She'd put a little pool of melted butter and sugar in the middle of the porridge pot. Each child had a long spoon and would take turns scooping out porridge together with a tiny bit of butter and sugar. If any of them tried to take too much butter or sugar, they got a clout from their mum's big wooden spoon. I loved that story. My teacher said my account of their childhood was one of the best in the class. She asked me to read it out.

I was very proud, but still, it made me more aware that I *did* have grandparents – my dad's parents – yet I had never met them and didn't really know anything about them. Surely they must have been sad about that too? After all, when my dad died, they had lost their only son – so you'd think they would be all the more eager to get to know their only granddaughter.

I badgered my mother a lot about this, telling her I really wanted to go and visit my granny and grandpa. I said it over and over again. At first she wouldn't hear of the idea, but I guess I sort of wore her down in the end. Eventually she relented, and told me that she was planning for us to travel out to New Zealand to stay with them over the Christmas holiday of the following year. Imagine that – New Zealand! It would be summer over there at that time.

It was a really, really long journey to get there, but I didn't mind that one bit. Going in an aeroplane across the whole world! I was so excited I thought I'd hardly be able to wait. But you can't stay excited for more than a year, so in the meantime I just had to get on with life as before.

Slowly time passed. Then, as the trip got nearer, things started to go wrong. First, Mummy told me that Grandpa had become ill, and Granny couldn't manage to have visitors because she was looking after him. Mummy said she was keeping in touch with Granny by letter and we'd hear about Grandpa's progress that way. Over the following month, Grandpa got worse and worse. Mummy said we'd have to delay our trip for a while.

One day, after another month or two, when I got home from school, Mummy made me come into the sitting room and sit down. I knew she had something awful to tell me. She said she was very sorry, but that Grandpa had died. I could hardly believe it. I was very, very upset. Mummy tried to comfort me, but it seemed so terrible to lose my grandpa when I hadn't even had the chance to meet him. I couldn't stop crying. Mummy stared at me and didn't say anything, but I think she must have been quite worried about me.

For days I felt miserable. Now I'd never get to meet Grandpa, and I thought poor Granny must have been so sad and lonely without him. I couldn't think about anything else. Mummy kept watching me. In the end she said maybe we could arrange for Granny to come and live with us in England, so she wouldn't be living alone.

This was around the time home computers were starting to become popular. Mummy liked things like computers. She had bought one and was teaching herself how to use it. She used it as a typewriter for writing letters to Granny. She called it a "word processor". She said that she was writing to Granny at least twice a week, and that Granny loved getting these letters.

About once a month, we received a reply from her. Mummy said old people like Granny didn't really know about computers, but she did have an old typewriter, and she wrote letters back to Mummy and me using that. Mummy explained that Granny didn't see so well, so the computer was a good thing because she could make the print large enough for Granny to read. When Granny wrote back to Mummy, she always enclosed a short letter for me in the envelope.

The post arrived after I had left for school in the mornings, so it was really exciting to come back home in the afternoon, and find a lovely message that Granny had written to me! They said things like:

Darling Lucy, I liked hearing about your school and your friends. Mummy tells me you work hard and do very well with your schoolwork. I'm so proud of you. It will be lovely to see you soon. Lots of love, Granny xx

I kept them all in a special folder with "Granny" written on it in red and gold lettering. I really enjoyed writing to Granny myself too. From time to time I would write and tell her something about my life, and give the letter to Mummy to add to her own letter to Granny. Sometimes I would draw a picture for Granny too, or write her a little poem.

Mummy told me she liked to give her letters some thought,

so she would write them on the computer later in the evening, after I'd gone to bed. In the morning, there would be our letters in their envelope on the hall table, waiting to be posted. I liked seeing the neat envelope with its coloured stamps and "Airmail" sticker, ready to be sent off to New Zealand. I liked to imagine Granny opening the envelope far away, and how she would enjoy reading Mummy's news, and especially mine.

Then, a few weeks later, hey presto! Mummy would hand me a lovely typed reply that Granny had written back to me! Sometimes Mummy showed me the envelope stamped "Christchurch, NZ", with its colourful stamps of exotic-looking birds. It was just brilliant. It made me so happy to think about Granny. I couldn't wait to meet her.

Maybe good things never last. A few weeks later a most awful, terrible thing happened. Mummy told me Granny had died too. It hardly seemed possible – it was more like a nightmare to me. How could she die – just when I was starting to get to know her through letters? I had been longing to get to know my granny properly, and for her to be close to me.

Mummy said we had to try to be positive. She said that of course it was sad for us, but we had to be thankful that Granny didn't suffer a long illness. She said that would have been worse for her. I tried to be grateful for that, like Mummy said, but it was hard, because Granny had always appeared such a fit and active person. Even though she was quite old, she wasn't *that* old. She used to go for walks in the country and ride her bike to the shops. I couldn't remember ever hearing about her being ill before.

Mummy was very strong about it – much braver than me. She didn't cry at all. But I guess as Granny was my dad's mother and not hers, Mummy didn't really love her as much as she did her own mother. It all seemed so sudden and shocking and cruel to me, though.

Chapter Twenty

1994

Lucy

As a smaller girl I just accepted what had happened to my grand-parents, and my lack of a father – why wouldn't I? – even though it upset me very much. It never occurred to me to ask more questions about them, at least not until I met Cassie. Most of my friends at school had known me since playgroup or Reception, so they were used to the idea that my dad was dead. I don't remember any of them asking me questions about him – but Cassie was different. Looking back, getting to know Cassie was a turning point in my life, but of course I didn't think of it that way at the time.

Cassie joined our class partway through the second year of middle school. Our form teacher, Mr Williams, introduced her one morning at registration. Cassie's dad was in the RAF, he said, and the family had moved around a lot. Cassie had been to lots of different schools, which had interfered with her education. She was perfectly clever, he said, but because of her interrupted schooling she was a bit behind with the curriculum. So she was joining our class, even though her age – she was twelve and a half – meant she should really have been in the year above. Having a September birthday meant I was one of the oldest in my class too – only four months younger than Cassie.

'I know you're all going to make Cassie feel welcome,' said Mr Williams. He turned to Cassie.

'They're a nice bunch of kids,' he said in his loud "give me your attention" voice, 'friendly, kind, polite and well behaved, even if they are a bit too gabby! Isn't that right, everybody?'

A wave of chuckles murmured round the classroom. We liked Mr Williams; I guess because he liked us too, and he was funny. Cassie stood unsmiling next to him. She turned her gaze from him to the class, her dark eyes scanning over us all like a search-light. They rested on me. She jerked her head, sweeping her dark hair back, like a horse flicking its mane.

'Now, let's see,' said Mr Williams, 'there are a few empty desks to choose from … over there next to Carl, but I don't suppose you'll want to sit there, will you, Cassie?'

Carl grinned sheepishly and his friends laughed and nudged him, making squeaty noises.

'Or, there's that seat next to Tiffany,' Mr Williams said, pointing, 'or there's a vacancy beside Lucy here …'

Cassie raised her face to him, then scanned the room again, stopping at me. 'I'll go and sit next to her,' she said, 'Lucy.' And she walked straight towards me without any hesitation.

'Hi,' she said, as she swung her body in next to mine. Her voice was low. She gave a trace of a smile. I carved my face into what I hoped was an equally neutral, indifferent smile.

'Hi,' I said, trying to sound casual, not too needy. My heart raced with delight. I could hardly breathe.

It was the start of one of the most significant friendships in my life. It wasn't that I was without friends or was shunned by other children; Laura, Jennifer and Megan, in particular, had been

92

friends since we all started school, but I sometimes felt that they preferred one another – that I was a bit of a "hanger-on", at the periphery of the group. With Cassie it was completely different; it was as if she had *chosen* me.

She was a striking-looking girl, really gorgeous. Her hair hung in two curtains at either side of her face. In the sun, it reflected streaks of red and gold. Cassie would fling her head to one side, sending a cascade of brown and copper colours over her shoulder. She had a habit of cocking one eyebrow in a quizzical manner when talking to people, and she loved to question everything, including the opinions of teachers!

She was the most confident person I had ever encountered, and at first made me feel as immature and unformed as a tadpole. Yet, even though I felt a bit intimidated by her, I discovered that Cassie was loyal and affectionate. She always appeared to value what I did or said. She was never scornful. In return, I grew more confident and relaxed in her company.

That first day, out in the yard, all the kids seemed keen to get to know her. Perhaps it was partly the attraction of her being a bit older than other children in our year, and maybe it was partly her air of friendly detachment. She answered the questions good-naturedly and responded by showing interest in other kids, but after a while she grabbed my arm and steered me to one of the benches.

'Come on, Lucy,' she said, 'let's just you and me sit and talk.'

I was swelling with pride, but tried to act cool. No one had ever shown so much interest in me before. When the bell rang and we headed towards the door, Cassie said, 'You know, I've never had really good friends before, 'cos we moved about so much, but I just knew you'd be interesting. I knew I'd like you.'

I had to fight the urge to fling my arms round her and hug her. Interesting, me!

* * *

Cassie's mother and father were lovely too, always warm and welcoming to me. We were both "only children", and they welcomed our friendship, unlike Mummy.

'Friends are so important,' Cassie's mum, Fiona, said over tea one afternoon, 'especially at your age, with the terrible teens not very far ahead!' She gave each of us a hug. She was always hugging me. It was really noticeable to me that Fiona – as she insisted I call her – was completely spontaneous in showing affection, whereas I always felt my mother's show of feelings was a deliberate effort. I know it sounds strange, but it was almost as though Mummy set herself a target for regularly assuring me that she loved me. Like she told herself "I must tell Lucy I love her at least twice every day". She was a bit fixated on numbers.

It was different when we came to Cassie's home after school. As soon as we stepped into the kitchen, Fiona's face would show instant joy. She really was genuinely happy to see us both, and would always greet us with something like 'Hellooo, my darlings! How are my gorgeous girls today?!' accompanied by a double embrace.

Being in the RAF, Cassie's dad Simon worked away from home quite a lot, but when he did come home, if I was there he would tousle my hair and call me "The Lovely Lucy". I was a bit shy of him, but I liked the way both of Cassie's parents always included me in the family.

My mother wasn't a huggy sort of person like Fiona. She never hugged Cassie – and even her hugs for me were saved for "appropriate" settings, like bedtime. I don't blame her for that. I knew she had a reserved personality, not outgoing like Fiona's. But I did wish she didn't make it quite so obvious that she didn't really like Cassie. She never actually *said* she didn't like her. She never prevented us from meeting, and accepted that Cassie would spend some time at our house, but she made it clear she wasn't at all enthusiastic about her, or our friendship. It was as if she felt threatened by Cassie.

'I do wish she wasn't quite so forward and pushy in her manner. I'm not sure I like that in a young girl.'

This was early on in our relationship. One time, while we were having tea at our house, Cassie looked straight at Mummy and said in her loud, cheerful voice, 'I'd much rather call you Alison than Mrs Brown, if you don't mind. Mrs Brown sounds so formal and old-fashioned, don't you think?'

Mummy looked uncomfortable and stiff. She frowned and turned away with a sniff.

'Very well, dear, if you wish,' she replied coolly, in her "I'm not happy about this at all" voice. She turned towards the sink. Cassie gave me a tiny smile and winked.

Chapter Twenty-One

1994

It was after Cassie and I had known each other for about three months, and were already firm friends, that I decided to tell her about an incident that had puzzled and preoccupied me for some time. I'd never mentioned it to anyone else before – certainly not my mother. Not Megan, nor Laura – and not even Claire next door. Claire was seventeen now, and had always been like an older sister to me. I still liked and trusted her more than almost anyone else in the world, but I hadn't mentioned this particular event. I'm not sure why – it was something that had bothered me a bit for about a year.

Of course, Mummy had talked to me about periods. I suppose most mothers did. In our case it had been a very uncomfortable discussion, mainly because, even at eleven years old, I could tell how embarrassed Mummy was, and that made *me* feel embarrassed. She talked really fast, as if she couldn't wait to finish the conversation, and then she showed me what she called "the necessary equipment". She said she had bought it in readiness and would put it away in her room for the time being. Being small and slight, I probably wouldn't "start" for at least a couple of years. (I didn't tell her that more than half the girls in my class had already started!) Nearer the time, she said, we could keep the equipment accessible in the bathroom cupboard.

If we hadn't had PSE lessons about periods and puberty two years before at my first school, I'm not sure I'd have made head or tail of what Mummy tried to tell me.

* * *

Some months after our conversation, I'd come home from school not feeling too well. Mummy made me a mug of sweet tea.

'Have a nice lie-down on the sofa, dear. I hope you're not coming down with something.' She felt my forehead.

'You don't seem very hot.'

'Maybe I'm just tired.'

'Have a little snooze then. I do need to nip next door and have a word with Susan about the jumble sale at the church this weekend. I'll only be gone fifteen or twenty minutes.'

'That's fine, Mummy.'

'Well, you know where I am if you need me. Just stay here and rest quietly.'

I wondered if I was coming down with something too. My head was aching and I had a gnawing pain in my tummy. Something felt wrong, different. I went to the toilet. That was when I saw it; in my knickers was a patch of blood. It was like being punched in the stomach – hit by a great lurch of shock, disgust and excitement all at the same time: I was growing up! It was thrilling. It was awful. I felt a bit like crying – I actually did cry, and really wished Mummy was there.

What should I do? I had to find the "equipment". I checked to see if Mummy had put it in the bathroom cupboard, but there was no sign of it there. So I went into her room to see where she might have stored it. Mummy didn't really like me going in her room when she wasn't there. But I had to find the sanitary towels, so I knew she'd understand.

There weren't many places to choose from. Her big wardrobe was neatly arranged with all her clothes carefully sorted: skirts, blouses and dresses one end, then some "slacks", as she called them, with coats and jackets at the far end, all ordered according to length. Shoes, on a rack at the bottom, were graded by colour: white on the extreme left, then beige, light brown and so on, to black shoes on the far right. Nothing else in there.

I gazed at the clothes for a moment and ran my hand across them. I like clothes, but there were lots of things Mummy didn't wear. Just very occasionally, she dressed up for some special events – a party or dinner with friends – and then she looked really lovely. But generally she wore the same sort of things all the time: slightly boring skirts or trousers and tops.

There were a couple of garments with full-length grey plastic covers on, I suppose to protect them from dust, maybe they were old. I pulled up the cover of one; it was a dull tweedy suit I'd seen Mummy wearing on one or two occasions, but not for a long while. I lifted the other cover and got a real surprise. Underneath was a vivid red coat I'd never seen before. Surely she'd never ever worn it? What a shame; she'd look so nice in a bright colour like that.

I pulled out the hanger and ran my hand over the rich red material for a moment. I stared at the coat. A strange shiver ran down my spine. I shook myself to make it go away. Then I pulled the grey cover back down over the coat, and replaced it in the cupboard, making sure to smooth it over and space the hangers again.

The chest of drawers held some geometrically folded tops, jumpers and underwear – no one was as neat as my mum! – but that was it. Next I tried her desk – a big old wooden knee-hole type. I opened each drawer in turn. Again, everything was carefully organised: stationery in one drawer, letters and documents in another; a file for household bills and receipts.

Inside the bottom drawer was a small carved wooden box I'd never seen before. It wasn't going to contain sanitary towels, of course, but I was curious, and picked it up to examine it. It was locked. I felt around for a key but there was no sign of one. I returned to the stationery drawer. There was a small ruler, some scissors, and a rubber stamp and inkpad. The stamp was very black with ink. I peered at it – of course you had to read it in mirror image. I worked it out; it said "Christchurch, NZ". I'd seen that stamped on Granny's letters to us. It must have been something you had to use on the envelopes going back to New Zealand too. Funny, I'd never noticed that, but then maybe I didn't see them just before Mummy posted them.

I opened the drawer containing the file marked "letters". I'm not sure what I expected to find. I opened the file. There was a folder with some boring-looking official sort of letters; some from Mummy's bank, one or two about rates, one from a solicitor, that sort of thing. Another folder was labelled "New Zealand". It seemed to contain copies of all the letters Granny had written to me. That was a surprise, but rather sweet of Mummy, I thought. If she kept copies of all Granny's letters to me, perhaps she really did care about her more than I'd realised.

Anyway, at the back of the drawer was a little tray for small items such as paperclips, board pins and so on. I noticed there were three little keys. Being nosy, I desperately wanted to see if one of them might open the wooden box, but I didn't want Mummy to come home and find me searching through her desk – and besides I was starting to feel blood seeping into my underwear, maybe staining my school skirt. I was anxious to find what I needed.

There was only one place left to look: the bedside cabinet. Sure enough, there was a Boots bag containing sanitary towels. I took them into the bathroom and sorted myself out. When Mummy came back, she was quite shocked to hear that my period had started so soon. I told her it was OK – I'd found the bag in the bedside table in her room. She blushed slightly when we talked about it.

'Oh dear, I am sorry – I should have given it to you sooner. Erm … did you find it … straight away?'

'Yes, it was no problem. It only took me a minute.'

'I'm glad you're such a sensible girl, Lucy,' she said.

'Hey, but you know what, Mummy? I saw such a brilliant coat in your wardrobe. D'you remember – the bright red one under a grey plastic cover? Why don't you ever wear it? It'd really suit you and—'

'Lucy! How dare you?' she interrupted in a shouty, angry-sounding voice. 'You had no right to snoop among my clothes!'

I must have looked a bit shocked, because Mummy stared at me and put her hands over her mouth.

'I wasn't snooping,' I said, feeling cross and upset that she was being so unfair. 'I was just looking for the equipment. You should have left it in the bathroom if you didn't want me to go in your room.'

'Yes … yes, you're right. I'm sorry – I didn't mean to snap, Lucy. It's just that … that coat … I've never liked it … it has bad associations.'

'What sort of associations?'

'Oh just … I don't know … oh, let's not talk about it now. The important thing is you found what you needed.'

She paused for a moment and smiled in a bit of a forced way. 'And here you are growing up already!'

'Mmm – I suppose getting my period means I could have a baby now!' I said, with a laugh. I wanted to lighten the atmosphere, but it didn't work. Mummy seemed to go pale. She reached for the arm of the chair and sat down, breathing heavily.

'Technically, yes,' she said. 'However, there's no question of a young girl like you considering having a baby for many, many years. You need to concentrate on your school education first, and then going to a good university – and embarking on a suitable career, long before you even think of marriage and babies.'

'I only meant it as a joke, Mummy.'

* * *

I didn't think much more about that evening for a while. But as time went on, when I was lying in bed waiting for sleep, my mind sometimes returned to that red coat. There was something that troubled me about it, and I wasn't sure what. Also, why had Mummy been so angry and upset when I mentioned finding the coat? I wondered if maybe she'd paid a lot of money for it and then didn't like it enough to wear it. She'd have hated that; she couldn't bear waste.

My thoughts kept drifting to Mummy's desk – as if there were secrets there that she wanted to keep from me. I wished I'd had the chance to look inside the wooden box. Once I started to think about it, I just couldn't seem to leave it alone. I'd have to wait for the chance to have another look.

101

Chapter Twenty-Two

Alison

Of course I was unhappy about Lucy finding the red coat. I hated seeing her so confused and upset. How could I not be concerned? I was furious with myself for leaving it in a place where she could find them. How stupid, stupid, stupid of me! It had never occurred to me that she might search in my room. I had burned the dark blue coat, the dark wig, and the children's clothes from that day in Riddlesfield, years ago, soon after we came to Newcastle. Somehow, I had admired the red coat and been loath to get rid of it at the time. I'd thought it was well hidden, and had forgotten it was still there all these years later – so very idiotic of me.

Yet, at the same time I couldn't help feeling just a little bit hurt by Lucy's reaction. I won't go so far as to say I felt betrayed, but I did feel a mother should be able to rely on the loyalty of a daughter. Surely I'd done everything to make her life perfect: safe, secure, stimulating, full of love and affection, and full of rich and educative experiences? Didn't I have the right to expect honesty and trust in return? Of course she had no reason to doubt that I was her mother, no.

Could Lucy possibly have memories of the red coat? No, surely not, she was so young. Far too young to have conscious memories from the age of two … yet … what if she did? The very thought sent icy shivers down my spine. I would have to be extra vigilant to see just how her active young mind worked. I should certainly make clear to her that she needed to respect my privacy – well, that we needed to respect one another's privacy. I don't believe in locked doors in my own house. I have to be able to trust Lucy. She would have to understand that my bedroom is "out of bounds" to her unless she obtains my permission first.

I suppose I should have been prepared that the time would come for Lucy to ask questions about her father, and, as a result perhaps, about her wider family. I'm not proud of having had to deceive her about her grandparents living (and dying!) in New Zealand. But when she became so questioning a few years ago, I admit I was caught off-guard. It was fortunate that I was able to think of some sort of story, which fitted the bill at the time.

Some might call it lying, but I don't think my explanations can be described in that way. They were constructed for the very best of motives – in other words, to help Lucy feel more at ease and to give her the security of feeling she belonged to an ordinary family, just like other children. Of course I was aware that hearing of the "deaths" of her grandparents caused her some distress. But then almost all children have to come to terms with the death of grandparents eventually – and after all she didn't *know* them, so her sadness must have been relatively short term. Also, the situation I invented for her relieved her of long-term bewilderment and anxiety, which I am convinced could have been much more damaging. What else could I have done?

103

Chapter Twenty-Three

Lucy

One Saturday a few weeks later, Mummy said she was going to nip out to the post office for some stamps and would I go with her? I told her I really needed to finish my French homework. Even though I was nearly twelve, Mummy didn't like to leave me alone in the house for more than a few minutes, unless she was just going next door.

'Well then I think I'll pop round to ask Auntie Molly to come and sit with you,' she said.

'There's no need, Mummy. You'll hardly be gone more than half an hour, and you know how Auntie Molly likes to talk and ask questions. I'll never be able to concentrate, and this French is really important if I'm to get an A. I'll just sit here and finish my work. Don't worry about me.'

That was a clever move. Mummy's face showed she was torn between not wanting to leave me alone, and her wish for me to get top marks at school. Top marks won.

'Well, all right … if you're sure, Lucy. But don't open the door to anyone, will you?'

After the red coat business, she'd had a serious talk with me about us respecting each other's privacy. It seemed to me she was more concerned about her privacy than mine. Mummy was always going into my room, but she made me promise I wouldn't go into hers unless she said I could.

I was about to break that promise. As soon as she shut the front door, I got up and raced to her room. I opened the wardrobe first – and gasped! Oh my God, it was gone! There was no sign of the red coat! I pushed each hanger along the rail to make sure, but there was no doubt about it; the red coat – and its cover – had vanished. After rearranging the hangers loosely and evenly spaced, as they were before, I shut the wardrobe door.

Next, I rushed to the bottom drawer of the desk. At first I was astonished to find that the wooden box had also disappeared. There were some cards and envelopes at the front of the drawer instead. I felt with my hand to see if there was anything else in the drawer. There was just a cardboard box with some pens and pencils. Disappointed, I began to shut the drawer, but then I noticed that the desk was quite deep. I opened the drawer again, further this time, carefully removed the box of pens, and felt with my hand right to the very back – and there was the wooden box!

My heart thumping for some reason, I took it out and put it on the desk. Then I reached into the stationery drawer and found the little tray at the back. The three small keys were still in it. I tried the first key, but that didn't fit. The second key slipped smoothly into the lock. I turned it and the box opened with a click. Inside was a yellowing newspaper cutting, carefully folded.

I noticed the date at the top of the page was March 17, 1985. I read the article slowly and carefully:

Police are continuing to question the parents of missing 2-year-old Stacy Watts about her disappearance on March 8th.

Detective Inspector Lawrence Dempster emphasised that the search for little Stacy was far from over, and that their questioning of her parents, Gary and Shelley Watts, was routine procedure. It is now over a week since Stacy went missing from outside her home in Frainham, Riddlesfield, and D.I. Dempster told reporters that the police are very concerned for her safety. He appealed to anyone who has any information about a child answering Stacy's description – however insignificant that information may seem – to come forward, either by ringing the special incident number (printed below) at Riddlesfield central police station, or by contacting their local police station.

At this stage of the search, he added, police have no reason not to believe that Stacy is still alive. However, Detective Inspector Dempster reminded the public that Stacy is a very young and vulnerable child, small and slight for her 2 years.

Stacy has fair hair and blue eyes. On the day of her disappearance she was wearing a yellow dress, a green knitted jumper, and black plimsolls a little too large for her. Police are particularly interested to interview a slim, middle-aged woman of average height, with mid-length brown hair, who was seen in the area. It is believed this woman was wearing a brown or dark blue coat and shoes.

Chapter Twenty-Four

I read the article again twice. Then I replaced it in the box and shut the drawer. I don't know why, but the cutting left me feeling puzzled and disturbed. Why was it there? Why had Mummy kept it? Should I ask her about it? Somehow I didn't feel I could.

My stomach felt jittery, like before an important test at school. In fact, I felt quite sick. I wished I could talk to someone about it, but there was no one who felt just right.

Not until much later, that is, when I had got to know Cassie better. Cassie didn't seem the least impressed though. In fact, she was completely underwhelmed when I first tried to tell her about it.

'Right ... so your mum had a nice red coat she never wears? Just as I would expect really – I mean she doesn't wear bright colours, does she? She tends to dress a bit dowdy. I don't quite get the point.'

'Dowdy?' I was hurt on Mummy's behalf.

'Well, maybe not dowdy, but conservative. It was probably an impulse buy that she was sorry for later, 'cause it's not her style.'

We were sitting on the floor of Cassie's bedroom and I'd been telling her about my finds: the coat and the cutting. I'd memorised the newspaper article almost word for word.

'I don't know … oh, I know it sounds stupid. But I keep thinking about it. There's something about a red coat … I can't explain it!' I felt heat working its way up the back of my neck. I pressed my hands hard on my eyes, as if I might construct a picture in my head that would make some sense.

'I don't know,' I repeated. 'It's just … like I've got a vague feeling that I've seen a red coat before some time … in my head … or kind of like in a dream.'

'Right …?' said Cassie. Her voice sounded a bit doubtful, but still encouraging.

'I expect your mum tried it on some time, and you saw it then.'

'Well … why did she get rid of it – the red coat, I mean – after she realised I'd been in her room? Why was she so annoyed I'd seen it? And that article about the little girl. What was that all about? Why had she kept it?'

'I dunno, Lucy. Maybe she knew the family. Maybe she thought it was a sad story … You seem to be linking the coat and the cutting, as if there's something important about them, just because your mum didn't like you looking at her coat. Anyway, the article didn't say anything about a red coat, did it? Just a dark blue or brown coat.'

'No, I know – but it's not just that. I don't really know what the problem with the coat was. It's so hard to explain, but I've sometimes had a feeling that … that … oh I don't know …'

'Come on … what sort of feeling?'

'A sort of feeling that there are things from when I was little that I can't remember – like there's some important memories there that I just can't reach. Like … there's a black hole or something.'

Cassie snorted.

'Well there are plenty of things from when I was little that I can't remember either. My mum's always telling me funny stuff I'm supposed to have done as a baby or tiny kid – and I can't remember a single thing about it. Nada!'

108

'That's just it, though. My mum never really tells me anything about when I was a little kid. No funny stories, like your mum. Just general things like "Oh, you were a beautiful baby". Sometimes I feel like I didn't exist.'

Cassie looked at me thoughtfully. She waited a while for me to go on.

'Look, Lucy, I know your mum is a bit odd, but I think you're making more of this than necessary. Maybe she's just not the sort of person to talk about memories …'

'She is not odd! Why do you say that? She's lovely. She's just a bit … reserved.'

'Well, I thought that business with your grandparents dying in New Zealand was a bit odd, didn't you? It was almost as if she didn't want you to meet them, or … as if they didn't even really exist.'

'Didn't exist? No, that's crazy. It can't be true. She did want me to meet them. Why shouldn't she? Anyway, I got letters from Granny. Quite a lot of letters.'

Cassie looked thoughtful.

'Hmm … you got typed up messages that your mum gave you.'

'So what? They were still messages from Granny.'

'Were they? Maybe your mum wrote them – maybe she got jealous because you were starting to love your gran.'

I was shocked.

'How can you say that, Cass? She loves me. She wouldn't try to trick me. Anyway, they had New Zealand stamps and post-marks, so of course they were real.'

I started to cry. It was like there was a deep well of sadness inside me. Once I started I couldn't stop myself.

Cassie put her arms around me and rocked me like a baby.

'Sorry, Lucy, 'course I'm wrong then. I know your mum loves you. Anyone can see that. It's just that she's not a very … relaxed sort of person, is she?' She gave me her piercing look. 'But anyway, you'd remember, wouldn't you? I mean, if anything special, or anything bad had happened when you were little, you'd remember?' Cassie said.

'Yes, I keep thinking that too. So I don't believe anything bad happened, except for my dad being killed. That was very bad for Mummy, but I was too little to remember it. You know what? However hard I try, I don't remember anything before Newcastle – well, not clearly at least. Sometimes I get these strange sorts of picture flashes, but I can't make proper sense of them. Don't you get bits of memories like that, from when you were very little?'

'Oh yes, I suppose I do,' Cassie said. 'Like you say, they're mostly just single images – I can't really remember many details. For instance, I have this memory – I think I was about two or three – and Dad was holding my hands and swinging me round and round in the garden. I have this picture in my head of trees and bushes whizzing by and him laughing. I remember liking it – but that's about all.'

We sat in silence for a few moments.

'What about other people, Lucy? Somebody must know – somebody who knew your mum from long ago, and your dad before he died – and you as a baby.'

'Well, that's another thing. Mummy says we moved here from Nottingham when I was about two or two and a half. But I don't know of a single person who knew us before we got to Newcastle. My dad had died, of course – I don't remember him at all – I wish I did. I suppose Mummy was so upset about losing him, she didn't have much to do with other people. She just wanted to get away to somewhere without all the sad memories and connections. To start a new life. And then her mother – who she adored – also died before we moved here. I don't remember that grandmother at all. I thought maybe I remembered a fattish sort of woman, but when I asked Mummy what her mother was like, she said she was very small and slim, and always dressed smartly, so I must have just imagined the fat one. And Mummy doesn't seem to have any friends from that time – or any other family.'

'Couldn't you look through some photos of your dad and his family with your mum – and then just ask her more about that time?

'No, I can't do that. Mummy doesn't have a camera. There are no photos of my dad – or of his parents, my granny and grandpa ...'

'None at all?'

'None at all. I don't even know what he looks like.'

'Phew ...'

Cassie turned to face me. She took hold of both my wrists.

'I think you really need to ask your mum some questions, don't you?'

111

Chapter Twenty-Five

It was a sunny weekend. The air was warm and soft – the first feel of long summer days to come. Normally, I loved that time of year. We were in the car, driving on the Spine Road, which ran parallel to the coast. Mummy had packed a picnic. It was in a basket on the front passenger seat, next to her. We were heading northwards up the coast, past little old villages, and great sweeping bays. I think we were going to visit a castle by the sea; Bamburgh or Dunstanburgh, perhaps. I can't remember exactly which one. We often went to castles or historic houses of interest at the weekend, or during half-term holidays.

Of course, I was sitting in the back seat strapped into my seatbelt – Mummy thought it was safer than the front. My hands were twisting a damp handkerchief, tying it into knots and untying them again. Maybe it was that position, behind Mummy, not having to look at her directly, that made me brave enough to ask her. Even so, I opened and closed my mouth several times before eventually I had the courage to speak.

'Mummy …'

'Yes, Lucy?'

'Where was I born?'

'Where …er?'

'Yes, where was I born?'

There was a long pause while she took some deep breaths.

'Well … you were born in Nottingham, of course. I thought I'd told you that. Nottingham was where I … we … lived before we moved to Newcastle.'

'So was Daddy there too?'

'Er … yes … yes, of course. Daddy was there … with us.'

'But then he died and we moved to Newcastle?'

'Yes. Lucy, these are serious questions, and it's right that you should ask them, but let's wait until we stop the car and have our picnic. I really have to concentrate on driving.'

I could see her eyes keep glancing at me in the rear-view mirror, but we sat in silence until we reached a car park in the dunes. She pulled in and parked the car. We carried our basket and bags over the humpy marram grass to find a sheltered spot overlooking the sea. The water sparkled in the sunshine, the sky was blue and for once the breeze was gentle. The beach stretched far to the north and the south, so extensive that people and dogs looked like figures in a Lowry painting, tiny and distant.

We put a rug on the pale sand and Mummy arranged the picnic in the middle of it. By this time I was totally dreading the conversation – and wished I'd never raised it. Mummy was very quiet. She handed me an egg and cress sandwich. I took a tiny nibble. My appetite had totally vanished.

'I … um … just thought it would be nice to know a bit more about you and Daddy before I was born,' I said tentatively.

Mummy was looking at me. 'Is there a particular reason for asking about it now?'

'Well …' I stammered, 'you don't talk about it much, about Daddy I mean, and I don't remember him. And why did we move, from Nottingham? Why did we come to Newcastle? I mean, it's not that I don't want to live in Newcastle. I like it here. But there are lots of things I don't understand.'

'What sort of things?' she asked quietly.

I didn't know why, but my chest was starting to feel tight and I could hardly breathe. I could tell I was going to start crying. I tried very hard to stop myself, but I couldn't. I squeezed my eyes tight shut, trying to block the tears, but still they started to seep out, like water escaping from under a closed door; slowly at first and then running down my cheeks in a hot flood. Suddenly, just like the tears, words seemed to come bursting out of me from somewhere inside. I don't understand exactly where the words came from. It was as if I had no control over them.

'There's something about that red coat and I don't know what it is. I don't know whether someone was wearing it, and I don't know who that someone might have been!' I blurted. 'That red coat in your wardrobe … I wasn't snooping, really I wasn't. I was just looking for the sanitary towels and I saw it. There was something special about it. Maybe it was as if I'd seen it before, or maybe it was just in my head … I just don't know …' I was running out of breath and stopped to gulp in air three or four times. My head felt funny and I was afraid I might faint. Mummy's face looked like it was made of stone. Still it was as if someone inside me couldn't stop talking.

'And … and … also, also, I didn't tell you this, and you won't like it, but I looked inside the desk drawers and there was an article from an old newspaper and it was about a girl called Stacy, and I think maybe I know Stacy, but I'm not sure. I feel she's someone, but I don't know who. Do I know Stacy, Mummy? Who is she? Do you know who Stacy is? Do you, Mummy?'

I couldn't go on talking because I was sobbing so much. Mummy put our sandwiches neatly back on a tea towel on the picnic rug, away from the sand. Her face seemed to be unsure whether to keep its stony look or change to a softer one. When she started speaking, her voice sounded hard and cold.

'Well! I was hurt enough when you searched through my wardrobe, Lucy! Now you tell me you've had another snoop around my room – looking in my desk, in my private drawers.

114

Do you understand the word "*private*", Lucy? Would you want me to rifle through all your private possessions? How would that make you feel?

'You certainly had a good search around my room, didn't you? Why didn't you think to *ask* me if you wanted to know what was in my desk? I was only next door. What exactly were you thinking? What *are* you thinking? How can you be so suspicious of me, Lucy? How can you? It's quite ridiculous to get yourself in such a state – you've just let your imagination run away with you! I have to say I'm very disappointed.'

After a minute she must have seen how upset I was – and by now I was very, very upset. What was I accusing my mother of? What vile thoughts and suspicions were going through my head? I had no idea. I could hardly believe what I had done. I was horrified by what I had said, what I had hinted at. How could I un-say it, undo it? I couldn't.

I could do nothing but cry and say, 'I'm sorry, I'm sorry, I'm sorry, Mummy …'

She reached for my hands, pulled me close and held me in her slightly rigid way.

'Lucy, Lucy, Lucy,' she said softly, 'Surely you know who Stacy is. She's in your own head! You imagined her yourself. I thought you'd forgotten about your little imagined friend long ago – do you remember Lucy, how you used to pretend? I don't know what made you call her Stacy. Maybe there was a little girl called Stacy at your nursery? I suppose I kept that article because it was about someone with the same name. How silly of me, I'm so sorry it's upset you, my darling Lucy. I don't know what you've been thinking of – you're Lucy and always have been. What has put these strange thoughts in your head, these fears?'

I'd never heard Mummy talking like this, and for so long.

'You're Lucy, lovely, special Lucy – my Lucy. And I love you very much. I always have and always will,' she continued. 'You poor girl, you've been worrying and worrying about this for some time, haven't you? You've got yourself all worked up and unhappy – and it's partly my fault – yes it is. I know I'm not all talkative and outgoing and lovey-dovey like Fiona or Susan. Maybe I should be. I wish I could be.

'I know I should have talked more to you about your daddy and the times in Nottingham. But I couldn't, you see, because it was such a sad and painful time. First losing Daddy, and then my dear mother too. Do you understand that, Lucy? I'd nearly forgotten about the red coat – until you asked me about it. Maybe I shouldn't have kept it all those years … I … er … I don't really know why I did. I suppose it was *special* … in a way. Special because your daddy bought it for me. Yes, he did. He liked red, so he bought it for my birthday. That's why I kept it.' She looked at me and took a deep breath.

'But then, after you found it, I decided to get rid of it because it reminded me of all that sadness; of losing Daddy. So … so I took it to a charity shop last week – I should have done so years ago. That's all. I don't know why it upset you so much. I never meant to worry you. Can you forgive me?'

We were both crying and hugging now. It felt quite nice but quite scary at the same time.

''Course I forgive you.'

She released me from her embrace and sat back.

'But, Lucy, I have to say, I am disappointed – and surprised – that you could ever think awful, sinister things about me. Surely you don't really think I'm sinister, do you, Lucy? I've tried hard to be a good mother. It isn't always easy to be a mother on your own …'

'I don't, I don't … I'm very sorry, Mummy.'

It was a relief for both of us when the discussion was over – if it was over. We wanted to think we had somehow sorted the situation out, at least I did. I felt washed out, weak and empty after all the crying – a bit like the cleansed but limp feeling you get after being very sick. After the picnic – which neither of us could eat – Mummy and I didn't speak about it again.

* * *

Later, Cassie asked me whether I'd managed to ask Mummy the questions I wanted to. I said some, but not all of them. I told Cassie both Mummy and I had got very upset, and she said in that case it was probably best not to talk more about it. She did look at me in a concerned way. Maybe she was a bit disappointed in me. Certainly I felt a bit of a failure myself.

She must have spoken to her mum, because Fiona took me aside and sat me on her knee, as if I was a small child, and put her arms round me. She told me that if I ever wanted to talk about sad or difficult things – in confidence – she'd be happy to discuss them with me. It felt good to think she cared about me enough to help me in that way. I thanked her, but assured her I was fine.

Mummy and I both wanted to put the episode behind us. But would that be possible? I guess sometimes we try to bury thoughts, yet maybe those thoughts don't always want to stay buried. Maybe they *can't* stay buried.

117

Chapter Twenty-Six

Alison

Perhaps I shouldn't have been surprised by Lucy's curiosity – I do remember asking Mother about my own background from time to time. I recall questioning her in a particularly persistent way, when I was about the same age as Lucy is now.

'If I don't know who my family is,' I had asserted to her, 'how do I know who I am?'

'You know exactly who your family is, and you do know who you are,' Mother had replied calmly. (She always remained calm, a characteristic that sometimes provoked further frustration on my part.)

'Just remember, Alison, *I* am your family. Whether a family is large or small is not important. Nor do I believe family is about who gave birth to you or what the "blood ties" are. It's about who you love and who loves you. I love you, Alison, and I hope you love me too. So you and I – just the two of us – are all the family either of us need.'

'I do love you, of course I do. But in most families children look like their parents. At any rate, like *one* of their parents. I don't look like you at all, do I? Our faces are different shapes and you have a long thin nose. Your eyes are brown and mine are blue. You have dark brown hair and I have fair hair. I'm already nearly as tall as you, so I shall certainly grow taller.'

'None of that matters. You are my daughter and I am your mother.'

'It matters to me ...' I had replied mulishly.

'Dear Alison, we have something about our relationship that is much more special than most mothers and daughters.'

'What do you mean?'

Of course I knew exactly what she meant, but I never tired of asking Mother to tell this story again and again.

'Most mothers and daughters exist purely by chance. They may or may not get on; they may or may not like each other; they may or may not have interests in common. Always remember, I *chose* you specifically for yourself. I walked up and down the rows of babies' cots in the Mother and Baby Home. I specially went to the girls' nursery and looked at all the baby girls. As you know, I had already decided I wanted a daughter rather than a son – and not many mothers are able to choose their child in that way. I looked at each little baby girl for a long time; I really studied them. Many of them were very sweet, very pretty. Some of them even smiled at me.

'But as soon as I saw you, I knew you were the one for me. You didn't smile. You looked at me very solemnly. Your eyes were fixed on me, staring at me, as if you wanted to look right inside my soul. That's how I knew you were the right one. My special little girl. That's who you were then, and that's who you are now.'

I loved to hear Mother reassure me in this way, and often returned to the topic over the years. I knew I could be a challenging child for her sometimes, though I never meant to be.

I found the company of other children trying. At the small private day school I attended during the infant and primary years, teachers were keen to mould me into a more conventional child.

119

People didn't talk about "social skills" in those days, but they did want to encourage children to "learn to share" and to feel "part of a team". As a child, I found playing or working in pairs or groups extremely difficult and even distasteful. Other people were so slow at solving problems and completing tasks. I found it dreadfully frustrating. Why struggle to perform tasks with someone else, when it can be done far more quickly and successfully alone?

Over the years I have learned to understand other people's expectations of me, but not then. At school I excelled at mathematics and some aspects of science. I was good at all memory and logic tasks, but none of these achievements ever seemed to be enough for the teachers. No, they were forever asking what I regarded as unnecessary and irrelevant questions, especially the "learning assistants" engaged to help me – as if I needed assistance to learn!

'Describe this picture, Alison,' one of them might say.

I would do my best to comply, providing the facts as I saw them, but my responses never seemed to satisfy the assistant.

'Yes, dear … that's all … good … but what do you think those people might be *feeling*? What do you think might happen next?'

They never considered that such deductions were impossible based on the flimsy evidence of an infantile drawing. My answers never seemed to please them. They were always wanting something different.

It was much the same with the other girls of my own age. They were forever preoccupied with topics that seemed to me of little interest or importance. This became even more noticeable as we progressed to the senior school.

'Look, Alison, have you seen Charlotte? Doesn't she look miserable?' one child might whisper to me confidentially. 'That's because she's fallen out with Sarah. Now Sarah refuses to be friends with her. What do you think? I think Sarah's being mean, don't you?'

'I don't know … I don't know anything about Charlotte or Sarah.'

I quite liked other girls talking to me, but was never sure how to respond, so would search around for something interesting to say. Having felt I had exhausted the topic of Sarah and Charlotte, I cast around for something else on which to comment.

'Look,' I ventured, 'I've noticed the wall over there is slanting slightly on the right-hand side. I think it needs to be reinforced, otherwise a crack may form, and it could fall down.'

'Alison Brown, you're so weird!'

It was a label that was frequently attached to me over those unhappy years. As time went on the other girls often saw me as a source of entertainment. They found they could tease, humiliate and torment me mercilessly and delight in the result, without any fear of sanctions from teachers. Their cruelty was predominantly verbal rather than physical. On the rare occasions that I complained to a teacher, I was told it was "harmless fun", and that I should simply "laugh it off" or stand up for myself. I recalled many painful scenes of this apparently harmless fun at break times, with my classmates surrounding me like a pack of wolves bent on attack.

'What's your favourite group, Alison?' one girl might ask.

'Group? Group of what?'

Gales of laughter followed.

'You know – music! Music groups.'

'Oh. Well … I especially like Bach for the intensity and orderly patterns of his music. I also like …'

'Oooh! Bach! Alison fancies Bach – even though he's been dead for about five hundred years!' they would shriek.

'No, actually he died in 1750, so that's two hundred and ten years ago.'

'He's still dead!'

'But his music lives on.'

They groaned.

'Which of the Everly Brothers d'you fancy – Don or Phil?

'Umm. I don't think I know anyone called Everly ...'

Screams of laughter.

'What about Bobby Darin or Elvis Presley, Alison?'

'Of course I have heard of Elvis Presley, and I believe he has rather a nice voice ... if you like that sort of music.'

'You are so peculiar, Alison Brown!' they howled.

This sort of exchange was reproduced with many variations over the course of my school years.

* * *

Home was my refuge, although even Mother could not always protect me from the unremitting demands of an unsympathetic world. When the strains became too great, I would sometimes come home, fling my schoolbag onto the floor and myself after it, and shout and stamp and scream like a banshee (Mother's description).

She would lead me gently upstairs to my room, switch on a soft, subdued light, close the blinds and let me pull the curtains, which she had specially made for me, around my bed. Inside this den, or cocoon, I felt safe. The harsh expectations of the day would gradually melt away. After a time, Mother would come upstairs carrying a tray, and enter the den. She would pour a cup of Earl Grey tea for each of us. We would sit quietly and companionably together drinking it, sometimes with a Rich Tea biscuit.

Occasionally, when it all became too much for me, I would have a similar collapse or "melt-down", as my teachers inaccurately called these times, at school. I would be secreted away to the medical room, or to the head teacher's office, for a period of reflection and calming down. It was always put down to my oddness. No one ever took the view that perhaps it was the behaviour of the other girls that needed to change.

Despite the fact that I achieved top marks in almost every assessment, my teachers seemed to feel there were issues about my development that warranted "further investigation". Poor Mother had to trail me first to our general practitioner, and then to various specialists. I was given a range of puzzles, tests and assessments to complete, most of which I rather enjoyed.

After analysing the results, all the doctors seemed agreed that I was highly intelligent, but suffered from what was variously described as idiosyncratic quirks of development, severe anxiety, poor insight into the feelings or thought patterns of others, rigidity of personality, lack of empathy, overly concrete interpretation of language, and on and on. Neither Mother nor I found these pronouncements very helpful.

'We're all individuals. We're all different,' said Mother, ever pragmatic.

'Why is it always me and my problems people fuss about?' I asked. 'Nobody takes Mary or Helen to see a doctor just because they're no good at Maths or French.'

'Quite right, Alison. I think you should just forget about the doctors and get on with your life. You're doing so well at school, and soon you'll be doing your A levels and applying to universities. There's just no limit to what you might achieve, a clever girl like you. But do you know what I think is going to make the biggest difference to your life, and especially to your future happiness?'

'What?'

'Having a child of your own one day. A lovely little baby to love, and to love you back, exactly as you are. Babies love their mothers. They don't judge their mothers or criticise them or try to change them. They just love them. Isn't that wonderful!'

Mother mentioned this potential solution to my problems on several occasions over the years.

At the time I had no experience of babies and small children, and was not particularly drawn to them, but the thought of anyone, beside Mother, loving me without judgement or criticism seemed very attractive. I never forgot Mother's words.

Chapter Twenty-Seven

Alison

1962 Durham University

Mother ran her fingers across the top of the wardrobe and turned to show me her still-pristine hand.

'Well, that's a good sign. At least they're keeping the place clean. It could do with a lick of paint, but never mind.'

'It's like a cell,' I said gloomily, trying to swallow the lump in my throat, trying to control the threatened tears.

'Now, Alison, I know it's … compact, but you've got everything you need. Look, nice comfy bed, wardrobe, chest of drawers, desk, and a useful shelf for your books and knick-knacks. Once we unpack all your things and put some pictures up, put your books on the shelf, it'll be much more homely.'

Mother was in her brisk, determined-to-be-positive mood.

'Look, dear, blue curtains! Quite pretty – they almost match your lovely eiderdown!' She held open one side of the drab greyish-blue curtains.

'Ooh, come and look out of the window! It's really lovely, Alison. You've got such a nice outlook onto the grounds. Don't the trees look glorious – the leaves are just starting to turn. Look at that maple – it's going to be deep scarlet in a week or two. Come on – come and see.'

Reluctantly, I joined her and gazed at the parkland outside. It was truly a fine view. Mother had written ahead to the principal to explain some of my vulnerabilities; that I was sensitive to noise, and needed peace. Perhaps the university staff had genuinely taken note of her request, and selected a quiet room for that reason. This thought restored some feeling of optimism in me.

The previous day, as we had finalised my packing, we'd had a long and serious talk about making the adjustment to university life – life away from home, and away from Mother. What I had to focus on, Mother had said, and I had to agree, was *study*. I loved to study. Everything else was secondary. I had to enjoy what I could, and gradually adjust to what was unfamiliar or difficult.

'You're right. It's good to be on the quiet and leafy side of the building. Let's unpack and get things sorted out.'

Mother's face relaxed and she smiled.

An hour later, as I was arranging my books in alphabetical order on the bookshelf, and Mother was putting the last of my clothes in the chest of drawers, there was a knock on the door. We stood open-mouthed for a moment. The door opened and a head peered around it. The head had a mass of curly reddish hair, and a pale white face with a sprinkling of freckles over the nose, and wore a big grin. It was quickly followed by a sturdy body, dressed in blue jeans and a green jumper.

'Hello! I'm Karen. I'm your next-door neighbour, on that side.' She pointed to the left of the door, and strode into the room with her hand outstretched, first to Mother, who shook it hesitantly, and then to me. I managed to return the handshake and smile at the visitor. She gave a snorting laugh.

'Wow! You've certainly got yourself organised!' Karen exclaimed, looking around the room. The three of us were standing in an awkward huddle in the tiny space between the bed, the cupboards and the desk.

'Do sit down, dear,' Mother said indicating the upright wooden chair, which she pulled from under the desk and turned to face the bed, making even less space. Karen sat and turned to me.

'What's your name?'

'Oh ... sorry ... I'm Alison and this is Mo ... I mean my mother ...'

'Dorothy,' Mother said.

'Alison ... and Dorothy. It's very nice to meet you.'

'Of course, I won't be staying long,' Mother said. 'I'm just settling Alison in. I need to get home soon.'

I looked at her, feeling panic start to creep up my spine again.

'Why don't I make us all a cup of tea?' said Karen. 'The kitchen's just three doors down the corridor. Have you seen it yet? It's very nice, very well equipped. Well, I'll just go and make us some tea ... oh, or would you rather have coffee?'

'Tea would be very nice, dear. We both take milk, if you have it, no sugar.'

'Right-oh. I'll bring three cuppas here – my room's an awful tip! Be back in a minute!'

Karen stood up and stomped noisily from the room.

'What a nice, friendly girl, wasn't she? Polite too. How kind to bring us tea.'

'Yes,' I replied, 'very thoughtful. I wonder what sort of tea ...?'

'Now then, don't forget what we talked about, dear. We'll just enjoy it, whatever sort it is.'

* * *

127

Later that evening I sat in the darkening room alone. Mother had gone back home to Nottingham. Karen had cheerfully said she'd call for me at around seven, so we could go across the yard to the refectory together and have supper. After she had picked up her mugs and left my room, I heard her voice and several other excited female voices in the corridor outside and in nearby rooms: greetings, exclamations, comparing rooms, shrieking and laughter. I could hear them asking each other questions and making conversation – just as Mother and I had practised many times. I knew I should join them, but I couldn't. I couldn't open the door.

Karen didn't call for me. I suppose she must have forgotten – she had so many other people to talk to. I couldn't bring myself to walk across the yard by myself, so I stayed in my room. I had a biscuit and an apple for supper.

Much later, when all was quiet apart from a few sighs and murmurings from behind some of the closed doors, I crept down the corridor in my dressing gown to the toilets and washroom, clutching my wash bag and hot-water bottle. After washing I filled the hot-water bottle from a kettle in the kitchen and hurried back to my room. I tried to calm my tense stomach by holding the warmth closely and curling up, like a prawn, Mother always said.

* * *

My interview with the college principal the next morning did not begin well. I found her terrifying. Dr Bessel (one of the second-year students had informed me at breakfast that her nickname was "Dr Bestial") was a tall, angular woman in late middle age, with lank, greying, dark hair pulled into an untidy bun. Her expression was severe and distant. Mother's letter was visible on the desk in front of her. She nodded towards the chair opposite. I understood this to be an invitation to sit.

'Your mother seems to think you are a frail and needy being, Miss Brown. Why exactly is that? You don't seem to have had any problems achieving top A-level grades.' She appeared to have a whole file of information about me.

'I … I find it difficult to talk to other people of my own age … you know – to make friends. I get … er … very nervous, very anxious …'

'That is not unusual in a young person, Miss Brown.'

'Mother thought I'd be better at a university like Durham, with the collegiate system; that it would be more … nurturing.'

Dr Bessel looked at me quizzically and did not comment.

'Um … I don't have the same sense of humour as most other people seem to have. In fact, I don't understand their humour most of the time. So they think I'm odd. Weird, they often say. Perhaps I'm too serious.'

Dr Bessel peered at me over her glasses. Her mouth puckered in a twitchy sort of way, as if she was trying to smile, but couldn't quite manage it.

'I have to say, Miss Brown, that your description of yourself accords remarkably with what has often been said about me. I do not consider a lack of the hysterical humour so many young people demonstrate to be a fault. Indeed, seriousness could be regarded as a desirable quality, particularly in an establishment devoted to learning and education, such as this one.'

'I see …'

'I suggest you devote yourself to study. Make that your priority for the present. Enjoy exploring your new courses. Make the most of the library and the other facilities the university has to offer. If you meet other like-minded students, all well and good – enjoy their company. If not, well you wouldn't miss them much anyway, would you?'

'No …'

'Make an appointment with my secretary to see me again in

four or five weeks, and let me know how you're getting on, will you? Good luck, Miss Brown.'

'Thank you, Dr Bessel.'

* * *

Karen and some of the other girls in my corridor did their best to "take me in hand". This appeared primarily to involve encouraging me to dress differently, to develop an interest in some of the male students with whom they had become friendly, and to join a number of clubs and societies. I was regarded as a sort of "work in progress", not unkindly, but slightly despairingly. Just like the girls at school, the other students expected me to participate in the current "youth culture" as befitted 1962, and to share with them a particular taste in fashion, music, films and politics. Their suggestions were delivered in good humour, and without the malice I'd experienced at school, but with some determination nevertheless.

'Oh, Alison,' Karen would exclaim as I emerged from my room, 'haven't you got some *jeans* to wear?' or 'What about taking that skirt up a couple of inches, or six ...?!'

Karen even took it upon herself to turn up the hem of my favourite skirt – cutting off the excess, so there was no going back. I agreed to wear it only with my thickest tights, and even then felt dreadfully exposed.

Durham was far too cold for wearing miniskirts.

* * *

I didn't *enjoy* that early time at university, but in some ways I did learn to adjust to the routines and expectations, and felt proud of myself for "settling in", as Mother called it. Yet, however friendly the other students tried to be, I felt their friendship to be superficial. Mother and I wrote each other long letters at least once a week. Every fortnight or so, I would wait for one of the telephones next to the Junior Common Room to be free, and would ring Mother. It wasn't very private.

'How are you getting on, Alison dear?'

'Oh all right, I suppose. Durham's very beautiful when it's frosty.'

'How lovely. And what have you been doing?'

'Well … working a lot, of course. Going to the library. Walking by the river. I love doing that.'

'That sounds nice … not too cold, I hope? You must remember to wrap up warm … and what about friends?'

'Karen's always friendly – and the other girls here too. There are some quite nice people in my Maths lectures. There's this boy called Phil who does the same subsidiaries as me and he's in my tutorial group. He bought me a cup of coffee in the library the other day.'

'Well that was good of him. Is he a … nice boy?'

'I think so – he was talking about calculus with me. The other girls say he's cool.'

'Cool? What does that mean?'

'I'm not sure. I think it means they like him.'

'Well, just be careful, dear.'

'Mother?'

'Yes, dear?'

'I miss being at home. I miss you, Mother.'

'I miss you too, Alison, but you're doing very well. I'm so proud of you. It won't be long 'til the Christmas holidays, will it?'

* * *

131

Towards the end of the first term (they called it Michaelmas term), Karen told me there was going to be a party at one of the boys' "digs" and we were all invited.

'I'm not very keen on parties.'

'Oh come on, Alison! This will be brilliant – a proper party – for grown-ups, not a kiddies' party. There'll be fabulous music, and dancing, and booze, and gorgeous boys of course. You'll love it, you'll see.'

'I'm not sure …'

'Now, I absolutely insist. We'll help you dress just right. You'd look beautiful if you weren't just a little bit … *square*. You'll see, the boys will love you.'

Penny, who was slightly built like me (I learned that "square" did not refer to my shape, but to the way I dressed), lent me a pair of close-fitting, deep-blue crushed velvet trousers. These clung tightly to my hips and thighs like a second skin, flaring out below the knees. I quite liked them, and at least they kept my legs warmer than the miniskirts. I had a white gypsy-style shirt of my own that the others approved of. This was topped by an embroidered waistcoat provided by Helen. Karen undid my pony-tail and brushed my fair hair out to its full length. The girls all crowded around me watching their handiwork progressing.

'I know!' shouted Lisa, and she rushed off to her room. She returned a few moments later clutching a long, silky purple scarf. I had worn hair bands as a child, in the style of an Alice band, but Lisa fastened the scarf around my head, crown-like, its loose ends flowing over my shoulders. The other girls shrieked with delight, as excited as if I were a snowman they had just created and decorated to perfection. They dragged me to the bathroom to look in the full-length mirror. I was astonished. I hardly recognised my reflection.

'You look amazing, Alison, absolutely gorgeous!' said Karen.

We tripped down the wooded pathways alongside the river, overshadowed as always by the cathedral – trying to avoid stepping in muddy puddles with our unsuitable shoes. They hadn't allowed me to wear socks. Helen was even wearing sandals – in December! The others linked arms and giggled about nothing in particular. We'd shared a bottle of wine brought by Lisa's visiting brother before setting out. Drinking wine always seemed to precipitate somewhat silly jolliness. I felt a little light-headed and dizzy.

The party was in a narrow three-storey terraced house up one of the steep, cobbled streets a little out of the centre of the city. It was rented by five male third-year students. When we arrived, the house was already bursting with people and noise. There was a lot of laughing and hugging as we greeted the hosts and other students we recognised. The music pounded through my whole body like a drill. I was starting to feel shaky. I realised I hadn't eaten since lunchtime. Karen steered me towards the kitchen, where there was a mess of dirty and clean cups and glasses and miscellaneous bottles. Phil, from my Maths tutorial group, was standing behind the table, talking to a girl I didn't know. He turned and saw us.

'Hi, Karen. Hi, Alison – oh wow! You look terrific! What do you want to drink, red or white – or beer?'

'Um … is there any orange … or water?'

'Plenty of water in the tap if you get thirsty. Here – start with this white.'

Karen disappeared upstairs with her drink. Phil kept looking at me, shaking his head and grinning, as if he'd never seen me before. He took hold of my hand and led me into the largest room, where some people were gyrating wildly to the thump of the music. Others in pairs grasped each other in tight clinches and shuffled about more slowly.

'Want to dance?' Phil asked and immediately started to throw his body about, as if in extreme pain. He reached his hand out to me and pulled me towards him. I sipped frantically at my glass of wine and tried to bob about in some semblance of what the others were doing. It felt ridiculous. I felt ridiculous.

The next hour or two were agony for me. My head was pounding as if keeping time with the relentless drum beat. Phil wanted to "show me off" to some of his friends, but since it was impossible to hear anyone above the noise, conversation was not an option. I wondered how soon I could reasonably make some excuse and leave. As the evening wore on painfully, Phil drew me closer and closer when "dancing". My only escape was to rush over to the table at the side of the room, where our drinks had been parked, and periodically take further sips. Before long I felt as though my head would explode, and waves of nausea churned my stomach, as if an octopus was waving its tentacles and swimming back and forth inside me.

'I'm feeling a bit dizzy ...'

Phil clutched me tighter and whispered in my ear, 'Just hold on to me. I'll look after you.'

'I'm going to be sick!'

I tore myself away from him and rushed up to the bathroom, just in time. I bathed my face in cold water, and drank its heavenly coolness.

Phil was waiting as I tottered down the stairs. He held out my glass.

'Phil ... I really need to go back. I ... I ... want a cup of tea, not wine, and I want to lie down.'

'That's a good idea.' He grinned at me. 'OK, I'll take you back, but it's still so early. Let's go to my place first, shall we – it's just around the corner. I'll make you some tea and ... you can have a rest. Then I'll take you back.'

'Oh, thank you,' I said gratefully.

Phil's digs were in a nearby terrace – a mean, shabby house.

'Don't you live in college? I thought all first years did.'

'I applied too late. All the college accommodation had gone ... This is OK. I'm more independent here. The landlady's old and deaf – she won't hear us. We'll be fine.'

He opened the front door and then unlocked a downstairs

room immediately on the left of a steep, narrow staircase. The room smelt of stale, burned toast. It felt damp and chilly. He locked the door, knelt in front of the gas fire and lit it with a match. I was shivering.

'Soon warm up,' he said cheerfully. He pulled me down to a threadbare rug in front of the fire and put his arms around me. 'Better?'

'Mmm ...'

He grasped my chin and turned my face towards him. To my surprise he kissed me on the lips, just gently at first, as if he was being friendly and comforting. I tried to move my head away, without being rude, but he held me fast. Then the shock of his exploratory tongue horrified me. I froze and pulled away.

'Tea ...?' I blurted.

'Oh ... OK.'

He got up and put a kettle on an electric hotplate in the corner. He pulled two mugs from a bookshelf. I hoped they were clean. The room was sparsely furnished. There was a narrow single bed with a faded, green eiderdown, a bedside table, an old wooden wardrobe, and a wooden table and chair. I headed towards the chair.

'Sit on the bed – it's much more comfy, and warmer.'

I sat uneasily. The bed felt lumpy and it was so high my feet only reached the floor by pointing my toes. Phil brought two steaming mugs and placed them carefully on the bedside table. It was marked with many rings from previous mugs.

'Sorry, but there's no milk.'

'Oh ... never mind ...'

I didn't get the chance to finish my sentence. Phil hurled himself at me, knocking me backwards on the bed. I was so astonished. I could do nothing but squirm on my back, waving my legs in the air, as helpless as an upturned beetle. I was amazed at how strong he was. He ground his mouth onto mine, his tongue pushing and searching once more. I think I made a strangulated squeak. I was afraid I would choke. He pulled back for a moment.

135

'Oh, you're gorgeous,' he gasped, breathing heavily.

'Phil, Phil, stop it!'

But he didn't stop. His hands were everywhere: reaching under my shirt, touching my breasts, reaching into my trousers. He grabbed one of my flailing hands and pressed it onto his crotch.

I screamed at the top of my voice and kept screaming. With all the strength I could muster I pushed him off and scrambled out from under him. I stood up still shrieking, and trembling all over.

'Stop it!' he hissed. 'You'll wake the whole street, for God's sake! What the hell is the matter with you? You were happy to come home with me – I thought you wanted it! Just stop screaming!'

'I'm going home! Leave me alone. Don't you touch me – don't ever touch me again!'

I grabbed my jacket and bag and rattled the door – which was locked – frantically.

'Open it! Unlock the door!'

He found the key and unlocked the door. 'Go on then – good riddance!'

Just before he slammed the door shut behind me, he spat out in a loud whisper, 'There are words for girls like you!'

I ran down his street, and the next, and the next, tripping on the cobbles, chanting under my breath as the cold air revived me, 'Never, never, never again! Never, never, never again!'

I ran alongside the river through the dark, suddenly illuminated by streetlights and then cast into the shadows again; past towering trees, and along more streets. It was late and few people were about. An elderly couple with a small white dog were walking arm in arm along the path. They stopped and turned to look curiously at me. A middle-aged man, starting to walk over the bridge, called out, 'Are you all right, pet?'

'No! No! No!' I shrieked, as I ran. No man will ever come near me again, I told myself, never, never, never.

I kept running until I reached the college residence. I pounded along the corridor to my room, flung myself on the bed and wrapped the eiderdown tightly around my curled body. I remained, prawn-like, until early the next morning. As soon as I was sure the main college building would be open, I ran across the courtyard and inside.

I rang Mother.

'Come and fetch me straight away! Today! I can't stay here another day. Not one day. I want to go home! I won't ever come back.'

* * *

Mother didn't try to persuade me. After a few weeks "to recover", she arranged – through a contact of her solicitor – for me to be interviewed to train as a junior administrative assistant in a large legal practice in the city centre. I found the work undemanding and was told I would have the opportunity to progress in time. Mrs Anderson had just started as office manager. She lacked any sense of humour. She was strict and discouraged chatter among office staff, all of whom were women and girls. Her regime suited me very well. I was thorough, applied and efficient. I felt secure. It never occurred to me that I would remain for more than twenty years.

Chapter Twenty-Eight

1997

Lucy

The year of our fifteenth birthdays was one of upset and difficulties. In August, three months after Cassie's birthday, the whole country was shocked by Princess Diana's death. Cassie and I talked about it endlessly. She was such a lovely person, who did lots of caring things for people, and anyone could see she wasn't happy being a princess. Her sadness made us love her all the more. Why should such a young and beautiful person be killed? It didn't make sense.

Mummy disapproved of what she called "mass hysteria". She thought the public displays of sorrow and bereavement – such as the growing mountains of flowers outside Buckingham Palace – were exaggerated and unseemly.

'It's not as if anyone knew her personally,' she kept repeating. 'It's not like losing a close friend or member of the family.'

Yet for Cassie and me, and many of our friends, it *was* like losing someone close to us. She was so beautiful, and so young.

We became interested and disturbed by death, especially when it happened to young people. I guess we were looking for answers. Cassie developed a particular interest in things like the occult, gothic stories, Eastern religion and psychology – anything that couldn't be rationally explained, as she put it. I took a secondary interest too, out of loyalty to Cassie, I suppose, but it wasn't really my sort of thing.

Anyway, Cassie hadn't had a party for her birthday in May. There was nothing special she could think of doing at the time. But later, in September, as *my* fifteenth birthday approached, Fiona suggested Cassie thought of a special celebration for us both, to cheer everyone up. Fiona said she could choose anything, within reason, as a late birthday party or activity. Fifteen was unique, she said, halfway from ten, which was still a child, to twenty, which was an adult. I loved the way her parents always took account of her wishes.

* * *

There was a cult psychologist called Hans Augenblick (I bet that wasn't his real name) who had a reputation for being an amazing hypnotist. He'd become quite famous. He had a regular television show, and he sometimes performed in theatres, doing things like message or thought transmission, "mind-sharing", suggestion and hypnosis. He claimed he could hypnotise anyone, even those who tried to resist.

Mummy totally disapproved of him. She said he sensationalised human weaknesses and suggestibility, and that he publicly humiliated people for entertainment and financial gain. She insisted his shows were all trickery. I wasn't sure about the trickery part, but I did secretly agree with Mummy's point of view – though I would never admit it, especially to Cassie. Cassie, on the other hand, loved everything about his performances.

By lucky chance – or maybe unlucky, as it turned out – Hans Augenblick was on tour in the North East with his current show, *Believe It Or Not*. He was to hold a performance at the Northern Life theatre in mid-September.

'That's what I want to do for my late birthday, Mum,' Cassie said. 'That would be absolutely brilliant!'

Fiona was very uncertain. She said she thought we were too young for the show. She thought it could be unsuitable, but Cassie begged and begged her.

'How can you possibly say we're too young, Mum, when you're the one who believes fifteen is nearly adult?'

'I didn't say "nearly adult" I said "halfway to being adult".'

'That's just playing with semantics,' retorted Cassie. She was always clever with words. I could never have answered Mummy back that way.

'Anyway, he's a real, qualified psychologist, a professional – not just some quack. It would be so brilliant to see him perform in person. There's absolutely nothing else I want to do. Please, Mum, please, please …!'

Funny how she could switch from sounding like a clever grown-up one minute to a little kid the next! Maybe that's exactly what Fiona meant by halfway between a child and an adult. I guess she just wore her mum down, because in the end Fiona agreed that she would take Cassie, me, Laura and Megan out for pizzas, followed by the evening performance of *Believe It Or Not*.

Predictably, Mummy wasn't happy about it. Not at all. She said it was an "inappropriate choice". After a long, uncomfortable discussion she agreed, very reluctantly, to me going, and then only because there was a group of us, and because Fiona would be taking us.

* * *

The man checking our tickets at the door to the theatre auditorium pointed out a number printed on the back of each one.

'You should each hang on to your tickets, girls – don't tear them up,' he said. 'The number on the back is like a raffle number – very significant. You'll see ...'

He tapped the side of his nose with his index finger and winked at us, as if this was a special secret he was sharing with us alone. Fiona handed us each a ticket to hold on to. The theatre was completely packed, the audience composed mostly of adults; just a few teenage kids like us. Our seats were towards the front of the stalls, near the stage. Cassie and Megan sat either side of me, then Laura, and lastly Fiona. The four of us were really excited. Of course, it was all a bit stagey, but I couldn't help being caught up in the atmosphere.

The lights in the auditorium dimmed. The curtain opened and Hans Augenblick stepped from darkness at the back of the stage into a pale pool of spotlight. He raised his arms and bowed deeply. There was a murmur of voices and loud applause. He wore a black evening suit, perfectly cut to his tall, thin frame. His black, patent-leather shoes reflected the light as he swivelled slowly from left to right and back again. His hair and beard were also black, sculpted into flawless smoothness by some sort of oil. He looked like a sleek, black raven.

He raised his head and his eyes were piercing. They swept over the audience, as if he were searching for someone he knew. He smiled and nodded his head slightly, as though conceding that the enthusiastic applause was no more than his due.

'What a showman!' I whispered to Cassie.

'Wait and see,' she whispered back.

'He certainly knows how to work an audience,' Fiona whispered across to us.

Hans Augenblick held his hands up in front of him, palms to the audience, and moved them sharply apart. At this signal, the audience ceased applauding instantly, and silence fell like a spell over the auditorium.

'Ladies and gentlemen,' he said, in a slightly high voice, with a hint of a foreign accent and only just loud enough to be audible.

'Welcome. Tonight, together, we are going to explore some of the mysteries of the human mind. Do not expect to understand everything you see. I have come to show you what a wonderfully complex and flexible phenomenon the mind is. I have not come to bring you easy answers.' He looked fiercely at the audience.

'No!' He raised his voice so suddenly, that on the "No!" people jumped and sat upright in their seats.

'No,' he repeated, more softly, soothingly, 'but perhaps I will raise some questions. Perhaps even some questions you did not know existed.'

He stared at the audience, as if challenging us to disagree. I had the strange sensation that he was looking directly at me. There was an intimacy in his manner that was unsettling.

'The mind is like an iceberg. What we see, what we know about, is just a tiny portion compared to what lies beneath the surface.'

Cassie and I exchanged glances and smiled.

'For tonight's exploration, I will need some of you to volunteer, to help me with my tasks.'

An uneasy muttering and shuffling greeted this announcement. Laura leaned across Megan towards Cassie and me.

'D'you think he's planted people in the audience?' she asked in loud whisper.

'Some of you may be wondering,' Hans continued sternly, 'whether these are genuine volunteers, or whether I have placed people among you.'

Laura clamped her hand over her mouth, made a wide-eyed face, and returned to sitting upright, a deep blush rising up her neck and cheeks.

Hans Augenblick held up some sort of remote control device. He clicked a switch, and lists of numbers appeared on a screen above the stage. At the same time, a green light played up and down the numbers, apparently at random, highlighting each for a split-second only.

Hans stepped to the front edge of the stage.

'Ladies and gentlemen, would one of you be kind enough to help me, please?'

There was a brief pause. Then a middle-aged man near the front stood up and raised his hand.

'Thank you, sir. Please join me here on the stage.'

The man walked self-consciously up the steps and to Hans's side. Hans reached towards him and they shook hands.

'Welcome, sir. What is your name?'

'Anthony.'

'How do you do, Anthony? Now, could you tell the audience, have we ever met before?'

'No, never,' Anthony muttered.

'Good. Now please take this electronic control.'

He handed the man a small black mechanism.

'Anthony, would you please turn to face the audience.'

The man did as requested, looking a little bashful.

'Now, sir, can you see any of the numbers on the screen behind you?'

The man shook his head to indicate no.

'Out loud, if you please, kind sir.'

'No, I can't see the numbers at all,' the man said loudly.

'That's good. In a minute, I want you to press that switch on your device. When you do, the green light will stop instantly, highlighting a particular number. The person holding the ticket with that number will be asked to volunteer – if they wish, only if they wish. Do you understand, Anthony?'

The man confirmed that yes, he understood. Hans turned to the audience.

'Please remember, ladies and gentlemen, that every number on the screen has an equal chance of being selected. Also, should your number be selected, there will be no pressure on you to participate, no pressure at all. It is entirely up to you.'

A murmur rose from the packed auditorium.

'Good,' said Hans, turning back to the man. 'So, whenever you are ready Anthony, and in your own time, press the switch to stop the green light.'

There was a slight rustling as people in the audience found their tickets and held them at the ready. The entire auditorium was suspended in tense anticipation. Everyone watched the green light racing along the rows of numbers. After a few moments there was a buzzing sound. The green light was still. It lit up the number 689.

'Good, good. Six, eight, nine, ladies and gentlemen. Six, eight, nine!' Hans Augenblick called loudly, making it sound as though number 689 was a wonderful, animate entity, with its own special personality.

'Six, eight, nine!' he repeated.

'Hey, that's me! That's my number!' an excited female voice from behind us called. She stood up and waved her ticket above her head. Everyone turned in their seats to see who it was.

'Excellent!' said Hans. 'Are you prepared to volunteer to take part, madam?'

'Ooh, yes.' The woman giggled and looked round at her friends. 'I suppose so …'

This procedure was repeated four times until four volunteers had been found.

'So, ladies and gentlemen, we now have four volunteers for the activities in the first half of our show tonight. After the intermission, I shall ask for two more.'

Anthony returned to his seat, while the four volunteers were guided onto the stage, where four chairs awaited them. Each in turn was asked to participate in "mind activities", as Hans called them. One, completely separated from Hans by a high screen, was given a tray with a row of ten coloured blocks. She was asked

144

to concentrate hard on one of the colours, while selecting a matching card of that chosen colour and holding it close to her heart. Hans closed his eyes. He looked as though he were in a trance.

'I see a warm colour,' he said. 'I see a colour of great depth. I feel a red, but it is not red like blood.' He paused and frowned. He screwed up his eyes and then pressed his palm against his forehead, as though searching the furthest corner of his consciousness for the colour.

'Dark red,' he announced. 'I see maroon.'

'Yes!' shrieked the woman. 'Eee, yes, that's right – it's maroon!' She jumped up from her chair and waved the maroon card at the audience, who clapped uproariously.

Each demonstration became slightly more complex and ambitious. The last of the four volunteers was a man in his thirties. He said his name was Rob.

'Now, Rob,' said Hans, 'I would like to put you in a very relaxed and suggestible state, so that you can follow some simple instructions.'

Rob nodded knowingly.

'Mr Augenblick,' he said, glancing at the audience and back again, 'I better warn you, I'm not at all suggestible. I'm a real sceptic about this hypnotism malarkey. I don't think I'm a good subject for this at all. Just to warn you – I don't want to spoil the show, like.'

Hans Augenblick faced the audience. He smiled calmly and nodded his head up and down.

'Thank you for warning me, Rob. That's fine. All people are different. Shall we just see how it goes?'

'Yeah, OK, it's your funeral, mate,' said Rob. The audience tittered.

'Let's hope not, Rob, let's hope not.'

Hans smiled broadly, resting an avuncular hand on Rob's shoulder.

Within minutes Rob was reclining peacefully in a leather chair, while Hans made a series of requests. He spoke gently but authoritatively.

'Raise your left arm please, Rob.'

'Comb your hand through your hair.'

'Stand up and face the audience.'

'Tell them what work you do, Rob.' ('I'm a gas fitter.')

'Wave to your family.'

So it went on, like a bizarre "Simon Says" game – and for each instruction Rob complied or responded appropriately, even when asked to turn his back to the audience, bend over and pull a face between his legs, making the audience laugh. At last Hans spoke more loudly.

'When I touch your shoulder and say your name, I want you to return to full alertness. You will remember nothing of the last few minutes.'

'Rob!' he said loudly, placing his hand heavily on the man's shoulder. Rob sat upright and smiled. He rubbed his eyes and stared up at Hans.

'See what I mean, mate?' he said apologetically.

'Yes Rob, I see what you mean. We all see what you mean, don't we, ladies and gentlemen? You have done fine, Rob.'

The audience exploded into applause and laughter. Rob turned towards the audience, looking puzzled and a little less sure of himself. He shrugged and returned to his seat. The curtain came down for the intermission.

* * *

'What did you think?' asked Fiona. We were all slurping ice-cream cones in the theatre foyer.

'He's amazing,' said Megan. 'I kept trying to work out how he does it – you know, what the trick is … but I couldn't tell, could you? He really does seem to get inside people's minds.'

'He must make use of a lot of non-verbal communication cues,' said Cassie, who knew about these things, 'to tell him what people are thinking and feeling.'

'Did you think it was exactly fair?' asked Laura. 'I mean, that Rob had no idea what he was doing or saying. Unless it was all an act.'

'It seemed pretty genuine to me,' I said, 'but I know what you mean, Laura. I felt uncomfortable about him losing control of himself too. He was kind of made to look a bit of a fool.'

'Mum, would you go on the stage if your number came up?' asked Cassie.

'I'm not really sure – I don't like the idea of being so exposed,' said Fiona, 'and remember, darlings, all of you – if by any chance one of your numbers comes up, don't feel you have to volunteer. It's entirely your choice.'

* * *

She didn't realise just how relevant that advice would be. No sooner had we settled back in our row than the curtain went up and Hans stood by his number screen again. The atmosphere in the auditorium was now truly electric.

'Ladies and gentlemen,' said Hans, 'welcome back to the second half of our show. Now we are going to explore the pliability of the mind in even greater depth. The first half was not exactly just "Party Tricks"' – a wave of chuckles – 'but what I would regard as some simple demonstrations of how mental suggestion and transmitting thoughts may occur. These next activities are more complex and may take much longer, so we will begin with two volunteers only. As before, we will use the number board to select our participants.'

This time, a teenage boy was given the light switch mechanism.

He faced the audience and after a few moments, pressed the button. Number 199 was lit up in green. With a terrible jolt, I realised it was my number. I stared at my ticket, not quite believing what I saw. My hand, holding the piece of card, started trembling uncontrollably.

'I ... I ... it's my number ...' I stammered.

Chapter Twenty-Nine

My voice sounded feeble, as if on a faulty telephone line.

Fiona and my friends turned to look at me. Hans Augenblick peered down at our row, frowning, as though not only my voice but even my image was too faint to make out clearly.

'M … my ticket is number 199,' I repeated shakily.

The process of selecting a second volunteer via the number board continued. Cassie clutched my hand.

'Are you OK?' she whispered.

Fiona was leaning forwards and looking at me. Her face looked anxious.

'Lucy, you don't have to do it. Don't go up on stage if you don't want to. They can choose someone else.'

Did I want to? Did I not want to? I had no idea. All I felt was shock and uncertainty.

The second person selected by the number board was a kind-looking grandmother. She got up straight away and started making her way up the steps at the side of the stage. She waved cheerily at her family in the stalls. Hans stepped towards her and then peered down at the audience.

'Welcome, madam, welcome,' he said. 'Now, where is my young girl? Where is number 199? Will you come up and join me, my dear?'

'Come on, pet,' said the grandmother loudly. 'Come on up here with me, clever lass. 'E won't bite, will you, Hans? It's just a bit of fun.'

The audience laughed. I could feel many eyes on me. Laura gave me a thumbs-up sign. I squeezed Cassie's hand and released it. I stood up and steadied myself for a moment. Somehow my legs propelled me onto the stage before I could hesitate further.

Hans grasped both my hands and held on to them. He asked my name and age. He spoke quietly and reassuringly. He asked me to sit in the reclining leather chair. I would go first, he said. There was nothing to worry about. The older lady was asked to sit at one side until it was her turn.

'Ladies and gentlemen! Now we have two very helpful people here. Lucy, who is nearly fifteen, just on the verge of becoming an adult, and Margaret, who is a little more than fifteen! So we will ask them about different periods of their lives.'

'First, Lucy, let us think about when you were just a little girl, a very young child. Not a baby, but perhaps two or three years old.'

Immediately my heart began to pound. I could scarcely breathe. How should I think about being such a small child? I couldn't possibly remember that time … and they were all watching me, waiting to hear.

Hans stood close beside me as I reclined helplessly in the chair. Sweat was gathering in the small of my back. My temples throbbed. Maybe I should get up, I thought. Maybe I should go back to my seat? Hans now loomed over me, like a great black crow. I remember some soothing words from him. I remember him stroking my hand, and then passing his cool hand gently across my eyes and forehead.

After that I remember nothing more until opening my eyes and seeing Hans gazing intensely at my face, as if looking for answers to a question I hadn't heard. I appeared to be lying limply on the floor. What was I doing there? Hans smiled and patted my hand. His face was bending close to me. He appeared to be in a strange haze, as if a sudden mist had descended. He smiled and exhaled.

'Lucy, you are here with us again. Well done, dear girl. You are fine now.'

"Fine *now*"? Had I not been fine before? Had something gone wrong?

There was silence from the audience. It was as if the world had suddenly stood still. I felt somehow absent, as if I had been transported into a different universe or a different time zone. Some time must have passed since he asked me to think about when I was a little girl, but I wasn't a part of that time. It had happened without me.

Hans drew gently on my hand to indicate he wanted me to stand, but my legs felt as weak and wobbly as a newborn fawn's. 'Try to stand, Lucy,' he said softly. 'I will help you.' With Hans's help I struggled to my feet. Sweat now trickled down my spine in a cold rivulet. He supported me with a firm hand holding my arm, and led me towards the chair at the side of the stage, where Margaret sat. We changed places.

Hans turned his attention to her. I assumed he had finished with me, but had no idea what had occurred. I felt horribly exposed, vulnerable. Had I made a fool of myself? At a distance, I heard the drone of Margaret's voice responding to Hans, but I couldn't concentrate on what they were saying. My head felt as if it was held in a tight vice. Waves of nausea rose and receded.

After a while, I heard laughter and clapping. Hans was helping me out of my chair. He held my arm on one side and Margaret's on the other, as if we three were actors taking a bow after a performance – which perhaps we were. The audience was applauding and whooping. Hans steered us gently towards the steps down from the stage.

'Go and sit back down, Lucy. I'll come and have a word with your mother shortly,' Hans Augenblick muttered softly to me as

I began to descend. Cassie was waiting at the bottom to help me. I staggered down the steps towards her, clutching the rail.

My mother? I thought. He must think Fiona is my mother. Why would he need to talk to her? I must have done something terribly wrong on the stage. What on earth had I done? What had I said?

Her arm around my waist, Cassie helped me back to our seats, her eyes on my face. I was panting rapidly, yet not enough air seemed to reach my lungs. Megan and Laura were looking at me in a puzzled way. Fiona regarded me searchingly and with concern.

'What's wrong?' I whispered.

'It's OK,' said Cassie. 'Nothing's wrong. You haven't done anything wrong.'

So why did Hans Augenblick call Fiona backstage for a private discussion while we girls waited in the foyer?

* * *

Everyone was quiet going home in the car. Fiona dropped Megan and Laura off at their homes and then drove Cassie and me back to her house. She made us some hot chocolate and gave us a plate of biscuits to take upstairs. She said she would telephone Mummy to come and collect me in half an hour.

In the quiet of her bedroom, Cassie told me what had happened. Downstairs, Fiona must have told Mummy.

152

Chapter Thirty

Alison

The hypnosis incident upset me terribly, totally – more than I can say. It was exactly the sort of scenario I had feared most. Why, why, *why* had I agreed to let Lucy go to that ridiculous show? I felt so furious with myself for allowing it. I didn't blame Fiona – well, not completely. At least she had been there to support Lucy, and I suppose she had been open in sharing her observations with me. She wasn't to know the true significance of what had happened. Or was she?

I started to wonder how much Lucy had shared with Cassie, and with Fiona. There was a time – until recently, in fact – when Lucy had told me everything, but lately I wasn't so sure. She had become more secretive. Was she sharing her life and her thoughts with others, rather than me, her mother? At the very least, Fiona must have been aware of how unsettling the whole episode had been for Lucy.

Of course, I didn't blame Lucy. She was the completely innocent party. I did deeply, deeply regret Lucy's participation, though. If only she had had the sense not to go on stage. If only I had been there, I would have discouraged – no, *prevented* – Lucy from stepping onto the stage, submitting herself to such a farce, like a lamb to the slaughter. But she must have found herself in a very difficult position, poor child. Perhaps she couldn't have been expected to refuse to go on stage herself, in the heat of the moment, even though she had clearly been very frightened. So my thoughts went backwards and forwards, like flotsam washed to and fro in shallow waves on the beach.

After putting together all the accounts from Lucy, Fiona, Cassie and the other two girls, I felt I had a reasonable understanding of what had actually happened – and the picture that emerged was not reassuring. Having singled Lucy out with his sinister number game, that dreadful Augenblick man had promptly put her into some sort of hypnotic state – a *trance* – which she was quite unable to resist, even if she had known how to try. He had then asked her to think herself back into her early childhood self.

'Imagine you are a very little girl, Lucy – just two or three years old perhaps – can you do that, Lucy? Maybe you are playing. Perhaps you have a teddy bear or a nice dolly to play with?'

I could just imagine his vile, soothing tone. Apparently, Lucy had immediately regressed into her two-year-old self. She spoke in a high, uncertain, infantile voice, with a strong regional accent. There she was on the stage, exposed for all to see (and hear!) in the undeveloped, embryonic state in which I had found her all those years before.

'It wasn't exactly a local accent,' Fiona had told me. 'I don't think it was Geordie. Mind you, I'm not very good at distinguishing accents. But no, I think it was more like Midlands or Yorkshire, but I can't be sure. It was really uncanny how she put it on – that little baby voice combined with the odd accent.'

She didn't mention Riddlesfield, of course; how could she? Fiona had carefully taken notes of all she could remember of the exchange between Hans and Lucy that evening, so as to retain as much information as possible. According to Fiona's account, Lucy had screamed at the top of her voice, a series of words or apparent words, in a baby-like tone: *'Dolly? Polly? Wy-yan! Wy-yan!? Tacy! Tacy! Lady!? Hair? Tain! Mam?! Mam!? No Mam. Tacy Tacy.'*

She had ended with a piercing shriek and the single cry of *'MAM!'*

What horrified me even more than the actual utterances, was Fiona's description of Lucy's simultaneous action; she had apparently slipped from her chair onto the floor, where she curled herself into a ball with her legs drawn up. She rocked back and forth in this position, pounding the floor with her fists, as if demented.

After this, it seems Lucy had been sobbing; the sound of her high wailing filling the auditorium. The audience had watched in uncomfortable silence, uncertain whether this was an intended part of the performance. Hans Augenblick – aware of their discomfort – had quickly intervened and brought Lucy back out of her trance. She had clearly been horribly distressed and confused. She had needed Cassie's help to return to her seat.

Fiona had been very concerned that Lucy was deeply upset by what she described as her "dream". Hans Augenblick, also anxious about Lucy's reaction, had approached Fiona, initially assuming she was Lucy's mother. He had spoken to her after the performance, while the four girls waited in the foyer. Fiona had explained that Lucy was not her child and she didn't know all of her background. Perhaps some early memories from Lucy's infancy had become distorted in her mind, she had suggested to Hans, and been transferred to a dream?

He had looked dubious. Certainly those words, so clearly scripted by her baby mind, derived from early childhood, he had told her. He was more inclined to think of it as an account of real events, rather than a dream. Fiona explained that Lucy had lost her father as a small child, but she didn't know the details. Ah, Hans had said, that could well be the root of the problem.

Later, when talking to Fiona about what had happened, I

decided it was best to go along with her description of a "distorted dream".

'The mind plays funny tricks,' I told her, 'especially with vague, long-past memories, and who's to know how confused she was by losing her daddy? Far too young to understand ...'

'Yes, it must have been a dreadfully confusing time for her, especially when she was too young to articulate any of her feelings or experiences. Poor Lucy. Maybe some bereavement counselling would help? Even after all these years?' said Fiona.

'Mmm, I'm not sure about that. It could just be more upsetting,' I said.

I took the same line about memories perhaps distorting into a "dream" in trying to explain the experience to Lucy herself. Thankfully, she did not remember any details of what had occurred that evening, least of all what had been said or had taken place during her "hypnosis". But this in itself made her feel desperately exposed.

'It felt like I'd done something awful, Mummy,' she told me. Colour suffused her face and neck.

'It was like I'd taken all my clothes off or something, and stood up there naked on the stage for all to see. I felt terribly embarrassed – but I didn't know what I had to feel embarrassed about.'

Of course, I assured Lucy that nothing like that had happened, but I did emphasise to Fiona most strongly that she should not speak to Lucy of exactly what *had* occurred. It would be too distressing and undermining for a teenage girl to realise she had made something of an exhibition of herself. Also, I said, would Fiona please ask Cassie to remain silent about the incident? I was not totally confident of Cassie's cooperation, and thought that maybe I should speak to her myself and try to gain her support.

Chapter Thirty-One

Over the years since Lucy had first become my daughter, I had rarely questioned my actions in taking her away from her home and biological family. Having devised the plan and then acted on it, I was confident that I had done the right thing. Looking at Lucy now, how could anyone doubt that she had benefited from having me as her mother?

Surely everyone would agree that those inadequate parents didn't deserve her, neglecting her as they did, leaving her to play alone in the street while they pursued their own pleasures. Any fleeting concerns I might have had centred not on the parents but on Lucy herself – and the possible effect the loss of her original home might have had on her. After all, however unsatisfactory, it was all she had known at that stage.

I have read that young children – for want of anything better – may develop a strong attachment to the most hopeless, even neglectful, of parents. Yet, how much better had Lucy's experience of care been; loved and cherished by me, over all those years. I had carefully stimulated and developed her through a wide range of experiences; through coaching, visits, games, reading and conversation. I had provided her with total security and appropriate examples and guidance. All this guided by my own experiences, my fond memories of dear Mother and her calm, methodical manner of child rearing.

By contrast, the birth parents had amply demonstrated their indifference to the welfare of their children. They had several other children besides Lucy (or Stacy, perhaps I should say) – far more than they deserved. I felt certain that they would hardly miss one child – and must have quickly got over the absence of Lucy. Perhaps her abduction had even been a blessed relief to them – one less mouth to feed, one less body to clothe, one less child to consider – if they actually considered any of them!

My conclusion was that Lucy's development and state of mind could only have been positively affected by her removal from her original family. Indeed, I believed that after the first year or so, any awareness Lucy may have had of her change in circumstances had receded – both consciously and unconsciously. This belief had only very occasionally been challenged.

One of the most recent – and certainly the most disturbing – of those rare and isolated occasions had been the hypnosis debacle. Exactly how that wretched charlatan had achieved Lucy's reaction – for the sake of public entertainment – was unclear to me. What might he have awakened in her impressionable young mind? If he could coax such a response from Lucy apparently so easily, how often might the past emerge again, and in what form? Could it be that my action, in removing her from her original home, had actually contributed to Lucy's distress and disturbance? Suddenly it felt like a situation that was totally – *frighteningly* – outside my control.

It had never been in my nature to discuss personal difficulties with others. Normally I felt perfectly capable of dealing with such matters alone, and in my own way. The thought of "opening" myself up to others, discussing my most intimate concerns, made me feel sick with horror. Yet I had to admit that lately I had found myself lying awake at night, brooding. I longed to sink into the relief of sleep, but rarely achieved it until two or three in the morning – and then only to wake again in the early hours, with cold, clammy fingers of anxiety clutching at my heart.

I even resorted to over-the-counter sleep remedies, but these – far from inducing restful sleep – only made me feel as though I had been rendered unconscious by a blow on the head from a large mallet. These pills did ensure I slept a little sooner, it is true, but I woke – still early – my head confused, my body leaden, my mouth a desert.

Susan, always a determined and loyal friend, had not failed to notice some changes in my appearance and demeanour over recent months.

'I'm worried about you, Alison,' she said. 'What's wrong? Just look at you! Great shadows under your eyes. You must have lost at least half a stone – and you didn't have it to lose in the first place.'

'Oh … there's no need to worry – I'm quite all right.'

'No, you are not all right, and you know it. Let's meet for lunch in the Bonjour Bistro tomorrow and have a proper talk. No excuses this time. I know you don't generally do "ladies' lunches" – but I won't take no for an answer!'

For once, I was grateful for Susan's persistence. For all her apparent superficiality, she had remained an affectionate and true friend – undeterred by what she regarded as my reserve and eccentricities.

Bonjour Bistro was one of Susan's favourite locations. Unlike me she was untroubled by its ridiculous name. She told me she liked the informality and friendliness of the staff; I found them a little over-familiar. Susan felt its "limited but imaginative menu" recommended Bonjour. I thought it pretentious and over-priced. However, I had developed a taste for wine lately – it seemed to help me relax – and Bonjour did have a good selection of wine available by the glass. It also had comfortable seats, and tables well spaced enough to allow private conversation, without every other diner nearby listening in. So, on the whole, I was content to be there.

We sat in a corner close to the window overlooking the park. Outside, a blustery wind was lifting last year's chestnut leaves and wafting them in little circular eddies. The sun filtered through the trees and lit up patches of the grass. Parents watched their young children playing in the little playground beyond the lawn and trees. I remembered bringing Lucy there years ago, when she was small. How simple life seemed at that stage.

'How's the job going?' Susan asked. I redirected my attention from the window to my friend's question. I had recently started a part-time administrative job in the office of Lucy's old first school.

'It's good – exactly what I wanted. I'm always at home in time for Lucy, and of course the school holidays are free. I know she's a teenager now, and thinks of herself as independent, but I still feel it's important to be there for her.'

'Yes, but I think you have to take care of yourself too, Alison. You must be busy what with work and maintaining Lucy and a home all by yourself.'

'Mmm. It's not very demanding really.'

'How's Lucy?'

It took me a while to consider this question. I realised I was on the brink of making some revelations about Lucy's background – and my own – which could alter the course of both of our lives irreversibly. I was frightened, yet I'd known for some time I couldn't keep all the secrets totally hidden for ever. It was affecting Lucy's mental well-being, as well as mine. Susan was a good and reliable friend, who clearly cared for us, and yet …there were so many dangers in revealing the whole truth …

'Basically, she's fine …'

'But …?'

I took a deep breath. There was no point in putting off what I wanted to say.

160

'Susan, if you found out I'd done something awful – well, maybe even illegal – in the past, would it make a difference to how you felt about me … could you still be my friend?'

Susan laughed. 'Oh Alison, I can't imagine you've done anything so terrible! I'm quite sure most of my friends have done something illegal in the past. Haven't we all? I know I have. What's the matter – have you been shoplifting or something?'

'No!' I said, shocked. 'No, of course not …'

'Joke, Alison.'

'Oh … yes, OK. But, if I had … broken the law … speaking as a lawyer, would you represent me, if necessary?'

She looked quizzically at me.

'Well, I'm a solicitor, not a barrister, so it would kind of depend on what it is you think you've done … but you must know, Alison, I'd always do whatever I could to help you.'

I was already beginning to regret having started this conversation. I concentrated on straightening the cutlery.

'Yes, thank you, I know you would. It's nothing, really. I've just been a bit upset by that hypnosis business recently.'

'Oh yes, you did mention that to me. I must say, I don't think it was a very good idea for such young girls to be taken to that sort of event. I was a bit surprised at Fiona.'

'It wasn't really her fault. If anyone was at fault it was me. I should never have let Lucy go – at least, not unless I'd been there too. That Hans Augenblick certainly shouldn't have used such a young and vulnerable child as a "volunteer". I'm really worried it's upset her terribly. She seems to have lost confidence. And she doesn't want to talk about it – not to me, anyway.'

'Well, it all sounded very unfortunate, but she'll get over it. Anyway, it was hardly *you* doing anything wrong, and certainly not illegal. You're not planning to murder Hans Augenblick, are you?'

I knew she meant this as a joke, but couldn't bring myself to smile. I ran my finger around my glass of Sauvignon silently, measuring its cool circumference. Susan watched me quizzically.

'Were you, Alison?'

After a long pause, I resolved to tell a partial truth. 'No, of course not. But I have done something wrong, which I think may be relevant.'

She studied my face expectantly.

'You see, I haven't told Lucy the full truth about her background, or you, for that matter, and I think I made a terrible mistake.'

Susan put her hand on mine. I felt the presence of her hand resting its weight on my own, heavy as a toad. Leave it there for a minute before pulling away, I instructed myself queasily.

'I've always let Lucy think that I'm her mother – her "real" mother that is – but I'm not, you see.'

Susan looked at me in puzzlement, astonishment.

'You're not Lucy's mother?'

'No. You see, Lucy was *adopted*, like me. I suppose that, somehow, that hypnosis episode must have accessed some subconscious memories of her birth mother, even though she was tiny when she came to me ... to us, I mean.'

I carefully slid my hand out from under Susan's, noticing my heart rate start to slow almost immediately.

'I should have told her the truth right from the start ... but at first she was far too young to understand, and then she was so unsettled at the time we moved up here – do you remember what she was like? When at last she started to settle down, I couldn't bear to risk opening new wounds again. It was wrong of me, I know. Maybe it was cowardly. But "the moment had passed", Mother would have said. By the time I thought Lucy might have been ready to hear the truth, it felt too late. It's not as though it made any difference to me – I couldn't have loved her any more than I did – and still do, love her. Giving birth – or not giving birth – seemed an irrelevance, a meaningless detail. It's just that ... I'm afraid she'll lose trust in me, if she feels I've withheld information about something that may seem important to her. Especially if any other memories were to surface …'

It was some moments before Susan spoke. Her expression was, at first, one of horror and disbelief. She stared at me, her mouth unattractively open. Gradually the lines of her face softened and she appeared to be trying to process what I had told her.

'Yes, I see … Oh Alison – how awful to have kept such a huge secret hidden all these years. How could you bear it? I'm so glad you trust me enough to have told me now – I feel honoured. But, oh my goodness, what to do now? My instinct is that it's always best to tell the truth and be completely open. Of course, now it's harder, more complicated. But Lucy's a bright and insightful girl. She may be surprised, maybe even hurt that you didn't say anything sooner, but I'm sure she'll understand. She may react angrily – you know how adolescents are – but I'm sure she won't hold it against you, not for long at least, if you explain it to her as you have to me. Of course, she may want to contact her birth mother one day, assuming she's still alive. Have you thought about that?'

Thoughts spun wildly in my head. No, I hadn't thought about that! I hadn't thought properly about any of this before. How lies reproduced, one spawning another, and another, in increasingly complex circles.

'That's just the problem. When Lucy's daddy was alive …'

'Russell …?'

'Yes, Russell. When Russell was alive, he was adamant that Lucy shouldn't know, that she should become our real daughter. He didn't want her ever to know, in case she should doubt we loved her as much as we would our own daughter …'

'Well, yes, he might have thought that at the time … but now …?'

'Yes, but you see, he felt it so strongly that he destroyed all records relating to her original name and her adoption – burned everything, every scrap of paper.'

Susan stared at me open-mouthed.

'What about the adoption agency? Surely they could give you some information. They must have to keep their records for years.'

'Her entire file – everything relating to the adoption; Russell burned it – he burned it all. The agency disbanded years ago. And the ghastly times that followed have erased everything from my mind.'

'Everything? But you must remember some details?'

'Not a thing. Russell's death, my bereavement, was so dreadful, so huge; it wiped everything from my mind. Plus losing my mother … I can't remember anything. For me, Lucy's life and identity – and mine too – began when I became her mother, and more particularly, when we arrived in Newcastle. It's as if nothing before that time existed – a blank page.'

'Oh Alison, you poor, poor thing. You must have been so traumatised.'

Chapter Thirty-Two

1997

Lucy

Following the hypnosis evening, Cassie was keen to return to the discussions we'd had a few years earlier, when I had discovered the red coat and the newspaper cutting. She seemed to feel there was some connection between those discoveries and what had happened when I was hypnotised by Hans Augenblick. Once she got the idea into her head, Cassie wouldn't – *couldn't* – leave the matter alone, though I begged and begged her to. She wanted me to *confront* Mummy again, to ask her questions, to probe further. She questioned me mercilessly at times, particularly about what I'd apparently said during the hypnosis session.

'What does "Wyan" mean, Lucy? What about "Tacy"?'

'I don't know, I don't know …'

Once Cassie got her teeth into something, she wouldn't let go; she worried at it and shook it like a terrier with a bone.

Cassie was convinced I had to "face up to'" what she believed were secrets Mummy was keeping from me. Of course I sensed there were secrets too, but Cassie didn't seem to realise how terrified I was. Opening up secrets could have unpredictable consequences: outcomes I couldn't begin to contemplate. Maybe Cassie hadn't thought about what those consequences might be – and I certainly didn't want to. Just starting to think about it made me feel quite ill. Worst of all, it caused Cassie and me to have our first argument.

'You don't know anything about my mother, Cassie – or me – you know nothing about us!' I shouted, on the verge of tears.

'Maybe not, but it seems that you don't either, Lucy.'

'Oh, you're so good at twisting my words …'

I stormed out of the room and stomped down the stairs. Cassie called to me from the top of the stairs.

'Lucy, please don't go! Please stay! I'm sorry – I won't say any more about it if you don't want me to. Let's listen to some music instead!'

I faltered at the bottom of the stairs, and heard Fiona call to me from the kitchen, her voice questioning and anxious.

'Lucy, sweetheart! What's going on? Are you all right …?'

I so much wanted to return to Cassie, to make it up, to be close as we always had been. I wanted life to be simple and fun again. But it wasn't simple. It certainly wasn't fun. I wanted to run to Fiona too; have her put her arms around me, cuddle me as she often did, and assure me that she'd make everything all right. But I couldn't go to Fiona, or to Cassie either. I was past staying there, in their house with them.

I opened the front door and slammed it behind me. I could hardly breathe. I staggered home, my face wet, my chest heaving, straining for air. Cassie and I had never argued in the past. Why did Mummy have to come into everything I did, everything I thought. Why couldn't she just be ordinary – an ordinary mother. There always seemed to be something mysterious about her, something unreal. I didn't understand what was happening to

Cassie and me, but even that felt like Mummy had something to do with it.

My life felt like a runaway train. Out of control. Speeding ahead, faster and faster. Changing lines and direction without warning. And I felt like an impotent, petrified passenger at its mercy – I wasn't even the driver – waiting for the inevitable derailment, waiting for the crash that would surely come. The brake was out of reach. There was no stopping it.

* * *

When I got home, Mummy was sitting reading in her favourite place: just inside the sitting room by the open garden door. The last of the evening sun illuminated her and the faded ochre velvet of her chair with a soft golden light – so out of keeping with my mood. She looked up when she heard me come in, and smiled. The innocent, genuine pleasure of that smile sent daggers of rage through my heart.

'Hello, Lucy. Have you had a nice time, dear? Here I am again, enjoying the last bit of warmth and sunshine. I'm so lucky to have this little shelter from that chilly wind. It's just lovely here – what bliss. I'm so glad we chose a west-facing garden, aren't you?'

'We didn't choose it, you did. I didn't choose anything in my life – you chose it all, didn't you?'

I don't know where the words came from. Like a doll or a puppet with an automatic, preordained script, I couldn't help myself. It was happening more and more these days. I could see Mummy was shocked and hurt, but I couldn't stop the wounding words. There was some sort of satisfaction in seeing her pain. I hated myself for feeling pleasure, yet it was as if I was compelled to continue.

'By the way, now that I'm fifteen, I think it's ridiculous to go on calling you "Mummy". It's so babyish, don't you think?' I glared mercilessly at her.

Mummy stared back at me. Her eyes glistened. She turned her head away from me for a minute. I could see the muscles and sinews of her frail neck working. Her chest heaved. She swallowed several times. Then, slowly, she turned back to me, her face white and chalky.

'No, I can't say I think it is babyish or ridiculous. Surely it's natural for a child to continue calling its mother "Mummy", however old that child is?'

I stared at her fiercely. She looked up into my face. Her voice was quiet and controlled. Yet there was a quaver lurking. We stared silently at one another. A muscle in her chin twitched. The corners of her mouth trembled downwards. I thought momentarily of how a small child might draw a "happy face" by making a curved line for the mouth point upwards. Right now, Mummy's mouth was not pointing upwards, it was pointing downwards – definitely a sad face.

I was aware of us having reached a critical point, a choice, a line beyond which there would be no return. Was I really going to cross that line? Of course not, I realised, as the seconds ticked by. I'm not ready. I'm not old enough to handle possible revelations that might change my life, both of our lives, for ever.

It was as if we had both screeched to a halt on the edge of a cliff, like Road Runner in the cartoon, applying brakes to our feet just in time. Smoke from the friction of our heels rose. We stared down at the abyss far below.

* * *

Of course, I cried upstairs in my room. I'd never felt so bleak. Mummy left me alone for a long time. As it grew dark she came upstairs. I heard her hesitate at the top of the stairs. She knocked on my door – something I don't remember her ever doing before.

'Yes …?' I called uncertainly. I was sitting on my bed.

She opened the door and came in. 'I've made us some leek and potato soup, Lucy.' It was a favourite of mine.

'I thought we could have supper by the fire and watch *The X Files* on the television. It's on at half past. Would you like that?'

I'd never heard her suggest watching television before. She didn't really approve, unless it was an educational documentary. A hard lump was pressing unpleasantly in my chest. I looked down at my lap and nodded. She came and sat next to me on the bed and put her arm around me.

'You do know I love you, Lucy, don't you?'

I nodded again, a lump growing in my throat.

'I need to tell you something, Lucy. I should have told you years ago, but I was too cowardly to do so. I hope you'll understand. I hope you'll forgive me for not telling you before. I think I was afraid you might love me less.'

She sighed and gently turned my face towards her. And then she told me. She and my dad had adopted me, she said. I wasn't really their child. They couldn't have children of their own. She told me how she'd chosen me from rows of babies in cots. She'd fallen in love with me the moment she set eyes on me. She knew immediately I was special.

It was a shock. Yet maybe it was also a solution. A new history. *I'd been adopted.* It explained a lot, yet it didn't really change much. *Adopted* – I could get used to that idea. Surely it made sense.

In time – after only a day or two, in fact – I talked to Cassie. I told her what Mummy had told me. We restored our close friendship. It was a relief for us both. By some silent agreement, we didn't refer again to my parentage, whatever it was.

Chapter Thirty-Three

2000

Lucy

Over the coming years, Cassie and I both concentrated on trying to demonstrate how detached we were from our parents – whoever they might be – and from their entire generation. We were assured of our uniqueness, of the originality of our thoughts, and how extraordinarily misunderstood we were. We became scornful, rebellious, moody and troublesome. We discovered causes, social and political issues and ideology, music and literature. We discovered boys and hesitantly began to explore sex. We tiptoed our way in and out of punk and goth culture. Cassie handled the adolescent years with relative ease – Fiona was relaxed about all her experimentation.

'It's what being a teenager is all about. Just make sure you respect your own autonomy and your own body, and you won't go far wrong.'

Cassie emerged at the other end of her teens with a clutch of good A levels, hoping to study Medicine at university.

My own experience of adolescence was much more difficult, as it must have been for my mother. She tried not to show it, but I knew she detested everything about my teenage years: the clothes, the hair, the drinking, the boys. Above all, she hated the inevitable distance that grew between us – seeing me unhappy, confused, vulnerable, self-harming at times – and having no idea how to respond.

During the late summer after we'd done our A levels, when Cassie was eighteen and I was soon to be, there were picnics and barbecues and parties galore. We were invited to a party at the home of twins called Aidan and Callum. Their parents were on holiday in Majorca, and had "trusted" them with the house. They were nineteen and were both considered among the most attractive and desirable boys in our circle of friends.

At the party alcohol flowed freely. Callum made a move towards me. We danced. We kissed. We drank. There were beer, wine and spirits of all sorts. I lost count of what I'd had to drink and how much. Cassie was dancing with one of Callum and Aidan's friends. She was watching me. I knew she was looking out for me.

'Take it easy, Lucy.'

'Take it easy? Plenty of time to take it easy when we're old!'

Callum laughed and kissed my neck as we danced. At some point in the evening he produced a couple of little pinkish pills – one for himself and one for me. We swallowed them and laughed. I felt great. The world was wonderful. Callum was wonderful. I wanted him. We went upstairs to his room and he locked the door. He kissed me some more. Then he took off his shirt.

'Your turn now,' he said, smiling at me and breathing heavily. The room seemed very small and dark all of a sudden. Music from downstairs was thumping through the floor and walls. The music was beautiful and very loud. It was so good to be there, with him. I was carried away by the feelings, the thrill of it all, by Callum. He was handsome; he was gorgeous. I wanted him so much. Yet my heart was pounding. He started to unbutton my dress. I gulped for air. I felt hot and cold at the same time. My heartbeat was a super-fast drill. My dress slid to the floor.

'Now me,' he said, unzipping his jeans, and pulling me close to him. I could feel his urgency, but the room was spinning. No oxygen seemed to reach my lungs, though I was panting and heaving for air. I was out of control. The room veered upside down. Suddenly I was on the floor, Callum standing over me half-naked.

'What the fuck is wrong with you?'

'I … I don't know … I feel weird – strange. Maybe it was the pill … I think I'm going to be sick …'

'Not on my fucking floor, for God's sake – get up.'

Callum got hold of my arms and tried to yank me upright. My legs wouldn't hold me. My whole body was shaking.

'Jesus! You better get out of here.'

He grabbed my heap of clothes and threw them at me. Trembling, I tried to put them on, but my fingers were too shaky and didn't work. I still couldn't breathe. I was afraid I would pass out. Callum pulled on his jeans and shirt and unlocked the door. He headed downstairs, his feet pounding on the stairs. A moment later, Cassie appeared. She took one look at me, and turned to shout furiously down the stairs.

'Arsehole!'

She put her arms round me.

'Lucy, Lucy, it's me. Don't worry, you're going to be all right …'

My whole body was shaking. I was wet with a cold sweat. She cupped her hands around my mouth and nose.

'Breathe, Lucy,' she said. 'Try to breathe steadily.'

After a few minutes the world stopped spinning quite so wildly. A strange moaning sound emerged from somewhere inside me.

'Come on, Lucy, it's OK,' she said softly. 'We're going home.'

Cassie took over. She wiped my face with some tissues, and helped me put on my clothes and fasten the buttons. I felt help-

172

less as a child, frightened and ashamed. Cassie made me drink a cup of water – that seemed to soothe my aching head. We pushed through the indifferent crowd and out of the front door. Cassie helped me stagger back to her house.

The hall light was on, but Fiona and Simon were already in bed. They must have heard us. We heard the murmur of their voices. Fiona emerged from their bedroom in her dressing gown. She took one look at me and wrapped me in a big hug. I held on to her tightly and pressed my face into the soft comfort of her chest. I sobbed like a baby. I felt I wanted to stay there for ever.

'Oh, you poor darling …'

Fiona and Cassie helped me upstairs and let me slump down on Cassie's bed. Fiona made us both some hot chocolate. I didn't want it, but she made me drink it. Then she tucked me into the bed. She bathed my face with a cool flannel and stroked my hair. Cassie pulled a mattress out from under the bed for herself.

I remember nothing more until Cassie brought me a cup of tea in the morning. Fiona had rung Mum the previous night to let her know I was there. She rang again in the morning to reassure her I was safe. I heard bits of what she said on the phone.

'Yes, it was a party, Alison. I think things got a bit out of hand. No, really, no need to panic – she's all right. They came home together late, a bit the worse for wear, I'm afraid. What? Well, I think you should ask Lucy about that – it's not really for me to say. Yes, we'll try to get her to eat some breakfast and bring her home after that.'

* * *

Simon pulled up outside our house. I could see Mummy waiting at the window. I dreaded having to talk to her. Simon patted my knee and gave me an encouraging nod. Reluctantly, I stepped out of the car and approached the house. She was hovering by the door as soon as I opened it.

'Why, Lucy? Why did you do such things? Was it to get at me in some way?'

'No, of course not. Why do you think everything is about *you*? Why do you think I have to do everything like you? Sometimes maybe I just want to do what I want!'

'I thought I'd brought you up to know what's right and wrong, how to behave … sensibly and decently. Not to take *drugs*! Surely you have more self-respect than that? I know men can be very persuasive – but you have to resist. You have to be very firm.'

'Oh, you'd know all about men, I suppose.'

'Lucy, there's no need to become offensive. It's unpleasant and wrong.'

'Oh yes, and you're very decent, and so honest. You wouldn't do anything wrong, would you? Well maybe just bringing up a child doesn't ensure she'll be exactly like you! Maybe I'm more like someone else than you … have you considered that?'

Her face was white and rigid. 'What do you mean?'

'I … I don't mean anything!' I sobbed.

I ran up to my room.

Chapter Thirty-Four

2000

Alison

Where have I gone wrong? Where is that sweet innocent child who flourished in my care during those early years in Newcastle? I'm so very frightened. I don't know what I can do to restore the former equilibrium. Everything seems out of my control. I live in a constant state of anxiety. How could Lucy have willingly – *willingly* – placed herself in just such a vulnerable, such a *dangerous* position as I desperately sought to escape all those years ago in Durham? I can scarcely believe such a thing. Sometimes I hardly recognise her.

How I hate the distance that seems to have grown between us. Other people may assert Lucy is simply demonstrating normal teenage behaviour. I'm not so sure. I feel Lucy is rebelling against *me*, against all of my values, against all I have tried to teach her. Coming from the family she did, with its total *lack* of values and principles, I always harboured a lurking fear – especially during the early years – that she might revert to type, and somehow become more like her genetic parents. I would try to reject these thoughts; they filled me with such horror. Indeed, over the years her personality developed in such a positive and delightful way, that my apprehensions faded. Until the last few years.

There can be little doubt that her friendship with Cassie has played a significant part in determining the direction of Lucy's recent development. Worst of all, Cassie appears to encourage Lucy to question all aspects of her past as well as her relationship with me, and this fills me with absolute terror. Thankfully, at this point, I do not believe Lucy seriously suspects her actual history, but how much more of Cassie's hints, suggestions and probing will she withstand?

I find myself struggling with these issues at all times of the day and night. I have frequently woken in the early hours, after a brief and shallow sleep, in a state of absolute panic about what the future may hold. How I wish those precious feelings of calm and "peace of mind" could be restored to me. Yet such a luxury appears totally beyond my grasp now.

With Lucy growing older, I had begun to have concerns about her documentation. Allowing Lucy to believe she was adopted by me helped to solve some of these anxieties. I have her birth certificate, which I was so proud to have arranged at the time of her becoming my daughter, but I had begun to worry about its possible imperfections. So far, it has never been put to the test. No one had required it when she started school, and as we have never holidayed abroad, we haven't had to apply for a passport.

But as she grows older, she may need to present her birth certificate to acquire a driving licence, say, or a passport? She may want to visit other countries at some point. I examined the certificate to check the details. Her name, of course, appears as Lucy Brown, the father's name as Russell Brown and mother's name as Audrey – rather than Alison – Brown. Her date of birth is listed as 20/9/1982, and we have always celebrated my Lucy's birthday on that day.

I had lain awake at night thinking of the problems any inconsistencies might cause – as well as the possibility of officialdom, if contacted, being able to link the original details with Lucy Brown's death. Now of course, Lucy being *adopted* provided a logical explanation for some of the apparent inconsistencies. If only I had thought of claiming adoption sooner, I could have saved myself many sleepless nights.

Chapter Thirty-Five

2001

Chief Superintendent Lawrence Dempster

I guess it's natural to reflect on your working life as you approach retirement. Most people do it – wonder how effective they've been, whether they've left their mark, whether all that effort has been worthwhile. We all like to feel we've made a difference, however small. I'd had no ambitions to reach Chief Constable – I'd been more than happy with Detective Inspector, but others further up had urged me to look further afield and apply for promotions. Now here I am at fifty-seven, back in Riddlesfield for my last years of duty, as a Chief Superintendent.

Like almost everyone I knew, I'd grown up in a small Durham mining community, following a long line of mine workers. By local standards, I was regarded as having done exceptionally well.

Barbara and I built our lives in Riddlesfield, with a few brief moves to other cities to take up promotion positions. But Riddlesfield was where we put down roots and brought up our three children. They all went to university and into good jobs. I was immensely proud of each and every one of them.

I was well out of the home village, but that didn't stop me feeling a huge sense of loss and heartbreak for those lost communities – yes, and a sackful of guilt on my back too. Dad had died of mesothelioma, like so many pitmen, just two years after he started drawing his pension. We'd go back to visit Mam regularly until she died, and each time the village looked a little more shabby, a little more down at heel.

So Riddlesfield had become my world – and there was no shortage of villains to chase. I rose quickly through the ranks and thoroughly enjoyed my work. Even if I say so myself, my record for solving complex crimes was exceptional. It wasn't just my doing – I led a good team. Always had a knack for identifying the most promising young officers and ensuring they were considered for promotion. I was never one for pulling up the ladder behind me. I demanded a lot of the team, mind, but they knew they'd get my full support, as long as they pulled their weight. I taught them to be thorough, meticulous – no short cuts – and to use their intelligence.

But for all my solid reputation, my success, I knew I'd be remembered for my one greatest failure. Human nature. No, it wasn't just public interest that drew me back to the Stacy Watts case time and time again. Stacy's abduction was the one unsolved crime that preoccupied me for more than fifteen years. I was certain it had been an abduction, and not just that the kid had wandered off and maybe fallen into a drain and drowned or something – which was one of the many theories. It was a persistent mystery, and one that regularly woke me in the middle of the night, frantically seeking the clue that I knew I must have missed for all those years.

Nothing had been heard about Stacy, no new developments, in over fifteen years. Yet, even before the letter – long before – I was convinced Stacy was still alive. There's no doubt that in most child abduction cases, if there's no sign of the child after a week or two, chances of finding her alive are very slim, almost zero. But there was something about this abduction that didn't feel like murder, didn't feel like a paedo, didn't even feel like the perpetrator was a man, in fact.

Not many people owned cars back then in the Rigby Street area – and a strange car would have been very conspicuous; it would have been noticed. But no one referred to a car – none had been seen. So I reckoned the abductor must have carried the child, walked with her, or, most likely, used a pushchair – must have had a pushchair ready.

Now, back then in the Eighties, how often did we see men on their own pushing a small child? None of your "new men" then – specially not in the Frainham neighbourhood. Men were macho, or liked to think they were. Someone would have noticed a man pushing a kid in a buggy. So, I told myself, the abductor was much more likely to have been a woman.

A dark-haired woman in a dark blue coat was seen in the area by several witnesses. A dowdy woman, neat, but not very smart, neither ugly nor very good-looking, not very old nor very young. A thoroughly unremarkable woman – unmemorable. But she was there, and some witnesses said they'd seen her with a pushchair. A few witnesses mentioned seeing another woman with a child in a buggy: a blonde woman in a red coat. But this woman definitely had a small boy with her, not a little girl.

Of course, we had considered whether these two women had been one and the same person, but could find no evidence of that, nothing to connect them. Still, whoever took Stacy, I was sure it was a woman, and a clever one at that.

Why do women steal babies or young children, assuming they're not completely psychotic? Maybe they've lost a child of their own: a miscarriage or tragic death. Maybe they're being pressured to produce a child by parents, or by a husband or partner. Perhaps the "biological clock" is ticking and no baby is appearing. Or maybe they know they're infertile and can't ever have a child.

Whatever the cause, they would be likely to have an overwhelming urge to have a baby of their own. If that was the case, it could have been good news and bad news for Stacy at the same time. Good news in that the woman would nurture and care for the child well. Unlike a male abductor, a woman would be unlikely to kill her. Bad news in that it might be many years before the woman and/or the child would resurface – if ever.

Gary and Shelley Watts had got some bad press, there's no doubt about it. The newspapers had it in for them, all right. They were seen as the "undeserving poor". If it had been a middle-class family – or even a good, solid "hard-working" working-class family, who'd lost a child in that way, they would have had a lot more sympathy. As it was, the tabloids had a field day, especially with Gary. Well, he was a waster, true enough, so who can blame them? The police and courts had known him intimately from the age of twelve. Never done an honest day's work in his life. Supplemented his benefits with petty thieving – and a bit of dealing on the side. He did nothing for his kids – or for Shelley for that matter.

Shelley was different, however negatively the newspapers tried to present her. One of the papers referred to her being "in thrall" to Gary. That was close to the truth. He certainly had complete control over her earlier on in their relationship.

Over the years I found I had a lot of time for Shelley, whatever her shortcomings. She kept in touch with me, regularly. I think I was the nearest thing to a father figure for her. That's what Barbara always said anyway. Somehow Shelley had got hold of our home phone number and called us up. I got a shock the first time, and was none too pleased. But as I got to know her, I began to feel some sympathy – and even respect for her.

Life hadn't dealt Shelley a good hand. She was just sixteen when Gary first got her pregnant. He was twenty-eight, and had

181

already fathered several children with other women. She'd had a rotten childhood – never knew what it was to be cared for, let alone loved. In fact, she'd been in and out of so-called "care" from the age of three, until Gary took over. She'd bunked off school regularly, although teachers reported she had some "potential". Shelley wasn't stupid – just never had a chance. She was looking for affection and security – desperate for it – and thought she'd get it from Gary, poor misguided kid.

He introduced her to some lovely habits. She knew nothing about looking after children, and – on Gary's instructions – barred the door to social workers when they tried to help her. Didn't trust them.

Neither Gary nor Shelley had ever cooked a proper meal in their lives. Those kids lived on chips from the chip shop, and whatever they could scavenge from school, or nick from shops. They were wild as savages and tormented the neighbours. It took losing Stacy and having the rest of her children taken into care to make Shelley see where her life was heading.

Gary was soon in jail again following his latest misdemeanour. That was it for Gary as far as Shelley was concerned – and a good thing too. After Stacy disappeared, Shelley was even less popular with the neighbours. She persuaded the council to re-house her in a different area, and got herself a job as a cleaner. After that she wouldn't let Gary near herself or the kids for long, except to give him the odd hot meal, and drop a few quid in his pocket.

Credit where it's due, she worked really hard to get herself on the straight and narrow. Eventually she even became a supervisor at her cleaning firm. Over time, she managed to get all those kids back from care. She was no angel, and sure as hell she was no super-mam, but she did her best to look after them, and straighten them out. But Stacy was still missing.

Shelley would ring us a couple of times a year, sometimes more. Her opening line was always: 'Any news, Inspector?'

Her plaintive voice nearly broke my heart. I couldn't let her know that though.

'News, Shelley?' I'd say, 'Yeah, the news is I'm getting older, like the rest of us. Fifty more grey hairs at last count.'

Barbara would frown at me and mouth: "Don't tease her!"

'Oh, come on, Inspector Dempster, you know what I mean. What about Stacy?'

'Sorry, Shelley, nothing new, I'm afraid. But the file's still open. Won't be closed 'til we find her, however long it takes.'

Sometimes Barbara would talk to her. She was good at that sort of thing. Motherly, like.

'How are you, Shelley? You still working up at Moorside? Yeah? Good for you, pet. Isn't Ryan doing well – fancy him having his own business! We heard he put in a bathroom for some neighbours of ours. And what about Ashley's twins? They must be getting on for ten now, aren't they? What …? Secondary school? Never! Where does the time go, eh? You what …? Uh-huh … I know, pet. You must miss her all the time, poor love. They never stop being our babies, do they …?'

Getting back to the letter. It came as a huge shock, of course, and yet, somehow, it wasn't really such a great surprise, if that makes sense. I call it a letter; it was hardly that. Barely even a note, written on a computer. It was printed on A4 paper, but the writing only took up a few lines; the rest of the page was blank. It arrived on 25th October, in a cheap, white envelope. An adhesive label with the address typed on it had been stuck on the front:

For the attention of:
Detective Inspector L. Dempster, Riddlesfield Central
Police Department,
Riddlesfield.

Inside, the following message was typed:

Dear Detective Inspector Dempster,

I believe that it is possible that I may be Stacy Watts,
who was taken from outside her home in Frainham,
Riddlesfield, in March 1985. I am now 19 years old
(at least I think I am), and of course, I have a different
name.

I have no proof and may be quite wrong. But I
have reasons to think my mother may have kidnapped
me as a toddler, although I don't remember anything
about it consciously. I can't reveal who she is because
I don't want to cause trouble and distress for her,
especially if my suspicions are without cause, as I
believe they may well be. She has looked after me
well in every way and I know she loves me, but questions about my origins arose in my mind a few years
ago, and have grown gradually.

Why have I written to you now? Because this suspicion – whether it is justified or not – has been a great
burden for me for some time, and I needed to share
the information with someone with an understanding
of the circumstances. I can't disclose more now –
perhaps one day I will.

Chapter Thirty-Six

Chief Superintendent Lawrence Dempster

That was it. No name, address or signature. The note had been typed on a computer, then printed, and posted in Worcester. I had no doubt that Stacy would have ensured it was posted some distance from her home. Could she be a student somewhere near? Could being away from "home" have made her feel lonely and isolated? Was she working in or near Worcester?

Somehow, I didn't think she'd allow that connection. More likely, the visit to Worcester (from where?) was a one-off. The envelope was the "ready-stick" variety – a strip to remove from the pasted section – no licking ensured no DNA. Same with the stamp – a self-adhesive sort. She was as careful and cautious as her "mother". It was sent to the lab, of course, but that just confirmed what I guessed: that it yielded no evidence or distinguishing features.

More interesting was the discussion with Eleanor Best, our exceptionally able forensic psychologist.

'I'd say the writer's honest about her age. She's young, certainly not more than the nineteen years she admits to.'

'Yes, well that would make her Stacy's age, of course.'

Eleanor looked up from the note and peered at me severely over the top of her glasses. She didn't welcome interruptions. She returned to her analysis.

'There's not a lot to go on, is there? Clearly she's not prepared to commit herself one way or the other. I'd say she's highly confused and perhaps anxious or depressed; she talks about the great burden of her suspicions. See here, she says she doesn't remember anything "consciously" – as though maybe she's had some unconscious intrusion of memory – a dream perhaps, or just a flash of recall, and been disturbed by it. Everywhere, when she raises a potential suspicion, she follows it with a "let-out clause", like "if my suspicions are without cause, as I believe they may well be".

'She's clearly attached to her supposed mother. Notice she refers to her as "my mother" although she clearly believes she is not, or may not be. Protective of her – but angry at the same time; furious, I'd say. I get a strong sense of controlled anger here. Notice too she says she has "reasons" – not "a reason" – for suspecting her mother kidnapped her. See here how she dates the note "September 2001" – but it didn't arrive until the end of October. I reckon she wrote it, and then had second thoughts about sending it. She must have hung on to it for several weeks in a state of indecision. Eventually, I guess the urge to share her secret became too great. Maybe new evidence has just arisen for her; maybe she's been totting up the reasons over time, until she's reached breaking point.'

Eleanor looked intently at the note. She tapped her pen on the desk thoughtfully.

'Also, possible identity problems. I wouldn't be surprised if she was brought up in a single-parent household – female, that is. I suspect she regards her mother as vulnerable. Could be she has some sort of mental health problems – the mother, that is. Well, if she did abduct the child, it goes without saying. She talks

186

about perhaps disclosing more "one day" – that sounds as though maybe she's thinking of waiting for her supposed mother to die before revealing the truth.'

I groaned. Eleanor frowned at me, and returned to her scrutiny of the note again.

'Missing a father figure, I'd say. That's probably why she chose you to write to.'

'That's me, reliable old dad figure.'

Eleanor didn't do humour. She regarded me with her formidable intelligence. I took a deep breath and tried again.

'Anything to be gained by me trying a response, maybe through a newspaper or on TV?'

'I'd say that could be counter-productive. For one thing, if the abductor found out, it could cause serious problems between the two of them. Even assuming that didn't happen, it could alienate the girl completely – she'll feel it's a betrayal of the very minimal trust she has shown in you. I think you have to wait for her to contact you again.'

'Do you think she will?'

'I do, but it could be some time. Something's triggered this contact, maybe some sort of personal crisis. She's very fragile. Could be you'll have to wait until something else happens, or perhaps until her current situation deteriorates.'

'How long might that be?'

'How long is a piece of string? As we don't know what her current situation is, I can't possibly say. Could be six weeks, six years or sixteen years. All I can say is, I think she wants to be "found". Have you thought about whether you're going to inform the birth mother about the note?'

I'd already been struggling with this question. There was some obligation on the police to keep parents informed of any new development – but how cruel it would be to raise Shelley's hopes, only to find out the letter was a hoax? And even if it really did come from Stacy, as Eleanor pointed out, she might not get back in contact again for years. Knowing Shelley, if she heard about the note, she'd be bound to attempt to send some sort of message back to Stacy, to try to get her to make contact – through television, internet or newspapers – and that could scare the girl off for good.

No, I thought, we're going to have to keep quiet about this, leave the press well out of it – and hope that Stacy's patience runs out before mine does.

So I put a couple of detectives back on the case to follow up any leads the letter might have thrown up, but in the end, as I said, she was that careful; she made sure there were no leads.

Chapter Thirty-Seven

2001

Alison

It was such a relief when Lucy finally emerged from those awful teenage years, almost like a rebirth. Although I had grown to appreciate Fiona and Simon for their loyalty and kindness, I still found Cassie difficult to like. I'm sure that initially she was partly responsible for steering Lucy towards the unsuitable clothes, make-up, behaviour – and above all the company – all of which were so out of character for her. I tried not to hold a grudge.

Very gradually, things got easier. Of course, it didn't happen all at once, but slowly I noticed small changes for the better. Eventually Lucy stopped finding it necessary to challenge everything I said, or to bat against every normal code of civilised behaviour that I suppose I must have represented to her. She no longer glared icily at me as though she detested and despised me, at least not so frequently. I had tried not to show how hurtful I found her attitude. Really, she had treated me with total contempt at times.

Then at last, the day came when she condescended to eat some of her meals with me again, and even chose to sit in my company sometimes, without freezing the atmosphere. To my astonishment, I noticed that occasionally she might even ask my opinion or advice – as she had done regularly up to the age of fourteen or fifteen, but rarely since then. In fact, I would go so far as to say that the "old", dear Lucy, who had all but disappeared and been replaced by a raging, ranting harpy, had reappeared at last.

Susan had assured me that all this was normal behaviour in adolescence, especially in adolescent girls, but I can't accept that this is the case. Many girls seem to go through their teenage years being quite amicable and pleasant. For example, I don't believe that Susan's daughter Claire ever demonstrated such unattractive traits at a similar age – and I am perfectly convinced that I myself remained serene, polite and compliant, and certainly never put Mother through such trials.

At her most difficult, some of Lucy's behaviour was extremely distressing, because it seemed to show not only a loathing of me – which perhaps I could have tolerated, though it wounded me deeply – but also of herself. I hated to see her refuse to eat, to become thin and gaunt. Worst of all, I hated to witness how she abused herself, beginning with those hideous piercings, and ultimately by deliberately inflicting wounds on her arms and legs. She tried to hide them from me, but of course I knew; I saw.

Paradoxically, in the end it was Cassie who helped both me and Lucy through this difficult time. I admit I had never greatly approved of Cassie, nor, I suspect, was she very fond of me. Over the years I had tried to warm to her – she was Lucy's closest friend, after all – but I just could not. However, I had to concede that she remained a steady friend and supporter to Lucy, and became, at my most anxious and unhappy times, reassuring and kind to me.

Once, after a particularly upsetting argument, Lucy had stormed out of the house in fury, abandoning Cassie and me in the sitting room together. In my despair I think I had murmured out loud something like, 'Oh Lucy, Lucy, why do you hate me so?'

Cassie had turned to me with a surprised expression on her face.

'Lucy doesn't hate you, Alison; she loves you more than anyone.'

Of course, I made no comment on this observation, but I did find it both touching and comforting.

* * *

Oh, what a joy it was to learn that Lucy had achieved top grades in her A levels.

I was delighted when, of her own accord, she showed me prospectuses from the four universities to which she was applying. We began to discuss the pros and cons of each course and institution. In the end, Lucy was accepted by her first choice of university – Birmingham – to study Psychology. I couldn't help regretting that she had chosen a location at such a distance from Newcastle, when Durham – only half an hour away by car or train – offered a similar degree. Of course, I had my own private reservations about Durham, with all its negative associations for me, but logically I realised that it made little sense to condemn the university – or the city – because of my distressing experiences long ago.

In any case, Lucy convinced me that the course content was what had decided her, and that the department in Birmingham was very well regarded. Meanwhile, Cassie was accepted to read Medicine at Edinburgh. How ironic, I thought, that Cassie, with her unconventional leanings should be off to that most traditional institution to study conventional Western medicine! Perhaps

Susan was right to assert that the wayward directions pursued by teenagers were not to be taken too seriously.

How lacking I had been in my understanding of adolescents. My only continuing concern was that Lucy seemed to have lost some of her former sparkle. It was as if there was a lingering sadness at her core.

* * *

The week before both girls were due to leave for their prospective universities, Fiona and Simon invited Lucy and me to a buffet dinner party at their house. Fiona had written on the invitation:

It was kind of her to arrange the evening – she is thoughtful about such social events in a way that I am not, and could never be. It was not the sort of occasion I enjoyed; supper parties – or any other parties – have never been a pleasure for me, but rather an occasional necessity to be endured. I still feel nervous about making conversation and have never really got the hang of "small talk", despite Susan's well-meant efforts to coach me. However, this time I was determined to overcome my anxieties and present a positive front, if only for Lucy's sake.

Cassie was there, of course, with her current boyfriend, Ed, an intelligent young man about to start his third year of Engineering studies at Glasgow University. Susan and Mike had also been invited, as was Claire, now twenty-five and home for a long weekend break from her teaching job in Leeds. Charlie, who had completed his first year of Computer Sciences, was spending the entire summer vacation travelling in Europe with a group of friends – a somewhat frivolous use of time, I felt.

Fiona had sensibly arranged for a buffet rather than sit-down supper. There were too many people to sit comfortably around the table. I was pleased to note how happy and relaxed Lucy seemed. She felt so at home in Fiona and Simon's house, and was familiar with everyone in the room. In fact, she had grown up with them all, apart from Ed, whom she had known for over a year. She obviously liked him and felt comfortable with him too.

I was trying to cut down on alcohol, which had become something of an anaesthetic recently during times of stress and anxiety. I knew there was a danger of becoming overly dependent on it, so I had initiated a gradual reduction of my intake. But tonight I decided to allow myself one glass of wine. It was a special occasion, after all.

Limiting myself to a single glass became increasingly difficult as the evening wore on. Simon – ever a generous host – was quick to refill glasses as soon as they were half empty. I noticed he made several advances on Lucy's wineglass too. It was hard to keep exact track of how much she – or I – had drunk; two ... or was it three? It could have been more.

'Special occasion!' Simon said amiably.

The food was delicious of course, with a Middle Eastern theme on this occasion; Fiona and Simon are both good cooks. There was plenty of it too. A long table had been set up at one end of the large sitting room cum dining room. It was laden with exotic dishes of every description. People were encouraged to make more than one excursion to the table and help themselves freely.

The young people seemed happy to remain sociably in the large main room together with the parental generation, seemingly quite uninhibited about raising their voices and offering their opinions, unlike me at their age. Conversation flowed along with the wine. Cassie could often be provocative in discussions, enjoying challenging others. She named one of the books on Lucy's reading list, which she had chosen to read herself out of interest rather than need. She asked if anyone else had read it.

Of course Lucy had, in preparation for her course, but none of the others. Lucy remained quiet and watchful from her place on the sofa opposite me. She took a long swallow of her wine. I

193

wondered if I could tactfully suggest she'd had enough and ought to move on to fruit juice or water. Before it was possible to act, Cassie began elaborating some of the book's themes.

'It's really interesting,' she said. 'The writer examines the influence of "nature" versus "nurture" in determining developmental outcomes.'

'Well, that's got to be a topic that particularly interests me,' Claire said. 'Of course for me as a teacher it's not just a fascinating subject, it's a crucial consideration. How far is a child's potential set by genetic inheritance alone, and how far can we change or improve that potential with the right learning conditions and stimulation?'

'So, what do you believe, Claire?' asked Fiona.

Please Come to an Informal Supper Party: To Celebrate Cassie and Lucy's Success, and To Wish Them Well for the Exciting Adventures to Come!

'I've got to believe it's the latter,' Claire said, 'otherwise, much of my job would seem pointless.'

'Do you really think you can overcome the potential – or lack of it – that a child is born with, Claire?' asked Simon. 'Surely there are innate differences in intelligence, interest, attention and so on, that with the best will in the world we can do little about?'

'Well, yes, of course I agree that nature, or genetics, determines ability and personality to some extent. But I also believe that through encouragement, good teaching, motivation – in other words, nurturing – we can vastly extend each individual's potential to learn and to achieve. Surely that's the theory behind a principle such as universal education?'

'That's an encouragingly positive view! Even after three years teaching in what's regarded as a "sink school", my daughter is an eternal optimist!' said Susan, raising her glass towards Claire with a smile.

'What about you, Mum?' said Lucy suddenly. Her speech was

slightly slurred. My heart immediately began to hammer painfully in my chest. Having the attention of the group diverted to me was exactly what I hated, as Lucy was well aware.

'You're the one with personal experience in this field, aren't you?'

An uneasy silence fell on the room. Susan sat bolt upright, as if preparing herself for protective action.

'Well, I mean, you're *adopted* aren't you, so you must know all about how much of you is down to what your adoptive mother nurtured in you, and how much is … well … a complete mystery?' Lucy continued. She giggled, adopting a facial expression of wide-eyed innocence. She took another hefty gulp from her glass. I felt colour burning my cheeks. She hadn't finished.

'And … of course, you adopted me as well! It was an *adoption*, wasn't it? So there I was: a tabula rasa for you to make of me whatever you wanted. You could nurture me in your own image! Hmmm? Oh, but maybe I wasn't completely a tabula rasa – maybe sometimes some of those nasty *nature* characteristics crept in, did they? Betraying my origins, despite your best efforts …?'

'Excuse us, everyone!' Cassie said loudly. She had stood up and put her hand on Lucy's shoulder. 'I think we should go out in the garden, Lucy, maybe get some fresh air.' She hauled Lucy firmly up by her arm, and guided her out towards the kitchen. Their departure left an awkward vacuum in the room.

'Well …' said Mike, 'kids, eh?'

Slowly, murmurings of conversation picked up again. I sat, mute and unable to move. Susan came and perched on the arm of my chair. She touched my arm gently.

'You look tired, Alison,' she said. 'Listen, Lucy can come back with Claire. Why don't I drive you home?'

Claire nodded her assent.

'Yes, leave your car in the drive, Alison,' said Simon. 'I'll bring it back for you in the morning, if you don't mind leaving the keys.'

I said my thanks and goodbyes, and gratefully slid into the front passenger seat of Susan's car. She studied me with one of her meaningful looks and then switched on the ignition.

'Simon's very hospitable, very generous with the wine, but I think Lucy had quite a few too many tonight,' she said.

'Young people can be very hurtful sometimes.'

'I know, Alison. But think of it as the wine talking, not Lucy. A term away at university will do wonders for helping her to appreciate her home and loved ones.'

I was glad of the lift, but didn't ask Susan to come into the house with me. I couldn't wait to be by myself, for the blissful relief of silence. Was Susan right? Would Lucy's time at university bring her closer to me again – or would she regret having to come home at all?

I paused in front of the mirror on the landing. I touched the familiar pewter surround and my fingers automatically slid over the cool relief pattern. In the cruel glare of the wall light, I stared at my reflection. I was fifty-eight. My face looked drawn and lined. Gravity had worked its relentless force on every feature. My forehead was marked by horizontal "worry" lines, which appeared to compete, above my nose, with two deep vertical "frown" lines, as if my face needed to allow for each emotional possibility, but was uncertain which to engage.

I looked at my eyes; the lids drooped, spaniel-like, at the outside corners; shadowy semi-circles beneath merged with my cheeks, which appeared to have sunk inwards. A line each side of my nose drew deep chasms down to the corners of my mouth, dragging them further down still, to end in jowls interrupting the curve of my jaw. My hair had lost its blond brightness, and though Susan had insisted I get a "colour rinse", it looked coarse and dry to me, and obviously disguised grey.

I could be more than sixty, I thought. I'm getting old. In two years' time I *will* be sixty, and ten years after that I'll be seventy.

Lucy had her whole adult life ahead of her, and I could no

more control her future than I could control my own ageing process.

Strangely, this was a comforting thought. All these years I had been trying so hard to be the perfect mother to Lucy. Now I was tired; desperately tired of the constant, deliberate effort. Part of me was terrified of her departure to Birmingham, of being alone. Yet, another part felt a degree of relief that, for a time at least, I could abandon all that effort. Lucy needed her independence, to forge her own directions. I could do little to influence her choices.

Chapter Thirty-Eight

2003

Shelley

There's a programme on the telly called *Blood's Thicker*. I watch it nearly every week. It upsets me something terrible, but I can't help meself. It's about people separated from members of their family as babies or young children – for loads of different reasons, different situations – sad situations. Often the children grow up longing for their true relatives, wondering who they are and what they're like. Even if they've been adopted by kind people, and well looked after, the kids seem to have this longing all their lives to find their missing family members, to know why they were given away or separated, to find out whether they were missed or loved. Or even just to find someone who looks like them.

The programme helps people find their missing child. Often they take a letter from the child to the parent – or the other way round – and there's lots of tears as they read it. Then the programme sets up a reunion. It's dead sad – but happy at the same time. That's when I can't stop crying, but I *have* to watch it, like. It gives me hope; hope that maybe one day me and Stacy will be reunited.

I love the bit where they manage to bring them all together. It's really touching to see how they first meet. How they hug and cry and laugh. They can't take their eyes off each other, almost like lovers. It's like they fall instantly in love with this person they've thought about for years. Sometimes it's like they find the other half of themselves.

I sit there watching, blubbing, and thinking about my Stacy – and how much I want to see her, and hold her in my arms, and know her. I want that so much it hurts.

Is she still alive? Is she out there somewhere, wondering about me, wondering if I ever loved her, if I still love her, and if I still care about what happened to her? If she is alive, does she remember anything? What might she remember? She was such a tiny, little mite when she disappeared. She must have cried and cried for her mam and dad; wondered why we didn't rescue her, why we didn't fetch her home. She must have been so confused.

It breaks my heart to think of it. Maybe she hates me for not protecting her from the kidnapper, for not finding her and rescuing her. Does she still think about me, about her family, after all these years? Or has she forgotten all about us? Stacy, Stacy, where are you? What are you doing? What are you thinking?

After my baby went missing, the police searched and searched for her for weeks and months on end – and never found her. Gary always said she must have been murdered by some maniac or paedo. I think he just couldn't cope with the situation, with not knowing. It was easier for him to think she must be dead, that we'd never see her again.

I never believed that – I still don't. As a mother, I'm sure I'd know – inside – if she was dead. I don't think she is dead. I've always *felt* her alive – I can't exactly explain it. Inspector Dempster believes she's alive too. He doesn't say it in so many words – I suppose he can't. But I know he does think someone kidnapped Stacy, and took her away. She was such a gorgeous bairn. If someone had really, really wanted a kid, someone a bit disturbed or mental, my Stacy would have been just the sort of little girl they might have gone for. She was so pretty and cute, like a little pixie.

Well, she won't be little any more. She must be nearly twenty-one. If I close my eyes I can just picture what she might look like; still pretty, blond, not too short, not too tall, and *slim*. That was the only good thing Gary passed on to the kids. He was dead skinny. Not one of them's fat like I was. Mind you, fat or not, I was a lot prettier than Gary! 'Til he turned me into an old baggage, what with all them pregnancies, and the drugs, and the tabs, and the booze – and the chips.

I try to look after meself these days. I cook proper meals, with vegetables from the market. You're no use to anyone else if you don't look after yourself. And I do help out with my kids, and the grandkids too.

The telly and the papers made out I never cared about Stacy. They said me and Gary only thought about ourselves and didn't look after the bairns properly. Maybe that was true about Gary; he couldn't look after his left foot, let alone a kid. But it wasn't true of me. Maybe I wasn't the world's most perfect mam, but I did love them. I did me best, even if it wasn't very good all the time. Trouble was, I hadn't had a proper mam meself, to help show me what to do, how to look after them.

In the end I learned though, I had to. I can see, now, I shouldn't have let them run so wild. I shouldn't have drunk so much, and I shouldn't have let Gary turn me on to the weed. After Stacy was taken I went to pieces for a while. I took to the drink in a big way. Some days I couldn't get out of bed. It was a terrible time.

When Dr Shah and the social worker, suggested "counselling", I didn't think much of the idea at first – didn't seem like something the likes of me would do. I wasn't very good at expressing my feelings, 'specially not with strangers. Well, no one had ever shown any interest in my feelings before, not even me. Only agreed to go on the course to get the bairns back. But the counsellor turned out to be a nice woman. She really seemed to care.

Gradually I got to trust her. She talked a lot of sense. Told me taking all the blame onto meself for what had happened was negative, that it didn't help. Blaming meself was different to taking responsibility, she said. She used words like that. At first, I couldn't understand her meaning – I could hardly see what she was on about. But I stuck with it, and slowly started to see what she said was true. It was hard, very hard. But in the end, it forced me to take a good look at my life, and to make some changes.

Gary being gone was a blessing in disguise. Having him out the way was the best thing that could have happened to me at that point. I feel sorry for him really, he's a useless drunk and druggie. Can't even rob an empty house without getting nicked. He's lost to me, and to the world now; homeless, sick, skint, hungry. He looks old, but I don't think he'll make old bones. I used to think he was that powerful – now I reckon he's just pathetic. I'll never refuse to help him if he asks me, but I'd never, never have him back.

I'm dead proud of how I managed to make a proper home and get a steady job to support meself and the bairns. Now they're all grown-up, and doing really well, every one. Even the eldest two – Dean and Leanne – have done all right in the end. Our Ashley's got her hands full with her twins – pity she didn't get some exams behind her first, but never mind. My own twins, Sean and Kelly, were always bright sparks; they both did really well at school and went on to college. I was so proud of them.

I was dead proud of Ryan too. When Stacy was taken the poor lad went to pieces, and he's never stopped missing his little sister. I can't forget those early months after little Stacy disappeared. Our Ryan would wake night after night screaming with a nightmare. Used to think it was his fault she'd gone. I told him he wasn't to blame; it was a "bad man" or a "bad lady" what took her. That just upset him more, though, to think Stacy was with somebody bad. 'What if that bad man or bad lady is nasty to our Stacy?' he'd say. Well, what was the answer to that?

After school, our Ryan trained as a plumber. Now he's making good money with his own plumbing and bathroom business. Never forgets his mam, though – he's a good-hearted, kind lad – gentle, even if he talks rough sometimes.

I know Stacy's grown up now too, but she'll never stop being my baby, and I'll never stop worrying about her. Inspector Dempster said he thought it was a woman what took her. But just like Ryan, I can't bear to think of that "bad lady" either. What if she was unkind? What if she hurt Stacy? I used to torture meself with thoughts like that. Inspector Dempster tried to comfort me by saying he thought she was someone who really, really wanted a baby and maybe couldn't have one. He said he was sure someone like that would look after Stacy well. I hope so, but nobody truly knows, do they? Not even him.

Chapter Thirty-Nine

2003

Lucy

The time at Birmingham was mostly wonderful. I enjoyed being a student and made some very good friends. No one quite as special as Cassie, of course, but important friends just the same. My friendship with Cassie had been so close, I could hardly imagine finding that sort of relationship with anyone else. Yet I did find trust and close companionship with others once I got to know them – and Cassie and I did still get to see each other during the vacations, when we each went home to Newcastle.

Despite that, nothing could beat the fantastic times we had when Cassie visited me at Birmingham, and the equally fantastic times when I stayed with her in Edinburgh – but neither of us could afford to make those trips more than once or twice a year.

The course was an inspiration to me – I loved it. Studying was no problem because I found the subject so interesting. I suppose I had to join in with the moans about workloads when I was with my friends – it's what everyone did – but really I liked nothing better than those long evenings at the library poring over books, high on coffee and elated by the thrill of knowledge and discovery.

For the first time in my life I felt uninhibited, free to express my personality. I missed Mum at first and worried about her, but not having her constraining judgement, stiffness and control, not always worrying about her approval, was a total liberation. I knew there were issues still to acknowledge and sort out, but I told myself I had a few more years of growing up to do before I needed to face them – and certainly before I *wanted* to face them.

Being away from home and Newcastle gave me the chance to see Mum more objectively, at a distance, for once. At the same time, that detachment meant I was forced to accept some of the unanswered questions about my background. There were times when I felt pretty down about it. So much so, that in my first year, I wrote a note to the senior police inspector in charge of the Stacy Watts disappearance in Frainham. It was a spur-of-the-moment decision, even though it took me a few weeks to actually take action and post it. The note didn't give much away – I wasn't ready to initiate a proper dialogue – but it did help me to feel I had taken a first step, opened an avenue that I could pursue if and when I felt ready, or not.

I took a train to Worcester early one morning, and posted the note there. I often imagined Detective Inspector Dempster receiving the envelope, opening it, and reading the note. I wondered if he would believe I really was Stacy. I still didn't truly believe it myself. I still didn't know what I believed. Maybe Inspector Dempster would just think I was some sort of crank, seeking attention. I wondered if that's what I was too.

From Worcester, I went on another train to Great Malvern and spent most of the day walking in the Malvern Hills to clear my head. I stood on the Beacon, where I could look eastwards and see the flat plains stretching away, with Worcester and

Birmingham in the distance, where I had come from. If I climbed over the brow of the hill a few yards further on, and looked westwards, the hills of Herefordshire and Wales disappeared in misty layers towards the sinking sun. The ridge of the Malvern Hills was like a division, I thought, separating two opposing worlds. A metaphor perhaps. Just like the two directions open to me. One, to the world of silence and concealment, a world of safety. The other, to the world of truthfulness – opening up any number of frightening and unknown possibilities. Which route would I travel?

* * *

The first time Mum came to visit me in Birmingham – it was during my first year at university – was odd, quite a shock. She had always been so definite in her views, especially about anything concerning me. We'd had some difficult times when I was younger, but I think that was mostly about me trying to assert myself and not being very good at doing it in a reasonable and adult manner. I'd either become stupidly upset, or else I'd be angry and confrontational. I shudder to remember some of the things I said to her.

Generally she managed to keep her cool, and just let me make a lot of noise. Her way of dealing with my behaviour was to withdraw into herself. That lack of emotional response drove me crazy with frustration at times, but I suppose in the end it forced me to calm down. Now, suddenly, seeing her in Birmingham, outside her own environment and in foreign territory – *my* territory – she seemed diminished, older, and unsure of herself. Sometimes it felt almost as if she was afraid of me. Perhaps that should have made me feel powerful, but it didn't; it just made me feel sad, and uncertain of my own place in the world.

Mum came to stay once or twice during each year that I was at university. We would go out for meals together, go for walks along the canal, explore St Paul's Square and other historic areas – and above all, we both enjoyed the feeling that we were building a more adult relationship, one of equals. Whenever I told her about my subjects, she picked up on everything in an instant. She actually helped me understand an aspect of statistics I'd been struggling with for ages. I only had to explain a new concept to her once and she understood it better than I did! She just loved me talking about my current area of study – it was as if she really came alive. We talked more than we ever had before.

I wish I could have asked Mum more about her experiences when she was my age. I know she went very briefly to Durham University, and that it was an unhappy time. She never told me exactly why, and I never asked her. She's so intelligent, it's a real shame she didn't stay at university herself. By some unspoken agreement we didn't touch on anything very personal in our conversations together. There was still so much to resolve between us, so much for *me* to resolve about myself, for which I didn't feel ready. Would I ever feel ready? I wasn't sure.

It was as if my visit to Worcester and the Malvern Hills was a turning point. It seemed to settle something in my mind. I made a conscious decision not to think about my background for the moment. Not at a time when I was delighting in all the experiences I was exposed to, the joy of discussion with like-minded people about topics that interested me: psychology approaches, personality, social issues, politics, and more. The whole exciting world was opening to me.

Chapter Forty

2003

Alison

How Lucy has matured during her time at university. Our relationship seems to have entered a different phase. I've missed her terribly and felt quite lonely without her. Yet when she returns for the holidays I feel we have been closer than for some time.

While she's less confrontational with me, she's more confident and assertive. What delights me is that her old loving and affectionate nature has returned. Sometimes I'm concerned that there's an element of desperation in her attitude, as if she senses things must change – and that terrifies me.

Before she left for university she seemed to be becoming distracted – obsessed even – with chipping away at her background. Her "history" she called it. Thankfully, her preoccupation with that quest seems to have receded for the moment. I suppose she has so much else to occupy her thoughts. I myself have thought much about sharing more information with Lucy, especially in the light of recent developments with my health.

It will have to happen; she will have to know – but I insist it is a subject over which I – and *I alone* – will have control. I *will* talk to Lucy in time, but *when* has to be my choice, as does the manner in which she is told. There are so many risks. My greatest fear is losing control over the situation, or even jeopardising any continuing contact with her. I couldn't bear to lose her, not ever of course, but especially not now.

Naturally I'm pleased that Lucy has made some good friends – maybe they will even dilute the intensity of her relationship with Cassie, which could surely only be a positive thing. Not that they have lost contact. Cassie has made several trips to Birmingham during the years of Lucy's studies, and similarly, Lucy has been to visit her in Edinburgh – at not inconsiderable expense. Unnecessary and extravagant I would say, given that in the vacations, Lucy has barely set foot in her own house, but rather she hurries off to meet Cassie, and to visit Fiona and Simon. I try not to let it upset me, but I can't pretend I'm not hurt.

I suspect that Lucy has found romance at Birmingham too. She hasn't confided any such thing to me, but sometimes I catch her staring dreamily at nothing in particular, and smiling in a secretive way. I'm not jealous, of course, but I find it a little irritating. I just hope she's being careful.

Chapter Forty-One

2003

Lucy

My final year at university was very strange, full of unbelievable ups and downs; Himalayan, you could say. I experienced some incredible, life-changing "highs" – followed by being plunged into deep chasm-like "lows". Meeting Guy was definitely one of the most significant highs. Guy Downing was doing his final year of Medicine. We met at a gathering at the house of a friend of Cassie and Ed's, another medic, of course.

The moment we set eyes on each other I felt an extraordinary connection. I could tell Guy did too. We talked non-stop that first evening. After an hour we'd exchanged phone numbers. By the time I went home, we'd agreed to meet for a drink the following evening. He had already taken possession of my whole consciousness.

That night I lay in bed and thought of him. I gave a small yelp of pleasure as I pictured him; I actually *smiled* as I recalled the soft curl of his hair around his ears, the way his mouth lifted on one side when he smiled, the shape of his hands, the slightly languorous turn of his eyes when he looked at me, the easy way he took my hand as he walked me back to my flat that night.

One single day before meeting Guy, I would have asserted that "love at first sight" was a ridiculous concept, invented by some fatuous Hollywood screenwriter. Now I had no doubt that this man, whom I had encountered only five hours previously, would mean everything to me, always; that our lives were destined to be entwined for ever.

Not long after the joy that was meeting Guy, came the greatest possible "low". It couldn't have come at a worse time for me, just a couple of months before finals, when I needed to focus above all else. I'd asked Mum to come and stay. I told her I had something important to tell her. It gave me a thrill to think of telling her about Guy, of being able to talk about our plans together. Surely she would be pleased for my happiness? Surely she would like him when she met him? *Surely* … yet there was nothing sure about it. Her reactions were never predictable.

I knew something was wrong as soon as she stepped off the train at New Street station, or rather lowered herself cautiously onto the platform, clinging to the support rail beside the train door. She had always been slim – but now she looked frail, quite scrawny, in fact. Her hair was greyish and wispy; it had lost most of its fair colour. Her face was pale, her eyes shadowed. Her cheeks seemed to have sunken inwards.

'Mum?'

'Hello, Lucy,' she said, holding thin arms towards me. 'How lovely to see you, my dearest girl.'

We hugged and I felt her sharp bones move about inside her coat as if they were no longer quite connected. She clung to my arm. There was a feeling of desperation in the grip of her fragile hand. Her body seemed to tremble slightly. She walked slowly, unsteadily, like a very old person. Where was her brisk, bird-like energy?

'What's wrong, Mum? You look terrible. You look … ill.'

'Oh dear, do I? I have been a bit poorly lately …'

'Why didn't you tell me? You never mentioned anything on the phone. When did it start? You didn't seem ill at Christmas. Have you been to the doctor? What's wrong with you?'

'Oh, my dear, so many questions. Here, help me with my bag. Let's get a taxi today. I'm a bit tired … after the journey, you know.'

I looked sideways at her. She never took taxis.

'Let's go to your flat and have a lovely cup of tea. Then we can talk properly, can't we?'

* * *

The taxi ride was a nightmare of dread. The driver did the usual cheery but banal conversation openers that taxi drivers seem to specialise in. I was incapable of responding other than in mono-syllables. But Mum seemed happy to talk in the same light-hearted manner, not normally typical of her. My body felt frozen rigid to the seat. Mum kept turning to smile at me, as if we were on a pleasure trip.

Back home in my shared flat, I prepared a tea tray with trem-bling hands, while Mum sat serenely in the sitting room. My flatmates were still out. We sat alone while she told me her story.

She'd had some symptoms back in February, she said. They got a bit worse so she'd gone to see the GP. He sent her straight to hospital for tests and a scan, after which she was given a diag-nosis of bowel cancer – 'Not very glamorous, is it?' she'd said. Even before the diagnosis, she'd guessed, what with the pain and the weight loss. The operation had been a qualified success. They'd removed a large section of her lower intestine, including "all they could" of the cancerous tissue. With cancer, they said, it was always a question of how much it might have spread. She'd clearly had it for some time before consulting the doctor.

The specialist was optimistic, she said. With treatment she could go on for some time, perhaps a year or two, maybe quite a bit longer. Of course, there were no guarantees. It all depended on whether they'd "caught it", and on how she reacted to the treatment. The chemotherapy was "unpleasant", she said. It drained her energy. She felt nauseous during the treatment cycles and had little appetite. She was most fortunate, though, she said; in between cycles she felt better, almost normal, in fact. She could do most things, enjoy her usual activities – and she still had most of her hair, for the moment, anyway.

'Like so often, it's a case of the cure being worse than the illness,' she said with a laugh. 'The latest chemo cycle ended only yesterday, so I'm just a bit low at the moment – but I didn't want to delay coming to see you – I was so looking forward to it. I'm sure I'll pick up in a day or two.'

I couldn't bear it, seeing her so reduced and vulnerable. I put my arms round her and sobbed. I thought of all the times I'd been hurtful, I'd been *cruel* to her.

'I'm so sorry, Mummy. I hate it. I hate to think of you ill – fancy having the operation all by yourself. It's awful. You should have told me.'

'Absolutely not! What could you have done, other than worry yourself? I wasn't alone – Susan was very good, and Fiona too. No, I'm only telling you now because I have to, because I can't hide it. But you must concentrate on your work and not think about me. You have important exams before long – that's what matters. The good degree I know you're going to get – and what comes after it. Everything is under control. The doctors are very good – well, most of them. I'm having the best possible treatment. I've insisted they tell me the truth, and I trust them to be straight with me. They don't like it, of course, they don't like to be pressed about timescales, and I know they can't be exact. Doctors want everyone to feel hopeful. Well, I do feel hopeful – I'm perfectly optimistic, but I don't need to cling to *false* hopes. After all, life is a terminal illness! There's no getting away from it. From the moment we're born, we're dying!'

She smiled, as if delighted at this thought. She grasped my hand.

'You don't need to worry, Lucy. I'm managing fine, and everyone's being very kind: Susan and Mike, Fiona and Simon, so kind. They all send their love to you, by the way.'

* * *

I made some scrambled eggs for Mum and me for supper. It had always been one of her favourites. She managed a few mouthfuls and a cup of tea, but then said she was a little tired after the journey, and would I mind if she had an early night? On previous visits, she'd slept on a sofa bed in my room, but I wouldn't hear of it this time, despite her objections.

'Really, Lucy, there's no need to fuss. I'll be perfectly all right on the sofa bed. It's quite comfortable.'

'Not as comfortable as the proper bed. You need a good sleep.'

I made up my bed for her with clean sheets and a warm duvet, and put a hot-water bottle in it, even though the weather was mild. She'd always felt the cold, and now she was so thin. It felt strange acting maternally towards her. I moved into the room next door. Hannah, one of my three flatmates, was away on a field trip for her dissertation. I knew she wouldn't mind me borrowing her bedroom.

It took me a long time to get to sleep; my mind wouldn't rest. How could it be possible? I picked and picked away at all she had told me, as if it were a scab, analysing it, searching my memory for clues to make sense of it, worrying about all the times I'd

213

been unkind to her. I hardly dared let my thoughts drift to the future. Would she really cope on her own? What if the symptoms became worse? What if the treatment didn't work? Should I defer my finals? Should I give up my studies to look after her? On and on and round and round. I wished I could talk to Cassie. I wished I could talk to Guy.

The next morning I felt weak and exhausted, but Mum looked a little better. There was a faint blush of colour in her cheeks. She ate a small piece of buttered toast for breakfast and had her usual cup of tea. Kate had left early. Orla came and joined us in the kitchen. She'd come in late and I hadn't had the chance to talk to her, to warn her about Mum being ill, but I could tell she was concerned to see how she looked.

'How are you, Mrs Brown? You look a little tired. Did you sleep all right?'

'Oh, very well, Orla, thank you for asking. In fact, I feel much better this morning,' Mum said. 'A good night's sleep was just what I needed. So, Lucy, if you have to go to a lecture or to the library, off you go. Don't worry about me at all. You mustn't let me interrupt your studies; I can entertain myself perfectly well.'

'Well, I've only got some reading to do today, Mrs Brown. I can be here and keep you company today if Lucy needs to go out.'

'No need, Orla dear. And please just call me Alison. It's kind of you, but I really don't need looking after. What I would like is to hear about your Pharmacy studies when you have time, though.'

Mum just loved discussing the details of their courses with my flatmates and friends.

'Yes, thanks, Orla,' I said, 'but I've kind of cleared most of my work for the next few days, to make sure I could spend some time with Mum while she's here. I've only got a couple of tutorials this week, and some reading to do. Mum, it's such a nice

214

day – if you feel up to it, I thought we could take a bus ride to the Lickey Hills today, and go to a nice café I know there?'

'That sounds a lovely idea, if the bus stop's not too far. I'm afraid my walking's a bit feeble at the moment.'

'I can drop you at the bus station when you're ready,' said Orla.

'I wouldn't want to put you to any trouble,' said Mum.

* * *

Normally, Mum would have enjoyed striding energetically around the entire country park, studying the labels on all the trees, shrubs and flowers, often jotting down details as to their Latin names and origins in her notebook. That day, it was enough to stroll round a couple of fields, close to the Visitor Centre, Mum holding on to my arm and remarking on the spring beds of perennials, just budding or starting to bloom. We found a bench under a magnolia tree, not quite in flower yet, and sat in the dappled sunshine.

When Mum's breathing had slowed down a bit, I poured her some hot tea from the flask I'd brought. She clasped the mug in both hands, closed her eyes and held her face up into the sun.

'Ah, this is lovely, isn't it? Clever girl to bring a Thermos.'

'Mmm. Not too tired, are you? Are you warm enough?'

'I'm just right, thank you.' She paused. The silence between us was filled with a potency that scared me.

'Lucy, there are things I need to tell you.'

'I've got something to tell you about too, Mum,' I said, hastily, thinking of Guy and smiling, wishing I could fill the silence with him.

She twisted her body slightly to face me. She smiled too and took my hand.

'I sensed you had something special to tell me. I want to hear all about it. But first, Lucy, I need to talk seriously, I'm afraid.'

'Isn't that what you've been doing?'

'Yes … but there's something else we need to talk about. You know there is.'

My heart began leaping wildly in my chest, like a captive frog desperate to get out. I took a deep breath.

'Is this really the right time, Mum?'

'Yes it is,' she said quietly. 'You know we must. I need to tell you the truth, the whole truth. Please. Before it's too late.'

Chapter Forty-Two

Alison

Once I had made up my mind to tell Lucy everything, my belief in the correctness of that decision was absolute. While the doctors were confident that the cancer was treatable at this stage, it was clear to me that my life would end before much further time had elapsed, despite their excellent efforts. In principle it was possibly a year or more, but equally possible that only months remained to me.

What if I left the full truth concealed? After my death, it was almost inevitable that details of Lucy's background would emerge. How would she cope with such a revelation at that time, knowing I had misled her and lied to her over all these years? I desperately wanted our relationship to end in closeness and trust. I wanted Lucy to remember me as a mother – yes, a *mother* – who loved her enough and who was brave enough, to tell her the truth.

Of course she would be shocked, distressed, and perhaps angry, to hear of her real background, but how much better to learn of it now, than after I am gone and unable to reassure and comfort her.

The more I considered my plan of action, the more animated I felt, and the more convinced I was that it was the right decision. In fact, I recalled the excitement of my original campaign to obtain a child; the thrill of first finding Lucy in Riddlesfield, and following the plan one step at a time, each stage meticulously planned, organised and executed. It was still a matter of some pride for me that I had successfully carried out the "abduction", and remained undiscovered after all these years, despite the extensive police inquiries.

At a different level, I also found myself feeling some sense of guilt – not regret, never regret – about the anguish caused to Lucy's birth mother, despite all her inadequacies, and a certain concern about what was a serious criminal act on my part, however justified by the circumstances. Perhaps, as all of us near the end of our lives, we feel compelled to contemplate death with "a clean slate". It is a compulsion that has grown in me daily in recent weeks. I have no doubts that telling Lucy the full truth is the right thing to do.

Chapter Forty-Three

Lucy

She talked for over an hour, pausing periodically to allow me to wipe my eyes, blow my nose and regain some control. She told me everything: she talked of her desperation to have a child, which was heightened by the death of her mother. How she had planned an abduction after seeing the grave of a tiny child; how – and I found this deeply chilling – it was a child called *Lucy Brown*. She told me about the intricate preparations she had made; how she had sent for the dead child's birth certificate (which is now mine), about her search of the streets of Frainham, seeing me for the first time playing outside a terraced house, and her certainty that I was the child she wanted, that she was *meant* to have.

She had returned some time later to carry out and complete her plan. She had coaxed me into a pushchair, dressed me as a boy – and exchanged her disguise of a brown wig and dark coat for her natural fair hair and a red coat. Oh God, I thought, *that red coat*. Then she had fled with me on the train to Newcastle, to the home she had created for us both, the home I had regarded as my own these past twenty years.

She talked of the extensive police search, the stories in the papers and the television appeals. I detected a tiny note of pride in her account of how she had evaded detection and outsmarted the police investigation, even though she seemed to express – reluctantly – some admiration for Detective Inspector Lawrence Dempster.

She told me of my "biological" (her word) mother and father, Shelley and Gary Watts, and their appeals for me to be found and returned to them. Hearing her speak their names sent something like an electric shock racing through my body. Cold sweat ran down my back. I shivered.

'So, so … you're really not my mother?' I blurted, though I knew the answer well enough. 'You're not even my *adoptive* mother?'

'My dear, darling girl,' she said, tears now rolling down her own cheeks, 'I cannot claim to be your real mother, in the sense that I did not give birth to you. And no, I did not formally adopt you. I have done something terribly, terribly wrong – something quite wicked, I see that now. But at the time, I honestly believed I was saving you from a cruel and unsatisfactory life, from neglect, and perhaps even from cruelty. As soon as I saw you – *ridiculous* as it sounds – I fell in love with you. Totally in love. I adored you then and I have adored you ever since – as any true mother loves her child.'

Falling in love no longer sounded ridiculous to me.

'So, all that story of adopting me, of choosing *me* out of rows of babies in their cots – so all of that was untrue? That was just lies; it was lie upon lie upon lie?'

'I've told a lot of lies, horrible, dreadful lies, and I'm deeply ashamed of them now. But one thing has never been a lie, Lucy: that I have loved you from the moment I set eyes on you, and will love you as long as I live. That is the absolute truth.'

'You think that's enough?' I screamed. 'You loved me, so you stole me? You took me from a family who … who may have also loved me. What about my real mother? Didn't she matter at all? Didn't you think about her? What are you, a psychopath, a monster? *What you wanted* – is that all that matters to you? Does that justify what you did?'

She stared at me in shock, tears spilling from her eyes. I clenched my fists and felt hot rage rising through me.

'Damn you! Damn you! Fuck you! How could you do such a thing? How could you?'

She cringed at my words and held her hands up protectively to her face.

'You're right, Lucy,' she whispered. 'You're right to be angry. I've done a terrible, terrible thing, and loving you didn't justify it. I was … misguided and stupid. Maybe I was heartless. I thought I was doing the right thing for you at the time, I honestly did.'

I looked at her, frail and trembling, her face thin and drawn – a picture of misery. I drew her into my arms and we sobbed together.

For a while, neither of us could speak. We held each other. We each felt the trembling of the other's body, the juddering intake of breaths. An elderly couple wandered near and, seeing our tears, our distress, hurried quickly past. They paused a little way ahead and we heard a disjointed, murmured conversation. Then the woman returned hesitantly towards us, her face full of concern.

'I'm so sorry, I don't want to intrude, but are you all right? Is there anything I can do?'

Mum straightened her back for a moment, took a deep breath, and looked up at the woman.

'How kind of you to enquire,' she said. 'Most people would walk by. My daughter and I are a little upset. We have just heard that I am very unwell, you see. Thank you so much for asking.'

A minute before, she had appeared in total collapse, an old woman, apparently broken, pathetic, at death's door. What an accomplished liar she had become over the years, I thought, so adept at making use of "half-truths".

'I'm sorry to hear that …' The woman paused. 'Things aren't always as bad as they seem at first, you know. I do wish you all the very best – you and your daughter.'

She walked on and rejoined her husband.

'You know,' said Mum quietly, 'after all these years, it still gives me a thrill to hear someone refer to you as my *daughter*.'

I shook my head in disbelief. We watched as the couple continued slowly on their way together.

'What are we going to do?' I wailed bleakly, like a helpless child. I *was* a helpless child.

'Well,' she said, 'I have been thinking about this for some time. I think it's quite clear, and all you have said just now confirms that to me. There is only one thing to be done, and that is to reveal the truth. I should have done so long ago, but I don't think I was quite ready at the time and perhaps nor were you – not to accept the truth, nor the inevitable consequences. I was terrified of the effect of the truth on you, and I was terrified of losing you, Lucy. Now I think I should contact Detective Inspector Dempster.'

'NO!' I shrieked. Mum jumped and looked at me in horror.

'No,' I said more quietly, 'not yet, not now. You can't do that now. Not when you're ill. Just think what would happen. The police asking endless questions. Maybe the newspapers too. You'd be arrested! You can't go to prison when you're ill. Do you want to die in prison? What would be the point?'

'The point is, Lucy, as you have made very clear, I committed a crime – and it was not a victimless crime.' She paused and looked thoughtful. 'At the time, I felt nothing for your parents. At least, nothing but scorn and disgust. I genuinely believed they were not worthy of being parents; that they were neglectful at the very least, and perhaps even abusive. I still believe that your father – Gary – was … *is* … not a very admirable man. But, despite what you say, I have been thinking of your mother a lot lately, of Shelley. I realise now that I condemned her without enough justification. Having been a mother myself, knowing how

222

much I love you, how it would destroy me to lose you, I came to see that *she* must have suffered terribly, losing you. How could I not see that before? I suppose I never wanted to consider her feelings, or even to acknowledge that she *had* feelings. She has a right to know you are alive and well.'

'OK, OK ... but not now, not yet. After all, she's had to cope all these years. Let's not rush into action just yet. We need to think this whole situation through properly.'

* * *

That night, over a simple supper, I told her about Guy. I'd rehearsed it many times, anticipating our discussion. Now the context had changed completely; our relationship had changed, for ever. I'd been expecting her to be stiff and cool about hearing of Guy. She'd never been keen on any of my boyfriends in the past, not even hearing about them. They were seen as a distraction from the true path of my future, and generally dismissed as inferior or undesirable. Perhaps, too, she'd seen them as coming between us; between her and me.

She listened intently when I talked about Guy, and interspersed my account with questions; interested questions, not hostile ones.

'A doctor? So he's already qualified?'

'Yes, but he's planning to specialise as a psychiatrist.'

'Mmm? A psychiatrist?'

'He's arranged to do his Psychiatry residency in Edinburgh, starting in the autumn. Actually, he and Cassie and Ed are friends, and have several friends in common. His parents live in south-west Scotland too, so Edinburgh makes sense for lots of reasons.'

'South-west Scotland ... so beautiful ... do you remember, Lucy, those lovely holidays we had there when you were small?' She gazed dreamily out of the window for a moment.

'I do, Mum,' I said quietly. She smiled that I still called her

223

"Mum". 'If we're living in Edinburgh, it's only about an hour on the train from Newcastle – and it's not so far to go and visit Dumfriesshire some time. Would you like that?'

'I would like that, if it's still possible … I'd like it very much. So you and Guy plan to live together in Edinburgh?'

'Yes. I know it must seem to you as though we haven't known each other very long, but we're in no doubt. We want to get married in time, but that may have to wait a while.

'Yes, well, such details don't seem to bother most people these days. What about your idea of doing a PhD?'

'Well, if I get a good enough degree, I hope to be accepted for a Clinical Psychology PhD in Edinburgh.'

'I have no doubt you'll get a good enough degree. But what if you don't get into Edinburgh for any reason? Would you consider anywhere else?'

'I've kind of set my heart on Edinburgh. It makes sense in every way. It would be lovely to be near to Cassie and Ed – and to be in easy reach of *you* – but, to be perfectly honest, I *have* to be where Guy is.'

'You love him?'

Her question shocked me. She'd never asked about such personal or intimate feelings before.

'Yes I do – I love him so much …'

I couldn't control my face breaking into a joyful smile, even if I had wanted to.

'And he loves you.'

It wasn't a question.

'Yes. We want to be together always. Mum, I really want you to meet Guy.'

'And I would very much like to meet him. I'm delighted you have found someone special, Lucy. That gives me great comfort.'

'But, remember, Mum, Guy doesn't know anything about you, and my background, and I don't intend to tell him until the time feels right – and that may be some time from now.'

Chapter Forty-Four

The meeting with Guy was arranged for two days later. It was a far greater success than I could have hoped for. I was amazed that Mum was not just compliant, but actually eager to meet him. He invited us to his flat for tea. I'd explained to him about her illness, and also tried to describe something of what she was like as a person. While trying not to prejudice him against her, I told him she was "a bit complicated"; that she could be tricky and sensitive, and that her thought patterns were not always like those of other people.

He couldn't have been kinder and more considerate towards her. He prepared a tray of tea and had even baked a coffee and walnut cake! I could tell she was impressed. She seemed to take to him immediately. There were some slightly awkward silences at first – well, awkward for me. It didn't seem to bother them much. Mum was engrossed in studying Guy's bookshelves, her head bent to the right as she walked along the row, studying the titles. Then we all sat down, passing cups of tea and plates of coffee cake, like children pretending to be grown-ups.

Neither of them was great with small talk. They quickly got into deep discussions concerning serious issues, about ethics and the rights and wrongs of different types of research, and about the merits of a medical approach versus a psychological one in treating various mental disorders. She seemed more at ease with him than I'd ever seen her in company before. She asked him about his interests, his background and his family. I had a sense that she was building up to something important. Despite what we'd agreed, I was horribly afraid she might be planning to reveal my "history" to him.

'Well, Guy,' she suddenly announced, making me jump, 'it has been a pleasure to meet you. I can see you are very fond of Lucy.'

Guy nodded. He gave her his full attention. He didn't flinch. I squirmed with apprehension, and intense embarrassment.

'But ... fondness ... even love, by themselves may not be enough ...'

'Mum!' I exclaimed, horrified.

She raised her hand to me, to quiet me.

'I don't want to appear a Victorian parent, but I do need to be sure what your intentions are with regard to Lucy.'

'Mum! You can't ask that of Guy!'

'It's fine, Lucy,' Guy said equably. 'I understand.'

'Lucy is very special to me, you see. Very special,' she continued.

'Of course she is,' Guy said with a smile, glancing in my direction. 'She's very special to me too. She always will be.'

'I believe that, and I find it deeply reassuring. For all sorts of reasons. It makes me happy. Lucy will have told you about my illness, and as a doctor you will understand better than most people that I may not live a lot longer. It is important for me to feel confident that Lucy will be all right when I am no longer here to support her. Having met you, I'm so glad to know she will not be alone.'

'Thank you, Alison,' he said. 'I can't promise you that our lives will always be easy and free of troubles, but I can promise that I will always love and care for Lucy.'

I could hardly believe that Mum was talking about emotions in this way.

'Hang on a minute,' I said, feeling a bit left out, 'it's not just a one-way relationship, you know – we'll be there for each other.'

'That's just how it should be,' said Mum briskly. 'Now I think we should go back, Lucy.'

* * *

Outwardly I tried to maintain an appearance of normal life, without revealing the huge burden I was carrying. Strangely, Mum appeared to manage it better than me. But it was never far from my mind. I woke each morning with a jittery feeling in my stomach, deeply anxious. The only thing that worked for me was concentrating my mind firmly on my studies – perhaps another way in which I resembled Mum.

The term ended. Mum was unbelievably pleased and proud when I got a First, despite the huge distraction and strain of her revelations, which she acknowledged had changed my life for ever. Academic achievement always meant a lot to her. It was one of the few areas about which she was competitive. She was delighted, too, when I heard that I'd been accepted to do my doctorate in Edinburgh.

'But I won't just want to do Psychology in the abstract – I want to apply it in the real world, with people who actually need psychological help.'

'People like me, do you mean?' said Mum.

'Yes! People like you,' I said savagely. 'People who cause psychological pain to others. People who are *feeling* psychological pain too. For whatever reason.'

* * *

Guy went to stay with his family in Cumbria for a few days and then went ahead of me to Edinburgh, to arrange somewhere for us to live. I spent a couple of weeks staying with Mum. She looked better than during her time with me in Birmingham. The treatment seemed to be working, but we both knew it was likely to be a temporary remission.

Now that I no longer had my studies to occupy me, I was increasingly absorbed by Mum's revelations. Any thoughts of the future, of what she, and I, might have to face, set off feelings of absolute terror – of near panic. I could concentrate on little else. In comparison with what lay ahead, everything else seemed irrelevant, insignificant.

Guy found us a two-bedroom first-floor apartment to rent in a lower Morningside tenement. The rent wasn't too pricey, and it gave us a chance to take our time about buying somewhere. We went to look round it together for the first time. I knew Guy was excited about it, and expected me to feel the same.

'Look, Lucy, I love these high ceilings; makes it seem so spacious and light.'

'Mmm? Could be expensive to heat.'

'Well … these main rooms face south, should get plenty of sun. That'll help.'

'When the sun chooses to shine, of course.'

Guy glanced at me.

'Come and look out of the window – there's a great view of the city.'

'I wish Edinburgh wasn't so grey. It's a bit depressing, isn't it?'

Guy put his arm round me and hugged me close. 'No, Lucy, I don't think it's depressing, I think it's a fine city, and I thought you did too. You seem down though. What's the problem?'

'Who said there's a problem?' I snapped. 'Just because I think it might be cold or … or draughty?'

'OK, OK,' said Guy. 'You just don't seem quite yourself at the moment, Lucy. You will tell me if there's anything wrong, won't you?'

'Nothing!' I said, louder than I meant, tears starting to spill over. 'There's nothing wrong.'

I hugged him and he kissed me gently.

Thoughts whirled round my head. I couldn't deal with them – I hadn't the mental energy. Guy and I were so close and discussed everything together, yet I still hadn't broached the most central concerns about my background with him. Somehow I thought it was possible to bury the whole issue in some remote corner of my brain, until later, until some "suitable time" that I hadn't yet defined. The truth is I was terrified. It began to prey on my mind constantly. What effect would it have on our relationship? I wanted nothing to change. Yet once the truth was out, everything would *have* to change.

The unshared knowledge became a barrier between Guy and me. There were times when I was preoccupied, fearful and depressed. Guy, increasingly aware there was something I was concealing from him, was becoming deeply troubled. It troubled me too. We'd had no other secrets from one another. Here I was, living with the man who meant most to me in the whole world, and I hadn't shared with him the secret that defined – and blighted – my whole life.

My moods were very up and down. On several recent occasions I couldn't get out of bed. I could barely eat. I was drinking to blunt my feelings, blur my thoughts. I knew Guy was anxious about these changes, and particularly about my reluctance to speak honestly about their cause. Often I felt him watching me with concern, and hated it.

Whatever we were doing, it was there between us: as we chose colours to paint the flat, picked out rugs for the floors, and discussed what furniture and equipment we could afford; as we sat side by side on the sofa; as we walked up Arthur's Seat; as we made love. It was not just "the elephant in the room" – it was the elephant that imposed itself between us at all times.

One weekend night, we were sitting on the sofa together. Guy was peaceably stroking my neck and shoulder.

'Shall I make a stir-fry tonight or would you rather have a takeaway?' he asked.

I was shocked by my own response. It came out of nowhere. 'What does it matter! Nothing is important!' I shrieked.

'OK, Lucy, we can decide later,' Guy said quietly. He looked deeply hurt.

I apologised later and we made up, but the pain and confusion was still there, for both of us.

'Why don't you have a day out with Cassie?' Guy suggested.

* * *

We met by the river and sat on a bench, as close together as children, with coffee from one of the stalls. Our breath, heated by the drinks, made steamy clouds in the frosty air.

'We're like a couple of horses,' she said, breathing more steam. We giggled and touched our heads to each other. It was so good to see her. My sadness hid away.

She looked round at me.

'You don't look great, Lucy.'

'Thanks.'

'Really, I'm worried about you.'

'Don't you start too.'

'Is it to do with Alison? Is she worse?'

'She's … not doing too badly at the moment …'

'Well then?'

'Look, there are some things I need to talk about, but first I need to talk to Guy.'

She looked intensely at me.

'Everything OK with you and Guy?'

'Yes, yes, it's not that. Can we not talk about it just now? Can we just have a fun day?'

Cassie leapt up and pulled me to my feet.

'We sure can!' she said in a fake American accent. 'Come on,

230

girl, a bit of retail therapy will sort you out. Let's go and spend some money!'

We headed straight to Jenners in Princes Street and wandered the fashion outlets.

'Hey, Lucy, look at this top! You'd look great in it. Try it on, go on. With some slinky black trousers, just imagine! Go on, take it to that changing room. I'll bring some trousers for you to try on.'

So the time went, trying on extravagant and unsuitable clothes, egging each other on, giggling like teenagers. We had a wonderful time and emerged from the fashion department carrying large carrier bags, and rehearsing what stories to tell Guy and Ed. It was so good to be with Cassie. Even though a dark shadow still hid on my shoulder, I hadn't felt so relaxed in weeks.

Then off to the café for a light lunch and a glass of Sauvignon, or two.

'Look at the cakes!' Cassie crowed. 'We've got to have one of those!'

'I'll never fit into those trousers …'

''Course you will …'

* * *

We sailed happily down the escalator and wandered out of the front exit. The cool air hit our flushed faces. We took some steps, arm in arm.

'So what's going on with you and Alison right now? I get the feeling something's happened. Can you tell me, Lucy? Lucy!'

Crowds scurrying past us suddenly moved in slow motion. The traffic seemed to stand still; buildings spun crazily. A wall of silence built around me as if I was under water. From far away, Cassie called to me, 'Lucy! Lucy! What's wrong? Come and sit down. Here, lean against me. It's all right, you'll be all right.'

People seemed to be standing all around me. What did they want? I was trying hard not to be sick. I didn't want to bring up that cake …

'What's the matter, Hinnie?'

'Go get her some water.'

'By, but she's pale, poor lassie …'

Then Cassie's voice: 'Just give her some space. Move back please. She'll be all right …'

Chapter Forty-Five

Eventually, the Scottish winter set in with frosts at night and misty mornings clearing to crisp and sunny days. We were preparing for Mum to come and stay for a few days. We planned to take her to meet Guy's parents. Guy wanted to tell them we were going to be married. We'd been together over a year and a half. I knew the time had come. It could not be delayed any longer. I told him there was something important I needed to speak to him about first. I was sorry, I said, to have held back for so long, and that I knew it had caused him stress, but he would understand once I spoke about it.

'Are you unhappy with me? Have you had second thoughts about us being together?'

'Oh, Guy, of course not! Please don't think that. Nothing could be further from my mind. It's just *because* I want us to go on being together always that I need to tell you something … fundamental about me, about who I am. I don't think it will make you feel any differently about me. Well, I hope not … It's … it's something that's very, very hard for me to talk about.'

Guy looked so pale I worried he was going to pass out. He frowned and studied me with an anxious, questioning expression. What did he think I might tell him? What was he imagining? A criminal past? That I was already married? That I was actually gay, was pregnant, had been raped, was about to emigrate? I had to put him out of his misery – and fast.

'Let's sit down, Guy. But first, get me a drink; get both of us a drink.'

* * *

Once I started, it was surprisingly easy. It was a story that had been lying in wait for this moment for so many years. Guy sat next to me on the sofa and squeezed my hand as I spoke, occasionally shaking his head or gasping, occasionally stroking me. I told him everything, everything that Mum had told me, all that I knew and all that I felt, from start to finish. It all came pouring out; I hardly had to think what I was saying. I was grateful that Guy made no attempt to interrupt. I omitted nothing. Guy put his arms around me. He nestled into my neck. He stroked my hair, my face. He wept with me.

'Oh Lucy, Lucy, I'm so sorry you've had to carry this … this confusion and pain for so long, you poor, poor girl. How could you bear it? Thank God you've been able to talk to me about it at last.'

We talked about it late into the night. I was so thankful that at no stage did Guy condemn Alison or pronounce judgement on her. His only concern was for me, for my feelings.

Knowing how long Cassie and I had been friends, how close we were, he asked me if she knew. I explained that she'd had suspicions about Mum and her relationship with me. She had sensed that something was not right, but that, no, she didn't know what really lay behind her feelings. We agreed to ask Cassie and Ed over, so I could speak to them as soon as possible, but that no one else should be told for the time being.

By the time we went to bed, I felt drained, completely washed out – but overcome by a lightness, a huge sense of relief.

* * *

We invited Cassie and Ed round to the flat for paella supper. As we prepared the meal, chopping the vegetables, adding the rice and mixing the salad, my tension rose. Guy glanced frequently and nervously at me, as if I were a bomb about to go off at any moment. He poured us each a glass of wine.

'I think we could both do with this,' he murmured.

We all hugged warmly when they arrived. Cassie embraced me particularly affectionately. I guess she suspected there was some significance in the evening's gathering.

'How's Alison doing, Lucy?'

'Not too bad. She's very frail, but still in remission.'

'Yeah, Mum said she'd lost weight. She and Susan are taking turns to go with her to her hospital appointments.'

'I know. I'm so grateful they're doing that. It means a lot to her to have a good friend with her. She told me it's really important to have another pair of ears listening to what the specialist is saying. She said it's impossible to take in all the information, you know, in the heat of the moment. Those appointments are so stressful.'

'At least she's responding positively to the treatment, for the time being, anyway.'

'Mmm.'

Cassie gave me a penetrating look.

'And how are *you*, Lucy?'

'Oh, I'm all right.'

She cocked her head to one side, as if to say "really"? Guy and I had agreed to leave the serious conversation until after the meal, but what with Cassie giving me meaningful and questioning looks, it was hard to relax. There was a definite – and atypical – tension during the meal. Everyone must have been aware of the atmosphere, not just me. Conversation was stilted, unlike our usual laughter-filled get-togethers. I could hardly eat a mouthful. I felt sick with apprehension. It was a relief when everyone finished eating. Guy had opened a second bottle of wine. He suggested we abandon the table and move to the comfortable chairs with our glasses. He went to the kitchen to make coffee.

Just as when I revealed everything to Guy, once I started, the story flowed without difficulty. When I finally stopped talking, Cassie came over to me and put her arms around my neck. She stroked my hair, my face.

'Wow, Lucy, this suddenly makes sense of everything. But what a revelation for you to have to deal with. How long have you known?'

I explained about Mum's visit to me at university. She whistled. 'So long!?'

Ed stretched his hand across and grasped mine.

'Jesus, that's a terrible thing she did. It's a wicked thing she did to you, your mother – I mean your *not-mother*, I mean Alison.'

'Oh come on, Ed – blame and condemnation's really no help,' said Cassie. 'She's a disturbed woman. Anyone can see that. At least, she must have been seriously disturbed at the time when she took you, Lucy. She has always seemed … unusual. It's all so complex … I mean, once she'd taken that initial action, I suppose there was no undoing it, no going back.'

'That's right. Just imagine maintaining that story for more than twenty years,' said Guy, his arm around me, holding me firmly but gently, as if I were a fragile vase likely to fall and shatter at any moment.

'Alison must have been terrified that any action she did take would result in her losing you,' Guy continued. 'What she did is unforgivable, but it's clear she loves you very much, Lucy, even if that love had seriously misguided foundations.'

236

'Unforgivable is right. You're all being very understanding about it – perhaps no one wants to condemn her … I mean, knowing how sick she is,' said Ed, 'but at the same time it's hard not to feel that there was a lot of selfishness in the way she lied to you, Lucy, over and over again, from when you were a small child up to a year ago. And the other thing I find hard to stomach is her complete lack of sympathy for your birth parents. I for one would be perfectly happy to go straight to the police about this.'

'Well, please don't, Ed! Don't even think of revealing any of this to the police!'

'No, Ed,' said Cassie. 'This is no one's story to tell, except Lucy's – if and when she's ready.'

I shot her a grateful look.

'I do understand what you're saying, Ed. Even though I don't know my birth parents, I haven't found it easy knowing that to Alison they were just "non-people". It was like she genuinely believed they didn't deserve to bring up children; they were unworthy. I think she got so caught up in the story she'd created, that after a while she actually came to believe in it herself – or at least, she justified it to the extent that it became the only acceptable reality for her.' My voice became a strangulated croak as I fought back tears.

'You're very generous, sweetheart,' said Guy.

'It's not generosity … The thing is …' I said, gulping and gasping as I tried to hold on to control, 'of course I *love* her too. I love her,' I repeated. 'I mean, I know what she did is terribly wrong … but she's the only mother I've had … or at least the only one I remember having – and she did the best she could for me over the years, even if she could be strange at times.'

There was a pause as everyone grappled with their thoughts. It was Ed who broke the silence.

'So what are you going to do now, Lucy? Are you really saying you're *not* going to the police?'

'No, no! I'm not going to do anything that causes her further

237

stress and pain at the moment. Having discovered her conscience, she's really suffering enough from that – as well as from her cancer. I'm so scared of what might happen to her once the police know who she is. I'm so scared of losing her too. I'm scared of everything right now.'

'What are your feelings about your birth mother, Lucy? Shelley, was it?' asked Cassie.

'Yeah, that's another whole minefield I don't feel ready to explore. Just now I don't have any strong feelings for her or about her, except maybe slight curiosity. It's as though … she's a stranger to me. I've no picture of her in my head at all. Maybe if I'd been older when Mum – I mean Alison – took me, I'd remember her – my birth mother, I mean. Oh Jesus, see how complicated it gets: my mother, my birth mother, Mum …! Anyway, I don't think there's much scope for an ongoing relationship with my *dad*, by all accounts. Oh God, that sounds strange to me – "my dad"!'

'You can't help feeling dead sorry for your mum – Shelley, that is. Just imagine what she's been going through since you disappeared. She must have spent years and years worrying about you and longing to see you. Parents always say losing a child is their worst nightmare, worse even than a child dying in some ways. Do you think you'll try to get in touch with her?' asked Ed.

'I don't know, maybe, some day. This is all so new for me. There are lots of emotions … lots of reactions I have to sort out. My feelings are all over the place at the moment. One minute I'm getting on with day-to-day things as if everything's normal, the next minute it hits me, and it's like my head's exploding. I'm going to need some help with it all – Guy's been great about it all since I told him, and I know I can rely on you both to support me. But to be honest, it hasn't properly sunk in yet. It feels like a dream – no, a nightmare – a lot of the time. I don't think I can do anything for a while.'

'I think that's the right decision for the moment,' said Guy.

'There's no need to rush into any action immediately. You need time, lots of time, to let it sink in. A good counsellor might help when you feel ready.'

'I agree. It's going to take a while to figure out exactly what you do feel,' said Cassie, 'but I think one thing that's really important is that you don't *ever* allow yourself to take on responsibility for what happens to Alison, Lucy. You've got to remember that none of this is your fault. I mean, absolutely none of it! *You* didn't do it. *It was done to you* – when you were a tiny child, and completely powerless.'

Chapter Forty-Six

2005

We'd agreed that I'd go to meet Mum off the Newcastle train on my own and take her home for a light lunch. I needed time alone with her. Guy wouldn't be home before teatime. Her train was due at 11.57. I'd been waiting for nearly half an hour, wandering around Waverley station, checking the arrivals board every few minutes. I wouldn't normally get there so early, but the idea of Mum – in her present state – arriving and not finding me there was unbearable.

For some reason, since discovering my mother was not really my mother, my feeling of protectiveness towards her had increased, not decreased. Counter-intuitive perhaps. I thought about her constantly; I worried about her constantly.

A bitter wind blew down the platform, penetrating my coat. Why are stations always so cold? I stamped my feet and gazed down at my new boots. Guy had bought them for my birthday and I loved them. Calf-height, black leather, fur-lined, with criss-cross lacing and neat heels. She'll notice those, I thought. It'll be one of the first things she'll comment on. Anxiety was starting to build up. My stomach was churning. I felt hot and cold at the same time. My spine tingled unpleasantly. Little spasms nipped at my hands. Why get so worked up? She's just your *mother*, for Christ's sake, I told myself. And then I remembered. I shook my head and smiled bitterly to myself.

Feeling a stiffness spreading through my joints, I stretched my shoulders and rotated my neck, first to the left, then to the right, as the Alexander technique trainer had shown me, to release tension. The train appeared at the southern end of the platform, looming large as it approached and rumbled slowly to a halt. I checked my watch. It was 11.58, only one minute late. Jesus, I'm getting as obsessive as she is.

Train doors were opening and people pausing as they descended the steps, looking around to orientate themselves, then scurrying along the platform, streaming towards the main body of the station. I stood firm, forcing them to separate to one side of me or the other, like ducks swimming round a rock in a river.

I scanned the length of the platform for her. Then I saw her emerging from the train about halfway along. A middle-aged man had lifted her small, wheeled case onto the platform. He was reaching up to help her down the step. She allowed herself to be handed down – something she would never have done some years ago: a curt 'I can manage, thank you,' would have been her most likely response.

I saw the man hesitate and watch her take hold of the handle of her case. She gave him a brief smile and nodded, as if to reassure him that she would be able to propel herself and her luggage onwards without further assistance. He raised his hand in a gesture of farewell and walked briskly away.

'Mum!'

I waved at her and started to walk towards her. She smiled. She reached me and we hugged. I thought I detected a small convulsive sob as we embraced, but when we broke apart she sniffed and pulled herself upright, like a child determined to be brave.

'Lucy, dear Lucy – how lovely! You look tired, my dear. Are you looking after yourself?'

'Of course I am, Mum. It's you who needs looking after.'

'What nonsense!' She shivered. 'Oh, but it is cold here, isn't it? What a wind! Let's walk, shall we?'

She stood still and looked down at my feet for a moment.

'What nice boots! Are they new?'

'I thought you'd like them. Guy got them for my birthday.'

'Mmm, lucky girl. He's got good taste. They suit you.'

'Well, we chose them together, of course.'

'Of course.'

I reached for her case. She raised her hand as if to stop me, but changed her mind and made no further protest. We walked slowly up the ramp to the bridge. The slope was clearly an effort for her. She hung on to my arm and we had to stop every twenty metres or so.

'What an old wreck I am these days,' she wheezed. She gave me an apologetic smile.

'You're doing fine. There's no rush. We'll get a taxi at the top,' I said firmly. Again, she didn't argue. This compliance of hers was a strange new experience. It took some getting used to.

* * *

'Mum, do you remember when I was a teenager, we once had a bit of a to-do over what I should call you? I wasn't happy calling you Mummy. Do you remember?'

'Yes …?' she said cautiously, placing her teacup down with a shaky hand.

'Well, I really don't want to upset you, but I'd like to start calling you Alison now, rather than Mum … if you don't mind.'

She frowned. She looked from me to Guy and then studied me intensely.

242

'Would it make any difference if I said I minded?'

Guy sat upright and shifted in his chair. He gave her a steely look, as if ready to intervene if this turned into a "scene". I glanced at him and turned back to Mum. We'd agreed we needed to have a meaningful conversation with her about a number of things. Names were one of them.

'Well, no, not really, because I honestly feel it's more appropriate to call you Alison … you know, in the circumstances.'

'I can't pretend I'll like it, but I won't argue with you this time, Lucy. I haven't the energy.'

'I know it may take a while to remember every time, for it to come naturally – for both of us.'

She sniffed. 'I'm sure we'll get used to it, in time.' One of her brisk responses.

'Alison,' said Guy, as if feeling the need to demonstrate use of the moniker I had newly assigned her.

'Yes?'

'You should understand that Lucy using your own name isn't just a sudden whim. It's part of what's bound to be a long and maybe difficult process – of dealing with the reality of what's happened and who you both are.'

'Mmm? I'm not aware of having any difficulty understanding or "dealing with" who I am.'

Anger immediately rose at this self-centred response. I stood up. 'Maybe *you* haven't, but *my* world has been pretty much turned upside down recently. I have to feel I can acknowledge the truth more openly, that I can make sense of it, if I'm to be able to accept it … psychologically.'

'Well, I'm not sure I'd use your terminology, Lucy, but I do agree that, for everyone's sake, there needs to be more open discussion. I haven't failed to notice that you appear overly anxious, nervous, these days.'

'I agree,' said Guy. 'I'm concerned about Lucy's state of mind.'

'Well, I don't know about that,' I said irritably.

Guy turned to Alison.

'I had wanted us to take you over to Dumfriesshire to meet my parents at the weekend, Alison. I think it's important for you to get to know one another – we both do. But Lucy isn't happy with the idea just at this time.'

'Oh?' She looked at me quizzically.

'Well, think about it, Mu … Alison. It doesn't seem right to launch into the whole saga the first time you meet my future in-laws – and it certainly wouldn't be right to pretend we're a normal mother and daughter, and then to have to revise the whole story fundamentally at a later time,' I said. 'I think Guy and I should speak to them first, openly and honestly, to explain the situation. It's going to take some time for them to absorb that information. It could be pretty shocking for them, but at least then there would be no secrets when you do meet them.'

Alison looked distinctly displeased.

'They're hardly going to want anything to do with me once they know the truth. But if you two both feel that's really best, I suppose I agree. I'll just have to go along with what you decide.'

* * *

Guy and I planned to marry the following year. The original idea had been to announce our intention to his parents and to Alison together, during our visit to south-west Scotland. I already knew Alison would be pleased about our union. She'd made it clear that she approved of Guy. I was sure that his parents, Liam and Julia, would be delighted too. I'd met them on several occasions and felt confident that they liked me as much as I liked them.

Guy had grown up in a talkative, argumentative and affec-tionate family, with a lively interest in politics and social issues. After growing up in the quiet of my home, my family consisting of just Alison and myself, I'd been astonished and a little intimidated by the noisy debates aired across the dining room table at Guy's family home. He was the youngest of three children and the only son. His eldest sister Martha was a barrister, and second sister Helena a social worker. Liam and Julia were both GPs, nearing retirement, but still practising in Dumfries.

It was a family with a strong belief in public service. Of course, they would have assumed I came from a relatively normal family too, in which case I'm convinced they would have approved of me as a daughter-in-law. But now that it was becoming clear my background was far from normal, how would they react when the truth emerged? My whole life had become one of uncertainties.

It would be a while before we could have our "open and honest" session with Guy's parents, and find out exactly how they would respond. Dealing with the sharing of information was turning into a major project, needing careful planning. After Alison returned to Newcastle, we decided to make a plan detailing exactly how we were going to progress the situation. We decided to start by making an action plan, listing and prioritising what we felt needed doing. Alison would have approved: she loved lists and timetables. However, Guy was shocked when he saw what I had written at the top of the list:

1 – Meet Shelley Watts.

'I thought you felt there was no great hurry to meet her yet?' Guy asked with an anxious frown.

'I know I thought that to start with, but it's the one thing I know I've got to do – and the thing that terrifies me most. I can't think about anything else. The longer I put it off, the more I'm going to obsess about it. Also, I can't get *Shelley* out of my head; how she must have been yearning for me all this time, all these years. How might she feel if she discovered I had known about

245

my background for some time but hadn't tried to contact her? If we're going to arrange to meet, isn't it best to do it sooner rather than later?'

Although I tried to speak firmly and with confidence, in reality the whole prospect terrified me. Yet, I knew in my heart it was the right thing to do.

Shelley Watts was my mother after all, my birth mother, my biological mother, my *real* mother – whatever that meant. How could we deprive her of the knowledge that her daughter, stolen by a stranger at the age of two years and missing for over two decades, was alive and relatively well? I was well, wasn't I? I was confused by the tangle of often conflicting feelings. Surely *I* should be longing to see her too, my own mother, who had clearly ached to see me? But how could I love a woman of whom I had no memory, whose face I couldn't picture, who was, in effect, a total stranger? What if we didn't even like each other?

I did not explain our exact intentions to Alison. I phoned to ask if we could stay a night with her in Newcastle. We had friends to visit in the wider area, I told her, and it would break the journey from Edinburgh, make it more manageable. She was delighted. Of course it wouldn't be too much for her, she assured us.

Alison's priorities had changed since becoming so ill. She had dispensed with some of her frugal attitudes. A pleasant Latvian woman, Elena, had been engaged to help with the heavier domestic chores on two days a week, cleaning, making up beds, washing and ironing, even a little shopping and cooking.

Alison had instructed Elena in how to prepare vegetarian stuffed pancakes for supper. It had always been a favourite dish of mine. Elena was a quick learner; her pancakes were delicious. Alison ate little herself, but took pleasure in watching our enjoyment.

'You should try to eat more, Alison,' said Guy. 'It's important to keep your strength up.'

246

'Oh I do, I do. Once this current round of chemotherapy ends, I'm sure my appetite will return.'

Although we hadn't yet told Alison about the planned visit to Shelley, we *had* talked of the need to tell certain carefully selected people the truth about my abduction. She already knew that Cassie and Ed had been told. Next on the list were those who had regarded themselves – and whom we regarded – as close, long-standing and loyal friends; like Fiona and Simon, and Susan and Mike. Alison was anxious at the prospect.

'The trouble is,' she said, 'that the more people who know, the more likely it is for the news to leak out somehow – and you've already made clear that you don't want that to happen at this stage, Lucy. I just wonder if we shouldn't wait a while – until after I've informed the police myself – "gone public" as you put it.'

'That's why we think it's important that *we* talk to your special friends, and explain the exact situation in as calm an atmosphere as possible.'

I felt considerably less confident about our prospective discussion than I tried to pretend to Alison.

After a leisurely breakfast the next morning, we said our goodbyes and drove to Cassie's parents' house nearby, where Fiona and Simon were expecting us. I introduced Guy and there was lots of hugging and hand-shaking. Of course, I knew Cassie would have spoken to them, would have told them much of the story, as I had agreed she could, so they'd had some time to process the information. I trusted Fiona and Simon absolutely. I told Guy they had been almost like second parents to me.

'Just how many parents can one girl cope with?' he had joked.

'This is going to be a very emotional, maybe traumatic, meeting for you, Lucy,' Fiona said. 'Are you quite prepared for that?'

'Yes, I think I am – with Guy's support. It may not be straightforward. For a start, we can't be completely sure we'll even find Shelley. Even if we find where she lives, she may not be home. We'll just have to see what happens.'

247

'Does Alison know what you're doing?'

'No, not yet. We'll have to prepare her very carefully for that. She's not strong mentally or physically at the moment. I'm so grateful for the support you're giving her.'

'I have to admit we were deeply shocked to learn what she did when you were a small child. We can hardly approve of her action. I know she's an … unusual person, but really there's no excuse for such a wicked act. At the same time, she's clearly very vulnerable now, and we know you would want us to help her as best we can.'

'I really appreciate that.'

'You're a very special girl, Lucy. This is an unspeakable horror to put you through – I'm really not sure she deserves your love and consideration in view of what she did to you – and to your original family.'

'Well at least Alison does now recognise the wrong she did. She really wants to face up to her crime – it's *me* who can't face the result just yet.'

'We'll do whatever makes the situation easier – or less awful – for you, Lucy darling.'

Fiona got up and hugged me.

'You do know there's been a setback with the treatment, do you? She's not doing so well lately.'

'Yes, she told us about it. She's looking more poorly, we thought.'

'Good thing you're here with Lucy, Guy,' said Simon. 'However it turns out, it's going to be tough. She's going to need a lot of support.'

* * *

Next, we had arranged to meet Susan and Mike in a quiet café not far from home. I was more apprehensive about their reaction,

248

as this would be completely new information for them. Since my teens, when my friendship with Cassie had become so central to my life, I had seen more of and become closer to Simon and Fiona. Still, I knew Susan had been an unfailingly loyal friend to Alison.

'Lucy! It's wonderful to see you – and Guy – how lovely to meet you! Come and sit down, both of you. What a pity Claire and Charlie aren't in Newcastle just now – they'd have loved to catch up with you. Never mind, Mike's here. He's just parking the car – he'll be thrilled to see you.'

'Thanks, Susan, it's lovely to see you too,' I said, 'but I'm afraid we can't stay long … I've really just come to talk to you … about … about Alison.'

'Yes, I know, she's taken a turn for the worse, poor thing. Listen, just sit down and I'll go and order us some coffee. Would you like some cake? Lucy, you look beautiful, but you're a bit on the thin side, darling. Are you eating properly? Oh listen to me fussing – all "Mumsy"! I'll be back in a minute.'

She bustled over to the counter. Guy and I exchanged glances.

'Oh God,' I whispered, 'I hope this is OK …'

* * *

They both looked absolutely stunned when I finished talking. For a few moments neither of them spoke. A range of horrified expressions passed over their faces as they considered what I had told them. Mike shook his head in disbelief. Susan covered her face with her hands. Her expression changed slowly from horror to fury.

'It's unbelievable,' she said. 'It's utterly unbelievable. How could she do that to you, Lucy? How could she have kept it up all those years? Lying to you over and over again, lying to *me*, lying to everyone. I tried to be a friend to her, even though she was jolly hard work sometimes! I gave her every chance to confide in me, but … but she just told one lie after another. I see that now. To pretend your father had died! And then your grandparents … When one lie ceased to work, she simply replaced it with another.'

Susan shook her head and looked from one of us to the other.

'You know what?' she continued. 'All this doesn't totally surprise me. Some years ago, I think she almost told me. She started talking of doing something wrong – she hinted at having committed a crime. Then I guess she chickened out from revealing the whole story, because she suddenly told me that you weren't her real child. She didn't say she'd *abducted* you; she claimed to have adopted you – do you remember, Lucy? It's what she told you too, isn't it?

'I never thought it rang completely true – not that I was actually expecting *this*, but I sensed there was a deep secret at the centre of her life, a dark secret. *Adopted* you indeed! What kind of a woman is she? How can anyone be so cold and calculating? She cared nothing for any of us all this time, did she? It's … it's frightening; it's sinister! Well, you're going straight to the police, aren't you, Lucy? We'll help you all we can. I'm a solicitor, remember – I've got lots of contacts in the legal world.'

I sat frozen, deeply frightened by Susan's reaction. I could not speak. Guy held my hand and squeezed me gently.

'Susan, Mike,' he said quietly, 'Lucy has been struggling to come to terms with finding out about her abduction. We're just on our way to try to make contact with her biological mother in Riddlesfield. Of course this news has come as a shock for you both, and we understand your anger and resentment, Susan. But Lucy – in fact, we both – take the view that Alison's action was part of a general mental disturbance, a personality disorder if you like. That is not to excuse what she did, or the lies she told – but we feel extreme vindictiveness or a desire for retribution is not helpful at this time, certainly not for Lucy. Imagine the effect on *her* if this news goes viral …'

'Oh that's all very reasonable, Guy, but has *Alison* given a moment's consideration to the effect on Lucy? I don't think so! If anyone has been vindictive it's her! She's stolen someone's child, for heaven's sake. I can hardly believe any civilised human being would do such a thing. She's lived with the knowledge of what she's done for nearly a quarter of a century! And done nothing to rectify it for Lucy – or Lucy's real mother. Quite the reverse. Surely she should pay the price? I, for one, believe we should go to the police about this. Right now.'

'Hang on, Susan,' said Mike. 'It's hit you hard, this news. You put a lot of effort into your relationship with Alison, it's true, and this has come as a real bombshell – but none of us know how much Alison suffered, keeping it to herself all these years. And, most important, this is *Lucy's* story. It's Lucy's life, and it's for Lucy to say what should happen next.'

* * *

It took another hour of begging, negotiating and tears for Susan to agree not to denounce Alison, on the understanding that it was for my sake only that she held back. We returned to the car feeling totally drained.

'Would you rather put the visit to Riddlesfield off for another day?' Guy asked.

I sighed. 'No, we've come all this way, and we'd only have to come back, go through it all again. Let's get it over and done with.'

251

Chapter Forty-Seven

It took a couple of hours to drive to Riddlesfield. Neither of us had been there before. No, of course that's not true. I *had* been there as a small child, but I had no conscious memories of it. Just as well: it's not a beautiful city; more of a post-industrial wasteland. Acres of small, smoke-blackened terraced houses squashed together in the central area. At the edges of the town, modern estates of cramped, close-built houses – interspersed with busy dual carriageways, run-down shops, power stations and the dreary remains of industry. A pall of polluted smoke hung over the city, a vision not improved by dark lowering skies and steady drizzle.

Guy had done as much research as possible into where the Watts family had previously lived. He had accessed the Riddlesfield phone directory online. It had provided several possible "Watts" entries to follow up. We knew that at the time of my abduction, my family had lived at 14 Tanners Lane, in the Frainham area of Riddlesfield. That was to be our first port of call.

Using an A-to-Z map of the city, we drove along City Road and turned into Holbrook Street, which led into Frainham. A few more turns and we found Tanners Lane and parked the car. Some of the small, narrow houses had been improved, with neat paved yards in the front, brightly painted front doors, and plants growing in pots. Some had extensions built into the back yards, allowing for enlarged kitchens, with an extra bedroom or bathroom above.

We made for the back lane onto which the back yard of number 14 and its neighbouring houses opened. Guy held tightly to my hand. I stared and stared at the back of the house I had apparently lived in for the first two years of my life. I screwed up my eyes and tried to think myself back into this place. Was this where I had played with my doll, Polly? Was this where my brother Ryan had run about? Was this where Alison had first seen me? My mind remained determinedly blank and empty.

We walked round to the narrow street at the front of the row and gazed into the small front yard of number 14.

'Can I help you?'

A youngish woman holding a toddler on her hip was looking over the fence from the adjoining house. She eyed us suspiciously. Guy walked towards the fence.

'Sorry to trouble you,' he said. 'Do you happen to remember a woman called Shelley Watts and her family? She used to live here back in the Eighties.'

''Course I remember *about* her – everyone round here knows about her. She's the one whose bairn was taken, isn't she? Why are youse asking?'

I joined Guy at the fence.

'Oh, we wanted to get in touch with her. I'm her … I'm a … relative of hers. I haven't seen her in years.'

'Oh aye?' She looked me up and down. 'Well, she moved away. Long before my time. Shirley might know where she's gone, like. Reckon Shirley's been here for ever. Number 16. Here, I'll come with youse and ask.'

The woman hitched the child higher on her hip and walked out of her own yard and into the yard of the house on the other side. She banged loudly on the door and shouted.

'Shirley!'

After a few minutes, the door was scraped open and an elderly woman peered out.

'Hiya, Shirley! These people are relatives of Shelley Watts. D'you remember? Number 14? D'ya know where Shelley went after she left here, Shirley?'

The old woman slowly surveyed first her neighbour, and then Guy and myself. I smiled and nodded, in what I hoped was an encouraging manner.

'Shelley Watts? Oh aye, poor lass. She left number 14. After that baby of hers went missing. Broke her heart, it did. That was a long time ago. They never found the baby. Reckon she musta bin murdered. So sad it was – she was a pretty bairn.'

A lump formed in my throat. I tried to swallow but couldn't shift it. 'Do you know where she moved to, after she left Tanners Lane?' I asked, my voice strangely croaky.

The woman stared at me and twisted the hem of her cardigan.

'They say she moved to Moorside. The council helped her, after her fella got put back inside. Good thing too, if youse ask me – he was a reet bad 'un. Them other bairns of Shelley's got taken into care. I heard she got them back later, though. I haven't seen her in years, mind.'

'There was an entry for S. Watts in Moorside,' said Guy, studying his notes. 'That must be her. Here it is – Belside Crescent. Let's go and see if we can find her. You've been very helpful. Thank you both very much.'

'She were a rough sort, mind,' added the old woman.

* * *

We parked along Belside Crescent at a slight distance from the address. We could just see it: 'a small, semi-detached house in a row of others, varying only in the colour of their pale exterior

254

wash. I stared at it. Guy stared at me. We'd been sitting there in the car for many minutes. I was trembling from head to foot.

'Shall I at least go and check it's the right house? That it's her?' Guy asked quietly.

'Just give me another minute.'

I tried to steady my breathing. Guy stroked my arm tenderly.

'Poor baby, don't worry. It's worse anticipating it. It'll be all right once we're talking to her.'

'Guy, what if she doesn't agree? What if she insists on going straight to the police or the newspapers?'

'Maybe it's a risk we have to take. We could still do our best to protect Alison – but I honestly believe she *will* agree once she knows the circumstances – if it's *you* asking.'

I sighed. 'OK then. You go and ring the bell and … and tell her. Then come and get me if it … seems all right.'

He kissed me and got out of the car. I watched him walk towards the house. I felt a strong urge to cover my face with my hands; to peek through my fingers like a child watching a frightening film. My heart was beating so loudly the sound must have filled the car.

Guy was at the front door. Nothing happened for a few moments. I held my breath. Then the front door opened and I saw a youngish, brown-haired woman step outside. I breathed out an ecstasy of relief. It was the wrong house! She was far too young to be Shelley. Thank God. We'd better just drive away. Try again another time. No need to submit to this agony just now.

Guy appeared to be talking to the young woman. She was nodding and saying something in response. They conversed for a while. Suddenly a small child appeared at her legs, maybe three or four years old. I couldn't see whether it was a boy or a girl. The woman grabbed the child and picked it up. She turned and went back into the house. Guy remained on the doorstep. He glanced over in my direction. What was he doing? Why didn't he just come back to the car so we could go? I was getting agitated. 'Just let's go, just let's go,' I said under my breath.

After a further age, another woman emerged slowly from the house. Guy retreated backwards in order to allow her to stand on the front step. It was too far to see the woman's features clearly, but I could tell she was older, perhaps in her fifties. She seemed a bit hunched and held her hands over her face, covering her mouth. She stood on the step looking at Guy, swaying backwards and forwards a little.

He reached for her and put his hands on her shoulders. It was a gesture I recognised. He was comforting her. The younger woman appeared behind the older one and put her arms around her, as if to support her. She seemed to have left the child inside somewhere. Guy said something to them and they both looked towards the car where I was sitting, frozen. I realised I had my hands clasped over my mouth too, as if in reflection of the older woman's gesture. Guy began walking towards me.

'Oh no, no, no,' I whispered, cringing into the car seat. He opened the door and reached inside to hug me, hold me.

'Come on, sweetheart. Don't be frightened. It's her. It's Shelley, and she wants to see you. She wants to see you so much.'

I started to cry immediately. He took my hand and led me to the house, with one hand under my elbow, as if supporting my weight.

She was still clutching her face. Tears were spilling from her eyes, which were open, unblinking, staring at me. The tears cascaded unchecked down her cheeks, over her hands. Her hands were red and broad, I noticed, lined and prominently veined. Her hair had the pale, frothy look of grey or white hair frequently dyed blond. We stood looking at one another for a moment. Then there was nothing else to do but fall into each other's arms, hugging and crying, standing back to look at each other some more, then embracing again. She was shorter than me, her build sturdy and square.

'Stacy, Stacy, my baby,' she sobbed. 'My beautiful little girl.'

It took some minutes before I could speak.

'I didn't expect to feel this way …' I said, 'I thought Alison was my mother; she always had been. I didn't know about you. I didn't know I needed you … so much.'

Tears coursed down my face. Guy, behind me, squeezed my shoulder.

'It's OK, sweetheart, it's OK,' he muttered into the back of my neck. I nodded, not taking my eyes off Shelley.

We were introduced to Leanne, my eldest sister apparently, who had opened the door to Guy, and Ruby, the youngest of her three children. Leanne's other two children were at school, they said. A new family was opening up to me, a family that had not existed until this moment. We were shown into a small sitting room, stuffed with large pieces of furniture. Ruby sat on the floor, gazing up at us, one finger in her mouth, the other hand holding a doll. An image of another doll flashed through my mind for a moment. Just as we were about to sit down, Shelley said she had to check something.

'It's not that I don't believe you and that. It's plain to see you're Stacy, but it's something I've got to do. I've been waiting all these years to do it; promised meself.'

'What are you talking about, Mam?' asked Leanne.

'Our Stacy had a birthmark, a brown diamond shape on the back of her neck. Would you mind? Will you let me look … to be sure?'

I turned around and lifted up the hair from the back of my neck.

Shelley gasped. 'Oh my God … oh my God!'

She started crying all over again. Guy and Leanne moved closer to peer at my neck.

'It's there, all right,' said Leanne.

'No doubt about it,' agreed Guy.

* * *

257

Somehow, amid fresh mugs of tea and plates of biscuits, we fitted more than twenty years into that first afternoon. I learned about my family, about lives linked to mine yet lived in my absence and without my knowledge. We were told about each of my other brothers and sisters, their partners and children: a great array of names to list and learn and one day to meet; a great deal of personal information about each of them to absorb.

Guy made extensive notes. He joked that he was making a list of names, like you might find at the front of heavy novel, to remind you who everyone was. They nodded and smiled.

We heard that my father, Gary, had lost touch with the family after his release from prison. It was thought he was living rough somewhere. His health was not good. His memory had suffered and he was often confused. It was the drink. Too much booze and drugs over the years had taken their toll, Shelley told me, and he consistently refused "rehab", treatment and even night shelters.

Occasionally, he'd drifted back into the orbit of Shelley or one of his children, just long enough to beg some money off them, have a good meal, maybe sleep on their sofa for a night or two, and then to disappear for further months or years. Shelley said she'd never refuse to help him if he needed it, but she 'would never have him to live here, never again'. She said she always half expected to hear that he'd had an accident and been killed, or that he'd collapsed and died on the street.

It was hard to absorb that they were talking about my *father*; the emotional gulf was too great for me to feel connected to him. In time, perhaps. Right now, any sympathy I felt for him was no more than I might extend to a stranger in difficult circumstances.

Of course, they wanted to know what had happened to me from the time I disappeared. I explained that although over the years I had begun to have occasional doubts and suspicions, they were vague and shadowy. I was afraid of them. It was only in the last year that I learned the full story. Before that I had simply assumed that Alison, my abductor, was my mother. It shocked them to hear that I had no real memory of my former life with my birth family, nor of the abduction itself, nor of the early days of living away from them.

My body and face flushed with illogical guilt. How could I be so heartless? Yet, at two years old, I could hardly be expected to remember the abduction. Despite that, the lack of memory felt almost like a betrayal on my part, when they remembered me and the loss of me with such pain, such intensity. How could I not remember? Surely a child should remember, mourn and long for her own parents and siblings? How could I just forget?

'You have to remember Lucy was just a tiny child when it happened,' Guy said, as if reading my thoughts. 'She must have been deeply traumatised. Young children have ways of protecting themselves if thrust into such difficult situations. After a while she would have had to find ways of attaching herself emotionally to her abductor, to Alison, because she had no one else.'

Shelley shook her head and reached for me.

'Poor baby. My poor, poor baby.'

It also shocked them that I did not describe Alison as the evil monster that had featured in their imaginations all these years, whom they had always believed the abductor to be. I had to explain that, on the contrary, she had brought me up with great love and care, and that I loved her too.

We talked for hours, until we were all exhausted. Ruby had fallen asleep on the smaller sofa. I told them Alison was terminally ill, that she was unlikely to survive more than a year. I could see, and understood from their exchanged glances, that they were tempted to rejoice over this news, but restrained their impulse to do so openly. I told them that Guy and I planned to marry and that I wanted desperately for Alison to live long enough to be present at the wedding. Finally, I told them that I wanted them to agree not to reveal my reunion with them beyond the close family members – and certainly not to go to the police or media. This was met with silent, closed faces.

'I know it's a lot to ask of you. I know you must have strong feelings of anger and maybe hatred towards Alison – and that it's justified – but I want you to understand that it would make *me* deeply unhappy if she were publicly pilloried and condemned by the press. I couldn't bear for her to be imprisoned for these last months of her life. We, Guy and I, *will* be talking to the police, but not just yet. I need that Inspector Dempster to cooperate too, and to understand that she's not all bad. And I need to prepare Alison.'

'Don't you think she *should* be punished for what she done to you, Stacy, and to our mam?' asked Leanne. 'She *stole* you for Chrissake. She broke our mam's heart – and the rest of us. D'you really think it's right she should just get away with it?'

'I understand why you might feel that way, Leanne. Really I do. But, you see, I believe she was mentally unstable at the time she took me. She'd just lost her own mother. She was all alone, and so desperate for a child, and she managed to persuade herself that she was doing the best for me. I also believe she's been punished enough with guilt and remorse over what she's done. She's terrified she's going to lose me, and she's so very ill now. I couldn't bear her to suffer more than absolutely necessary, not now at the end of her life …'

Leanne folded her arms and shook her head.

I tried again: 'Now that we've found you, now that we've met, I want to stay in touch, stay close to you all for always – and to meet the rest of the family. *You're* my family now, and I never want that to change, but if the truth were out in the open, we couldn't be together. I'd have to hide away, to protect Alison.'

Silence hung in the room, as everyone considered the conditions I had set out. Shelley, sitting next to me on the sofa, clung to my arm.

'All these years,' she said, 'I've been sure you were alive. It's what kept me going. But I've had terrible nightmares that whoever took you might have treated you bad. That was what was hardest to bear. Well, what she done, this Alison, was wrong. Taking you away from your mam and your family was wrong, very wrong; it was cruel, it was *wicked; terrible, terrible wicked* – and she's caused me a whole lot of heartache. I can't tell you just how much. She thought I was just some useless slag, what couldn't fetch up a child properly, like. Well, she was wrong there. Maybe I wasn't the best, but I did love you. I always loved you. I loved all my kids.'

She paused and shook her head, tears springing from her eyes again.

'But at least she didn't hurt you. At least she's been good to you, Stacy, and I'm so, so thankful about that. I don't know if I can ever forgive her, not really, but for your sake, I can *try*. If she'd 'a hurt you, treated you bad, I'd 'a wanted to kill her. I don't mind admitting it. I'd 'a happily cut her throat. But she didn't. She treated you well. I can see that, from how much you care about her.'

She squeezed my hand and stared into my face. Leanne stood up and paced the room, sucking on a cigarette.

'Yeah, OK. That's all very well, but it might not be very easy to get everyone else to agree to keep quiet, might it not?' she said. 'What about our Ryan, for instance? You know how badly he took it, how it upset him something terrible.'

She turned to me. 'He's never stopped missing you, Stacy. You were his special little sister. He thought he were to blame when you went missing.'

'Yeah, well, I'll talk to Ryan. I'll talk to all of them,' said Shelley, her eyes steely, her mouth set firm. 'Just leave it to me.'

'Thank you, Shelley. That means so much to me,' I said.

'Here now, what's with this "Shelley" business? I'm your mam, aren't I?'

Guy and I exchanged glances.

'You are my mam, and I'll never deny it, or you. But for years I've been calling *Alison* "Mummy" or "Mum", and I've just told her that can't go on; that I'll be calling her by her name instead from now on. I'd like to do the same with you. Otherwise it could get so complicated and confusing. Calling you Shelley doesn't mean I think of you as anything less than a mother.'

Shelley wrapped me in another tearful embrace.

'Who'd 'a thought our Stacy would turn into such a clever and thoughtful lass?' she said.

'I'm going to have to sort something out about *my* name too,' I said, looking at Guy, 'about "Stacy".'

'What do you mean?' said Shelley. 'Stacy's the name you was given when you were born. It's your name.'

'Well, I know that, but I'm not sure I feel like Stacy any more. For all these years I've been called *Lucy*. Ever since I was taken. Lucy's the only name I can remember being called. But I have to admit I don't exactly feel sure about Lucy either now … Lucy was the name of a dead child. Alison saw it on a gravestone and decided to use it. My name was stolen too, just like I was. It just doesn't seem quite right any more.'

Chapter Forty-Eight

2006

Alison

It wasn't easy hearing about Lucy and Guy's visit to Shelley. I'm not one to overdramatise, but it made my blood run cold. My feelings were very confused. On the one hand I felt an overwhelming need to hear everything that had happened, on the other hand it caused me great pain; coming to terms with how *wrong* – how shallow – many of my perceptions had been, especially about Shelley, with whom, reluctantly, I now had to share the term of "mother".

My need to know Shelley in every detail – what she looked like, how she spoke, what sort of person she was, and above all, how she had reacted to seeing Lucy for the first time – bordered on desperation. I drew every drip of information from them, almost as if I were a parched traveller lost in the desert, attempting to draw water from a dried-up well.

'Was she very ... upset?'

'Well, first of all she checked the birthmark on my neck to make sure it really was me,' Lucy told me.

I gasped in astonishment at this. 'Really? Did she? So she did know! She *had* seen it,' I mused. 'Well ... that was very sensible of her.'

'Yes, and she had lots of questions. They just tumbled out of her, one after another. She was very emotional, as you might expect, but actually she appeared mostly really happy to see me.'

'I see ...'

'She wanted to know,' Lucy continued, 'if you'd treated me well, if I'd had a happy childhood. That was what seemed to be most important to her.'

'Oh? So ... what did you tell her?'

'What do you think? Of course I told her you'd treated me very well, that you'd loved and cared for me as if I was your own child ...'

A heavy lump gathered in my chest, making breathing an effort. I scrabbled in my bag for a handkerchief and dabbed my eyes. Lucy paused; I looked at her, waiting for her to finish the sentence.

'... and that, on the whole, I'd had a happy childhood.'

Oh, the relief. I released a long breath and shook my head. 'She must have been very, very angry with me. I would have been, in her place. How she must hate me. The whole family of course, they must all despise me ... and rightly so.' I sighed and gazed out of the window, imagining their loathing.

'She'll have gone straight to the police after seeing you, I suppose, so I must expect to be arrested any time now.'

'At first, I guess she must have thought she would tell the police, but I asked her – I *begged* her – not to, nor to make the information public in any way – at least, not at the moment.'

Lucy's words struck me like the blow from a fist. I turned to look at her in shock.

'Did you, dear?' I tried to control my faltering voice.

'Of course I did. Why does that surprise you? *She* was surprised, as you might expect. She found it hard to understand why I would ask it, but when I explained *why* I wanted her to keep it all quiet … when she heard how well you had looked after me … when I explained …'

'Yes?'

'When I explained how much I love you … well, in the end she agreed.' Lucy paused reflectively. 'I told her about your illness.'

'I expect she was rather pleased to hear about that, and who would blame her?' I said.

'Actually, she wasn't. I think Shelley is a very kind woman, a very … sensitive and generous woman.'

I fought my impulse to contradict Lucy's view of this woman, whom I had despised and resented all those years.

'Yes,' I replied, 'she does sound it. I had no idea.'

'My eldest sister, Leanne,' Lucy continued, 'took a bit more persuading, but in the end she agreed too.'

'Your … *sister* …?' I could hardly speak the words; they seemed so unreal.

Guy had been sitting silently, watching and listening. Now he stood up and came to sit with me on the sofa.

'Lucy has a whole family down there, Alison,' he said quietly. 'So far we've only met Shelley, Leanne and the youngest of Leanne's three children, but there's Dave, Leanne's husband, and their older children too …'

Guy opened his notebook and glanced at it.

'Sorry, it's still hard to remember them all – it's all so new. Yes, let's see now … there's Dean too, Lucy's eldest brother, and all of his family. Then there's Ashley. She has twin boys of seventeen. She works in a library apparently. Sean and Kelly – Shelley's own twins – are next in age. Kelly works in human resources. She's not married – quite a career woman by all accounts. Sean's a paramedic. He's married and has two children at school. Lastly there's Ryan. You may remember – he's nearest in age to Lucy

265

– just two or three years older. He has his own successful plumbing and bathroom business. He's married with one little girl of about two, and they're trying for another baby.'

I was completely dumbstruck. I stared at Guy in amazement. How could it be true? I had always assumed they were just a hopeless, dysfunctional family. I stood up and started pacing back and forth. I covered my face with my hands and shook my head. I turned and looked at Lucy and Guy beseechingly.

'What have I done? What have I done? I thought none of them would amount to anything. I thought Shelley was a dreadful failure of a mother; neglectful, stupid and selfish … but … she's not, is she? She seems to have done very well. They all seem to have done rather well.'

Drained, I slumped down on the sofa again.

Lucy came over and sat on the floor in front of me. She put her lovely head on my lap. I stroked her hair. She looked up at me.

'*Assumed* is the right word, Mum. You didn't know them. How could you judge? They're human beings, with the usual mixture of strengths and weaknesses. Flawed perhaps, just like the rest of us.'

266

Chapter Forty-Nine

Lucy

Back in Edinburgh, our lives were hectic on all fronts. Cassie and Ed were supportive to us both, as always. Cassie had begun working as a GP in a busy practice, but she and I managed to meet up for lunch or an early evening drink about once a fortnight. Ed, an engineer in the oil industry, spent regular periods away from home, so Cassie was often on her own.

Following his psychiatry training, Guy was working at the Royal Edinburgh Hospital. Somehow, through all the ups and downs of the last years, I had completed my PhD, and found a job working three days a week at a clinic supporting disturbed adolescents and their families.

With two reasonable salaries, even though mine was part-time, we had managed to buy a modest terraced house on the southern edge of Morningside. It had a sunny, narrow garden, which was my joy, and my haven.

We had planned a simple, small, civil marriage for the following May, with only closest family and friends present. However, now there was the added complication of exactly who constituted close family members. We decided to keep strictly to Guy's parents and sisters, Alison, Cassie and Ed – and now of course, Shelley. How would my numerous "new" brothers and sisters, their partners and children react to Alison being included, while they were being excluded? The prospect of explaining the arrangements to both Alison and Shelley – who had not yet met of course – and to the wider family, drove me to near panic.

There was so much to think about, so many complications, that we decided to put the marriage plans on hold for the moment – to enjoy a couple of years of normality. How naive to imagine that were possible. There were further complications lurking in store for us.

268

Chapter Fifty

2007

My anxiety increased exponentially once more when we discovered, unexpectedly, that I was pregnant, the baby due in February the following year. Despite the shock, we rejoiced at the prospect of a child – *our* child. We invited Cassie and Ed round for supper to share our news with them. They were equally delighted. Cassie wrapped me in one of her bear hugs.

'Lucy! Guy! That's fantastic! Not that I'm totally surprised – I thought you were looking a bit podgier than usual lately, Lucy!'

'Podgier! Do you mind …?!'

'No, just a tiny bit. You must both be so excited. Wow, fancy you getting to the "parent stage" – I guess that means we must be grown-up now,' said Cassie.

'I'm not sure I feel grown-up enough. It feels pretty scary at the moment: the idea of being totally responsible for another human life.'

'You'll make a great mother, Lucy,' said Ed, 'and Dad here will be pretty good too.'

'That's what I keep telling her,' said Guy.

'You know, every time you two come to see us, I feel like we have momentous news to impart,' I said.

'Yes, you do. We'll expect nothing less from you. No boring small talk, just earth-shattering revelations every time. So what's next?'

'Well I don't know about earth-shattering, but I do have something else to raise with you.'

They all looked at me expectantly, including Guy.

'I've been thinking about this since Guy and I met Shelley ...'

Guy regarded me apprehensively. "Now what?" his eyes seemed to be asking.

'Whatever it is, maybe you should talk to Guy about it first,' said Cassie, her gaze flicking between the two of us. She was always sensitive to non-verbal cues and atmosphere.

'I did mention this in front of Guy some time ago, so he does sort of know. The thing is, I've told both Alison and Shelley that I can't call either of them "Mummy", "Mum", "Mam" or any other mother-specific name. To do so would risk upsetting one or other or both of them. Nor does it feel natural, or even *possible* for me, knowing everything I do now. I decided I can only call them by their first names. They didn't like it, but they seem to have accepted it.

'Well, that sounds reasonable. It makes sense,' said Cassie. 'I'm glad they've both accepted it.'

'The thing is, I think the problem may extend to me too.'

'What do you mean by that, Lucy? How does it extend to you?' asked Ed.

'Well, think about it. Alison thinks of me as Lucy. Shelley thinks of me as Stacy. It doesn't feel fair to stick with either name – and somehow, I feel sort of detached from both of them now ...'

'So what do you want to do about it, sweetheart?' asked Guy, his face a picture of anxiety.

'I've been thinking maybe I need to choose a new name altogether.'

270

'A new name? What a weird idea. Have you thought of one?' asked Cassie.

'Well, not exactly; it's not very easy. First I wondered if I could combine Lucy and Stacy; you know, use the beginning of one name and the end of the other. But they both end with a "y", so it doesn't quite work. So then I looked at using the beginning of one name with the vowel of the other. But then you get either "Stucy", which sounds ridiculous, or "Lacy", which is equally weird, and vaguely reminds me of that 1980s American TV police drama!'

Everyone laughed at this.

'So ...?'

'So, I thought maybe I had to come up with a completely new name.'

'Go on then – what is it?'

'I don't know, I haven't thought of one yet ... I wondered if you might all help? You know, we could try sort of brainstorming ...?'

Nobody spoke for a few moments. They all looked at me.

'Oh God, it sounds ridiculous now ... It *is* ridiculous, isn't it?'

'It's not ridiculous, Lucy,' Cassie said, 'but how will you feel connected to a new name? How will we? How will any of us feel it's *you*?'

'Obviously it would take some time to get used to it,' I said feebly.

'I'm not sure,' Guy said, frowning. 'When your whole identity – and your concept of who you are – has been so deeply undermined by recent events, is it really a good idea to introduce a new name as well? Surely you've been Lucy for as long as you've been conscious of having a name. I think taking on a new one could be very disturbing.'

'I agree,' said Cassie. 'I mean, I know we've talked about how you have to keep reinventing yourself as you go through life and take on new roles and responsibilities ... We all have to do that, but adopting a new name at such an unsettled time seems a step too far. We all think you're pretty fragile at the moment, Lucy.'

'Thanks very much. Now you think I'm mad too.'

'I said fragile, not mad. Of course you're fragile after all you've been through – and are still going through. Anyone would be. Wasn't it you who had a panic attack in the middle of Princes Street after you found out about your past? If that isn't a sign of unbearable stress, I don't know what is.'

'OK, OK.'

'Mmm,' said Ed, who was always less ready to venture opinions in matters psychological. 'I'm no expert in this sort of field, but it seems to me that what you need most at the moment, Lucy, is permanence, not more change.'

They were right of course, I could see that. In uncertain times, I was looking for certainty, but in the wrong direction.

That evening, I told Guy that I planned to write another letter to Inspector Dempster. I wanted to inform him of how things stood, but I needed to remain anonymous until it was time for the full truth to emerge. He agreed it would be helpful to share the situation with the man who knew more about my history than almost anyone else.

Chapter Fifty-One

There followed a period of relative calm, to everyone's relief. Guy was kept busy with his work. I enjoyed combining my part-time work with some intensive home-making: painting and decorating our flat and making it ours, and our future child's. Alison had been in remission again for an extended period. We alternated between visiting her in Newcastle, and seeing Shelley and my new-found family in Riddlesfield. It was a relief to have postponed our marriage plans for the time being – there was so much else to think about.

We all knew it couldn't last. Everyone was waiting for the "next step", and of course I was procrastinating as usual, hoping against hope that the problems would disappear if I ignored them. I knew I couldn't expect my birth family to wait much longer. In the end it was events out of my control that took over. One grey, damp day in the autumn of 2007, Susan rang.

'Lucy, you'd better come down. Alison's back in hospital. I'm afraid she's not well. The cancer's spread.'

It was what I had dreaded. We went down to Newcastle for a dismal meeting with Alison and the oncologist the following day. Alison looked terrible: wan and exhausted. She was adamant she wanted no further chemotherapy. The specialist agreed it was a case of palliative treatment only, to control her pain as far as possible, and ensure some quality of life for the last few months.

The following day I composed a letter to Inspector Dempster:

October 2007

Dear Detective Inspector Dempster,

I wrote to you some years ago to tell you that I believed that I might be Stacy Watts. I didn't feel sure, nor was I ready to admit it fully to myself at that time. Things have moved on since then. I now know for certain that I <u>am</u> Stacy. The woman who abducted me, and whom I have regarded as my mother throughout my childhood, has admitted everything to me. Although it was an abduction rather than an adoption, I shall refer to her as my "adoptive mother", for the sake of clarity.

I know you have had ongoing contact with Shelley Watts and have provided her with some support. Following my adoptive mother's admission, my partner and I went to Riddlesfield and found Shelley, my birth mother, and spoke to her and to my eldest sister. It was an understandably emotional reunion. I asked Shelley not to go to the police, nor even to tell you, which she had wanted to do. I particularly asked her not to make news of my "return" public, until I feel it is the right time – and she has agreed. So I would be grateful if you do not press her for information about me. I will briefly explain the situation.

At the time she abducted me, my adoptive mother believed she was doing the right thing by removing me from what she then regarded as an inadequate home. I believe she was at least misguided, and

274

possibly mentally disturbed at the time. She has brought me up with great care and love, and is deeply attached to me, as I am to her.

She – my adoptive mother – now has terminal cancer, and may have only a few months to live, perhaps even weeks. She has come to recognise that her action, in taking me, was wrong, and she is tortured by guilt.

I myself am expecting a baby, which is due in February next year.

My adoptive mother will readily admit her role in abducting me and is prepared to face the consequences, <u>but I am not</u>. I do not want her to spend the last weeks or months of her life in custody, and I ask that you can give me some assurance that this will not be necessary.

I am now becoming close to my birth mother, Shelley. I have come to regard her as a very admirable person. She has agreed to cooperate in not making any complaint against my adoptive mother. I'm sure you will understand that to protect my adoptive mother, I cannot yet give you any direct contact details for me, but I ask that you write a letter of assurance to me <u>via Shelley Watts</u>, whom I trust to send me the letter in confidence.

I am also putting my trust in you.

My thanks.

Whose name to sign: Lucy or Stacy? I left it unsigned – he would know who I was. Although Shelley had given me Detective Inspector Dempster's home address, I sent the letter to him at the central police station in Riddlesfield; it felt more formal somehow. I knew he might well have retired by this time, but surely it would be forwarded?

After one of my visits to Alison, I took the sealed envelope and drove all the way to Riddlesfield. I deliberately posted it near to Shelley's house. If the police attempted to trace where it had been posted, the only information they could glean would be that I had been near Shelley's home – and I had already explained my contact with her, so it was nothing new.

I had explained the letter to Shelley, and she had agreed to forward any response from Detective Inspector Dempster to me in a plain envelope, which I left with her, ready addressed. In case her home was being observed, further visits to Shelley would now be possible only after hearing back from Detective Inspector Dempster, or after "going public".

About a fortnight later, an envelope dropped through our letterbox. It contained the following letter:

8th November 2007

Dear Stacy,

(I can only address you by this name, in the absence of information as to what you might now be called.)

I am very pleased that you felt able to contact me again after these last several years. Please be assured that <u>everything</u> that could have been done to find you after you were abducted, <u>was done</u>, but sadly, our search was unsuccessful. That was partly due to the very careful planning of your "adoptive mother" (to use your own terminology). However, the case remained open, and you were <u>never forgotten</u>.

I was always convinced that you had been abducted and that you were still alive. After your last letter in 2001, I was greatly concerned for your welfare. Reading your letter I got the impression that you were confused, unhappy and vulnerable. I hoped you might contact me, or the police service, again – and am delighted that you have now done so, even though some time has passed.

I am glad to hear you have made contact with your birth mother, Shelley Watts, who never gave up hope of seeing you again. Her heart was broken by your disappearance. Shelley has spoken to me on regular occasions over the years, hoping for news of you.

It is helpful to have information of your "adoptive mother", and her initial motivation and possible state of mind at the time of taking you. I can understand that, despite the wrong she did, you have become deeply attached to one another, and for this reason, I am very sorry to hear of her serious illness.

Let me outline what might happen should your "adoptive mother" present herself to me directly or at a police station, and admit her role in your abduction. It is likely she would be formally arrested, though this need not involve a dramatic scenario of sirens blaring, handcuffs, police vans or photographers. Most likely she would be interviewed in a quiet room and a statement taken in writing, so that her account could be investigated. In all probability she would be detained in custody overnight, presented to the court the next day, and then <u>possibly</u> even bailed – having satisfied the court that she would reappear at the police station at some appointed time later.

In view of the seriousness of the crime, I have to suggest that it is unlikely that the Crown Prosecution Service would agree not to prosecute. Again, it is <u>possible</u> that the crime would be marked as "detected", and "no further action – not in public interest to prosecute". This would be on the basis of taking into account the state of health of the perpetrator (your adoptive mother) and the wishes of the main victims of the crime (Shelley, as birth mother, and you yourself) not to make a complaint or press charges. However, in view of the extreme seriousness of the original offence, it is much more likely to be felt necessary to demonstrate that such a crime would not go unprosecuted or unpunished.

Despite the uncertainty of the outcome, I hope your "adoptive mother" will feel able to present herself, perhaps accompanied by you, to myself or to one of our police stations, and that this action will ultimately ease her mind, and yours.

Yours sincerely,

Lawrence Dempster (Chief Superintendent, retired)

Chapter Fifty-Two

2008

Alison

Oh what joy! My beloved Lucy has had a beautiful baby boy. Lucy and Guy have named him Milo – a somewhat unusual name, I feel, but it is their choice. I expect I'll get used to it. He weighed nearly eight and a half pounds at birth; quite a hefty weight, apparently, especially for someone as slender as Lucy. Even so, he looked impossibly small to me.

Lucy had had a long and arduous labour. There had been some question of a caesarean section towards the end. She had reached a state of exhaustion, poor girl, and there had been concern that the baby was also showing signs of distress. But, thankfully, after a few more strong contractions, she had managed to push him out, safe and sound, all by herself. What an achievement! I'm sure I could never have managed such a terrifying task myself.

Guy – who had been present throughout the birth, of course – described every step of the whole procedure to me. Young people seem quite unabashed at sharing such intimate details but, in truth, I was glad to know. It made me feel closer still to Lucy; closer to both of them, in fact. I am indeed fortunate in my son-in-law. Well, he isn't really my son-in-law, though he performs that role. I was disappointed that they decided to postpone their marriage, until a "more appropriate time". Well, I suppose it could have turned out to be an awkward occasion. Guy laughingly referred to himself as my "son-out-of-law". He can make a joke out of any situation, however sensitive.

I'm quite surprised at how fond of him I have become. If I'm honest, he is the first young man I have truly got to know. What a relief it is to know that Lucy will have the support of such a loving and caring "partner" (I hate that term; it sounds as though they've gone into business together!) when I am gone. Partner or husband, he's been so kind and accepting towards me too, despite all the revelations and turmoil of recent times.

Despite my fatigue, I was desperate to see Lucy and the baby as soon as possible. The day after Milo's birth, Guy met me at the station in Edinburgh and drove me to the infirmary. Lucy and the baby were in a side room. I was shocked by the sight of her. She looked pale as a ghost, and tired, her cheeks hollow, her eyes shadowed. I felt a rush of anxiety – near panic, in fact – but I forced myself to breathe deeply and contain my feelings.

It seemed quite extraordinary to imagine that barely twenty-four hours previously, little Milo had been *inside* Lucy! Yet here he was, robustly feeding at her breast, his tiny, perfect hand spread star-like against her smooth skin. Lucy had smiled wanly as I entered the room, and reached her hand out to me. I grasped it and bent to kiss her. The baby writhed for a moment, disturbed momentarily from his rhythmic sucking. He gave a faint mew and thrust his head back towards his mother's body. He smelt faintly of milk and soap, and something more primeval and unfathomable – yet not at all unpleasant. I stroked his smooth, downy head and he sighed softly.

'Hello, little Milo,' I said.

Lucy looked at me, smiling.

'What do you think?' she said.

'He's beautiful,' I said. 'He's perfect.'

She nodded. Then her smile faded. 'Alison, you don't look well. You're so thin.'

'Oh, I'm all right – all the better for seeing you and this little one. I'm just a bit tired after the journey – and I haven't even the excuse of having given birth! *You* must be exhausted, my dear. Are you getting enough rest?'

Milo had relaxed into a deep baby sleep, his breathing steady and his body limp. Guy lifted him very gently from Lucy's arms, and lowered him into the plastic, transparent cot beside her bed.

'There now, little man,' he said, 'let your mum have a break.'

There was no question of a "lying-in" these days. In the past, I'm told, new mothers spent a few days, or even a week, in hospital recovering from the birth. No such luxury these days: Lucy was due to go home with Milo the following day. Even after such a difficult birth, it seems, mothers are sent home after a night or two in hospital. I suppose the medical staff must know what is best, but it seems a harsh regime to me.

I was determined not to reveal to Lucy just how unwell I have been lately. There is no doubt that the cancer is progressing steadily and relentlessly, despite the efforts of the excellent oncology department. I am dogged by nausea and lack of appetite, and have been unable to eat much. Increasingly I notice how painfully my hip bones protrude against the hard surface of the bath – so much so that I have taken to having showers instead.

I am able to control the level of analgesia myself to some extent, but am reaching a point of pain that even the strongest medication is unable to eradicate completely. One of the most distressing symptoms, I find, is the extreme fatigue. My energy levels, both mental and physical, are plunging. But at the same time I sleep badly, waking frequently and rarely able to sleep at all beyond four or five in the morning.

It is clear to me that time is running out. I am aware that my life is approaching its final stages, yet I feel so fortunate that the major "milestone" that I had prayed to be able to reach – the birth of Lucy and Guy's child – has now passed by safely. For some time I had been telling myself that if I could just live long enough to experience that joyous event – and, if it is to be, their wedding in a few months' time – I would be quite content to pass on to the next world, if indeed one exists, which I have always considered doubtful.

But despite the relief of living long enough to see my first grandchild (all right, I know others might not agree that Milo is truly my grandson), I am still anxious. Not about death itself – I have no fear of dying, which surely cannot be very different from falling asleep – but about leaving Lucy. Yes, I am reassured by Guy's presence, but I can't help worrying about Lucy's state of mind.

First, there was the whole distressing business of her name. I was so thankful that Guy and Cassie helped her to decide that she should remain "Lucy" – the person she has been for as long as she can remember. I thought it best not to communicate any opinion of my own to Lucy herself, but it was such a relief when she decided in the end to retain her own true name.

Of course I couldn't bear the thought of her returning to "Stacy", as if the last twenty-three years had not happened. Perhaps they *should* not have happened as they did, but she was formed into the person she is by those years – and by me – and that person is no longer Stacy, but *Lucy*. I was thankful that even Cassie agreed that a change of name could have been damaging at this time when Lucy appears so "psychologically vulnerable", as Cassie described her.

She is indeed worryingly agitated and appears dreadfully "stressed" all the time. Years ago the word "stress" was scarcely mentioned. Nowadays everyone seems to complain bitterly about how stressed they are – by their work, their boss, relationships, concerns about money, the behaviour of their children, the politics of the world, and so on and so on. I find it most tiresome.

Even so, while it is not a concept I have previously considered helpful, I can see that the word does apply to Lucy's current state. I had thought she would make a cheerful and calm mother, and at first it seemed just so, despite her exhaustion following the birth. Increasingly, following her return home with Milo, she has become anxious and preoccupied with details of the baby's care. She fusses over minor symptoms such as wind, or the slightest of rashes, despite the health visitor assuring her that these are quite normal in a young baby.

When I have seen how tired Lucy becomes and have offered to relieve her of Milo; to hold him, rock him, or take him out in his pram for a while in order to let her rest, she has become fretful and agitated, insisting that only she can comfort him. She is inclined to become tearful at innocent comments regarding the baby, interpreting them as criticisms of her care. Had these observations of Lucy's behaviour been mine alone, I might have dismissed them as my own excessive anxiety – but Guy is equally concerned. I am deeply worried about her.

Chapter Fifty-Three

Lucy

I'm so tired – so, so tired. I wish I could sleep, but it's dangerous. I have to watch him, keep him safe. They expect to take him from me, as if I can't look after him. I'm his *MOTHER*! It's my job. Can't they see that? If I can't comfort and protect him, who can? Even Guy doesn't always seem to realise. Today he put Milo – sleeping helplessly – on Alison's lap.

'Give him to me,' I said.

'He's fine, sweetheart,' Guy said. 'Let Alison hold him for a few minutes.'

He just doesn't understand. None of them do.

'I want him. I need to hold him. Give him to me,' I repeated, getting angry.

Guy sighed and looked at me with a shrug.

'Of course you want to hold him, dear,' Alison said. 'Here you are. Go to Mummy, Milo.'

She passed him to me. I buried my face in Milo's warm tummy.

Sometimes he's restless. I try to calm him. It worries me if he's restless; I should be able to soothe him. I'm his mother. Sometimes he writhes about and doesn't feed well. He's got to feed properly or he won't grow, he won't thrive. The health visitor watches and watches me. She says he's doing well. She doesn't seem to notice how he turns his head away from my breast. I know some babies fail to thrive. Inadequate mothers have babies who fail to thrive. Then they take the babies away.

I need to protect Milo. There are so many dangers. The others don't always see the danger. I'm so afraid of losing him. The world can be so very dangerous for a small baby. The others don't realise how dangerous it is for a helpless little baby. Someone may try to take him away. The front doorbell rang today. Of course I grabbed Milo and ran upstairs to hide him, to keep him safe.

Guy kept saying, 'It's OK, Lucy, it's just the postman.'

Little do they know! If I don't protect Milo, anything could happen. They have no idea.

So when the bell rang I quickly took Milo into our bedroom and grabbed the sewing scissors from the drawer. There's a space in the corner of the room beside the wardrobe. You can't be seen there, not unless someone comes right into the room, right up to the corner – and then there are the scissors to help protect us. I wrapped Milo in the big woollen shawl and crouched with him in the corner. I gave him my finger to suck to keep him quiet. We stayed there a long time. Milo fell asleep. After a while Guy came up.

'It's all right, Lucy,' he said softly. 'You're quite safe, both of you. Come downstairs. There's no one here, just us. You're perfectly safe.'

Maybe this time.

Chapter Fifty-Four

Alison

The health visitor knows how worried we are about Lucy. She is visiting every day. Guy says Lucy has become moody and withdrawn. The health visitor feels she has become deeply depressed. She asked Guy to take Lucy to the GP as soon as possible. He managed to arrange an appointment this afternoon. Apparently Lucy sat clutching Milo close to her, refusing to look at the doctor, or respond to her, but simply looking terrified.

It seems there is now some talk of Lucy being taken to a special mother and baby psychiatric unit. I am so desperately sad to see her like this, and search my brain constantly for some solution; something I could do to help my poor girl; anything.

I decided the first thing I needed to do was to return to Newcastle, and leave Lucy and Guy to sort out their problems together. I told them I needed to be at home for a few days to attend medical appointments – which was true – and that then I would return to Edinburgh.

On the train back home I began to mull over the past few days, and just how desperate was Lucy's state. I was determined to do what I could to help her, but hadn't revealed to Lucy and Guy the various options I had considered. There were not many possibilities. Suicide was one. Once in Newcastle I collected my latest prescriptions from the local chemist. They included several boxes of strong painkillers, bearing strict warnings not to exceed the stated dose. These instructions were always emphatically reinforced by the pharmacist.

At home I laid the pills out in serried ranks on the kitchen table, and estimated how many I would need to ensure a fatal dose. Suicide clearly had certain possible benefits. My death would ensure that Lucy and Guy need not consider me in any of their future choices. It would also enable any lingering doubts in Lucy's mind, however erroneous, that I might have the intention of abducting *her* baby, to be removed. It would free Lucy to develop a relationship with her birth mother and family, without needing to concern herself with my feelings in the matter.

However, I felt that these positives were counteracted by several negative outcomes that taking my own life might impose. Firstly, the circumstances of my death from suicide – whatever method I chose – would inevitably cause shock and distress, not simply for the unfortunate person who might find my body, but to a small number of people who cared for me, especially Lucy herself. This distress struck me as unnecessary, as in any case my natural demise was likely to occur in the very near future anyway.

Secondly, it would draw attention onto myself, which was the last thing I wished to do at this time.

Thirdly, it would appear a cowardly act, and one that denied members of Lucy's birth family – such as Shelley perhaps, or even Lucy herself – a sense of rightful justice. Finally, I had a strong feeling of unfinished business, which I decided I must attend to while I still could.

After much reflection, I put my medication away in the medicine chest, and turned my mind to other possible courses of action. It was clear to me that there was only one thing I could do that might have some beneficial effect. That was to go to Riddlesfield myself and speak to Shelley. While I was nervous at the prospect of meeting her, perhaps I could get her to accept that I was doing this for Lucy's sake, and that we could present a united front, to convince Lucy that we both feel the same, we two "mothers".

In other words, that Lucy is an excellent mother – and that all will be well with Milo. There were no guarantees that it would do any good – and Shelley might simply reject me entirely. She might even attack me. That would be an understandable reaction – *but I had to try something.* I felt Lucy's mental condition was becoming critical.

As it happened, before I could put the second part of my proposed arrangements into practice, I was overtaken by terrifying events.

288

Chapter Fifty-Five

At about ten-thirty on my second evening home, the telephone rang. I had just had a shower and was in my nightclothes, making a cup of camomile tea. It was unusual for me to receive calls at such a late hour. Even the infuriating recorded advertising messages tended to come during the daytime. I approached the phone with a strange sense of foreboding.

'Yes?'

'Alison, it's Guy.'

I could hear immediately from his voice that all was not well.

'Guy ... what's the matter? Has something happened?'

'Alison, are you on your own?'

'Yes ...' I said, my heart starting to pound.

'Listen. I want you to go and sit down. Will you do that straight away?'

Now I was really frightened. I sat on a kitchen chair clutching my mug of tea. 'I'm sitting, Guy ...' I whispered.

'OK. I'll try to tell you everything that's happened. Please just let me finish before you ask questions or interrupt.'

I heard him take a deep, juddering breath.

'As you know, Lucy's not been herself lately. I know you've been worried about her, as I have.'

I mouthed "yes" silently.

'Well, over the past couple of days she's got worse. More detached, more withdrawn. She was fantasising constantly that someone was going to steal Milo. She believed someone was watching the house, waiting for an opportunity to kidnap him. No amount of my reassurances made any difference – she was absolutely convinced. Every time the doorbell rang she picked the baby up and ran upstairs with him to hide. I'd find her crouched somewhere, hugging him, absolutely terrified ...'

I heard a sob in his voice.

'Oh Guy, I'm so sorry ...' Then I remembered he had asked me not to interrupt, and stayed silent.

'The GP asked a psychiatric social worker to call, which she did the day before yesterday,' he continued. 'She's called Ruth. She's very nice, very sensitive. Ruth felt Lucy was sinking into a kind of postnatal form of psychosis. It's worse than just postnatal depression. It's rare, but ... it happens sometimes. Maybe some people are more prone to it than others. I wondered ... well ... if Lucy's early experiences might have predisposed her to this reaction.'

'Oh ...' I gasped inadvertently.

He paused. I heard him blowing his nose and taking some deep breaths.

'Anyway, there's a specialist centre for mothers and babies quite nearby, where she could get highly specialised treatment and counselling, and support in a small unit. She'd be able to keep Milo with her. I'd be able to go into the unit and be with them every day. You could come in too in a while, once she's better. They assured me she'd get better, Alison, although it might take a few weeks, or even months. Ruth said there was a place becoming vacant in a couple of days and they'd reserved it for Lucy and Milo ...'

His voice broke again.

'Well, but it's wonderful that such help is available, Guy ...' I ventured cautiously.

After a long pause, he said, 'Well, yes, but ...'

'But ...?'

'But, the thing is ... she's gone missing, Alison.'

'Missing ...?'

'Very early this morning I heard her get up. It was about five a.m. I thought she was just going to feed the baby. He sometimes wakes about that time. I must have fallen asleep again – I'm so tired. Oh, Jesus, I'll never forgive myself ...'

'Guy?'

'When I woke again, she still wasn't there, I mean, in bed. Sometimes it takes a long time to settle Milo back again ... so I got up and went to the baby's room to see what was happening. They weren't there. I searched the house, but there was no sign of them. Lucy's coat was missing and she'd taken some warm clothes and shawls for Milo, and his carrier ... and the front door was locked, but the backdoor was open.'

I gasped.

'So, what did you do?'

'I rang the police straight away, and the GP, and Ruth, and Cassie. Anyone I could think of. I was just in a total panic. I raced up and down the street looking for her and calling, but there was no sign of Lucy or Milo. The police are searching for them. They've been really good and understanding. I'm so scared, Alison. They've been missing for sixteen hours. I'm afraid she might do something silly ... like hurting herself ... or Milo.'

Cold fingers of fear wrapped themselves around my spine.

'Now, no, no ... that's not possible, Guy. I can't believe Lucy would do any such thing. That's not how I've brought her up,' I said firmly. 'If she took warm clothes, it shows she's thinking of Milo's welfare. She would never, ever do anything to harm him.'

'No, you're right. I'm just so worried about her, about both of them. Oh God, I just want her home.'

Picturing my confident, intelligent "son-out-of-law", with all his psychiatric knowledge and experience, in this desperate state of agony and doubt pained me greatly.

'You must stay strong, Guy. They'll find her, I'm sure they will. I shall take the first train I can up to Edinburgh. I'll get a taxi from the station. Stay at home, won't you, in case she comes back, or tries to contact you? I've got my mobile phone if you need to reach me.'

I put the receiver down. I was trembling from head to foot.

Chapter Fifty-Six

Lucy

We were ready. He was all snug in his carrier, wrapped up warm in his furry teddy bear suit, with the shawl tucked round him for extra protection. I slipped on my warmest coat, with its thick padding and hood. Perfect; it fitted round Milo too. I zipped it up. He would stay cosy in there against the warmth of my body, insulated from the bitterest of weather.

I took some spare nappies, together with a bottle of water and some bread and cheese, packed into a small bag. That would do for me, and Milo was still on breast milk alone, so needed nothing else. I was enough for him. I was everything he needed.

I looked out of the back door. The garden was dark and silent. Anyone could be out there, hiding in the bushes. I pulled the back door shut quietly, leaving it unlocked and crept silently through the kitchen and the passageway to the front door – I opened it and looked out into the street. The streetlamps cast soft pools of light onto the road and nearby front gardens. No movement, no sign of anyone about. My heart was thumping, Milo's heart beating rapidly against mine. But he was safe. I would protect him, keep him safe always. No one could take him. I would die rather than let anyone steal him.

I pulled the front door closed, hearing it lock with a soft click. We hurried eastwards towards the park. A cold wind was blowing. My arms around him kept him warm, peacefully sleeping. I heard the sound of a milk delivery van. It rounded the corner and stopped ahead of us. The milkman pulled two bottles out of a crate at the back and began walking up the driveway of the house to our right, the bottles clinking slightly in his grasp. He saw me.

'Morning,' he said, looking curiously at me.

'Morning,' I mumbled, and hurried on. I did not turn round.

Chapter Fifty-Seven

Alison

A part of me prayed that by the time I reached Lucy and Guy's house all would be restored to normal, that she and Milo would have returned, or been found somewhere, safe and well. Where would she go? Cassie was an obvious choice, but Guy had spoken to her. I thought about Shelley. Might Lucy have taken Milo to see her? Guy met me at the front door and immediately enveloped me in a long embrace, rather than our usual brief hug. I looked up into his face hopefully.

'No word yet,' he said, reading my expression.

'Have you tried phoning … Shelley?'

'Yes, she hasn't heard or seen anything. She's really worried too.'

He took my bag and I followed him into the kitchen. A uniformed female police officer sat at the table. Guy introduced her as Constable Bingham. He called me "Lucy's adoptive mother".

'We're searching all the likely places, anywhere familiar to Lucy, any locations with which she may have had connections. Photographs of her and the baby have been circulated in the local press, free papers and local TV stations. I know it's terrible for you all waiting for news, but it's all we can do at the moment,' said Constable Bingham. She grasped my hand. My throat constricted. I tried to clear it.

Guy made us all a cup of tea. I noticed his hands were shaking. He paced the floor.

'It's getting dark,' he said, fretfully, pausing to look out of the glass door, which led into the garden. 'I can't bear to think of them spending another night outside. It's so cold out there.'

We sat in silence most of the evening. The front doorbell rang at about eight. We all jumped in alarm and raced to the door. It was another police officer – a man this time, Constable Mason – who had come to relieve Constable Bingham. I accompanied her to the door. She clasped my arms and smiled at me.

'Try not to worry too much,' she said, her voice full of concern. 'I'm sure they'll be found soon, safe and well.' A foolish assertion.

'Thank you, Constable, but none of us can know that,' I replied.

I heated some tinned soup, but neither of us could eat more than a few spoonfuls. Constable Mason said he'd had his "tea" before starting his shift, but thanked me politely. He seemed a pleasant young man. My mind returned to the question of whether to submit myself to Shelley, and to Inspector Dempster.

Perhaps I could raise it with Constable Mason? Perhaps the police ought to know the background to assist them in their search for Lucy and Milo? We were all sitting in the kitchen. I asked Guy to accompany me to the sitting room. He looked surprised, but picked up the telephone and followed me.

'Guy, while we have this young policeman with us, I think it may be an opportunity to share with him the information about me removing Lucy from her original home and family ...'

'What?' he said incredulously.

'Well, surely the police here should be told something of Lucy's ... unusual history. They may want to contact the police in Riddlesfield. It may help them to find Lucy and Milo. I mean, what if she tried to take him there, for some reason … what if she tried to find her original home, and became lost … oh I don't know, Guy, I just feel I should admit the truth to them.'

'Absolutely not! Look, Alison, I really can't think about this right now, but I know Lucy was adamant that she didn't want to go public about it at this stage.'

'But I think …'

'It's not about what *you* think. It's about what Lucy wants. It would be terrible to start a process when she's not even here – just another thing about which she'll feel she's lost control. Promise me you won't speak to the policeman, or anyone, Alison. Our priority is finding Lucy and the baby, and for her to get better. Do you agree?'

'Yes, of course. I agree to whatever you think is best.'

'Now, it's getting late. I'm going to get you a duvet and I want you to lie down here on the sofa. You look very tired. I'll stay with the phone.'

I knew there was no point in arguing, and in truth I was exhausted. I felt sure I would not be able to settle, but shortly after lying down I slipped into a deep sleep. When I woke, dawn was showing through the curtain. I staggered into the kitchen, where Guy was sitting slumped over the table, still clutching the phone. Constable Mason was sitting quietly in the corner. Guy sat up as I entered. His eyes were deeply shadowed. A dark growth of stubble covered his chin and hollow cheeks. He looked worn out.

'I'll make us some tea or coff—' I began.

At that moment, the phone rang. Guy leapt to his feet and picked it up. He pressed the speaker on.

'Hello, Guy? It's Cassie. Lucy's here with me. She's quite safe and Milo's fine too …'

Guy dropped the phone and collapsed on the floor, sobbing. He covered his face with his hands and leaned his back against the kitchen cupboard. Constable Mason and I jumped up and rushed to him.

'Guy ... Guy? Are you there? Did you hear me?' Cassie's voice filled the kitchen.

He picked the phone up and took some deep breaths. 'I'm here, Cassie. Thank God, thank God ...'

'Guy, Lucy wants to come home. I'm making her some hot food just now, and then I'll bring them home ...'

'I can come and ...' began Guy.

'No. You stay at home. Let the police know, and anyone else who needs to be told. We'll be with you in about an hour.'

'Oh Jesus ... thank you, Cassie, thank you ... Alison's here too.'

'Is she? OK, Guy, but I think it might be a good idea if Alison went home ... if she wasn't there. It's just that Lucy's very confused, very anxious about Milo. Maybe Alison could come back when Lucy's feeling better ...?'

Guy looked at me, and I nodded my head vigorously to show I had heard and understood. It hurt to know I was thought to represent any sort of threat, but Lucy was clearly unwell, and delusional.

'And, Guy?' Cassie's voice continued.

'Yes?'

'We spoke about the centre ... the mother and baby unit? Lucy's very, very scared, but she agrees it's a good idea, for a while. She says she'll go tomorrow with Milo, if you take them. OK?'

298

Chapter Fifty-Eight

2008

After Lucy and Milo had been in the specialist unit for six weeks, Guy suggested I return to visit them there. Lucy was already much better, much stronger than before. Guy had kept me informed regularly of her progress.

It had touched me deeply to hear him talk of his relief at being reunited with Lucy and the baby, when Cassie had brought them home after their disappearance.

'I was totally beside myself to see them here, safe and sound,' he had told me on the phone. 'It was so wonderful to be able to hug them both – I just didn't want to let them go, ever again!'

I could hear his voice breaking as tears had flowed – tears of joy, I suppose. He was never one with "macho" inhibitions about showing his feelings.

* * *

Guy met me at the station and we drove to the unit. It was a low-level modern development, built on the site of a demolished, former mental hospital. The building was light and airy, with pleasant gardens, where a few young women sat chatting, or playing with infants. The entire unit and its gardens were surrounded by a tall security fence. I had been surprised to see Guy ring at the entrance and announce who we were through an intercom. After a few moments a member of staff came and checked Guy's identity card through the glass window of the door.

'This is Lucy's adoptive mother, Alison Brown,' he said, and we were admitted.

Guy showed me into Lucy's room, where she was playing with Milo on the bed. A nurse sat near the door. Lucy got up, smiled, and embraced me – what joy. She looked pale and wan, but something of her old spark had returned. She suggested we all went to one of the small sitting rooms, and that I could give Milo his bottle if I wanted.

'I would love to, Lucy, but aren't you breastfeeding any longer?'

'I've had to give up because of the anti-psychotic medication I'm on. It's not safe for the baby.'

It surprised me to hear her talk so openly of her condition. While Guy went to make Milo's bottle and some tea for us, Lucy talked readily of how ill she had been.

'I was so afraid. I don't know why, but I was so sure Milo would be taken away, that someone wanted to steal him. I thought someone was watching the house, waiting for an opportunity. That's why I had to take him away, to keep him safe. I left the back door open... to make it look as though we'd gone out that way, but actually I crept out of the front door. I didn't know where to go or what to do. We wandered about for hours. It was so cold. We went into department stores and cafés to try to keep warm. I found women's toilets where I could feed Milo without anyone noticing. After some time though, Milo was getting unhappy, he was crying, and I was so tired. So we headed for Cassie's house.'

'You poor girl.'

'I'm so sorry to have worried Guy, and you. Cassie explained that it wasn't true, that no one wanted to steal Milo. She told me my head was playing tricks on me, but at first it was hard to believe – I was so frightened.'

'Well, you'd been under a lot of stress, and I know that was mainly my fault. It's not surprising things got a bit mixed up in your mind.'

'I'm sorry, Mum ... I mean Alison. I didn't want to worry everyone. I was just trying to do my best to look after Milo.'

'I know you didn't, dearest girl. No one looks after Milo better than you ... and I would never do anything to harm him or you in any way ... not ever.'

Now I was crying too, and poor little Milo, disturbed by the emotional atmosphere, joined in with loud wails.

Guy came in with Milo's bottle, and our tea. It was a great delight for me to hold his sturdy little body in my arms, and feel him relax as he drank hungrily, while gazing up into my face. His little hand reached up to touch my blouse and my face. I was overwhelmed by love for him, as long ago, I had been for his mother.

* * *

I learned that Lucy was being treated for what Guy called "her disturbed thoughts and beliefs" with a combination of close and understanding care, counselling, and some appropriate medication, all in a safe and sensitive environment. I was so, so thankful a place was available to her in this wonderful, specialised facility, now at such a critical time.

The severity of Lucy's problems highlighted to me just what

a burden I must have placed on her, from the moment I took her from outside her original home as a tiny child. I have never been a great believer in the "subconscious" – yet now I wonder whether the trauma of her experiences in infancy – the sudden deprivation of her birth mother – may somehow have contributed to her recent problems, when she herself has become a mother.

I will not try to excuse my actions, but I did genuinely believe that by taking her from such an impoverished life and family, I was providing her with improved circumstances. Instead, it appears that, unbeknown to me, and certainly unintentionally, I may have been imposing a nightmare on the one person I have loved, and continue to love, most in the world – my dearest Lucy. It had been clear to me for some time that I had to take action to relieve her of this burden – now I explained to Lucy and Guy just what I planned to do.

'It's made me so happy to see how much better, happier, and more settled you are – both of you … and I am infinitely thankful for the wonderful care you've received here. But I'm also aware that you should never have had to go through such trauma,' I began.

'Well, let's not go back over old ground,' said Guy. 'Let's look to the future …'

'That's exactly what I mean to do, Guy. Your future and Lucy's – and little Milo's. The time has come for me to acknowledge my part in the past, and to "bow out" now.'

'What do you mean?' Lucy asked, her face drawn with anxiety.

'I mean that the time has come for me first, to visit Shelley, to admit to all the wrongs I have done …' Lucy, wide-eyed, opened her mouth to object, but I raised my hand to silence her.

'Then, once I have told Shelley the full truth – whatever her reaction – I intend to seek out Inspector Dempster and give myself up to him. Please understand that I have no fear of the consequences; I feel it is right for everyone to know exactly what happened, what I did.'

302

Lucy looked at Guy and then said, 'Don't you want to wait until one or both of us can go with you?'

'No, my dearest. I want you and Guy to be together with your beautiful son, and for you to concentrate on getting completely better. It was me who inflicted these problems on you, and it should be me who resolves whatever I can by being honest about what I did. I shall return to Newcastle immediately – I want to relieve you of having to consider the welfare of anyone other than yourselves and your precious Milo at this time.'

The room echoed with their silence.

'If you're absolutely sure about this, Alison, I'll take you back to the station,' Guy said.

'No, Guy, stay here with Lucy and Milo, but I'd be grateful if you would call me a taxi.'

* * *

Within a week I was on my way to Riddlesfield. I had confided my plan to Fiona. I knew Lucy had spoken to her, and to Susan and Mike too. It had upset me greatly that Susan had felt so let down and angry with me, although her reaction was quite understandable. Yet Susan was the one friend I was convinced would always stand by me. She had always professed total loyalty.

Clearly I was not a very good judge of character. It had been all Lucy and Guy could do to persuade her not to go straight to the police, which just goes to show, that even those you regard as close friends, do not always conform to the expected. It confirmed my view that you can rely on no one but yourself, particularly in extremis.

By contrast, Fiona, to whom I had never been so close, had been kind and understanding. I was particularly touched that she had even offered to accompany me to Riddlesfield. In fact, she had advised me in the strongest terms not to proceed with my plan on my own.

'Surely if ever there's a time for needing a friend, this is it? Have you really thought about what might happen, Alison?'

'I have thought of little else these last few days.'

'Lucy's birth family may react very strongly. They may even become violent. You can't be on your own.'

'They would be quite justified in attacking me, verbally if not actually physically. Thank you for your support, Fiona. I really appreciate your offer, but this is something I must do on my own.'

Chapter Fifty-Nine

May 2008

How different was this day from that damp and gloomy afternoon when I first arrived in the town long ago; nearly a quarter of a century previously, in fact. As before, I came by train. Last time, I had stepped out of the station into the chill of a late winter's afternoon. This time the air shimmered with spring sunshine, casting a glow on the stone buildings, giving them a soft warmth, so unlike the unremitting grey I remembered.

Riddlesfield was still far from a prosperous town, but the local authority seemed to have made an effort to improve the urban environment of the city centre, which had been transformed by a neat pedestrian shopping area. Churchill Square bristled with cafés among the "boutique" shops; a brave attempt to emulate a continental atmosphere, perhaps, with people sipping coffee at outside tables and chairs, though little could be done to alter the bracing Riddlesfield breeze. Paved walkways led from the square into a park-like area, with grass and flower beds, and recently planted silver birch trees. Children kicked balls and sped around on scooters, while older people relaxed on wooden benches.

The last time I came, I recalled, I had walked through the square from the station and straight into the dreary and dilapidated town centre, towards the adjoining streets of old terraced houses in Frainham.

This time I hailed a taxi by the park. The driver put my bag on the back seat, and sped me towards Moorside, a pleasant suburb of predominantly council houses. From the range of different front door styles and colours, and the varied alterations to the front gardens, it was clear that many were now privately owned.

I had memorised Shelley's address from what Lucy and Guy had told me, following their first visit there. Belside Crescent was a long, curving street, consisting mainly of modest, neat semi-detached houses. Most were painted white or cream, with an occasional non-conformist pale pink or green. I asked the taxi driver to drop me at the top of the crescent, so that I could approach the house on foot and in my own time.

'You gonna manage your bag, pet?' he asked, looking at me doubtfully.

'Yes, thank you. It's not too heavy, and it's got wheels.'

I identified on which side Shelley's house, number 34, would be. I walked slowly, shakily, keeping to the opposite pavement alongside the odd house numbers. I was glad of my walking stick. Anyone looking out would see nothing more interesting than a thin, elderly woman making her unsteady way, I mused. No one would pay me much attention; I was almost invisible. I'd always been almost invisible.

Every few houses, I paused to rest, get my breath and lean against a gateway, or sit for a few moments on a low wall. It wasn't far now. I came to number 43 on my side, opposite 38. I sat on the wall of 43. Just ahead I could see what had to be number 34. I trembled uncontrollably. All was quiet. A middle-aged man pushed a pram past me in the direction from which I had come. He gave me a polite nod as he passed. Two teenage girls walked past me and smiled. Someone closed a window upstairs at number 41. I took some deep breaths. No use sitting here for ever, I told myself, better go over the road and ring the bell.

Just as I started to raise myself, a van drew up on my side of the road, directly opposite house number 34. It was a dirty van, with one or two dents and scrapes, but otherwise looked business-like enough. On the side of the van were printed the words "R.A. Watts, Plumbing and Bathroom Services" in large black letters. I knew the name Watts, but it took my tired brain a few moments to process this information.

A stocky, youngish man got out of the vehicle. He had light brown hair and wore a white T-shirt, with some design I could not make out, and the long, camouflage-style shorts young men seem to wear these days. He spoke briefly through the open window of the van to someone inside. I stared at him as he strode across the road and approached the front door of number 34. He appeared to ring the bell, and then turned around and began to walk away again, like a mischievous child ringing a doorbell and then running away.

'Dad!' called a child's high voice from inside the van.

The man – I had realised by now that he must be Lucy's brother, Ryan – walked back towards the van.

'Coming, Lola,' he said.

A dark-haired young woman emerged from the passenger door of the vehicle. She stood and stretched her spine in a curve, her hands clasped on the small of her back. I could see she was heavily pregnant. Recalling Guy and Lucy's account of the family, I concluded the young woman must be Ryan's wife. I stood up and watched as Ryan opened the driver's door, scooped out a little girl and put her down on the road, holding on to her hand. The child was small and slight, with fair hair. She wore a pale yellow dress. My heart began thumping. I jolted forwards in shock.

'Lucy ...?' I said, clutching my stick and almost falling as I staggered closer. I took a few tottering steps towards them. 'Lucy,' I repeated.

Ryan turned around with a smile. 'Nah ...' he began, looking at me, 'she's called Lola, not Lucy ...' The smile faded on his face, overtaken by a look of puzzlement, and then the beginnings of enlightenment.

'I Lola,' said the little girl.

'Fuckin' hell,' Ryan said, staring at me, horror-struck. Thought processes, questions and deep frowns alternated, traversing his face, like the shadows of clouds drifting across a field on a sunny day.

'You're her! You're that woman, ain't ya?' he blurted, violently nodding his head, like a puppet.

He bent to pick up the child again, with stiff, jerky movements. He clutched her to him as if he was afraid I would snatch her and run away with her. The young woman had waddled around the van and approached us now. She held out her hands and took the child from Ryan, who stood limply, staring at me. The little girl wriggled free and skipped towards the front garden. I could hardly take my eyes off her, so unsettling was her resemblance to the infant Lucy.

'Ryan? What's going on? Who is she?' asked the young woman, looking from him to me and back again.

He lurched towards me, his fists clenched. I stood still, unflinching, waiting for a blow, not from bravery, but because I was incapable of moving. He stood before me, bending his face inches from mine, contorted with rage.

'What are you doing, Ryan? What's wrong?' repeated his wife. The child, standing on the front door step, had turned to watch us. She began to whimper.

'She's ... she's ... the ... one ... she ... stole her ...' The words burst out of Ryan one by one with each stertorous breath. His

308

face was so close I could see beads of sweat oozing from the pores of his forehead. His wild eyes bored into me. I could feel his breath on my face, his spit, his hatred, his fury. His fists still hovered over me, trembling.

'Yes,' I whispered. 'I'm sorry … I'm so, so sorry …'

'Ryan!' An older woman had come out of number 34. She took hold of the child's hand and stood shouting from the gate.

'Ryan! You stop that! Let her be.'

Ryan, looking down like a scolded small boy, withdrew his threatening hands and clasped his head, his shoulders hunched and shaking. I felt a surge of sympathy for him. My own head felt strange. I wobbled and began to topple to my left side. The young woman lurched towards me and supported me, holding my arm. She held me firm with amazing strength.

'Shelley, who the hell is she? What's going on?' she asked, looking at me as if I were a strange, foreign specimen, one she had never seen before.

Of course, the older woman, I had realised by now, was Shelley. She looked me up and down. Her face, revealing no emotion, had a bland, almost resigned expression.

'This is Alison …' she said flatly. She gave me a questioning look. 'She's the woman what stole our baby, our little Stacy. Kept her these last twenty years or more. Am I right?'

Her eyes swept over me, challenging me to deny her accusation. She started to walk towards the house. I noticed she had a slightly lumbering gait, although she was no longer as heavy as I remembered her from the television appearances of long before. She stopped by the front door and half turned.

'Well come on, woman, don't just stand there. You might as well come in.'

Ryan's wife, still holding me up, gaped at me.

Shelley clucked in irritation. 'Give over, Brenda,' she said. 'What you waiting for? Just bring 'er in, will you.'

We made an awkward procession; Shelley leading the way, Brenda and I shuffling after her in silence together, with the little girl Lola-Lucy prancing around us. Ryan, grimacing – as if in extreme agony – followed at the rear.

Chapter Sixty

Once inside, my nerves calmed. We sat in the sitting room Lucy and Guy had described to me, with its large sofas and glass coffee table. The child Lola played with a plastic kitchen set on the floor in one corner. A small circle of dolls and stuffed animals had each been served with miniature plastic crockery. Every now and then Lola brought a tiny cup and saucer to one of the adults and offered it to them.

'Want tea, Nan?' she trilled, thrusting a pink cup up to Shelley's face. Shelley took the cup and smiled at the child.

'Yeah, darlin'. Two sugars please.'

Lola approached me next.

'You want tea, Lady?'

'The lady doesn't want none, darlin', said Shelley, glaring at me. 'Leave 'er be.'

Brenda had been given the task of making adult teas. She could be heard clattering in the kitchen next door. Among the rest of us there was a tension, an atmosphere of proceedings not having started yet, but being about to – and that therefore there was no point in beginning to talk. We sat in silence, regarding one another across the inflammable space of the room. Brenda carried in a tray with four mugs, a small plastic cup of squash, a jug of milk

311

and a bowl of sugar. She handed them round, beginning with me.

'D'you take milk and sugar, um ... Alison?'

'Just milk, thank you.'

By unspoken agreement, Shelley was in charge of leading the conversation.

'So how's Stacy doing in that hospital place, bless her? Her and the baby?'

'Stacy ...? Oh, she was doing very well, when I saw her last week. Guy goes in for a few hours every day. Little Milo is thriving. He seems to have adapted well to the bottle ...'

I faltered. Was I talking too much?

'I thought she was breastfeeding?' Shelley said, frowning.

'She was, but unfortunately she had to stop because of the medications she's on ...'

'Poor kid, going through all this upset.' She fixed me with a hostile stare. 'How long's she got to stay in there?'

'They haven't said for certain. It depends on the progress she makes. They thought for a few weeks anyway.'

Shelley sipped her tea. Her eyes scarcely left me.

'And you, Alison? Why have you come here? What do you want?'

How strange was this situation, sitting drinking tea with the family from whom I had stolen their youngest child. How to answer her question, to encapsulate why I was there? Why had I exposed myself to this ordeal? Why had I exposed them to *me*, or myself to them? Why *was* I there? I leaned forwards, my cup rattling wildly on its saucer. I steadied it with my other hand and put it carefully on the coffee table.

'Well, I suppose I feel the need to apologise ... I know it's futile ... it's stupid to try to say sorry for something so terrible, so enormous ... I ... I want to try to explain what I did ... but I don't expect understanding from you, and certainly not forgiveness. I can't begin to know how you must hate me and resent me for what I did.'

'No, that you can't,' Ryan snarled.

Their eyes were all fixed on me. No one else spoke. I began a stuttering, inarticulate account; I told them of my early life with Mother, the difficulties I had experienced at school and university, about my longing for a baby, and my great sorrow at Mother's death. I described how by chance I had found the grave of little Lucy Brown in Nottingham, and how at that point, I decided to take a child, a child who I thought needed "rescuing" from her circumstances. I explained how I realised *now* that my idea of poverty and disadvantage, which I had used to justify my action, was stereotypical and wrong in every way. I stopped and looked around, slightly breathless, mulling over how to continue.

'So, this is all about you, Alison,' Shelley said slowly. 'Sure, you've got all the fine words. There's no way I can talk like you ... but really you haven't begun to say why you've *really* come here.'

'No, you're quite right, ...er ... Shelley. This isn't about me – it shouldn't be – it's about *Lucy* ...' I paused, aware that their looks had become more hostile again.

'I'm so sorry, but I can't think of her as *Stacy*. I know she's Stacy to you, of course she is, but she's always been Lucy to me ...' Pausing again, I fretted about the inadequacy of words.

'What I did should never have happened, no, never – but ... but it did ...'

'It didn't *happen*, Alison. You *did* it. You made it happen,' Shelley said, her face rigid with anger.

'Yes, yes, I did it. I never should have done it, but I did. Stacy became Lucy, and that's who she is now. She's been trying desperately to do the right thing for both of us mothers ... I mean, you, Shelley, and me ...'

I heard Shelley's sharp intake of breath, sensed the rage in Ryan's stare. The nerve of referring to myself as her mother. I ploughed on as best I could.

'Poor girl ... trying to be both Lucy and Stacy for our sakes has been tearing her apart, making her ill. That is entirely my fault. I accept that.'

Shelley nodded her head slowly, as if she agreed wholeheartedly with this last statement.

'What I'm trying to say … is that I should never have stolen Lucy from you. Even though I loved her deeply, and I think she came to love me, *she should never have been mine*. I hadn't realised it at the time, but I can see it now. Lucy should have been brought up with *you*, her true mother, with Ryan as her brother, and all of your family – her family. Had that been her childhood, I'm sure she would have grown up a happier and more secure person.' I took some gulps of my tea and continued.

'I can never undo the terrible wrong that I did, but perhaps I can try to repair some of the damage …'

'How the hell d'you think you can do that, now, after all these years?' spat Ryan bitterly.

'No, I can't, not completely. What I did can't be undone. You're right to be angry. All I can do, and will do, is to "bow out" now. Look, I'm not asking for any sympathy, but I think you must all know that I have a … terminal illness.'

Shelley and Ryan nodded their heads, while Brenda looked at them both.

'The thing is, I won't be here much longer, perhaps only a month or two. Maybe that's a good thing – I'd understand if perhaps you feel glad … but it's going to be hard for Lucy. She's going to need you, all of you, during the next period, and for the rest of her life. She has her wonderful husband-to-be, Guy, and now she has her beautiful baby Milo … but …'

'Aye, he's a good lad, is Guy,' said Shelley. 'We like him a lot. And yes, we know about you being ill, and … well … for all you done a terrible thing … I'm sorry. Not for you – I'm sorry for Stacy's sake, like.'

I smiled. My throat constricted and tears sprang to my eyes. I swallowed again and again, struggling to control my voice.

'Thank you. I'm fond of Guy too, very fond. And I trust him to be there for Lucy, but she needs more than just him to restore her sense of who she is. She needs to know that the family she was born into, the family she came from, accept her and will always be there for her.'

'There's never been any doubt about that. Of course we'll be there for her,' said Ryan. 'She'll always be one of us. She's our lass.'

'Yeah. Even though you've brought her up sort of ... posh,' said Shelley, 'I felt a bond the minute I set eyes on her. There was no distance, no strangeness. There's no side to her ... she's not proud, our Stacy, our Lucy. You don't need to have no worries about us being there for Lucy. Yes, and you know what? I'm going to call her Lucy from now on, for all it takes a bit of getting used to. I'm going to call her Lucy, not for you, but for *her* – 'cos the last thing I want is her getting herself all mixed up and upset about who she is. Of course she's been thinking of herself as Lucy for all these years – she didn't know no different. She's going to have to stick with it, and so are we.'

She said these last words loudly and emphatically, glaring around at Ryan and Brenda, as if daring them to challenge her.

Ryan leaned forwards, shaking his head, and sighed. 'Aye,' he said, 'mebbe.'

'Thank you for that, Shelley, and Ryan too – I'm so grateful to all of you for your understanding, which I had no right to ask for or expect, no right at all.'

Shelley stood up and paced between the coffee table and the largest settee for a moment.

'Never you mind being grateful – my understanding's not for you! Let me tell you something ... *Alison*. Although you took my precious child, my Stacy, who I've cried for all these years, even though you done that evil, wicked thing, even though it was like you stuck a dagger in me heart ... in some ways, you done me a favour too ...'

Ryan stared at her in puzzlement. I was confused too. Perhaps I had misheard her?

'Yeah, I wouldn't wish losing a child on my worst enemy. It nearly killed me. I didn't want to go on living, and you never gave me, or us, a single thought. But I'll tell you how, in one way, it done me a favour. Losing our Stacy, or Lucy, was what made me take a proper look at myself and change the path I took in me life. If I hadn't have lost her at that point ... I reckon I'd have ... sunk. I might have ended up in prison, like your dad. I might have drunk meself to death. I might have – I'm almost sure I *would* have – lost *all* me children, including you, Ryan.'

Ryan, weeping freely now, walked around the back of the sofa and put his arms around his mother.

'But ...' she continued, 'let me tell you something else ... *Alison*. You had Lucy – *my* baby – as she growed into a toddler and a little girl, and then a schoolgirl. You had her for all the years of her childhood. You had her as a teenager and a young woman – up to now in fact. You *stole* all those years from me and me family. But you know what? I feel sorry for you – 'cos you're not going to have her much longer, are you? You'll not see her and Guy married. You'll not see Lucy have another baby. You'll not see Milo go to school or get to be a teenager, or grow into a young man, nor any other children they have. You'll not see Lucy become a mature woman. She'll not keep you company when you're a right old woman, because you're not going to get much older. All that part of Lucy and her life is for me, and for us. It's not for you. You'll have none of it.'

I sat bleakly, unable to speak, as I absorbed all she had said, knowing it was true, knowing I deserved it. I nodded.

Brenda took this as a natural break in the difficult conversation. She began to gather the tea things and put them on the tray.

'Shall I make us another cup, Shelley?'

'Aye, go on, pet.'

'Um … there is another reason I came to Riddlesfield today – and in fact, another favour I need to ask of you,' I said.

Brenda stopped in her tracks, clutching the tray of used tea mugs. Everyone looked at me expectantly.

'Fuckin' hell … another *favour*? You mean as well as keeping our Stacy the last twenty-odd years? Never mind sodding tea then!' Ryan said. 'If you've got more to say, we're going to need summat stronger than that before you start over. What have you got, Mam?'

'There's that vodka left over from Christmas – that do? Go on then, Brenda pet, take that lot out to the kitchen. Then go and look for the bottle in the bottom cupboard next to the fridge. And the glasses are at the top.'

Chapter Sixty-One

By the time Ryan had served everyone with a generous half-tumbler of vodka, the atmosphere in the room had shifted. He had ignored my tentative attempts to limit the amount poured into my glass. Nor did he react when I mumbled plaintively about never having tried vodka before.

'There's a first time for everything, Alison,' he said with a grim smile.

I couldn't read his tone. Was his remark meant ironically? I'd always had trouble with irony. His expression seemed not altogether unfriendly either. Was it possible his anger was now spent?

We sat quietly for a few minutes, sipping our drinks, perhaps fatigued by the strain of our previous engagement with one another. It didn't take long for the vodka to course through my body. I pictured the alcohol as a hot, raging torrent, constricted by the confines of my arteries, forcing its way onwards to the furthest reaches of my brain and limbs; softening my muscles, releasing the words that swarmed through my mind. It gave me the courage to embark on my next announcement.

'The thing is … I'm going to hand myself in to the police,' I said.

All eyes turned to me.

'Yeah, well, that's not needing any favours then,' said Ryan, in his previous hostile tone, "cos if you *weren't* gonna go to the police yerself, I'd 'a taken you there, an' no mistake.'

'Just think on,' said Shelley. 'Does Lucy know what you're planning? 'Cos last time she talked to us, she still wanted to keep it all quiet, for now, like.'

'Aye, and look where it's got her – made her right ill, keeping it all inside,' said Ryan.

'It's true, Shelley … you're both right. Lucy couldn't face the truth emerging. She couldn't face the trouble that would follow … for me. But, as *you* say, Ryan, trying to protect me, while dealing with the emotions resulting from what I did – well, it's torn her apart, poor girl. It's led to her breakdown. Concealing the truth has caused a lot of problems. It's gone on long enough.'

'Aye, maybe, and at least she has Guy to support her.'

'You going to the police – mightn't *that* be very hard for Lucy, very upsetting for her, like?' said Brenda, contributing for the first time.

'It might, but I think it's got to be done. I will continue to assure her it's what I want.'

'You do know, you'll likely get put away, for a long time,' said Ryan. 'I mean, 'til you …'

'Until I die? I realise that. I'm quite prepared for it.'

I glanced at my small case in the corner of the room. Everyone was quietly thoughtful for a few minutes. I was the first to break the silence.

'Lucy has had some communication with Inspector Dempster. She wrote to him – anonymously – some years ago and again more recently. He's the only one who has direct knowledge of the … of the situation as it occurred.'

'He's a good man, is Inspector Dempster, and his wife's canny too. Barbara, they call her. But you know he retired a while back. He was a Chief Superintendent at the finish,' Shelley said.

'I guessed he would have retired, but I still thought I'd prefer to give myself up to him, rather than to a complete stranger. I believe you've had some contact with him over the years, Shelley?'

'Aye, I have.'

'So, do you know where he lives?'

'Yes, I do.'

'Well, I would like to go to see him at his house.'

'I've got his phone number. Shouldn't you ring him first?'

'I'd rather just turn up and let him respond naturally. Ryan, would you be prepared to drive me over there?'

'I'd be happy as Larry to see you arrested ...'

'Ryan, that's enough now,' said Shelley.

'When d'you want us to take yer?'

'Now, please.'

* * *

Ryan parked his van in a tree-lined street of large semi-detached Edwardian houses. I hadn't realised such an area existed in Riddlesfield. From our position, opposite the entrance, the house could only partly be seen, screened as it was by tall trees and shrubs, but an imposing front door was just visible at the end of a short, curving drive.

'Thank you so much, Ryan – I'm very grateful. There's no need to wait. I've taken up quite enough of your time. You just go.'

'I canna do that. What if naebody's in?'

'Well ... then I'll call a taxi – I've got a mobile phone – and ... maybe I'll come back a bit later.'

'That makes no sense. Where would the taxi take you? Are you sure you want to do this?'

I took a deep breath. 'Yes. I'm sure.'

'Then, if there's no one home, I'll bring you back later. Go on and ring the bell, woman.'

'Thank you …' I hesitated, my hand shaking on the van door.

Ryan sighed, got out of his side and walked around to help me out. He lifted my small case down and handed it to me.

'Come on, I'll come with you far enough to see if they open the door.'

'You're a kind man, Ryan – I don't deserve it,' I said, my voice breaking into a sob.

'No, you don't. Let's gerron with it.'

He took my arm and led me slowly to the open gates into the drive, from which there was a view of the front door.

'OK, I'll stay here. If someone comes to the door, I'll be able to see, and I'll leave you to it.'

'Yes, thank you.'

He released my arm. I began to walk towards the house, leaning on the handle of my case as it bumped and growled through the reddish gravel in the drive, my feet crunching uncomfortably on the small stones. Once level with the front door, I could see a double garage, its doors closed. There was a dark blue car, which had been hidden by the foliage and the curve of the drive until this point, parked in front of the garage. My heart lurched; that meant someone was likely to be at home. I turned to look at Ryan. He nodded his head and made a "shooing" gesture with one hand.

I heaved myself up the three shallow steps at the front door. Suddenly I was overcome with exhaustion. The door had a large, tarnished knocker. It seemed too loud, too intrusive to use that. I noticed a doorbell to the left of the door and pressed it quickly, before I could change my mind. All was quiet for a few moments. Relief flooded through me; perhaps no one was home after all.

Then I heard muffled footsteps approaching and the sound of an inner door opening. The front door swung open and a woman in her mid- to late sixties stepped forwards and smiled at me. She had neatly cut grey hair with pale gold streaks, and a pleasant, round face.

321

'Hello?' she said.

'Hello …' I replied, suddenly at a loss to know what to do or say next.

The woman glanced past me in Ryan's direction. I turned around and waved uncertainly at him. He raised his hand and withdrew.

The house suddenly appeared to sway at a strange angle. My case fell over on the step, and I struggled to remain upright. My thoughts retreated into a fog. The woman reached down and picked up my bag. She put it on the threshold and gave me a quizzical look.

'Are you all right? You don't look at all well …'

I swayed uncontrollably. She leaned forwards and grasped me. 'I'm sorry … I …'

'Come inside and sit down for a minute, dear.' She called into the house, 'Lawrence!'

A moment later a tall, grey-haired man appeared, a handsome man with white at his temples. I still recognised him after all these years.

'Inspector Dempster …' I said aloud.

The man and the woman looked at me, and then at one another. Then, one each side of me, they led me into a light, spacious sitting room and lowered me into a chair. Inspector Dempster pulled up a tall wooden chair and sat down in front of me, facing me.

'Barbara, would you mind fetching a cup of tea for this lady, please.'

His wife – I remembered that Shelley had said his wife was called Barbara – nodded and disappeared through a door on the other side of the room.

He squinted at me, moving his head from one side to another, as if a more favourable angle might help to identify me.

'Do I know you?' he asked.

'No, not exactly,' I replied, 'but I think you know *of* me.'

Chapter Sixty-Two

Chief Superintendent Lawrence Dempster

Barbara says it's easy with hindsight – she's not easily impressed – but I reckon I started to have suspicions as soon as I saw the woman stood on our front doorstep, before she'd even uttered a word. Certainly when she said my name – well, who else would call me "Inspector Dempster"? She had to be someone from the past, didn't she? Now here she was, sat in front of me, in our house, in our sitting room.

Phrases kept coming back to me from the investigation long ago: "an average sort of woman, neither tall nor short, of middle years, wearing a brown or blue coat, a bit mousey, ordinary, dull, unmemorable ..." Yet there was no doubt in my mind that the woman about whom I'd built a detailed picture all those years ago was far from ordinary and dull. No, she was exceptionally clever – highly intelligent in fact – as well as ruthless, single-minded and determined.

Could this frail, slight, nervous, elderly woman trembling before me, clasping and unclasping her hands, her eyes flicking round the room – anywhere rather than making eye contact –

could she really have carried out the crime that had haunted me since 1985?

The age would be about right. I reckoned she'd been about forty or a bit more when Stacy was abducted, so she'd be maybe about sixty-five now – about my age, in fact. I recalled the contents of Stacy Watts' recent letter: "terminal illness". This woman was clearly far from healthy. In fact, I was worried she might expire right there in front of me. I couldn't let that happen, not before telling me her story anyway.

Barbara brought in a tray with the tea things.

'I hope you don't mind, it's Earl Grey,' she said. 'We've run out of ordinary tea – I need to put it on the shopping list.'

The mysterious woman looked up. She looked directly at Barbara, animated for the first time, and *beamed*.

'Oh, I love Earl Grey – it's my absolute favourite tea,' she said.

Barbara looked a bit taken aback for a moment, but she quickly recovered herself.

'Well, that was a lucky choice then,' she said, in her effortlessly friendly, warm way. 'Now, I'm going to pour you both a nice cup of tea, and then let you two have a talk. It is Lawrence you wanted to talk to, isn't it? I'll just be sitting over there, out of the way.'

Barbara sat herself in an armchair in the far corner of the room next to a window. I realised she was acting in the role of chaperone, protecting me, in case of any possible subsequent allegations on the part of this stranger – a potentially unhinged stranger.

I let the woman have a few sips of her tea. She seemed to almost breathe it in like a drug. She leaned back in the chair and closed her eyes for a moment. She looked exhausted.

'Now then,' I began, 'it's clear to me that you know who I am, so that puts me at a bit of a disadvantage, doesn't it? I'm just guessing you've known about me for some time, some years in fact. Am I right?'

'Yes, Inspector Dempster, you are right.'

'It's Chief Superintendent now … or at least it was when I retired, but no matter. Inspector will do just fine …'

I finished with a gabble. She gazed impassively at me. Why on earth had I started on this? What did it matter what she called me, for Christ's sake? Was I just trying to establish my authority in the situation? I straightened my back and cleared my throat.

'I would also guess that your visit is in connection with the disappearance of Stacy Watts?'

She nodded.

'Well then, rather than ask a lot of questions, or put words in your mouth, I'll leave you to say whatever you want to me, in your own words. However, you must understand that depending on what you say to me, I may be obliged to take further action. I may need you to accompany me to police headquarters to make a full statement.'

She nodded again.

I spread my hands in a gesture meant to indicate that the ball was in her court. She sipped her tea again and put the cup down shakily on the table.

'My name is Alison Brown,' she began. 'About quarter of a century ago I decided to take a child. I planned it all carefully in advance. I was living in Nottingham at the time. I was all alone. My mother had just died and left me her house and all her money. I had a great longing for a child …'

The woman spoke for twenty minutes or so, scarcely drawing breath, describing in minute detail how she had planned and executed Stacy Watts's abduction. She was gasping and shaking, her voice growing weaker. After the words: 'So we took the train from Riddlesfield to Newcastle. I named the child Lucy … Lucy Brown. Sorry … excuse me …' she was unable to continue.

She took a deep breath and reached for her tea. I watched as she lifted the cup with a trembling hand and took some gulps before dabbing her mouth with a paper serviette Barbara had left for her. I waited silently for her to continue her account, which she did after a while.

'I loved her from the start, and I believe she came to love me, but there were some very difficult periods. I had not foreseen how complex would be the web of lies and deceit I had to spin to convince both Lucy, and our friends and acquaintances. Lucy turned out to be a highly intelligent and sensitive little girl. On a few occasions, she appeared to demonstrate some flashback memories, which she could not understand, of course, and which distressed her. It was only much later that she developed some suspicions about her true origins. I know that she wrote to you at around this time, first as a university student, and then again more recently …'

She paused again and looked at me. I nodded to encourage her to go on.

'Some time ago, when she was in her final year at university, I shared the full truth of her origins with Lucy, which, inevitably, she found very difficult.'

She looked up at me again and then turned to glance in Barbara's direction; an uncertain look, as if to check what effect her words were having. She was rocking backwards and forwards slightly. Her fingers worked a continuous sequence of movements, almost as though she were knitting the story. She told me that Lucy had given birth to a baby herself, but that following the birth she had developed severe anxiety. Her difficulties had intensified to the extent that she had a severe breakdown requiring specialist treatment.

'I realise all this must be my fault,' she continued. 'Thank goodness she is now slowly recovering.'

Alison Brown covered her face with her hands for a moment in a gesture of despair. Then she lowered her hands, bent her face downwards and closed her eyes. She was clearly drawing together the threads of her story, concentrating on what to focus on next.

'At the time I revealed Lucy's full background to her, I had recently been diagnosed as having cancer. I have been fortunate to have had excellent treatment and several years of intermittent remission. However, I'm told that the cancer has spread. My illness is now terminal, and I am not expected to live more than a few weeks. Lucy and her future husband, Guy, have met her birth mother Shelley Watts, and her extensive birth family. They have welcomed her back into the arms of the family with great warmth. Needless to say, my initial judgement on the family was totally unjustified. I realise that now. I have met Shelley, and have to say I admire her, and other members of the family, enormously.

'My wrongdoing – and my guilt – is a terrible burden, but it is not one that Lucy – or indeed Shelley – should have to carry in any way. Lucy has asked Shelley not to inform on me to the police, but I do not feel that either of them should be weighed down by such a responsibility. My reason for coming to you, Inspector … I beg your pardon – Chief Superintendent – is to make a full confession of my crime. I hope this may go some way towards relieving Lucy, and the Watts family too, of their suffering, all of which has been caused by me.'

She looked up, nodding first at me and then at Barbara, as if to say "that's it; that's all I have to say."

Barbara, who had been discreetly looking at a newspaper, got up and perched on the arm of Alison's chair. She patted and stroked Alison's arm gently, leaving her hand resting there.

'Well, Alison,' I said. 'May I call you Alison?'

She nodded.

'I appreciate that you've been very honest with me today, and that's a good thing. But I have to say, it's taken you a very long time to get to this point and admit the truth.'

Barbara looked at me sharply. I recognised that look. You can't live with a woman for over forty years without becoming familiar with her repertoire of expressions. That look said "Do you really have to bring that up now? The woman's sick, for heaven's sake.

She's used all her energy and courage to come here today and tell you her story ..."

'But,' I added hastily, 'I understand there were many reasons why it's taken so long. Um ... perhaps we don't need to go into those at this time ... The important thing is, you've decided to make a full confession now ...'

Barbara's face shifted almost imperceptibly. "That's better, Lawrence", it was saying, "now's not the time for criticism ..." Her head gave the slightest of nods.

'Now then, Alison, you do understand that I have to do something with the information you have given me? You've confessed to a very serious crime, very serious. We can't just leave it at that. The truth has consequences.'

She looked at me expectantly.

'What I suggest is this. I'll ring one of my colleagues at the station, a sensitive, understanding female officer – Lara Collins – with years of experience in dealing with ... complex situations. So, I'll ring Detective Constable Collins and ask her to come here to meet you and have a little talk. Then she and I would accompany you down to Riddlesfield station together. No handcuffs, no sirens blaring, you understand. We'll not make a drama of it. Just a quiet ride in the car. How does that sound?'

Her face was pallid. I was afraid she was about to pass out. She opened her mouth and shut it again, as if trying to formulate a response. Then she opened her mouth again, and started to speak, so quietly it was barely more than a whisper, barely audible.

'Yes. Yes, I see. So what will happen then?'

'Well, having made a confession, you'd be formally interviewed and asked to make a statement, which would be written down or recorded. You'll be advised that you're entitled to have a solicitor with you. You would probably be charged and held in custody overnight. We'll make sure the doctor comes to check you over and that you have any medication you may need. You'll be well looked after. After you've been presented to the court, you may or may not be bailed. Bail might be granted on the basis of your poor health, and on the assumption that you can assure the court you're not going to do a runner, and that you'll turn up at the appointed date and time for the case to be heard. You're not going to try to run away now, are you, Alison?'

I smiled – it was my attempt at a little joke, at lightening the atmosphere. Not very successful, judging by the look on Barbara's face.

Alison had nodded wearily all through the explanation.

'I have no intention of "doing a runner", Chief Superintendent Dempster. I will be pleading guilty, of course. What would be the outcome, do you think?'

'I can't say for sure. The court would want to take account of your poor health, but they would also feel compelled to mark the seriousness of the crime, and the fact that you withheld your confession for so many years, causing the girl's birth family untold trauma and distress. I'm afraid the judge may insist on a custodial sentence.'

Chapter Sixty-Three

2009

Lucy

Alison hadn't always been considerate in her dealings with others, but with regard to her final act, it was as if she planned and timed it to cause the least possible inconvenience and hardship to everyone else.

Following her arrest, she was charged and brought before the court the following week. I found it all very, very distressing. By Alison's own admission, she was guilty of the crime of child abduction. It was so hard to know the court was not just discussing child abduction in the abstract, but *my* abduction. Sentencing was delayed for medical and psychological reports. While these were being researched and assembled, Alison was remanded to Riddlesfield Prison.

Shortly afterwards, she suffered a serious health crisis, and was taken into the hospital wing of the prison. She deteriorated rapidly over the coming two weeks, and was semi-conscious for the last three days. Knowing how ill she was, I barely left her bedside. Guy often accompanied me. We were allowed to visit freely and Alison loved to hear about our lives at home, and especially about Milo. She was kindly treated by the staff, her pain was reasonably managed, and above all, *it was where she wanted to be.* "Just desserts" she called it, with satisfaction.

When the end approached, we were able to stay with her. There were no last words, no last-minute revelations. She slept more and more; her breathing became laboured, and slow. Eventually, the staff told us she was unlikely to last the night. She hadn't woken for more than eight hours. The three of us were sitting around her bed – Shelley had asked to visit her too. We were conversing quietly, in the hushed, slightly hysterical tones used in the near presence of death.

Suddenly, Alison's eyes flickered half open. She struggled to sit up but couldn't manage it. Guy and I lifted her upper body gently – she weighed nothing – and propped her up with two extra pillows. She wheezed and panted, exhausted by the effort. Her face was a sickly white. A fine film of perspiration glazed her forehead. She squeezed my hand with one bony claw. With the other she reached for Guy.

'Thank … you … Guy,' she whispered.

Then she withdrew her trembling hand from him and with effort reached it out to Shelley's hand on the other side of the bed.

'Forgive me …' she said.

She closed her eyes. She did not regain consciousness, and died peacefully soon after midnight.

* * *

Characteristically, Alison had left infinitely detailed instructions for her funeral, together with payment to the undertakers to cover

331

the cost of the service itself, flowers (to be distributed to me and any guests who wanted them – she didn't approve of the waste of flowers left to rot at the crematorium), the venue, the food and music.

I felt very low for some weeks afterwards. I was thankful to be able to talk to Guy and to good friends – above all, Cassie. Yet, despite the sadness I was not depressed; I felt confident, strong and balanced. I knew Guy was relieved that my vulnerable psychological state was a thing of the past. I rejoiced in our beloved child. I was so happy with Milo. Sometimes it was hard to take my eyes off him.

Every day brought exciting new developments: he pulled himself up on the sofa, standing wobbly for a moment before landing back on his bottom; he said a new sound combination; he pointed at something of interest. I felt calm, relaxed and at ease with him – and with myself as a mother. If only Alison could have seen more of us having fun together. At least it felt good to have Shelley with us, sharing our lives.

Like now, only five months after Alison's death, the kitchen was filled with laughter. Milo was on my lap, helping himself to bits of my lunch – sucking on a piece of bread, banging his hand on the table, gnawing a carrot stick with his two tiny teeth, and looking up to check my face. I burrowed my face in the back of his neck, blowing raspberries against his skin, kissing him, making him giggle. Guy was gazing at us, a thoughtful smile softening his features.

Cassie grinned and shook her head. 'So what do you think, Guy?' she said.

It took him a moment to turn his attention to her question. 'Oh, sorry, Cassie. I was miles away … What were you saying?'

'We were discussing, you know, the best location. Lucy thinks the Dumfriesshire coast. It was a favourite place from years ago, for both of them. No negative associations, just happy memories.'

'Yes, sounds fine by me. It's where we went with my mum and

dad too when we were kids, for days out and long weekends. It's a good choice – and my parents have already said they'd put us all up. They've plenty of room for everybody.'

'They must have a bloomin' mansion then!' said Shelley. 'Didn't she say nothing? I mean, Alison, didn't she leave any special wishes, like? I'd a thought she'd 'a had everything worked out, just like the funeral.'

'Yes.' I chuckled. 'That was planned like a military operation, wasn't it? Every poem, every reading, every piece of music – not to mention the food for the gathering afterwards!'

'I loved that part,' said Ed. 'I absolutely loved it. Just like the birthday parties my mum used to organise when I was a kid – all those little sausage rolls, and iced buns, and jelly …'

'Reckon she was just reminding everyone that she *was* a mam, don't ya think?'

'Probably,' I said, reaching out to touch Shelley's arm.

'Where exactly is Dumfriesshire, anyway?' Shelley asked.

'The nearest part of the west coast of Scotland. About two hours' drive from here,' Guy told her, pointing in a vaguely westerly direction.

'Don't feel you have to come, Shelley,' I said. 'I mean, it's a long way for you – and it's been just great having you here in Edinburgh. Thank you so much for coming, and staying with us. I'm really glad you've seen our house. That feels really special.'

'Nothing to thank me for, pet. It's about time I saw a bit more of the world. And now I'll be able to picture the two 'a youse and the little fella in your own home, it'll not feel you're so far away.'

'Getting back to Alison, though,' I said. 'She didn't leave any special instructions about her ashes at all. Maybe that's a bit surprising, but then she wasn't at all sentimental about things like that. She didn't feel her ashes would be *her* any longer. All she said was "don't make any fuss – just do whatever *you* want."'

So we did just that.

Chapter Sixty-Four

Susan had been reconciled to Alison's and my history during those last weeks. She told me she'd regretted the strength of her initial reaction.

'I suppose it was the shock. But, after all, we have to accept she was probably mentally ill – or suffering from a personality disorder at least.'

Alison had been thrilled when Susan visited her in the prison hospital. Fiona had visited too. We'd thought hard about who to invite to Alison's funeral back in April. As well as Cassie and Ed, there were Susan and Mike Harmon, Claire and Charlie, Cassie's parents Fiona and Simon, and Molly Armstrong from next door – now a feisty widow of nearly ninety – Frank having died a few years previously, along with family, and a number of more recent friends, neighbours and colleagues. It had turned out to be quite a lively event.

'Just as well Alison's not here in *living form*,' Guy had said wryly. 'She never did like parties.'

In the weeks and days leading up to and following Alison's death, I found it difficult handle all the emotions and sorrow coursing through me. I was afraid of being overwhelmed and had to find ways of protecting myself through practical arrangements. Keeping busy helped. Above all, Guy's constant support and understanding helped too. It had been agony visiting Alison in the secure hospital wing of the prison, in which she had spent her final few weeks, with uniformed prison officers constantly sitting in the room. Alison herself had assured me she was perfectly comfortable and content.

'This is the right place for me,' she had asserted more than once.

* * *

I was adamant I wanted the disposal of the ashes ceremony in Dumfriesshire to be a "family affair", much quieter than the funeral. Only our closest friends were to be included. So as well as Guy, Milo and me, there was just Guy's Mum and Dad, Cassie and Ed, and Shelley and Ryan to represent the Watts family – though I knew they had only agreed to come as a gesture of support for me.

For once the September weather was kind; it was a mild, dry evening with a gentle breeze. We found a rocky promontory sticking out into the sea. We all clambered out to the end of it. I opened the box and shook it.

'Bye, Alison!' I yelled into the gloom.

A soft wind scattered the ashes into the waves below. We staggered unevenly on the rocks to stand in a tight circle, clutching one another in a "group hug" – even Ryan – though he looked distinctly uncomfortable. The waves dispersed what remained of Alison. Shelley and I stood wrapped in each other's arms for a long time.

'Thank you so much for coming, Shelley – you and Ryan. It really means a lot.'

'It's you means a lot to me, pet,' she said.

* * *

The colours had leached out of the sky, leaving the seascape a monochrome bluish-grey. The fire made a dancing pool of light on the beach. We sat on the sand eating barbecued fish, falafel, corn-on-the-cob and vegetables, with our fingers, watching the stark white of the foam as the waves ran up the beach. Above us an arc of stars like Christmas decorations illuminated the sky. Milo slept in his carrier.

Guy put his arms round me. 'Well, I think we gave Alison a pretty good send-off, don't you?' he said.

I gazed out at the dark sea. 'Yes, I think she would have approved – as far as you could ever tell with her.'

'Do you feel you've laid her to rest, Lucy?' asked Cassie. 'And laid some of your own demons to rest too?'

'In a way, perhaps …' I said thoughtfully. I looked up at Guy. 'But there is just one more thing I want to do.'

Chapter Sixty-Five

2010

Lucy

Although Alison had spent her entire childhood and the first twenty years of her adult life in Nottingham, she had rarely talked to me about it until the final months of her life. Perhaps I hadn't known what questions to ask. Then, latterly, she had told me about the house she shared with her mother – her *genuinely adoptive* mother, Dorothy. Dorothy, who was the nearest thing I had to a grandmother, and whom I had never met.

Alison talked to me about her own room in the house – her haven of peace – about Sylvia, the next-door neighbour, whom she'd never contacted after our move to Newcastle, and who was now sadly long- dead; and she told me about the girls' grammar school she had attended, which had been such an ordeal for her. I mourned for the troubled child and adolescent she had been, the anxious student and the troubled woman she became. I still mourned for Alison, and the sadness of her confused life, of which I was a part.

* * *

We stood and gazed at the neat Edwardian terraced house where she had grown up. Guy, holding Milo, watched me carefully. He always worried about my reactions, afraid perhaps that, at any moment, I could revert to my disturbed and deluded state. Yet I felt little as we studied the grey stonework with its sturdy symmetry. I struggled to feel any connection.

A young woman opened the front door and came towards us.

'Hello. Can I help you? Are you looking for something?' she asked.

'Sorry, we're just being nosy. My ... er ... mother lived in this house some years ago, at first with her mother, and then on her own for a while. It was sold round about 1985, and I've never seen it before. We didn't mean to intrude.'

'No problem, would you like to have a look round inside? You'd have to excuse the mess.'

'It's kind of you to offer, but I'm sure it's changed a lot since my mum was here, and I've never actually been here myself, so it wouldn't mean a lot to me.'

'Wouldn't your mother like to come and see the house again?'

'I'm afraid she died a few months ago.'

'Oh, I am sorry,' the woman said. 'What was she called, your mother?'

'Her name was Alison Brown, and *her* mother, who lived here 'til she died, was called Dorothy Brown.'

'I remember those names from the deeds. I think there have been three owners since your mum sold it. We love it here. It's got all its original features – not all modernised like so many houses of this period.'

A little boy of five or six appeared in the doorway. 'Mummy!' he called.

'Sorry, I'd better go,' said the young woman. 'Are you sure you don't want to come in?'

'No, thank you, we should be going.'

So this fairly nondescript house, this quiet, pleasant area, was where she had started; where she grew into who she became; where she lived before *me*, before Newcastle. Now I would always be able to picture her in this house. It felt good to be able to anchor my thoughts and memories of her to this solid place, yet it gave no clue as to how or whether her environment had contributed to the complexities of Alison's personality. I picked Milo up and carried him back to the car, where Guy was waiting and watching.

But there was somewhere else I needed to see too. Somewhere where *I* had started.

* * *

The caretaker emerged from the lodge at the entrance gate, and gave us directions where to find what we were looking for. I'd never spent much time in a graveyard before. This one was beautifully cared for. I could imagine Alison's pleasure in the quiet, and in the trees all around it, and in the neat, well-kept graves and paths. The graves of the recently dead stood out with colourful floral arrangements. Even the areas allotted to the long-dead, to which visitors no longer came, where no one placed fresh flowers, were brightened with borders of flowering perennials and shrubs.

Milo, in his pushchair, sat alert and erect as a new shoot. He had his tiny index finger at the ready, eagerly waiting to indicate anything of interest.

'Twee!' he shouted, pointing. 'Man! Bird! Fower! Swiwwel!'

Suddenly there it was. Lucy Brown's grave. The shock of seeing her name – *my name* – on the sad little gravestone took me by surprise. A pain rose from my chest and gripped my throat. Tears ran down my face. Guy put his arms around me, and nuzzled the top of my head. We gazed at the inscription.

In memory of our dearly loved little girl
Lucy Sarah Brown aged 2 years
Born 20-9-1982 – Died 16-10-1984
Safe in the hands of Jesus

It was like staring at a notice of my own death. Yet Alison would have believed it was more a notification of Lucy Brown's *birth* – or perhaps *rebirth*.

'It's OK, sweetheart, it's OK,' Guy said, squeezing me. Milo looked up in concern.

'Mummy … cry?'

'No, no, Milo. Mummy's not crying, not really.'

I pointed to the writing on the grave. 'Look there. It's a story … about a baby. It's a sad story. It made me feel sad for a minute, but I'm happy again now.'

'We've brought flowers for the baby, Milo,' Guy said. He delved into a carrier bag on the back of the pushchair and extracted a wrapped bunch of flowers and a large glass jar.

Solemnly, he poured water from a plastic bottle into the jar, and fixed it securely on the grave, just in front of the headstone. He handed the flowers to me.

I took the cellophane wrapping and silk ribbons off the bouquet. The bright reds, yellows, oranges and blues seemed fitting for a child: a supermarket selection, not too subtle. I knelt down and arranged the flowers in the jar. I tied the silky ribbons round the arrangement.

'Yep,' said Milo, 'pwetty.'

Guy swept him up and put him on his shoulders.

'C'mon Milo,' he said, 'let's leave Mummy in peace for a minute, and go see if we can find any *squirrels*!'

'Yeah! Swiwwels!'

They galloped off together.

I felt the sun gently slanting through the chestnut trees behind me, warming my back.

I am not this Lucy Brown, I thought, I am *myself.* I am Lucy Brown Watts now. Lucy Brown Watts is married to Guy Downing. She is the mother of Milo Downing. We are a family. My background is complicated, but I have an extensive family; a living mother and one who has died. I have several siblings. I have in-laws who accept and like me for who I am. We are all family. We have good friends; we have work we enjoy. We have a future. I am loved. I am truly blessed.

Guy and Milo came haring back. I pulled Milo off Guy's shoulders and hugged them both.

'We've got a long drive back to Edinburgh,' Guy said. 'Shall we make a start?'

'Yes,' I replied. 'Let's go home.'

Acknowledgements

Many thanks to Bill Goodall, my agent at A for Authors, for his kindness, support, and belief in my work. Also to Nia Beynon, my sharp-eyed editor at HQ, for saying 'yes'!

Special thanks always to my family for their support and insightful opinions; Terence, Luke, Jo, Thomas, Rose, and Harvey. Also to my good friends; Anna, Barbara, Christine, Heather, Judy, and Margaret, for their willingness to express their thoughts and responses.

My appreciation to Neal for his insights into police procedures, and to Michael for his guidance on legal matters.

Dear Reader,

Thank you so much for taking the time to read this book – we hope you enjoyed it! If you did, we'd be so appreciative if you left a review.

Here at HQ Digital we are dedicated to publishing fiction that will keep you turning the pages into the early hours. We publish a variety of genres, from heartwarming romance, to thrilling crime and sweeping historical fiction.

To find out more about our books, enter competitions and discover exclusive content, please join our community of readers by following us at:

🐦 @HQDigitalUK

f facebook.com/HQDigitalUK

Are you a budding writer? We're also looking for authors to join the HQ Digital family! Please submit your manuscript to:

HQDigital@harpercollins.co.uk.

Hope to hear from you soon!

If you enjoyed *Finding Lucy*, then why not try another gripping read from HQ Digital?